48 South

Charles Manning

INNER CIRCLE

There are reasons more terrible than tigers
which will prove to him
that wretchedness in his duty,
but he accepts humbly
this felicity, this glimmer.

Jorge Luis Borges, 'Someone'

Copyright © 1990 by Charles K. Manning

First published in Great Britain in 1990 by
Inner Circle Books Ltd of London

British Library Cataloguing in Publication Data

Manning, Charles
  48 South.
  I. Title
  823.914 [F]

  ISBN 1-85018-086-5

Phototypeset in 11/12pt Linotron Times by
Phoenix Photosetting, Chatham, Kent
Printed and bound in Great Britain by
Billing & Sons Ltd, Worcester

Chapter 1

Midsummer in Patagonia; the morning wind already boist-
erous with dust; a smell of chronic dryness on the air; and
salt, and gasoline. On the new concrete, warming in the early
south-east sun, two sea-grey aeroplanes; two long-shadowed
figures, black flying suits, black baseball caps, peaks down
against the glare, dark glasses, Waiting.

'How far out there to *Las Malvinas*, Carla?' He spoke with
an air of passing the time.

She squinted at the sea horizon where the sun hung low in a
yellow sky. 'I don't know, Capitán. Seven hundred
kilometres?'

'Seven hundred and thirty-two, exactly, to Puerto Stanley
where the British Governor has his flag,' he said. He was
Capitán de Fregata Francesco Monegario of the Comando
Aviación Naval Argentine and it was his job to know this.

She was Teniente de Corbeta Carla Souza, also CANA,
and nearly as tall as her commander. Springy raven hair
spilled from her cap and moved in the gritty half-gale. Where
Monegario had three broad gold stripes, her epaulettes carried
a single thin gold band, and above her left breast she wore the
same gold CANA pilot wings as he. She shook her hair.

'Is it so important? For us?' she asked.

'Carla, Carla! One hundred forty-seven years that flag has
been on our islands, since 1833. Is that not important?'

'Of course, sir. Of course!' she said. 'But look, they are
coming, the English!' They spoke the soft Andalusian
platense dialect of the Rio Plata basin.

They waited. Close on their right, the tall white control

1

tower with its octagonal glass belvedere. Behind and left, a curving row of five dull green hangars; out ahead, the airfield, three runways, then drab arid scrubland to the ocean. Immediately behind, between them and the first of the hangars, the two aircraft.

A green bus had appeared around the far hangar. It traversed the six hundred metres of concrete parking apron, drew up before the waiting figures and decanted its eight passengers.

Capitán de Navio Perez, commander of Base Aerea Naval Roca, returned Monegario's salute and said to the seven civilians with him, 'Gentlemen, I am to introduce you Capitán Monegario, Air Group Commander, and Teniente Souza – she is like midshipman, for you. And also, too, our Argentine Corsair! You recognise it, eh? This is the secret weapon of our Special Group for Attack, Grupo Especial de Ataque, or GEA.' He pronounced it Gaya.

There was a good deal of silence. The seven, newly arrived last night by clandestine routes from the cold northern hemisphere, stared unbelievingly at the aircraft. Corsairs! Blunt, awkward things, with thick, cranked wings, tail-wheels and great four-bladed propellers, cockpits far down the fuselage behind the high nose, World War II planes. Out of production for thirty years. Museum pieces.

'They cain't,' said one of the new arrivals, none too quietly, 'they just cain't be bloody serious!' The rest were speechless.

As for the pilots! Monegario all right – there was that about him that credentialled him with the British fliers. But a girl, a woman? A circus act?

'OK! *Vamos, Comandante, por favor!*' At the base commander's imperative Monegario and the woman turned towards their planes. 'This way, gentlemen!' Perez indicated the control tower.

Nobody took any notice of him. The seven, in assorted dress, stood bemused on the concrete, most eyes on the lithe black-clad figure of the woman. She ducked under the wing of the right-hand aircraft, thick black hair bouncing at each step, mounted the wing-root and with practised ease pulled herself up to the high cockpit. When she had fastened her seat harness, pulled on her helmet and made a few small

2

movements around the cockpit she looked across at the other aircraft and gave a thumbs-up. In his cockpit Monegario circled his right hand. With a grinding whine the engines laboured on their starters and burst into life. Propellers blurred and fanned back a thin haze of blue smoke and the big radials settled down to a low throb. The girl's Corsair had four pods of air-to-ground rockets under its wings; the commander had four fat green bombs.

'Gentlemen! Please!' The captain shouted above the racket, gesticulating like a traffic policeman. 'This way . . .!' They caught him up.

'Where did you get them, Captain?' one asked. Short hair, short beard, light grey eyes and a symmetrical cragginess of features, he was the one, it might have been noticed, to whom the others made small deferences, as to a leader. His name was Hicks, and he was trying to make sense of what he was seeing. After all the secrecy, the intrigue, the urgency, since that first meeting with Cassián in Rotterdam, he had expected something special – a fleet of used jets, Skyhawks or early Migs, and something novel in the way of weapons. But this – this beggared the imagination! If this was Cassián's Special Attack aircraft, the Chance-Vought F4U Corsair, last great fighter-bomber of World War Two, then he'd got it wrong and the novelty was in the aircraft! Or was it a joke?

'We make zem!' Perez replied. The Corsairs taxied out towards the airfield, heavy and ponderous with their flailing propellers.

'How many?'

'Many! Plenty! 'Ondreds!'

They clattered on up the staircase of the new-smelling tower.

'And are there many – girls?'

'Gurlz? Gurlz . . .?

'Senioritas, Senioritas pilotas.' Hicks experimented.

'Ah! *Las muchachas! Si.* Maybe quarter.' Stranger and stranger, thought Alice, thought Hicks.

And then they were out in the tearing wind on a high walkway around the belvedere. On the west side, in the shade. Southward lay the airfield. To the west they had a view of flat, empty scrubland to the horizon. A mile out in the

3

desert three old-looking battle tanks sat inside a rough white circle. The sound of the departing Corsairs trailed thinly on the air.

The base commander had taken his cap off. A sleek seal-like man of medium height, flat black hair, thin moustache, his khakis carried pilot's wings and a double row of medals as well as the four gold rings of command. He spoke, quite ignoring a vicious gust of wind that had the British clutching the hand-rail:

'It is understood you are surprised to see these planes, gentlemen.' The English had a highly manufactured ring. 'So, before we begin to work, we think it is good we have some demonstration. Attack will begin at eight hundred hours.'

It did. Out of the dust-haze, well over to their right, a Corsair appeared, very low. At two miles it lifted its nose, zoom-climbed to about 3,000 feet and rolled in towards the tanks in a shallow full-power dive. They picked up the super-charger whine at about the same time as flames and smoke began pouring from its underwing pods. An avalanche of rockets streaked out and down towards the tanks. Fierce as Chinese crackers, shock-waves from the supersonic missiles rang out hard across the plain. The girl's aircraft banked, showing its belly, and roared away low to the west as the projectiles slammed thunderously across the target circle engulfing the tanks in fire, smoke and thrown earth. The other Corsair released its bombs from a near-vertical dive at about 4,000 feet and begin a hard pull-out, the straining engine note audible as it too turned away west. The bombs plunged and exploded among the hanging debris of the rocket attack, throwing up fountains of earth, rock and smoke. The control tower quivered with the shock.

The south-west wind carried the dust cloud away to the right, leaving the target area exposed. One tank appeared untouched; one lay on its side, outside the circle; of the third, no visible sign remained.

After a very low pass over the tower the two Corsairs circled to land. The base commander led the group back down to ground level where they walked out to meet them, as they taxied in.

The performance concluded with a synchronised shut-down. The pilots climbed down, came around to the front of their aircraft, not so spruce now, sweat patches staining armpits, hair awry. They pulled off their gloves. The *teniente* freed her hair with a shake of her head, finger-combed it roughly and pulled on her cap as she took her place beside the commander.

'*Muy bien, Comandante!* Very good!', Perez called. He didn't smile. He turned to Hicks. 'Commander Monegario – he like these planes!'

'Thank you, Captain.' The baseball cap and dark glasses hid the commander's eye's but white teeth smiled. 'I think also my Number Two did OK, eh?'

'*Si. Excelente! Excelente! Ola . .!.* Zis is Commander Eeks and the British *consejeros.* I think now they like to look at the Corsairs before we go to headquarters. You show zem, please . . .' He looked at his watch. 'They should be in HQ at nine hours. Zey have much programme today. OK?'

'*Si,* Capitán.' Monegario saluted, as did the tall young woman at his side, and the base commander walked away towards his waiting car.

'Captain!' Hicks called after him. Perez stopped and turned.

'I would like your permission for a short flight. Now.'

The two men regarded each other across ten yards of concrete. After an almost indecently long pause the captain's face hovered on the edge of a smile. He snapped his fingers to his chauffeur. The man went to the rear of the car and got out a valise which he carried across and placed beside Hicks. It contained a set of flying kit.

'We were afraid you would not ask! Have a good flight – but nine hundred at headquarters, please!' Perez got into his car and was driven off.

Hicks had never flown a Corsair. He had cut his teeth on pistons and had a few hundred hours in the Douglas Skyraider, the Able Dog, last and biggest of the single pistons. But that was long ago. Many years ago. And he knew the Corsair's vicious reputation. But he needed to fly it: ever since that first meeting with Cassián he had been working to prevent himself – and the others – from becoming mere employees. He'd had enough of being an employee. If he

5

couldn't master the brute, he'd at least go out in style!

In a packed twenty minutes Hicks grunted and sweated his way through successive barriers of fear towards a nirvana he thought he'd forgotten. The Corsair was slow, heavy, and cacophonously noisy and propeller torque was something he'd forgotten all about, but the power thrilled him, his adrenalin flowed and he was conscious of a deep-grooved sensual pleasure as he rolled and looped, dived and turned. He had no time for more than a glimpse of the physiognomy of the landscape below, registering only its lunarity, and the closeness of the ocean.

He finished with a low-level loop, and a tight circuit to land. It was the landing that gave him most satisfaction: the Corsair's rearing nose completely obscured the runway on the approach but he nevertheless managed a fair three-pointer.

'Nice one, Jeff!' the youngest, fair-haired Briton called as he climbed out. They were standing in a group beside the other Corsair, with the girl.

'A good flight?' asked Monegario, grinning.

'Average,' replied Hicks. It was enough, between those two. Hicks thankfully shed the flying suit. The bus was waiting.

'Commander Eeks?' He turned his head. It was the *teniente*. She was close enough to touch.

She said, 'They say you 'ave no fly ze Corsair before today?'

'That's right.'

'Zen, I salute you! Zat was good flying!'

'Thank you. You also, *Teniente*. Good flying! Good shooting!' He turned towards her, grey eyes appraising, until at some length and with easy deliberation she removed her sunglasses.

What happened then had the quality of a soft detonation that stopped the clocks of Hicks' life, and in the long moment that followed he knew with uncomfortable certainty that when they started, they would never run the same again. She was not pretty, nor even handsome. The mouth was too small, the small nose a little hooked; the whole face too small and pale for the lank figure. But it had authority, the sort that lives in old portraits, high-bred, Vizigothic. An opulence of black hair bushed from under her cap and some of it strayed,

6

Hicks noticed, untidily inside her collar to lie against her neck.

All this was there before. But now the eyes: brown almonds, flat-cheeked and high-browed, they fanfared somthing that went deep into Hicks and left him eighteen, gauche, and bewildered. Already in some difficulty with a shirt button, he fumbled, squinting at her, and thought he might have managed to cover his confusion. Then they were boarding the bus, leaving the Argentine pilots standing in the sun, in front of their Corsairs.

The half of Hicks that wasn't taken up with answering eager questions about his flight, as they drove away, was swirling with a mess of emotions that he barely recognised. And he found it very hard not looking back.

*

Could all this happen in three months? Rotterdam. The phone call in the bath. 'Commodore Cassián, Argentine Navy' with a proposition 'which I think you will find very interesting'. It had taken Cassián fifteen minutes, in the hotel bar that evening, to outline his offer. Hicks remembered particularly the eyes, black and lively, and like the rest of Cassián, small, close-set, dark and round. The English was adroit, heavily accented, suggesting one who read more than he spoke. Nature had been over-generous with the lips, but he managed them quite well, Hicks thought as he listened with increasing interest and excitement to the little man.

'That is my proposal, Captain Eeks. The basic idea. Details can come later. Now, will you let me buy a drink?'

'No thanks,' Hicks's glass was empty.

'Then you will excuse while I buy for myself?'

'Of course.' Cocky little sod. The bar was filling up. Hicks' first officer waved from his barstool between the hostesses: Hicks had told him he probably wouldn't be joining them, this evening. His eyes took in the over-familiar scene, a fashionable down-town hotel bar, the cheerful expectancy of early evening borne on chattering voices. Prosperous people pleased with themselves in a way that nowadays eluded him.

As an aircrew nightstop hotel you couldn't ask for better: for Hicks, it had gone stale long ago.

Now, in the last few minutes a rare exhilaration had gripped him. It dimmed the sights and sounds around, and deep inside him long-abandoned expectations stirred.

But for the Commodore, returning to his seat with a fresh glass, it would have been impossible to guess, from his politely interested expression, that Captain Jeff Hicks was effervescent with excitement.

'If I understand correctly,' he said, 'you want me to recruit a team of pilots to help you train an Attack Group for the Argentine Navy. I don't pretend to understand South American politics, so most of what you have told me I will have to take on trust. But there are some practicalities you did not mention.'

'Of course.' The man really was insufferably smug.

'First,' continued Hicks, 'the pilots would I suppose be classed as mercenaries. There is the question of payment.'

'Each one who completes his contract will be paid a quarter of a million pounds sterling,' Cassián said quietly while examining the contents of his glass.

There was a longish pause.

'High-class mercenaries!' Hicks allowed himself to sound impressed.

Cassián looked straight at him. 'I want the best, Captain Eeks. And to anticipate your next question, it is possible to make ironcast arrangements through English lawyers for the money, with English banks. Ironcast.' He frowned at having to raise his voice as a mixed party of noisy Dutch infiltrated around the next table.

Cassián sat back; smooth, neat, poised, expectant. They could not continue their discussion in this place, but the Argentine commodore had left the ball with Hicks. Let him wait: Hicks' brain was racing. The prospect of returning to military flying had been exciting enough – but a quarter of a million! The money was important mainly for its implications – something big, expensive, sophisticated, in which he, on account of his naval background, was being offered an important part. Cassián's brief sketch of Argentina's current political and military scene, aimed at establishing a context for

8

his proposed 'Special Air Attack Group', was of only peripheral interest to Hicks, who had left the Royal Navy some years ago after a lifetime in naval aviation, most of it actively flying. He had been driving an Anglo Continental Fokker F27 back and forth across the North Sea ever since, and had lately begun to feel trapped. Congenial monotony, the secret of happiness, he had once read, had become uncongenial boredom. Now, here, out of nowhere, this little man was holding open a door back into the world of real flying. All Hicks' instincts cried out yes! yes!, but there was more to it than that. He needed time. Not much, but a little . . .

'Shall we go somewhere quieter to eat?' he asked, at length.

Cassián beamed. 'I have already anticipated that pleasure, Captain Eeks!'

The Isidore Penthouse restaurant, exclusive and expensive, was of a world beyond Hicks' orbit. If his slightly up-market dog-robber's outfit jarred, the shock was barely noticeable as the establishment enfolded the two men. Their table, like all the others, was placed to afford privacy without isolation. Cassián was a model host.

Hicks had still had little time to think. In the taxi, Cassián had startled him by asking after his wife, Pauline, and his sons. He even commiserated upon the recent death of the family Labrador, Bonzo, pronounced Bontho. As his host ordered apéritifs, Hicks was thinking their relationship was becoming uncomfortably asymmetric.

'I'm no politician, Commodore, but the government you represent, the military government of Argentina, is not exactly popular – anywhere. Am I right? There is, for instance, the problem of disappearing people. How many is it? Twenty thousand? Thirty thousand?'

'Captain Eeks, you do well to ask zis!' Cassián gave no sign that he thought the question discourteous. He took a sip of his Pernod, leaned forward and spoke intently:

'Your country,' he said, 'has a political system which prevents excesses. You are fortunate. But you should not think this is a natural state of national affairs. Argentina is a young country, and there are deep divisions. On the land, in the *haciendas*, a Spanish aristocracy. In Buenos Aires, the business classes. And then the workers and their unions who despise and envy both. And under all this, the old British economy, dead now, railways and beef. Nothing since has been so good.'

Absent-mindedly, Cassián took the menu from the waiter, laid it down unopened and went on earnestly. 'Not blaming the British – do not think that! But do not be too quick to judging our ways. We do not like what we have to do to control our country, but our enemies will do the same to us, if they have control. Oh yes! And we happen to think Argentina is a better country without communism. These things don't happen in England? Of course – but I repeat, you are fortunate. These are the methods of primitive states, and you know they are used every day in Russia, or Iran, or South Africa – a dozen other countries. Northern Ireland maybe –' and here he became conspiratorial; 'Tooth and claw politics, Captain Eeks. Be grateful you only need to put a cross on a paper.'

Hicks change tack. 'The pilots I could get are not particularly young men. What aircraft are you using?'

'I cannot tell you that'. There was no regret in Cassián's statement, and he chose this moment to summon the waiter. When he continued, it was on another theme.

'Would you agree, Commander,' – the use of his Royal Naval substantive rank instead of the airline 'Captain' was not lost on Hicks, slewing their relationship towards the intimacy of professionals – 'that modern warfare has produced what we might call an oscillating equilibrium of offensive and defensive systems – and that there is a great advantage in being the first to innovate?'

Hicks smiled at this. 'Of course – but this is nothing new. It was true of the bow and arrow.'

'You are correct,' the Commodore nodded, 'but with modern technology the rate of innovation has become greater than ever before – too great, because of cost, for the system to accommodate! In the air, faster planes need faster planes to catch and intercept. Better weapons need better defences, but better defences need better weapons! But consider how it would be, in this situation, when somebody comes in with the

10

big innovation, *radicalismo*, a new departure! Something totally new!' There was a new animation in the deep black eyes.

'Kamikazes,' said Hicks.

'Excuse me?' Cassián looked politely puzzled.

'Kamikazes. Classic example of dislocation caused by the introduction of contradictive variety into a stable situation. They played hell with the US Navy – for a while, anyway.'

Cassián beamed. 'A beautiful example! The first cruise missile! And what were your words? 'Contradictive variety'? Contradictive variety! I like this expression very much!'

For the first time since they met, Hicks felt some warmth for the strange little Argentine. 'I assume you are not seeking pilots for the Kamikaze role?' he asked.

Cassián laughed. 'An attractive concept, Commander – the mercenary suicide! No indeed. We want you and your men for their brains. But they will fly, of course.'

'What in?'

'I may not tell you here about the equipment. But be sure the Special Attack Group will be a "contradictive variety" in modern warfare. And we believe with this advantage we can radically alter the political and military balance in South America – in our favour. Up to now, we are rationed. By the US. They don't want any of us so powerful to dominate the continent, or so weak we let in the communists. Now, in Argentina we want to make our own decisions, our own destiny. And with the Special Attack Group we can do it – because it is unorthodox. I can tell you it is very unorthodox!'

Hicks ate, trying to visualise South America, the continent, Argentina. He was unsure of the scale of his mental picture, imagining distances in thousands of miles, pampas and jungles, the Andes, endless coasts. The idea of a single air strike group enabling one country to dominate a sub-continent struck him as improbable. But this man was no fool.

A chilling thought caused him to pause, glass half-raised. He fixed Cassián with a cold questioning look and was about to speak, but the Commodore forestalled him with one of his cherubic grins.

'And if I may anticipate your next question, Commander – the attack group will use only conventional weapons. Not nuclear, not chemical, not biological.'

11

Hicks drained his glass and pushed his plate away. Damn the man! If he was so clever, and if he knew so much, and if he had gone to the trouble of arranging this meeting, he must know I'm not going to turn this down.

'I've always thought,' Hicks said in a voice with a new edge to it, 'the most important quality in a military commander is the power of anticipation. Allow me to congratulate you, Commodore. Of course I accept your offer.'

'Excellent!' Cassián showed no surprise. 'This I promise you, my dear Commander, you will not regret.' He poured for a toast and raised his glass. 'To our futures – and to the Special Attack Group! May these two lie together in success!'

He produced a paper and passed it across the table to Hicks. Hicks read a list of names, familiar names. Contemporaries. But more than that, these were probably the only pilots among all those Hicks had served with who he would have said lived and breathed to fly, men who had passed up promotions and pensions to go on doing dangerous things in fast aeroplanes. Fliers all, and good. Hicks pondered the list for a while: an inside job, from somebody who knew the Navy's pilots as well as he did. It made him, if anything, happier about his decision to go along with the Commodore.

'You want me plus six?'

'Yes. Seven,' Cessián answered with a quiet smile.

They had talked late and hard and found a lot of common ground. Before they parted, Hicks was given a London address, in Vauxhall Bridge Road, for future contact.

Back in his hotel, Hicks had lain in the dark, a roundabout of questions in his head; excited, but not troubled. Two years' operational flying in Argentina, even if it was to be almost incommunicado for security reasons, was something nobody in his right mind could turn down. The quarter of a million was still peripheral, but it made him think of Pauline, at home in Norfolk. No, not *at* home – she *was* the home. He came and went, always had. He loved her warmly, as he loved his home, the Aga warmth of its untidy kitchen, the redolence of children. She would be a little sad, but she would not question: they had always trusted to each other to maintain a balance of sacrifice and advantage throughout their long and comfortable marriage. And she, like all sensible wives of naval fliers, had from very early days erected around her a protective scaffolding of her own interests so that, if the ever-dreaded call should come, her life would not collapse. She would have no trouble coping with two years on her own. And then, afterwards . . .

But how did the Argentines get those names . . .? And who were they going to be fighting . . .? Seven Samurai? Or The Magnificent Seven . . .? Hicks had gone to sleep with a smile.

Chapter 2

Hicks resisted the overwhelming desire to look back. As the bus took them away from the two Corsairs, he tried to put out of his mind the oval face and almond eyes – he fancied, now, there might have been an edge of green around the pupils, eerie, ancient. He forced himself to re-engage with the others and their lively questions. The bus drove back along the fronts of hangars on a vast expanse of concrete. More concrete than Hicks had ever seen. Corsairs were parked out, in groups, and the hangar doors were open now revealing many more. The place was coming to life. They turned left around the last hangar, up a road between new buildings. There was no green, just grey earth, now concrete, tarmac, and swirling grey dust.

It had been very easy to persuade the others to drop what they were doing and come with him. He would have been surprised otherwise. They met in a London hotel in October. Jock Munro, big grin full of teeth, big aggressive ears, guttural brogue unameliorated by twenty years south of the border. The loud and legendary Pierre LeStrange: everything the man said laden with bullshit and inflated with hot air, but an effortlessly good pilot. Trixy Tracey, the baby, a fair-haired Peter Pan with his deceptive air of transparent innocence. Mike Finch, crew-cut, blue-eyed and alert, expensive-looking, very self-assured. Tim Blount, a medium man, balding, rotund of build and with a close indoor expression, might have been a small farmer or a butcher in a good neighbourhood; close friends of Hicks, wife not long died of cancer. And Miles Channing, serious, tousled hair, moustache, stock figure from the staff-room of a busy comprehensive. All recently ex-Navy, and, in their day, the best. Two weapons specialists, two tactics instructors, two flying instructors, and Hicks himself, weapons. Each for his own good reasons had needed no persuasion. So far, they seemed not quite dismayed by Cassián's Corsairs, but not enthusiastic, either, except perhaps for LeStrange, who had flown them long ago.

'Fantastic aeroplane, Trixy!' he was booming, to Tracey. 'Go for miles. Carry anything, stay up hours, and *beautiful* to fly!'

'Heapa junk! Propeller, for God's sake! How fast?'

'Four hundred – in the dive.'

'Geez!' Tracey had never had a propeller. 'What've I got myself into now!'

*

'So now you have seen Argentina's secret weapon!' Cassián looked incongruous in full uniform whites, with much gold. Without it, he could have been an onion-seller, or an academic, Hicks thought. He occupied the narrow rostrum of a small lecture-theatre in the HQ building. The place smelled of new wood and paint and the air-conditioning made Hicks' sweaty clothes cold on his skin.

'I am Contraalmirante Cassián – Commodore in your navy. You would call me 'Commodore Corsairs'. I have special responsibility for the Grupo Especial de Ataque based here at Roca. GEA.' He pronounced it 'gaya'. 'I will presume to anticipate some of your questions.' Hicks smiled to himself. 'First – where do we get these planes? We build them, here in Argentina. We start the factory four years now. We make all here, except propellers. How many? Several hundreds!'

'Several *hundred*!' Tracy sounded incredulous. Numbers like this were outside the British experience.

'Yes, hundreds.' Cassián was enjoying himself. 'So if you multiply what you see this morning by maybe a hundred you will obtain an imagination of the potential of the Grupo. Old design, yes. But modern weapons, modern engineering, and modern tactics. And – most important – numbers. Lenin, I do

15

not much admire, but he it was said quantity has a quality of its own. It's true. The Corsair is primitive, OK. But when GEA is trained and operational – with your help – it will overwhelm any modern air defence system. If you are doubtful of this, ask yourself how any modern system could respond to a hundred, two hundred, dive-bombers in a single raid?'

Hicks wasn't doubtful at all: numbers like that had gone out of fashion. They would swamp anything even the super-powers had nowadays in the way of air defence.

'Here at Roca we have five squadrons – Numbers One to Five – each forty planes and fifty pilots.' Hicks was beginning to feel overwhelmed himself by the scale of this extraordinary group, as the little commodore went on: 'And in the Headquarters Squadron are three Flights: A Flight is Flying Training; B Flight is tactics; C Flight is weapons, development and proving. The role of GEA is attack! The aim is to be operational within one year and half – by the middle of next year, 1982. Your job is to advise and assist with this training. You will work in Headquarters Squadron, two in each flight. Commander Eeks works with Commander Monegario. Your ranks will all be the same – *Capitán de Corbeta* – except Commander Eeks who is *Capitán de Fregata*. And you are all subject to Argentine military law for the period of your contract. You have operational status, from today.'

The big question, to Hicks, was where GEA fitted in. He felt he knew as much as any outsider about the Argentine military, from reading. If it weren't for its size GEA could be a private venture, by Cassián or, more likely, a patron. This would certainly fit in with the endemic rivalry and distrust between the leaders of the three armed services, and could account for the secrecy attending all his dealings with Cassián. But an air force on this scale, not to mention the manufacturing enterprise, was a national effort. So what was behind it, and where did the money come from, in a country reputed to be bankrupt?

Cassián leaned towards his audience to emphasise his next words. 'It would not be the first time Englishmen have made a big name in South America, eh? You know about O'Higgins? And Cochrane?' He beamed around. 'So – welcome aboard! I salute you! The work you will enjoy. The play you must work

16

at! In two years you will leave as wealthy men and honoured friends of Argentina. Now, you will have many questions . . .?'

'Why did you choose the Corsair?' Finch barely waited for the Commodore to finish.

'We did not choose.' Cassián was taking a chair to the centre of the rostrum. He sat down and continued calmly: 'We had drawings for the Corsair, and only the Corsair, from the American factory.'

'Are they all here?' asked Finch again, abruptly.

'Yes. You will see. We have special arrangements. We have to think about spy satellites. Secrecy, surprise, these are very important.' The Commodore was puffing on a cigar, relaxed in his chair.

'Who is the enemy?' Channing asked mildly.

'Any enemy of the Argentine State is your enemy.' The reply was bland. Hicks was uneasy with this, for a reason he couldn't put his finger on. He moved back onto firmer ground.

'How far have you got with the training programme?'

'The first four hundred pilots have been trained to one hundred and fifty hours on propeller planes. All these have started conversion to the Corsair. At this point, we find we need help. Fifty pilots started one year before, and are now about 450 hours. These are selected for instructors and leaders. One you saw flying this morning.'

Teniente Souza. Carla. Built like a gaucho, riding a Corsair, blasting tanks in the pampas. Hicks couldn't get her face to go away.

'How many females?' he asked, again.

'Twenty-six per cent. Why females? We wanted many good pilots in a hurry. We discover no difference in psychometry or psychomotor tests in girls' performance, so why not use them? They are good – as good as the men, and probably more patriotic.'

Finch spoke again: 'If our role is attack, who provides escort?'

'Organic? Is that the word? We are an autonomous unit. Zis is your problem. Defence against fighters, ground missiles and guns you make within the Grupo. You must work on weapons and tactics for this.'

17

'Within what limitations? I mean what are the resources?'
Finch snapped the question.

'No limitations. You want something, you get it. And we have full engineering on the base.'

The booming tones of LeStrange rang out: 'May I ask, sir, why you don't use Argentine Navy experts. You have one carrier and a Naval Air Arm already, I believe?'

Hicks sensed reluctance in the pause before Cassián replied. 'Our Fuerza Aeronavale is small, its officers are career professionals. They do not have great experience of large flying training organisation or maritime air, like you.' He paused again to examine the end of his cigar from which the ash had just dropped to the floor. 'There is, too, as you know, much rivalry between the armed forces in Argentina. GEA is a big project, important for our country. It will change the course of Argentine history. Control of GEA would give too much power to either our Navy, or our Air Force, for the other to accept. Or the Army. Remember Argentina is ruled since 1976 by a junta of the three forces. GEA must be neutral, so we avoid using our own officers if possible. There are some, you will meet soon.'

'Then why not US Navy pilots? There must be thousands, certainly hundreds as good as us – willing and eager.' LeStrange persisted.

'Politics! This is the US backyard – or so they think. They would find a way to stop GEA. We could not risk CIA to discover us. With you, I don't think they will, eh?'

'OK,' pronounced Tracey from a near-horizontal position in his seat. 'I like the idea . . . sir. Great! Fantastic! But these bleeding aeroplanes, these Corsairs, I've never even seen one before. Never flown anything like it. Never even had a propeller! Am I supposed to be an expert?'

'I think so. Tell me, how many of the pilots in this room have you flown against in practice air combat? And how many won?'

Tracey craned his neck, not really looking, then said: 'All of them I guess. And none.'

'So, you write the book on air fighting the Corsair!'

'Thanks a bunch! When do I get airborne in one of these heaps then?'

18

'Pretty soon.' Cassián got up, walked to the side of the dais, threw his cigar butt into a tin trash-can with a loud clang, and came back to face them, rubbing his hands. 'Another thing. Our working language is Spanish. Some pilots have some English. Many have none. There is a language laboratory and you start language study tomorrow. For the beginning, you each have an interpreter who will also be your assistant and guide. Your right-hand man, yes?'

'Or woman?' Munro got it in first. The others laughed.

'Why not?' replied the Contraalmirante.

They read, they studied, they flew, they explored. The *consejeros*, they were called. The advisors.

They soon found themselves appreciating the Corsair's advantages; its agility, its range and endurance and load-carrying potential and the superb avionics the Argentines had built into it. Most promising of all, in the context of air combat, was the absence of jet-exhaust: without a plume of hot gas for infra-red seekers the Corsair was immune to all but the latest air-to-air missiles. No jet could hope to out-manoeuvre it in a gunfight; and with heat-seeking missiles slung under its own stubby wings the Corsair would be death to any jet that came within a mile.

They didn't like the gunsight, which would have to double as bombsight; they found handling the power-plant, the 2300 bhp Pratt and Whitney double-radial and the 13½-foot propeller, hard work, after jets; there were no airbrakes, and the weapon carriers were totally inadequate. And worst of all was the physical effort required to manoeuvre the Corsair, especially at high speed, without power-controls. They didn't see how female pilots could cope.

The Corsair took a lot of getting used to. Blount and Tracey, early on, met up at 10,000 feet and fell to circling, like high-tailed cats or sumo wrestlers, or fighter pilots. The circle got smaller as they pulled tighter, going for each other's tail. Holding the very unfamiliar aircraft warily on the stall buffet, Blount, with very little experience in heavy pistons, was running out of ideas. Through the throttle gate into 'War Emergency'? Better not. Speed one-ten. Down combat flap and go for the yo-yo. Nose down suddenly and roll left and cut

19

across the circle. Keep her on the buffet! God it was hard work! Panting and grunting, he cursed the lack of power controls and electric trim. You're out of condition, Tim! Young man's game? We'll see! Tracey had countered. But was the little bastard using flap? They crossed in the centre of the circle. Blount waited until Tracey's Corsair passed down his left side and disappeared from view, then rolled savagely right, using a lot of rudder, to reverse the turn, hauled the nose up, with enormous effort, towards the vertical and looked back over his right shoulder for Tracey.

Bastard! The kid had done exactly the same, and the two Corsairs were poised, nose high, no more than 200 yards apart, Blount could see Tracey's head through the plexiglass, against the bright sky. Then – *shit!* What the hell's happening? Blount's Corsair had developed a mind of its own and began to roll viciously left, out of the turn, shuddering like a wet dog. A *spin!* Stupid *Bastard!* Panting through clenched teeth Blount jerked the throttle shut and took a two-handed grip on the stick and held it rock centre and waited. Spin? Or hammer-stall? If it spun, well he'd read the book. But that enormous long nose! He didn't fancy it.

It didn't spin. Without torque, the roll stopped and the Corsair's aerodynamic stability took over. Blount hung with zero speed, half-inverted, nose-high, cursing, until with a sickening swoosh the long nose cut down through the horizon in a hammer-stall and he was looking at the ground a mile below. Blount rolled the wings level, eased on some power, pulled the Corsair up to level flight, and breathed again. The air he drew in was heavy with fuel vapour. Warm with adrenalin, he gave a little grunt of pleasure at being alive.

'Dagga-dagga-dagga!' Tracey's voice, quietly, on the R/T. Bugger! The kid was on his tail. Blount's head jerked round but the other Corsair was out of sight, probably in his deep six. Oh well! – it wasn't the first time! Nor the first time he'd nearly killed himself hassling with Tracey. He rocked his wings. Tracey's Corsair emerged under his right tailplane and moved forward into the #3 formation position.

'Love fifteen! Big deal! I'm RTB for a clean pair of underpants!'

Tracey replied: 'You have the lead – and your slip is showing!'

Blount looked quickly around his cockpit, momentarily puzzled. Then the flap lever caught his eye, showing 20 Down. He moved the little lever to the fully up position, adjusted the trim and made a V-sign across sixty feet of space at Tracey's girlish grin. He felt a bit sick. The fumes. A drink would be good. A large gin.

Tracey's first comment on the Corsair was characteristic: 'Like flying a bleedin' iron foundry! But I'll tell you what, Tim,' he said to Blount, 'there's only one jet I know's going to be able to hassle this thing with a couple of 'Winders on it!'

'And what's that, Trixy?'

'Bleedin' Harrier! Good job there ain't any round here!'

There was no airfield boundary, no wire or fences separating the base from its desert-like surroundings. On the east side the airfield was bounded by the sea. Five-hundred-foot cliffs dropped sheer to the Atlantic. The cliffs extended seemingly forever, broken only occasionally by small shelving bays and beaches such as lay at the end of the rough track north of the base. They were told that Roca Zone was a circle of fifty miles radius and no Corsair was allowed beyond this. There was no other airfield within flying range, they were informed, but Roca had three good runways to allow flying in the fickle, gusting winds and dust storms that were a local feature.

From above, Hicks thought it looked like a different planet. For fifty miles south-west the cliffs continued. Twenty miles north-west, the coast turned back west, forming a blunt promontory beyond which the monotonous cliffs went on. There was no human habitation on or near this inhospitable coast. Only in a few wide ravines was there any vegetation, and a few poor-looking *estancias*, with sheep. From the air, the new airfield was a stark intrusion on this desolation. A new black-top road ran north to the horizon.

Early on, Hicks discerned the reason for the Corsairs' unusual paint scheme. They all had a swept-wing planform painted in black upon the upper wing and tail surfaces, and the long cylindrical front fuselage was painted to a point half way along. The rest of the upper surface being sea-grey, the effect, viewed from anything above a few thousand feet, was to disguise the Corsair as a small delta-wing jet, not unlike the A-4 Skyhawk in service elsewhere in Argentina.

The new base would have been registered by reconnaissance satellites, US, Russian, or both, but it would require a dedicated effort – or serendipity – to uncover the Corsair. Looking down from 5,000 feet, Hicks could appreciate the cost of the project, an enormous construction effort in an inaccessible wilderness. He tried estimating, adding in several hundred Corsairs, and gave up at around a billion sterling – or maybe two? He assumed he was looking down on a good slice of Argentina's foreign debt.

Indeed he was driving a purring package of it through the clear Argentine morning air – how incredibly clean the sky was after Europe! And how good it was, after four years of bus driving, to fly even a last-generation warplane, full of power and purpose. The Wasp was running sweetly, all gauges steady, and after only three flights he was beginning to appreciate the chunky, battleworthy feel of the Corsair. He played a while longer, looping and rolling, hauling, grunting and panting until his arm ached. Presently he throttled back, opened the hood and started down for home.

Home. The word didn't fit Roca yet. Not this concrete excrescence on a Patagonian wilderness. Home was Norfolk, England. A warm kitchen, a rambling garden, a loving, warm and welcoming woman, now so remote. Unbidden, entirely unbidden, a face intervened; a small pale face framed in a mass of dark hair, small features, almond brown eyes. Then there was the slender length of Teniente Souza's black-clad figure. But mostly the eyes . . .

*

Roca had the usual operational, engineering and domestic areas of any air base. The bulk of young pilots were cadets – *guardiamarinas* – and lived in barracks. The advanced cadre, the *tenientes*, lived in a block of the officers' quarters where the seven British and other officers had chalets arranged around a grassless square. All officers shared the restaurant and bar facilities of the Rancho.

22

On the Saturday after their arrival, the *consejeros* were enjoying their first relaxed evening. 'Hell,' said Blount after dinner, 'if the women eat steaks like that every day, perhaps we shouldn't worry!' They had been talking again, about the Corsair's stick-force problem.

'G forces pretty high too. You forget,' said Hicks. They walked into the bar-anteroom that was the focus of Roca's social life. Tracey and LeStrange waved from a table in the big pillared room. Hicks thought, as they went over, how the khaki uniforms emphasised their new circumstances.

'What a week!' LeStrange was drinking beer. 'Four days ago I was in my local. Now here I am God knows where on the other half of the world, getting ready to play Biggles in somebody else's war!'

'You know you're loving it, Pierre,' Blount said. LeStrange was one of those pilots for whom time between cockpits is time wasted.

'Who's complaining?' LeStrange grinned. 'I like the beast.'

'My arm aches.' Tracey flexed his right arm, wincing.

'Extra wheaties, Trixy, that's what you need,' replied LeStrange.

'Like flying a bloody flat-iron! I don't know how some of these girls are going to cope when they start putting bombs on. They're going to be spearing in all over the place 'cause they can't pull out of dives!'

'What a waste! But they're not all Jane Austen types, you know. Carla did all right on those tanks. Some woman, that. She's over there with her boyfriend.' LeStrange looked past Tracey towards where Carla Souza sat with a fair-haired male *teniente*. Tracey turned, and the girl turned her head. Hicks thought she was looking at him.

Monegario said, 'May I join you, gentlemen?'

There was a lot of shop-talk before the subject of stick-force came up again. 'I don't think you should worry,' he said. 'They all train for two years already, like marines. Men and women the same. Every day they have, how do you say? . . . *gymnastico?*'

'PT,' said Hicks.

'Oh boy!' Blount drained his glass.

Monegario twisted around in his chair. He beckoned

Teniente Souza. She and her companion got up and came across. They too wore khaki drill, the girl's bony felinity emphasised by the smooth drape of her skirt. Something twisted inside Hicks as he watched her move. Monegario rose and gestured the girl to take his seat, saying a few words in Spanish.

'Another demonstration, gentlemen.' He asked them to clear the low glass table. 'Try your strength –' Monegario invited Blount who was now sitting opposite Carla. She pulled forward, placed her right elbow on the table, arm vertical, and smiled at Blount.

Blount gave a short laugh. He looked around, as if for help. The others were silent, embarrassed. The contrast between the powerful, wiry girl and Blount, half-tipsy, bright-eyed and podgy and looking not at all at home in his aviator's khakis, was stark. Blount licked his lips, pulled forward, made great play of getting his position right, and with a jokey remark about not wanting to take unfair advantage of a lady placed his hand in hers. They pushed. Effortlessly, the girl flattened Blount's arm on the table.

'Bravo, Carla,' said Monegario quietly.

'Bravo indeed,' said Hicks.

'He wasn't ready – were you, Tim?' boomed LeStrange, laughing.

'No. Wasn't ready. Here . . .' Blount offered his arm again. 'Wait . . . wait,' he fidgeted around, then: 'Now!'

They pushed. The result was the same.

Blount withdrew his hand. His smile was stiff. 'Comes of having short arms. Never was any good at that – stupid game!' He picked up his empty glass and walked away in the direction of the bar.

'Anybody else?' Monegario was looking at Hicks, smiling.

'I will!' It was Finch, from the rear of the standing group. The young Argentines started to make way for him.

'I think Commander Eeks.' Carla's voice was high and clear. 'He is highest rank, so he should be *campeón*. Come – Commander Eeks!' She indicated the empty chair.

Their faces were a foot apart as they clasped hands. 'Ready?' asked Hicks, glad of his beard. Carla's small face wore a look of serene superiority. He noticed a little curl to her lip. There was iron in her steady eyes. '*Si*. Ready,' she replied.

They pushed. Hicks felt no give. No give at all. He poured power into his arm. But his effort was completely unavailing. His power peaked without producing the slightest movement of the girl's arm. He could feel the sinewy strength in her hand, and behind that a power he doubted he could match. Well, he'd go for stamina. He held on, concentrating on feeding his arm with energy. She ought to tire first. He became conscious of her face again.

Carla's small lip quivered, the faintest tremor. He watched, fascinated. With its little carpet of dark down, it lifted in a semblance of a grin. Still willing every ounce of his strength into his arm, he looked now into her eyes. Iron, he thought. Iron eyes. Iron arm. His own arm hurt. He sensed defeat. But, God damn it, this was a woman! Again he summoned his reserves, calling in unused energy from all over his body for one last push. Eyes steady . . . don't signal it . . . count . . . one, two, three, and push! Now! Their arms quivered. Hicks saw Carla's eyes tighten, could see more of her teeth. Small teeth. Anger rose inside him at the closeness of defeat. But he had spent his strength and had no more. He felt his arm begin to give under the girder-like pressure. Then suddenly it was over. He was pressing still with animal ferocity, her hand limp, and warm, under his on the table.

'*Muy bien!* Commander Eeks is *campeón!* He is too strong for me!' Carla's voice was amazingly light and feminine. Her smile, like a pretty frock, changed her from combatant to woman. She withdrew her hand and massaged her arm.

'Well done, Jeff!' cried LeStrange. 'Saved our bacon there, old man!'

'Only just!' Hicks rubbed his arm wryly.

Carla demurely declined further challenges, and the offer of a drink. Instead, she excused herself and stood up. Lightning forked inside Hicks as she smoothed down the khaki skirt. She left with her young blond friend. The circle of onlookers broke up in a chatter of Spanish.

Monegario sat down again. 'I apologise,' he said with a smile, 'but these young people, they give up everything to be

GEA pilots. For them, is more important to be GEA pilot and fight for Argentina – and maybe die – than anything else. They live tough, they train tough, they are tough. Carla, she is one of the best. A natural pilot, *muy intelegente*, strong like a tiger. But they are all good. You see now, GEA is serious business!'

'As if we didn't know! said LeStrange.

'I've just been talking to some of the cadets,' Channing said. 'They're a bit like students. It sounds a tough life. I asked them why they did it.'

Monegario smiled. 'And they said?'

'Patriotism, basically. They do it for Argentina.'

'Bit of a change from our pinky pacifist lot, eh?' LeStrange brayed a short bar-room laugh.

'Marines? Or students?' quipped Tracey.

'Well I wouldn't have believed,' Channing said, 'in 1981, you could get their generation, anywhere, fired up like this lot. It amazes me!'

'You need to understand Argentina's politics,' said Monegario with a mixture of pride and apology. 'How can I explain? It is not easy – even for many Argentine people. You see, since Perón, there is great *nationalismo*. After the war, many people leave Europe and come here, make new homes. They want Argentina to be a great country. For their children and grandchildren. Many different poeple, but anybody who is Argentine knows this is the best country in South America. All is needed is a little more time, to show the world. GEA will do it.' He spoke confidently. As if the thing were already accomplished.

'Where do you start?' asked Finch. 'We're on the Atlantic coast, aren't we?'

'Yes. This is Patagonia. As to where we start, this is not for me to say. I don't know. But remember Clausewitz? Possession of power makes its use unnecessary? I don't know what the politicians intend.'

'You have to show off your power, though,' Channing put in, 'and the only thing of interest over here is the Falklands, isn't it?'

'*Las Malvinas*,' Monegario corrected, less genially. 'No. GEA is not for this. Argentina could take *Las Malvinas* any time, very easy. There are about forty British marines.'

'That's what I thought,' said Finch, looking slightly puzzled.

When Monegario left them, Hicks felt the group relax. There was a discomfiting intensity about the Argentine commander that was hard to put a finger on. Perhaps it was his attitude to work that jarred after the easy-going ways of the peacetime armed forces at home. But since it was apparently shared by every member of the Grupo, including the raven-haired Carla who Hicks could see laughing with her boyfriend a few tables away, it was hardly remarkable in their leader. Was it? Anyway, he was glad the Falklands had been mentioned. He'd been worrying about that ever since they found out where Roca was, but Monegario had put his mind at rest. The idea of waves of dive-bombers assailing a sheep-farm was obviously ludicrous.

Composing himself to sleep, Hicks' thoughts were of home, and Pauline. His accommodation was an ample suite; sitting-room, bedroom and bathroom; french windows; stylish furniture. The large double bed had reminded him of the French Navy's *Cercles Navales* – naval officer's clubs in Brest and Toulon, where single beds were not available. But now, his mind was in Norfolk; five a.m., Pauline asleep in their room with its familiar odours and little noises, above in their bed; the house dark and silent, young Bonzo II keeping the Aga warm in the kitchen. There was a palpable loneliness in the room where he lay. It had been there when he first walked in, as real as the new furniture. It hadn't bothered him, he thought: just the latest in three decades of cabins and hotel rooms. Ten, twenty years ago the newness of it all might have thrilled him. Not now.

There was a small knock on his door.

It was Carla. Hicks, expecting Blount in search of a drinking companion and prepared to give him a tactful send-off, had a towel around him as he opened the door. Carla stood, unsmiling, in the corridor.

'I come in?'

Seconds passed as Hicks tried to find the rational response he knew existed, somewhere. But it was a consciously futile effort. He held open the door.

'Please.'

She came in, still wearing the uniform skirt and shirt, with a black shoulder-bag.

'Sit down.' Hicks indicated an easy chair in the sitting-room and switched on a light. 'Excuse me, please.' In the bathroom he combed his hair and beard, washed his hands and put on a red towelling bathrobe.

'Would you like a drink?' he asked. Carla had not moved. There was an impenetrable assurance about the way she sat.

'Thank you. I do not want drink.'

'Coffee?'

'Maybe. Yes. Some coffee would be good.'

Damn these people, Hicks fumed to himself as he prepared the coffee. Being anticipated was becoming a habit. Must be getting old. He put her cup down and asked: 'So?'

She looked up. God damn it – it was like falling into a bottomless black pit. Down and down. He struggled inexpertly to get a grip on his emotions.

'I want to sleep with you,' she said simply.

Still falling through the black void of her eyes, the best Hicks could do was: 'Why?'

'I like you. What is you name?'

'Jeff. Jeffrey.'

'Cheff-cheffrey.' The lip curled. 'I don't like Cheff-cheffrey very much. I call you Eeks, yes?'

'All right. Eeks, if you like – Carla.'

'Yes. Carla.'

'So now. Why does Carla want to sleep with Eeks?'

'Carla likes Eeks.' Her face was wide open.

'Eeks has son same age as Carla – nearly.'

'Is no matter to Carla.' She sat there, thin black eyebrows arched, her small old-fashioned face framed in a cloud of black hair, looking back at Hicks with all the innocent directness of a small girl.

Hicks lowered his eyes to the tantalizingly small breast swelling her shirt; to the long curves of her thigh; to the thin hands cradling her cup.

The loneliness was gone from the room, dispelled by this strange woman, this creature of the pampa. He could not tell what her motives were, nor the eventual outcome of what he

28

was about to do. His need for her was not overwhelming, but to let her go now was unthinkable. He could not have said what it was that made her bald proposal attractive to him. She was neither beautiful nor pretty. But here was a woman who could fly a Corsair as well as a man, a proud, strong woman who could have humiliated him in that ridiculous game but chose instead to let him win. And now she was offering the comfort of her body.

'You want I should sleep with you?'

'Yes. I would like that very much.'

She relaxed. 'Good!' She mimicked, gently: 'I also would like that very much!' Hicks was pleased to note the relaxing tension in her: her assurance then was not so doubly sure.

They talked, on what struck Hicks as a comically incongruous businesslike level. Carla asked genuinely about his wife and children, but it was soon clear she was more interested in his career, his flying, and ultimately in why he had chosen to join GEA. He tried to explain. It was a salutary exercise to have to put across his reasoning without using long words.

'I come here because all my life I have been in military aviation. But in my country now there is no place for me. No war. No prospect of war. Here, you have need of help with your war. Here is a place for me. So, I come.'

'But it is not your country. Not your war.'

'No matter. If Argentina has problem with agriculture, or engineering, or medicine, she will get help maybe from my country. Or Italy. Or Germany. Anywhere. There is no difference. I give Argentina professional assistance with her war.'

'But being engineer or doctor is not so dangerous; not get maybe killed in their work.'

'No. But doctors and engineers not so exciting. Not so interesting, I think!'

'Good!' Carla looked pleased. 'I think so too!' She became serious again.

'But to kill is different. Doctors and engineers do not have to kill. You do not . . .?' she looked around for the word, gave up, gestured with slender hands, 'This is not problem for you?'

29

'Mind. I do not mind. No. This is in the job. My work is to kill and maybe be killed. Between professionals, this is no problem. It is the oldest profession. And I do not operate against civilians. I do not like even to work against conscripts.' Hicks paused, wondering if she understood the word. They were sitting apart, and their talk had distracted him. A fresh awareness set off the vertiginous lightning in his belly.

'*Conscriptioneros*. I understand. But our *conscriptioneros* are so stupid!'

'That is no reason to kill somebody, Carla.'

'But if they try to kill you, even stupid?'

'Then that is reason to kill. But you, Carla – you are a woman. Why do you do this? This is not woman's work.'

'In England maybe. But here in Argentina we have not so many people, and is necessary everybody work for the country. To make Argentina great.' There was nothing of the zealot in the way Carla spoke, more a child saying its creed. 'So, if a woman can do something, she do it. I can fly pretty good, so I fly, in GEA.'

'You don't want husband? Children?'

'Of course!' She sounded surprised. 'After. Plenty of time after. I want many childrens. Four. Six!'

'Good! *Magnifico!* It would be a sin to deprive the world of your offspring.'

'Excuse me?'

'No matter.'

'Oh . . . Eeks . . ' For the first time since he had known her, Carla looked hesitant.

'Yes?'

'I 'ope you don't . . .' she tailed off, groping.

'Mind?'

'*Si*. I 'ope you don't mind. But tonight, for just tonight, you must not touch me. I 'ave – how you say – *la maldejada* – so we just sleep. Is all right?'

The curse! God damn! What sort of . . .? How . . .? Hicks burst out laughing at himself. But Carla looked so unhappy he stopped abruptly, leaned across and took her hand in both of his. 'Is all right, Carla. Tonight, we sleep. Come!'

In bed.

'Eeks?'

'Yes?'

'Your wife – you love her?'

'Yes. Very much.'

'She is good woman?'

'She is very good woman. Beautiful and good.'

'Yes. I think she is good woman.' Carla was silent in the dark. Then: 'You think she . . . mind?'

Hicks thought. About seven o'clock now at home. Pauline was an early riser. She would be up now, and organising her day.

'No. Pauline would not mind.'

The indescribable solace of the girl's presence beside him could not, he convinced himself, be a bad thing: there is, after all, it is well known, a unique intra-male distress, an anthropological thirst, that can only be relieved by the closeness of a woman.

He slept.

Chapter 3

Six months later, Hicks looked back with mixed feelings on the time that had passed since their arrival in Roca.

On a personal level, although his relationship with Carla had settled into a pattern of baffling, sometimes maddening unpredictability, he was conscious that she had worked a change in him that would be permanent, a new theme in the symphony of his life. They had slept together, regularly and tempestuously. On a wave of passion, he had neither thought nor cared where they were going. She let herself into his rooms, used them as her own. They talked. He learned a lot about her childhood and family, and incidentally about the fierce politics of Argentina. They argued. She never paused to consider a problem, never hesitated with an answer; she either loved a thing or hated it with an unself-conscious frankness that fascinated Hicks. He noticed – it surely wasn't imagination? – that wherever she went she enhanced the current of life around her. Things happened. Knives cut.

But he didn't have Carla to himself. Her affection had a feline inconsistency that allowed her with apparent insouciance to desert him after a few days and return to younger company. He would be treated with friendly indifference if their paths crossed. The first time this happened, he was devastated. And when, after some days, she walked back into his room at ten o'clock one evening, complete with the black shoulder-bag, Hicks was so cross he nearly spoilt everything.

'You just walk out without a word and treat me like a stranger for a week. And who is that *boy*,' he stressed the word, 'you've been with? His name is Funk, isn't it? What's special about *him*? Who *do* you like anyway – him or me? Or don't you know?'

'His name is Rudi.'

'Rudi Funk! A German!'

'I like 'im.'

'His name is ridiculous!'

'Not more ridiculous than Jeff-Jeffrey Eeks! And he is good Argentine, not German.'

'And you like 'im,' Hicks had mimicked. 'Then why are you here?'

'I don't have to like just one person! Why should I? You are nice. Rudi is nice. Most people I no like, but I like you, Eeks, and Rudi, and some others – not many. And I do what I like. And I hate jealous people – so please, Eeks, don't be jealous. I like you too much.'

'Jealous!' He had stood up, raised his arms in mock supplication. 'The most beautiful girl in South America sleeps with me for a week and then runs off with some Kraut kid, waving her goddam hair all over the place. And the way you wear that uniform would drive anybody wild – you know that don't you!' She was smiling with the corner of her mouth. He stormed on. 'So what am I supposed to do – just wait around till you can fit me into your schedule? That means programme – *pro-gramme*!'

'You want me go? I go!' Carla was quite matter-of-fact. She picked up her shoulder-bag from the floor and put it on her knees.

Hicks felt panic. He stood in front of her, looking down.

'What do you think?' he demanded roughly, disturbed by her blandness. 'Of course I don't –'

She interrupted. 'Then I stay! Only I don' like you be angry, Eeks. You got to be nice to me!'

Hicks was nearly speechless, 'Who's angry, for God's sake? I'd just like to know why you think you can go round like a goddam princess picking up people here and there – I mean do you have a list or something?'

Carla smiled. 'A short list. I told you.'

Hicks sat down facing her. He felt secure again. But what was he doing? A game of musical beds with a girl young enough to be his daughter! Ridiculous! But he was in the game, willy-nilly. He knew it as he looked into Carla's small face with its small smile.

'Are all Argentine girls like you?' Sternly.

'Maybe. No. I don' know. Why?' She unzipped her bag.

'Do you want a drink?'

'Of course.'

At the sideboard, pouring two glasses of Argentine white, Hicks asked over his shoulder: 'Have you ever thought of being a princess?'

'*Princesa* – foo! I rather to be *comandero* of Corsair squadron!'

'Or empress. For Argentina's new empire! A new Eva?'

'You speak *ridicolo*, Eeks.'

'But you would enjoy it – you would have such power.' He gave her the glass.

'I 'ave power,' Carla said, smiling, her long fingers brushing his, and something resonated inside Hicks.

And so it was. She came and went at will, a big beautiful cat, confident of his affection. Hicks didn't know if she slept with Funk, or anybody else. He didn't ask. He didn't much care. Recognising his own besottedness, he eschewed self-contempt in favour of self-congratulation: he was after all nothing if not a seeker of experience, and he had never been besotted before. Let it run its course.

The mettlesome Corsair dominated the other side of all their lives.

Cassián chaired progress meetings every Monday. At the first of these, back in January, they met the commanders of the Grupo's five squadrons, and Cassián had set out their aim: to prepare the unit for operations against defended maritime and land targets, optimising the Corsair's distinctive characteristics. They had eighteen months.

To Hicks, Cassián's aviation knowledge and his decisiveness were equally remarkable. He was soon persuaded that if the Grupo was to be all-weather capable it must have a two-seat instrument trainer, and authorised work to start at once to provide twelve tandem Corsairs – a decision that was to affect all their lives in a way that could never have been foreseen. He agreed to acquire some jets, to develop air-combat tactics. He talked fluently about electronic countermeasures, a cornerstone of modern war, and assured them they would have the best. It seemed resources were indeed unlimited: all this would have taken years of committee work at home; here, it was done in minutes.

When they came to the crucial question of the Corsair's weapon fit, Finch was the expert, but when Cassián asked him for his recommendation he gave the consensus British view. His rapid delivery soon had the Argentine CO's rolling their eyes helplessly as they gave up trying to follow him.

'Your Corsair can be adapted to carry any weapons up to certain size and weight limits and it has very good AC and DC power. This gives you plenty of scope. However –' Finch paused, set his pen vertically in front of him and looked up and down the table, 'I've been involved with weapon trials and development over ten years, and I can tell you that, starting with a raw airframe like your Corsair, you are going to be lucky to have anything operational inside twelve months! So your weapon choice is under very strict discipline. Design, engineering, testing and development in one year, to allow six months' training and work-up! I suggest you can only have the most simple and robust, and the choice must be made now!'

'And what is your choice?'

'Iron bombs and Sidewinder.'

'And why?' Cassián asked. There was some muttering from the Argentine officers.

'Iron bombs are robust, reliable, and the various types and sizes have a common delivery profile which reduces training. Sidewinder too is robust, reliable, easy to fit, and effective against jets. Guns and cannon are out since the Corsair will never get behind a jet. Sidewinder also gets around the gunsight problem. With these two, the Grupo would have the offensive power you want, and effective defence. So, bombs and Sidewinder – simple, feasible, effective!'

'We also have Exocet!' said Cassián, to a murmur of approval from the Argentines.

'I know. And I don't doubt the Corsair could carry it and its radar, but I also know how long it took the French to marry it to the *Étentard*!'

Hicks broke in: 'You'd certainly need help from the French, but that's not the only point. Surely it would compromise the whole philosophy of GEA, which is strength through numbers.'

There was an intermission. Cassián excused himself and lapsed into Spanish. A vigorous discussion took place among the Argentines. 'Exocet', 'Sidewinder' and *'bombas'* were tossed back and forth. Hicks thought they didn't much like what Finch had said, but when eventually, Cassián held up his hand for silence and spoke to them in Spanish, they showed varying degrees of agreement.

'We have decided,' he said in English. 'Because of the time, we go for bombs and Sidewinder, immediately. Others we will develop too, but not to interfere with these. Immediate is now! This meeting is closed. Capitán Monegario will coordinate. Progress meeting here in one week and every week. Thank you, gentlemen.'

'Commodore.' Hicks spoke as Cassián stood up. 'If all your Corsairs are here, what about a pre-emptive strike? Are you not worried? We haven't seen any AA defences.'

'All the eggs in one basket?' Cassián smiled. 'But who is going to attack Roca? Who knows we are here? Who is near enough? Nobody!'

'People come, people go. Can you be sure?'

The Commodore sat down, turned to Monegario and said, 'Explain.'

Monegario said, 'Nobody leaves Roca, except the Contraalmirante, and nobody comes in. There is *entrepôt* facility some distance north where drivers and pilots change places. They may not meet or talk, ever, so nobody on the other side knows where is Roca. They don't even know it exists, ever since we build this place – four years. There is total prohibition of airspace for two hundred kilometres. Going out is one secure landline. No radio. All personnel are like you restricted to one letter each week written and sealed by machine, after censoring. For satellites, we paint the Corsairs like Skyhawks from above, and we keep many covered. We think we can keep GEA secret until the right time!'

'And the rest of the Argentine armed forces?' Hicks asked. 'The Navy and Air force must know about GEA!' He was trespassing, but there was nothing to lose by pressing on. Monegario's face clouded and he looked to the Commodore. Cassián pulled himself forward and said, looking down at his papers, 'Some do – of course. But this is no problem and does not concern us here.'

Hicks made a point of walking out of the room with the Commodore. 'Tell me,' he said casually, 'would I be correct in saying the latitude of Roca is forty-eight south – within a degree?'

Cassián grinned. 'Very good! But for the Royal Navy, this was not difficult, I think?'

'No, not difficult,' replied Hicks, 'but not necessary, either, I think! It was obvious we would find our latitude, so, why the secrecy?'

The Commodore shrugged. 'Eeks. I am responsible for GEA, as you know, but I do not make all the rules. You must excuse our system, please!'

But Hicks persisted. 'We've had unrestricted access to everything here except this one thing – the latitude of Roca. Why would your bosses want to conceal from us the position of Roca – you admit it has already probably been photographed by satellite!'

Hicks sensed hostility, or annoyance, as Cassián stopped at the door of his office. 'I cannot answer you this,' he said stiffly. 'And it is not important!' Then in a more friendly tone, 'I hope you accept my word?'

'OK,' said Hicks. For now, he added mentally, more convinced than ever that Roca's position was significant.

'It's about as far as they could get from Brazil and Chile and Peru. Who else would they want to zap?' Blount had come back to Hicks' office.

Hicks went to the wall-map. 'Forty-eight south on the Patagonian coast just happens to be the closest you can get on the Argentine mainland to the Falklands, that's A.B, Cassián and his bunch sitting here talking Exocet. And C, the whole thing a deadly secret. What d'you make of it, Tim?'

'Blowed if I know, old mate. Last I heard, Exocet was a sea-skimmer, anti-ship. Not a lot of good for anything else.'

'So? They're thinking ships.'

'And the Falklands, Malvinas. But as the man said, they could walk in there any time. But if they did, can you see HMG doing anything about it? How far did you say it was?'

'Eight thousand miles.'

'There you are then. Not a chance in hell. I mean, it would need a whole invasion task force! Not these days, Jeff!'

'I suppose you're right,' Hicks said, staring at the map. The word 'but' hung in his head.

*

Patagonian winter brought no change to the landscape, just more cloud and even more oppressive winds. Such little rain as fell came down briefly, and loudly, often with thunder, and did nothing to relieve the swirling aridity of the place.

For realistic bombing practice, the Argentines decided upon a towed seasplash-target. The target itself was a simple affair: a sort of surface hydroplane, it scooped up a tall plume of water, making a highly-visible moving target. But it had to be towed, usually on a thousand-yard wire, and facilities for operating the towing vessel had to be provided, within the discrete framework of GEA. And again the British were dumbfounded: within a few weeks of Cassián's approval, it was done, and this on an exposed coast with a ten-metre tidal range. Another example of the apparently unlimited backing the Grupo enjoyed. From whom? And why? the questions nagged Hicks.

The big thirty-knot *Armada* patrol boat was ideal for the task. Roca's SAR helicopters flank-marked the fall of shot, and the bomb-sight calibration programme accelerated.

On a rough morning in July, Blount and Finch had been collecting data in a series of practice dives on the splash. As Blount pulled off the target in his last dive and turned towards the coast, a cylinder retaining stud in his engine had sheared. The cylinder moved fractionally on its seating, cracking the second of the four retaining studs. A rocker cover shook loose and oil sprayed from the feed lines onto hot metal. A low vibration set in, and the Corsair lost about twenty knots of speed.

Blount knew he had a failure in one of the Wasp's eighteen

cylinders – a cracked head, or a broken valve maybe. He was not too worried. Six miles to the field. He could accept a slow descent, keeping the engine running as it was. 'If you have an engine problem, leave it alone.' He lowered the Corsair's long nose and transmitted:

'Red Two, Red Leader – I've got a rough runner. Stay with me.'

'Roger,' answered Finch. 'You have some smoke. Not much.'

Big rugged engines these, Blount told himself. Everybody said so. And the oil tank held twenty-three gallons. 'Let me know if it gets any worse.'

'Wilco. Going line astern.' Finch slid out of sight behind.

'Roca, this is Red Leader. Five miles out on runway 24 with a rough-running engine;' as he spoke, his eyes were on his engine gauges. 'I want emergency straight-in on 24. Over.'

'Red Leader, roger. You are clear immediate landing any runway but be advised surface wind is 060 degrees, 30 knots, gusting 45.'

Blount felt a tightening in his guts. He could wreck the Corsair in a ground-loop, or worse, if he tried to land in such a strong tail-wind. He would feel, and look, foolish, when all he had was a little power loss and vibration. He could do a safe, normal landing on runway 06, into the wind. He checked the gauges again, then swung left, turning downwind, making room for a descending right turn onto 06 runway.

But, as he admitted later to Hicks, he blew it. Too much wind. He never made the runway. When he tried opening up the engine, he said, he felt a thud and the cowling exploded. He described to Hicks what happened next. He didn't get the fuel off – no time, before the wheelless Corsair hit the ground with a bone-jarring crash. Finch, watching from above, thought he might have got away with it. The aircraft slid on in a spray of sand and might have stopped safe and erect. But at about forty knots its nose fell into a deep, stony gully and the Corsair flipped over onto its back.

Blount regained consciousness quickly. His head throbbed fiercely. His arms dangled untidily somewhere above him. He saw earth and small stones against the windscreen. Above, below him, the canopy was still in place and intact, and by moving his head as much as a painfully stiff neck would allow, he discovered he was suspended over a gully, with about two feet clearance between the top of the canopy and the ground.

He wanted to get out. Right in front, between him and the engine, was the main fuel tank with about 150 gallons of AvGas left in it. He could smell the stuff. And he could hear the high tinkle of contracting hot metal.

He pulled hard on the canopy emergency handle. One hand, two hands. Then savagely, feet on the instrument panel for leverage. It wouldn't move. He tried the normal handle, hoping to slide the hood back. It jammed solid after two inches. Twisted fucking rails! Blount swore. Bugger you then! – I'll stay here. Panting, very tired, he closed his eyes and relaxed. Everything so bloody difficult and awkward. Drowsy. Sick. Too lazy even to be bothered when he smelled smoke.

His right leg felt cold, a wet cold as if somebody was trickling iced water from a jug down inside his trousers. It reached his knee and spread, icy chilli-hot, down the soft private skin of his thigh. When the petrol reached his genitals, burning like acid, Blount was stung awake. His hazy mind threw up an image of the charred skeleton of a crash-and-burn victim he had once seen, long ago. And here he was hanging upside down with his balls soaked in AvGas and smoke everywhere!

He screamed.

They found him, conscious but speechless, ten yards from the burning Corsair.

Blount's injuries, from smashing his way out through the canopy with bare hands, were more painful than serious. But although he was out of hospital within a fortnight, it seemed to Hicks, at first, quite likely his friend would never fly again. Hicks spent a lot of time at his bedside in the first days, holding him in his shouting, sweating nightmares, or talking through the tense remoteness of his waking hours. As the shock receded, Blount trembled less often and he could talk about the accident, the engine, his mistake, the final power failure, even the impact with the ground, but not about the inverted cockpit, or how he got out of it. And the sight or smell of roast or fried food sent him into convulsions of

40

vomiting and trembling. Hicks feared permanently psycho-logical damage, and asked Cassián to repatriate him to England.

'I am sorry, Eeks,' the Commodore replied, 'I know Commander Blount is suffering. But he cannot leave Roca.'

'He can be no further use to you!'

'I disagree. He is still a weapons expert, no? And it will be better for him to work.'

'Commodore,' pleaded Hicks, 'he needs to get away from this place! He needs a psychiatrist.'

'*Active Service*, Eeks! Remember?' The steel in Cassián's voice belied the roundness of his face. 'Capitán Blount remains. He is not the first casualty – and he will not be the last!'

Hicks took over Blount's flying.

Some of the *tenientes*, noticeably Funk, didn't trouble to disguise a contempt for Blount's weakness: he'd had an accident, hurt himself a bit, but that was no excuse for the shivering and vomiting fits that afflicted him long after his release from hospital. 'Typical *Englander*' was Funk's comment to his friends on one such occasion – 'no guts!' As this view gained currency among certain of the young, making the Rancho uncomfortable for him, Blount took more and more to his own company, his own bottle. Hicks was delighted, therefore, when a *guardiamarina* called Conchita, a fierce little girl who had been a shipyard welder, moved into Blount's suite. Her companionship visibly eased the tension in Blount and the unbridled ferocity with which she deployed her shipyard vocabulary shielded him in public, even made him smile.

Relieved, Hicks remarked to Carla, 'Conchita is good medicine for Tim. He is lucky she is so kind to him.' Blount was not the most attractive of men.

'*Si*, Choncita is good,' agreed Carla. 'She is my friend, she do what I ask.'

'You ask?'

'Of course! Poor Teem. He is sick, and afraid, and lonely. Is not good for him.'

'Carla, how did you get to be so beautiful?'

'Pah! You talk silly, Eeks.' Carla contrived to look annoyed.

41

Chapter 4

Roca Engineering and its chief Bolsano, untrammelled by bureaucracy, worked miracles – or that is what they would have been at home, thought Hicks – in response to the demands of the weekly *comités*. Undercarriage doors were strengthened for use as divebrakes; bomb-fusing and Sidewinder fire-control circuits installed, all from the drawing-board up. The gunsight was modified. Most impressive, in two months Bolsano produced a prototype two-seater for Channing and Munro to test, apologising for the unsightly raw metal.

Bomb-racks proved more difficult and were to be a standing problem. And the US government's strategic embargo on the fusing manual for their 1,000 lb bombs threw them back on their own resources for design and manufacture of a new fuse, a job in which Blount got deeply involved.

Using four ex-CANA Skyhawk jets, the *consejeros* and the Argentine CO's soon confirmed predictions that even this relatively agile jet could not get into a firing position behind an averagely well-flown Corsair, and conversely no averagely competent Corsair pilot could fail to force the Skyhawk out ahead where its exhaust would attract the Sidewinder's heat-seeking eye. They were relieved also to confirm that Sidewinder, at least the AIM-9G's they had, would not lock-on to the Corsair.

The more they worked, the more promising the Corsair looked. The wings, stripped of wingfold and guns, held 85 gallons of fuel a side, and with this and a centreline droptank it could fly for ten hours, a radius of 600 miles with bombs.

Munro and Channing tested the new two-seater. The back seat was uncomfortable and appallingly cramped after the spacious front cockpit, and the forward view virtually non-existent, but it would do.

The 'Trainer' was not popular. Instrument training was unglamorous, unpleasant, and difficult. To the British such skills were basic. But as the numbers of 'Trainers' increased and 'Inst' appeared more frequently against their names on the flight boards, the young Argentines began to object. Funk and his faction used 'Inst' in their campaign of denigration of the British – they were frightened of the Argentine weather, of the Argentine cloud; it was not necessary to expend so much time on their ridiculous 'Inst' when there was an enemy to be fought, bombs to be dropped . . .

It took another near-fatality to stop this talk. Munro was flying on a late afternoon in September, in one of the 'Trainers'. In front, Guardiamarina Cuevas, a close friend of Funk, was doing an 'Inst' Test, under the hood. A good pilot, but an arrogant kid who had made no effort to hide his disgust at this indignity, as he saw it. Munro had seen enough. Nice technique, good feel for the aircraft, thinking ahead. Good stuff. Do a lot better if he wasn't so bloody bolshie. Munro looked around before deciding which way to ask Cuevas to turn for descent and recovery.

So far, he had managed to keep out of cloud. He knew there was the odd thunderstorm about, could hear them on the radio, but with so much other cloud you never knew where they were. He was going to have to enter cloud to get down. It looked thinner to the left, and he instructed Cuevas on the intercom.

There was no reply, but Munro felt the throttle and pitch levers move as Cuevas lowered the nose and began a descending turn. They entered cloud. The vapour closed thickly in on the Corsair, a clammy grey womb, claustro-phobic. Munro tensed, right hand lightly on his stick, feeling what Cuevas was doing.

'Level off at ten thousand.'

'Okay.' It was about all Cuevas had said the whole trip.

Munro saw rate of descent reducing, felt the throttle edging forward again. Nice, he thought. Then with no warning what-soever, the deafening roar of hailstones on metal and a sickening drop. A cu-nimb! Straight into the downdraught! Munro waited for the wing-tearing crash that came next. He had been here before. It might not be too bad. Cuevas was still flying the Corsair.

'Hold your attitude!' Munro yelled. '*Attitude!*' Without a gyro horizon, he couldn't tell yet, from his primitive instruments, what if anything Cuevas was doing about the sudden descent. The safe thing was to do nothing.

Cuevas said nothing that could be heard above the din, but Munro felt the throttle slam forward and the stick move back as he tried to raise the nose and climb. Munro's grip tightened and he pushed forward, against Cuevas.

'*I have control!*' he shouted. Cuevas said nothing, though he must have heard. Instead, he pulled even harder back on the stick.

Munro pushed. Cuevas pulled. There was another thumping crash, and the noise died away. They were in an updraught, and the wings were still on, but Munro knew their troubles weren't over. He was still fighting Cuevas for control of the staggering Corsair. They were being carried upwards, speed unwinding through 100 knots and the turn needle full right. The Corsair, its controls effectively locked, was heading for a stall and going out of control.

'*I have control!!*' Cuevas should have acknowledged and released the stick.

Munro yelled again, louder, adding, '*Let go the fucking stick!!*' Cuevas's English was fair.

It was too late. The airframe shuddered. Before Munro could pull the throttle shut, the Corsair torque-rolled clumsily around its propeller and sliced down into a spin to the left.

The stick suddenly came free. Cuevas must have let go at last! Munro tried centralising everything. It didn't work. They were spinning through 8,000 feet, and it was getting darker.

There was a loud bang, a rush and roar of icy wet slipstream and engine noise. The canopy had gone, just a fragment of plexiglass hanging from the crude latch by his left shoulder. Munro struggled with slitted eyes to see his instruments and was only peripherally aware of something going past him in the slipstream. He slammed the rudder pedals hard over and pushed forward on the stick, both hands. The book figures

44

came into his mind: 130 lb on the rudder, 80 on the stick. It felt like it! His face contorted, eyes fastened on the turn needle, the needle . . . the needle . . . come on you *bastard*!

The needle moved. Munro jerked stick and rudders central and held them bar-rigid. The die was cast. He could do no more. The sickening yaw-roll stopped. The airspeed shot up, 100, 150. Munro levelled off. 2,300 feet. He set the engine up for cruise and looked around him as best he could in the battering slipstream. Cuevas was gone.

Still in cloud and rain, Munro could hear nothing in his earphones. He steered east until he was safely over the ocean, and let down slowly through the overcast. He saw the sea at 1,500 feet, turned back west, followed the familiar coastline to Roca and landed safely.

Guardiamarina Cuevas had a broken leg and an irreparably damaged ego which he tried to salvage by putting the blame on Munro. The gringo had interfered while he, Cuevas, was flying, and he had seen him put the plane into a spin. He baled out because he thought the English had gone mad. He was shouting. Munro had some sympathy: cunimbs were always terrifying. But Cuevas had failed a test of discipline. His reversion to cadet status was red meat to the growing anti-gringo faction led by Funk.

*

'I think it's time we had a chat,' Hicks said to Blount, standing in front of his wall-map.

It had been a particularly vicious October Monday, unflyable, Roca's people scurrying from door to door cursing the Antarctic wind that howled in from the desert intent, it seemed, on scouring clean the face of Patagonia.

And at the morning meeting, a new reserve in the Argentine commanders, with most of whom the *consejeros* were by now good friends. Wary looks, hushed tones, and again and again in their quiet conversations, *Las Malvinas* . . . *Las Malvinas* . . . like a keynote.

Hicks convened a meeting after dinner, in his suite.

'I've heard Malvinas, in the bar,' said LeStrange, who spent most time there.

'So what?' Finch snapped. 'We all know they're besotted about the bloody islands! I can't see what all the fuss is about. What's the problem, Jeff?'

'No problem, yet, Mike.' Finch's abrasiveness didn't bother Hicks, but he often wished he knew what it hid. 'Just this. I can only make sense of Roca, as GEA's base, in one context. The Falklands. *Las Malvinas*. And now, all of a sudden, Malvinas is the flavour of the month. You have noticed?'

'Of course I've noticed. So what?' It was rudely said, but not untypical of Finch.

'Yeah, Jeff,' Munro cut in. 'There's no but a few sheep-farmers out there. The Argies could take the place in an afternoon if they'd a mind. Wi'out us. What's it got to do wi' us?'

'Nothing, Jock,' Hicks replied patiently. 'You're absolutely right. But if they did invade, what happens next?'

'Well,' said LeStrange sonorously, 'there's not much we could do about it, is there?' Then as an afterthought, 'We – the UK I mean!'

'But if the UK did want to do something? What would they do?' Hicks persisted.

'Send the Navy, of course,' declared LeStrange unhesitatingly.

'Exactly! And how do you think a handful of modern ships would get on against say four waves of fifty Corsairs?'

There was a long silence.

'They wouldn't!' But Tracey sounded a little uncertain.

'Wouldn't what?' Finch was sharp.

'Send a task force! Not down here – it's how many thousand bleeding miles? With troops, and all their kit, and stuff? Rubbish!'

'I'm not so sure,' said LeStrange uneasily. 'With any other Prime Minister, I'd probably agree with you, Trixy. But can you really see this one just letting them get away with it?'

Blount said grimly, 'My guess is, the Hon Prime Minister would be down here with a task force before they got their field latrines dug, and she'd be ashore with the first wave, laying in with the lead-weighted handbag!'

'Crying "for cough – for cough" in haughty tones!' chortled LeStrange.

They all laughed. 'And serve the bastards right!' chortled Tracey.

'Yes, but, *mes enfants*,' Hicks raised his voice, 'If the Junta go for the Falklands; if the Navy comes down; if GEA is used to sink British ships and earn Argentina the undying gratitude and admiration of every man, woman, and child in South America – where the hell does this leave us?'

Hicks desperately wanted to know how the others were going to answer. His own naivety had not long survived Carla's stories of life in Argentina under the Junta, but at the same time he was beginning to feel a genuine affection for the contrary Argentines. It wasn't their fault they were stuck in a confusion of attitudes rooted in the past – like Northern Ireland, as Cassián had pointed out. Even their national arrogance, being self-confessed and based perforce on the achievements of tomorrow, had to him an endearing quality of its own. It was from Carla he had learned the depth of their emotion for *Las Islas Malvinas*, and had got the first inkling of a Falkland play by a desperate Junta. But most disturbing was to find, after less than a year in this place, that he no longer knew exactly where he stood on the question he had just posed.

The remnants of the day's wind fretted the dark windows. The *uligán*, a new word in local parlance, from Tracey's constant lament, 'Blowin' a bleeding hooligan again!'

Finch said eventually, 'I still don't see the problem. You guys can read, can't you? "Operations against any enemy of Argentina," the contract says. And if you read the papers, I'd have thought it obvious the UK was on the short list!'

LeStrange looked astonished. 'That's bloody ridiculous, Mike! You're not seriously suggesting I'm going to launch off in my Corsair and bomb the white ensign – my old buddies – just because some dago –' He stopped, speechless.

'You signed!' Finch replied with a smile. 'Didn't you read it?'

'Well, I won't do it!' LeStrange said emphatically.

Tracey poked himself in the chest. 'Me, I thought we were down here for some fun – couple of little banana wars, something like that, then home with the loot.' A suggestion of Geordie entered Tracey's speech when he got excited. 'Surely the RN's not going to come whistling down here just for a bunch of bleeding sheep? I mean, it's ten thousand bleeding miles, isn't it?' he pleaded, looking at LeStrange.

'I hope you're right, Trixy, but I wouldn't bet on it!' LeStrange said, worried.

'Miles, what do you think?' Hicks said.

Channing made a wry smile. 'Well, we've talked about it, haven't we? Very interesting! As I see it, *amigos*, the contract is clear, and we could have been expected to anticipate a Falklands move by the Junta. Personally, I didn't take it seriously, but it's all there in the history books,' Hicks' raised his eyebrows at Blount as Channing continued: 'So there's no argument about the contract – we honour our side of it if we want to get paid. But –' Channing paused and looked around the quiet group, 'honour is about obligations, and there's the conflict. Three obligations as I see it. First, to the contract, very simple. Second, to our country, not all that simple. We would be aiding the Queen's enemies in time of war, effectively. I don't know where we stand in law on that one, but morally I'm happy that earning a living that way is no more an offence than making and selling weapons to prospective enemies of the realm. Like frigates to Argentina, for instance, and etcetera. I don't want to face a treason charge, but the morals don't bother me.'

There was silence until Hicks asked, 'And the third obligation?'

'To ourselves. The "why am I here" question!'

'Well I can tell you why I'm here!' Finch sat forward in his chair. 'And I'd be surprised if my reasons are much different from anybody else's. My job is war. It happens to be what I like doing, as well as being the oldest of the professions – bar none. I don't want to spend my life earning a wage and saving it up in the hope of living long enough to enjoy it before I get old, fat, sick and silly. I'd rather enjoy myself, maybe go out with a bang. A short working life, so I sell myself dear. *My* third obligation is to me. I fight!'

'Bravo!' Munro exclaimed. Then, less loudly, 'I mean – that just about sums it up, doesn't it? We're all in this for the money. And the kicks!' The last was an afterthought. Hicks knew the sacrifices Munro and his wife were making to educate their four children. Which was the more mercenary then, Finch or Munro?

'Tim?' Hicks looked at Blount.

Blount examined his shoe for a while. Then he spoke: 'I don't think a country should expect a monopoly of anyone's affections – or loyalty. Or employers, or football clubs, or even family – it's the same thing, affection and loyalty have to be earned. I think patriotism, at least nowadays, is an invention of politicians, to get people to play their games. Soldiers, real soldiers, don't need patriotism. Never have. They fight as a way of life; the cause is incidental. Take the samurai . . .'

The door opened and Carla walked in. In uniform, with her black shoulderbag, she came as near to looking surprised as Hicks had ever seen.

Hicks smiled and rose. He broke the sudden silence. 'Hello, Carla.' The others stood, too, as he went to greet her.

'Ello, Eeks.' Carla gave a nervous little smile. 'You are busy. I come back later maybe.'

'No.' Maybe not. 'It's all right. We're just talking.' Hicks steered her to the seat vacated by Blount. 'Some coffee?'

'No. I want to hear what it is you talk. Is very interesting, men talk!'

Room was made for Blount. 'All right then. Tim, you were getting romantic, I think?' The warmth of Carla's thigh struck into Hicks' soul.

Blount cleared his throat. 'Well, never mind all that! For what I'm worth – now,' he grimaced, 'I'm in!'

Five counting me, thought Hicks, relieved. Blount had been ill-used by the navy: a brilliant officer, but too outspoken for his own good. The system had smothered him and his career came to nothing. He had resigned, embittered. His vivacious wife had died of cancer last year. Nursing him, seeing him in the raw, had left Hicks with a very special feeling towards Blount.

Should he have been surprised at the high level of acquiescence? All except Finch, it seemed, had been as naive as he. Like himself, they had all left homes and jobs to come here, so like him they probably saw the Argentine as the culminant job of their careers. And why should he be the only one to experience a sea-change in the South Atlantic? Finch would go along because he said he would, Munro for money, Channing out of intellectual curiosity, and Tim, poor Tim, because he had to. Tracy? Well, he had always seemed a morally absent sort of person who would follow his inclination, and the crowd. LeStrange Hicks had never understood; but he sensed the simplistic buffoonery hid qualities. He might give trouble.

Hicks hesitated to involve Carla, but the opportunity was too good to miss.

'Carla,' he said, 'tell us what you think about the Malvinas?'

'*Las Malvinas!*' Her voice was high with surprise. 'Why you ask this? *Las Islas Malvinas* belong to Argentina. And Great Britain take them since one hundred fifty years, and this is very wrong. Soon, we get them back!'

'But why?' Channing asked her. 'For a few sheep?'

'They belong to Argentina. Not Britain!'

'And how will Argentina get them back?' Channing pursued.

'I don't know. But we will. Soon!'

'Do you think GEA will be used?'

'For *Las Malvinas*? Probably. Why not? But not for bomb the islands.'

'For what then?'

'For sheeps, of course! Our army takes *Las Malvinas*, Britain sends sheeps, we bomb sheeps – poof!'

Silence.

Then Carla smiled. 'Now, I understand your talking here – you think you have a problem to fly with GEA to bomb British sheeps! Yes – is a problem. But you know about this before you come, eh?' Nobody smiled back.

Later, when they were alone, Hicks said to Carla: 'You should do something about your hair.'

'I don't know what you mean, Eeks. You don't like my hair?'

'It's too black. Too curly. Too everything. And it bounces up and down when you walk.'

'I know. I 'ave much trouble with it. Maybe I cut if off.' She pushed it up with both hands. Her head was really very small.

'Then people could see your ears.' He touched one. 'And that would send them crazy.'

'Is no good then. I keep it.' She let the dark mass fall, trapping his hand.

'*La Princesa de Las Malvinas.*' Hicks said softly, very Spanish.

'*Si* – I will rule the sheep!' Haughtily.

'And the men?'

'Is the same thing, Eeks. The same thing. Don't you know?'

Hicks lay long awake that night beside Carla. Late on, it struck him forcibly that he couldn't remember when he had last thought of Pauline. What was happening to him?

Chapter 5

Hicks detected a subtle acceleration in the affairs of Roca, more pressure, more urgency. The focus of this was less obvious than its direction. Eastwards.

Cassián began to send *Sylvestre*, the target tug, far out into the ocean, four hundred miles or more, and increasingly large waves of Corsairs to seek her out with bombs. He got the use of an Air Force Grupo One Boeing 707 from Commodoro Rivadavia and devised an attack plan using the Boeing's Inertial Nav system and Tactical Nav Tacan beacon to provide a radio bearing to guide the Corsairs to their target. The Boeing was call-signed *Kondor* and the plan was *Hayrake*: the Corsairs flew wide line-abreast down the designated bearing raking a path up to thirty miles across. It never failed.

Other things did. Engines, very occasionally. Bomb release, much too often still. Fuel transfer, often enough to make it the big bogey: fuel was fed from the Corsair's wing tanks by air pressure, and loss of pressure or a stuck valve outside about 300 miles could mean a ditching. Transfer failure plus bomb hang-ups meant almost certain ditching. The best range of Roca SAR helos was about 200 miles.

At first Hicks hated and dreaded these flights. A hundred single-engined planes coasting out for a five-hour flight, climbing east, each with its little cargo of fear. The weather forecasts, mere guesses mostly, sometimes dangerously wrong. The mounting tension as the hundreds of miles of water opened out behind them. The inevitable struggle, when they found the target, to get enough height for dive-bombing.

He agreed with the others though, that every trip was a little less terrying than the last one.

One hundred aircraft to 400 miles was Cassián's first demand. With fighter escort. They did it at the fourth attempt, and put 150,000 lb of bombs on and around *Sylvestre*'s splash target for the loss of two Corsairs and one pilot.

Cassián was not satisfied. When all the data on 'Strikex Four' had been collected, he stood on the plot on the operations room tactical floor and summed up. 'This mission had problems. Bomb hang-ups, fuel transfer, still too many. And weather – the wind, the cloud, this occlusion –' He rapped the symbol on the floor with his pointer. 'But this is the South Atlantic, it is winter, and you must expect these problems, eh? GEA must operate through, or under, or over the weather – any weather – and drop its bombs! The only limit is the hours of daylight, but we will if necessary launch and recover in the dark.' The pause which followed did not invite comment from the assembled senior officers.

'However after *Sylvestre* was located, there was problem with dive-bombing because of the cloud. Our bombers then are useless in winter? Is this so?' The question was put directly to Hicks, but Finch broke in.

'It's obvious cloud restricts dive-bombing.'

Cassián smiled patiently. 'So. How does GEA attack ships in cloudy weather, please?'

'Commodore,' Hicks said, 'there is no problem. There is an alternative attack. Lay-down. This is accurate and effective in any weather except fog. The aircraft flies very low over the target. The bombs have delay fuses.'

'But now,' protested Cassián, 'the pilots are all trained in dive-bombing!'

'Lay-down is easy – not like dive-bombing. It will be quick and easy to train all the pilots for both attacks.'

A loud whispered discussion had been going on among the Argentine CO's. One of them, Moreira, spoke up: 'We suggest, Contraalmirante, we use both attacks at the same time. Dive-bombers coming from above, and this "lay-down" attack from below.' He showed them with his hands. 'Make the ship divide its fire, no?'

53

'Good idea. I like it!' exclaimed Munro.

'Standard tactic, old boy!' drawled LeStrange. 'The old one-two!'

'This will not be too complicated?' Cassián asked Finch.

'Depends on the numbers. Speaking of which, why fighter escort when there is no hostile air? It seems a waste of resources.'

'You cannot assume the absence of air opposition,' said Cassián.

'Then it would help to know what it is.' There was an edge to Finch's voice.

'I mean, fighters four hundred miles east of here?' asked Tracey. 'Gotta be a carrier!'

'Obviously!' replied the Commodore.

'And another thing,' Tracey went on with a half-wink at LeStrange, 'if we're out there –' he pointed at the model *Sylvestre* on the floor, 'and we have a problem, fuel or something, there's an airfield on the Falklands, just south, about here. Very handy. Can we use it as an divert field?'

LeStrange joined in: 'Come to that, Commodore, there must be a weather station on the Falklands. Why don't we ask them for a weather ob when we're in their area. I'm sure they'd be delighted!'

'I mean, the Falklands could be quite useful to us, one way and another!' Tracey rounded off.

'The Malvinas,' said Cassián, with the same air of patience, 'are Argentine property, illegally occupied by Great Britain since one hundred and fifty years. Their return to Argentina is a matter of national honour which must soon be settled. You will do nothing to compromise this.'

'We might even assist?' suggested Channing quietly.

'I think not,' replied Cassián with a smug smile that Hicks had seen before. 'The army can take *Las Malvinas* tomorrow if they want. It needs only a few hundred men.'

'But –' began Tracey.

'No!' The Commodore held up his hand. 'The recovery of *Las Malvinas* is not a problem for GEA and we need not discuss it. Maritime strike is our function. This exercise will be repeated, and repeated. Bigger formations, more distance. Now, Capitán Bolsano –' he turned to the engineer,

54

'you will please examine, most urgently, how to get more fuel on the Corsair, as much as possible and still carry two bombs. Another tank, I don't know. I want, if possible, another two hours' fuel. Report in three days. Now any more questions, gentlemen? No? Then that is all today. This was the beginning. Next time, more planes, more bombs, more distance. And then more. Four hundred bombers to five hundred miles, this is what I want.' Putting down the pointer, Cassián picked up his cap and turned to Hicks with a smile. 'Capitán Eeks – I hope you would find it convenient to come to my office at eleven o'clock?'

Channing followed Hicks back to his office. 'Well? Wind of change, or change of wind?' he said as they went in.

'A firming-up!' Hicks' window was boarded up. Glass crunched underfoot. A returning bomber had crashed and exploded in the twilight the evening before. 'There's no doubt now, this is an ambush! Not a pleasant prospect! I had a feeling the quarter million was too good to be true. Tell me, Miles. Last time we talked about this, you said if we were to sink a British task force, it might be no bad thing. You weren't joking?'

Channing sat down. 'No. I think you feel the same as me – that compared with the most likely opposition, the British forces are in pretty pathetic shape. Russia has enough of everything to snuff us out and hardly notice. And yet, always, we go for quality – so-called! Quality counts, we're told. No matter a few squadrons of fighters against three thousand Russians, it's the quality that counts – and ours are always the best in the world! That's bullshit. Politics and big business and greasy palms. It's a cosy fallacy and it needs a shock, cold water treatment – unless we want to start the next war the way we started the last two, flat on our backs!'

'Strong medicine, Miles!'

'Serious condition! Possibly terminal?'

'Do we have the right to prescribe it? Administer it?'

'It's already been prescribed. By someone else. The list of names?'

'People will die.'

'You know what they say!'

55

'If they can't take a joke –'
'They shouldn't have joined!'
Horribly flippant. But Hicks recalled, in one of those unbidden, random tricks of memory, standing in a cathedral during the two-minute silence, a Remembrance Day service not long ago. An Army officer in the row in front held a small child. Playing absently with her father's Sam Browne, the child observed Hicks intently. Towards the end of the silence, she had asked in a high clear voice, 'Daddy, why is that man crying?'

Cassián's window had already been repaired. He sat with his back to it. Hicks, opposite, could see the whole airfield, Corsairs landing, taking off, taxying, silent and remote against the grey sky. English grey, he thought. A patch half way down the westerly runway showed where the bombcraters had been filled in and tarmacked.

'Time for cards on table, eh? my friend?' Cassián said with an arch look.

'The Falklands?'

Cassián frowned. 'I don't know what you mean by Falklands, Eeks, except perhaps *Las Islas Malvinas*?'

'*Las Islas Malvinas* . . . "jewel in the crown of Argentinas"' Hicks quoted from the patriotic school song, not in mockery but to show he understood.

'*Exactamente!*' Cassián relaxed. '*Las Islas Malvinas!*' He spoke the words broadly. A verbal banner at last unfolded. 'There has been some political difficulty, but now the Junta is decided. Operation Goa is approved.'

'Operation Goa?'

'From the example of India to recover occupied land from the Portuguese. I have a little hope – that soon your ever-expanding language will have a new word: Goanise, Goanisation.' Cassián gave a short little laugh. 'So. To apologise. It has been necessary for me to at least pretend to keep secret GEA's first task. Until now. I hope you understand?'

'Perfectly. But as you said, you don't need GEA for *Las Malvinas*.'

The Commodore got up, crossed to the wall-map. 'Tell me, Eeks – after we take back *Las Malvinas*, when the Argentine

56

flag flies there, the next morning – what will your government do?'

'I don't know. They seem to have no great interest in the islands.'

'So, they will do nothing?'

'They might.'

'But they might not?'

'With any other government, any other prime minister since Churchill, you could expect a complaint to the UN, resolutions, sanctions maybe; and then, after a while, nothing. The British Lion would roar and snarl, but eight thousand miles is too far for him, these days.'

'But this government? This prime minister?' Cassián asked eagerly.

'This one would probably feel an urgent need to deGoanize.'

'And could she? Think of the resources, the distance, the cost!'

Hicks thought. 'Yes,' he said. 'She could.'

Cassián seemed relieved.

'Is that the plan,' Hicks asked, 'GEA attacks the ships?'

The Commodore went back to his large chair and swung it to face the window, his back to Hicks. Only the wind was audible.

'Figures in a landscape,' he said, at last. 'A military landscape. That is what we are, eh? You, me, those –' he gestured at the Lowry-figures bustling on the concrete pan. 'And we don't like for our landscape to be spoiled, by outsiders. By politicians! And worse, by business men and money! How do you think I got the names?'

'From another figure in the landscape.'

'One who knows this part of it very well. An authority, you might say.'

'This is a small club.'

'An authority with a vision.'

'A very small club!'

'A club of one, at his level, I imagine!'

'No.' Hicks was looking far beyond the drab scene outside the window. 'No. More than one I think' he said slowly.

Cassián swung around to face him. 'I needed only one. I

57

know him many years. We often talk about this problem, modern weapons, so expensive. It's ridiculous! I hinted my solution – GEA. I told him of my problems with the conservatives, the reactionaries. He was sympathetic. It seems all navies have allergy to innovation. Later – I had almost forgot our talk, he gave me names. You know this man.'

'I know him.' Hicks knew one, maybe two men – there might be more – now in high rank in the Navy, zealots, iron men of burning vision whose talents had protected them while they stood against the current. Most had been swept away, like Blount. But he wanted to be sure. 'Did you discuss the Falklands? The Malvinas?'

'Of course not. It is not necessary.' Hicks believed the Commodore. The list of names bore him out. But suddenly, like a shop-window reflection, he had a vision of himself and the others, as seen by the writer of the list: dependably amoral, a-patriotic, disenchanted. The image was startling, disappointing. Unfair. He didn't feel like that. But in another way it was comforting to know he had been appointed here – almost like the old days!

The silence was sensitive.

'Now.' The Commodore sat forward, squarely facing Hicks. 'Our plan. The Army takes *Las Malvinas* – when the Junta is ready. A cordon sanitaire is established around the islands. We wait for the task force. The army remains in occupation, but not too many – not enough for Britain to think it impossible to recover their Falklands – their sheep! Then, when the task force comes, GEA attacks – in the British way, clean and quick, no waving of arms or blowing of whistles. The task force will be destroyed. Only the warships. Not troops or tankers, or other ships, just the warships. These are like the ones you sell us, soft-skinned and inoffensive! It will not be difficult.'

'The rest will turn around and go home, and three things are accomplished: the Argentine flag flies over *Las Islas Malvinas* – as it should; Argentine has defeated a world naval power; and I demonstrate my thesis that numbers is still, like Clausewitz says, the fundamental idea of warfare.'

A vision of burning, smashed, sinking ships, torn steel, rushing water, drowning men. Hicks kept it at bay with a screen of rationale; the ships, effete, expendable; the men, professionals, figures in the military landscape who knew what winds blew there. And violence is neutral. But was he ready for his appointed task? Had he the guts to do it? Or not do it? He really didn't know, yet. He opted out of the dilemma, for the moment.

'And you see no irony in using British mercenaries, considering Britain is supposed to be responsible for nearly all the ills of Argentina?'

'On the contrary. Britain has done much good in Argentina. On this, somebody recently wrote that the ills suffered by the Argentine people have not been caused by the British but by the Argentine bourgeoisie, military and government during decades of offensives against their own people! This opinion is rarely admitted, naturally, among the bourgeoisie, military, or government! But it cannot easily be denied. So there is some logic, you might say, in using British talent to help make this final adjustment in our relations!'

Walking back alone to the Rancho for lunch, Hicks pondered on Cassián's use of the first person singular. It confirmed that although the Commodore obviously enjoyed high patronage, he was the main thrust behind GEA. Hicks could not decide whether this, and the fact that the wraps were off GEA at last, should help him sort out his emotions about the whole set-up. It surely should. But it didn't. As it turned out, there wasn't time.

Chapter 6

That night, Munro was murdered in his sleep. LeStrange found him, when he failed to appear, lying in his blood-soaked bed, his throat cut. The killer, whom it did not take long to discover, had used a very sharp, heavy knife with savage force, severing at one stroke the windpipe, jugular and carotid. There was no sign of a struggle.

Guardiamarina Cuevas made only token attempts to hide his guilt. He cleaned the knife, washed his bloodstained shirt and trousers, and entered upon the morning programme as far as his injured leg allowed. But pride soon overcame discretion. He could not contain himself, and in the rising tide of outrage, he began to drop broad hints. Word was carried. By the time the MPs arrived to arrest him, Cuevas was positively swaggering.

He was taken straight before Cassián. Handcuffed, standing crookedly between two heavily-armed MPs, his thin face sneered defiant satisfaction.

'The gringo shamed and insulted me! He said I jumped from fear. I panic and jump! He is the hero! He save the plane! I am a coward – and incompetent! My friends, they all laugh –' he drew himself up and looked proudly at his escorts. 'Now nobody laughs, eh? The gringo is dead!' He practically spat the words.

Cassián stood behind his desk. 'And for this stupid reason you do this terrible thing?'

'Not stupid, Contraalmirante! It is my honour. The gringo took my honour. Without this I am nothing. Now he is nothing!'

'Honour! You kill a sleeping man and talk of honour?'

Cassián was burning with anger. Shame too, thought Hicks, observing from one side. Two small men. The Commodore sleek, clean, fastidious. Facing him an apparition from Argentina's past, from north-side Buenos Aires, lank, gaucho-minded, knife-handy, a creature of instinct. Street-corner man. Hicks' anger at the shocking crime was beginning to boil over in disgust and contempt at the pathetic, rat-faced little man, as Cassián continued, loudly for him: 'And did you think about the Grupo? These English are our friends. We need them. They are important to the Grupo and the Grupo is important to Argentina. You know this? But your "honour" is more important than your country!' He made a grimace of disgust.

Cuevas said simply, 'I do not like the gringos. I don't see why we need them here!'

'I need them! More than I need you! Take him away!'

Alone with Cassián, Hicks said, 'Munro never said those things.'

'I know. And I would not expect it. But it is enough for a man like that to imagine an insult. I am very sorry about this, Eeks. It could have been anticipated and avoided. You see, these people, like him, they have to have tragedy. They seek it out and make it. They cannot help themselves.'

'You think he reads Borges?'

'Him? Unlikely! They don't have to. They get it in the streets.'

'"Figures in a landscape?" The pampa!'

'So they think!'

'Then who are we to condemn?' Hicks was still angry, but in place of contempt he now felt a tinge of respect for Cuevas.

'Oh I do not condemn!' said Cassián surprisingly. 'But I regret Munro. Do you think he would have understood?'

'Would that make it better? Or worse?' Cassián didn't answer. 'Will there be a court martial?'

'Yes. Immediately. They will condemn.'

Cuevas was arraigned on a charge of murder. He made no defence beyond what he had already stated to Cassián and accepted with equanimity the court's verdict of guilty and the sentence that he should be shot.

His plaster-cast had been removed the day after the murder. After the trial, while arrangements were being made for carrying out the sentence, Cuevas was only lightly guarded in a guardroom cell. There was no point in him escaping, nowhere for him to go. He thought otherwise, and left by the toilet window, made his way down to the flight line where he chose a fully-fuelled Sidewinder-armed Corsair and took off.

Circling overhead, he called the tower and demanded to speak to Cassián.

'Contraalmirante. You hear me?'

'This is Contraalmirante Cassián. I hear you. What do you want?'

'I want you get all those gringos! Put them on the field, in front of the tower. Six of them now, I think?'

'Get Capitan Eeks!' Cassián barked to the duty officer. Then, in the same breath, into the microphone: 'Cuevas! This is a bad thing you do! It brings no honour to you, or to the Grupo. You think nothing of this? I can't believe it!'

'You think nothing of the honour of Argentina! *You* bring these gringos here!' The harsh voice was mingled with engine noise.

'What do you want them for?'

'First, I want to look at them.'

'Stand by.'

'What you mean, "Stand by"!' The voice became shrill. 'Listen, Contraalmirante, I am to die, yes?'

'That is the law.'

'OK. I will die. We must obey the law, eh?' There was a high laugh. 'But now I can choose how I die. And if I don't see those gringos out front in ten minutes, I take this plane up to ten thousand feet and then I dive. I dive onto the control tower at four hundred fifty knots. There will be nothing left. I die. You need a new tower! How do you explain this to Admiral Anaya? Get the gringos!'

'They have been sent for. Stand by.'

'Ten minutes.'

Hicks was on the phone. Cassián explained. 'Get everybody down here. Except Tracey. Bring Tracey's uniform. Tell Tracey to get to No. 1 Hangar – fast!' Then to Monegario who had just arrived: 'Arrange for somebody in the tower, anybody, who resembles Tracey, to put on his uniform and join the British outside.' He picked up the radio mike.

'Cuevas?'

'*Si*, Contraalmirante, go ahead.'

'The English are coming.'

'Good. Make them hurry!'

'Cuevas?'

'Go ahead.'

'What do you want?'

Silence. A long silence.

'Cuevas?'

'I want to do something for Argentina! I show you. You get the gringos!'

'You think you know better than me what is good for Argentina?'

'Gringos never did any good for Argentina. Especially English!'

'These English are good men. They too are men of honour.'

'So you say!'

'Cuevas. How long are you in the Navy?'

'You know that!'

'Two years? Me? Thirty-five years, working for Argentina. I love this country. I want to see it proud and strong. GEA will do this. Only GEA. Listen, Cuevas. You mention Admiral Anaya. You know him perhaps? He is a good Argentine, yes?'

'Admiral Anaya is OK.'

'This Admiral put me in command of GEA. He know I use English *consejeros*. He is in the government – your government!'

'So?'

'But Guardiamarina Cuevas disagrees? He thinks the government, the Admiral, all are wrong? Guardiamarina Cuevas knows better than all these? This is ridiculous! You talk like a girl! People will laugh!'

'Where are the gringos?' Cuevas snarled back.

'They are coming out now, see?'

Six figures in khaki drill were walking out onto the airfield below.

63

'Further! Away from the tower! To the edge of the runway!'
Cuevas was getting excited. The message was passed by portable radio to Hicks. After some hesitation, the six resumed their walk until they stood, small and remote, by the edge of the runway.

'Tell them take off caps! Stand to face the runway!' They did. Cuevas's Corsair left its orbit to fly low and slow along the runway, flaps down. Hicks could almost see his face.

'OK, Contraalmirante,' Cuevas called as he powered up and away from the runway, 'tell them stay there. We see how brave they are, these gringos!'

Hicks got the message. The six stood still, in the middle of the silent airfield. A lazy black dot, Cuevas' Corsair, moved across from their right, descending, descending, and straightened up, two miles and soundless yet, pointing.

There was no shelter, anywhere, from a suicidal paranoic with a thirteen-foot four-bladed scimitar. Hicks called out, 'When he gets to the other side of the runway, drop! For God's sake don't try to run! *Comprende?*' Tracey's stand-in nodded wordlessly.

The first sound was the reptilian hiss of the wing-root supercharger intakes, at about a quarter of a mile, then propeller roar, then engine. The elbows of the Corsair's cranked wings were nearly scraping the ground as it hurtled towards them, and by the time it reached the far side of the runway, fifty yards away, they could plainly see the whirling propeller.

'Drop!' Hicks fell flat and pressed himself to the earth. The Corsair roared over in a blast of slipstream, leaving a stink of exhaust. Five Britons were unscathed, but 'Tracey' who had tried to run, had died a quick and bloody death.

'Fuck this for a game of soldiers!' yelled LeStrange. 'I'm off!' The others scattered, streaking for the nearest buildings. Hicks stood, bespattered beside the mutilated body, feeling terribly responsible.

A new noise came from behind. Hicks swung round. With a bull-like roar, a Skyhawk under full power emerged accelerating fast from No. 3 Hangar, swerved across the apron and lurched across the rough in a fountain of dirt to reach the runway halfway down still cornering fast. Tracey went past Hicks with a wave and thundered away down the runway. The Skyhawk hardly seemed to lift, but the wheels came up and it went on out low across the desert still throwing stand. The whole breathtaking manoeuvre had taken about half a minute, Hicks judged. Had Cuevas seen it?

He had. Up at two thousand feet, he turned in pursuit and tried to lock his Sidewinders on the jet. Too late. Tracey already out of range, was still accelerating. The A-4 could fly twice as fast as the Corsair. Cuevas could only watch the small shape until it vanished at about five miles. This made him angry.

'Eh, Contraalmirante!' Cuevas was shouting, panting with excitement still from the satisfying thump of propeller on flesh, oblivious to the vibration of the bent blade. 'What is this Skyhawk? Who is he!'

'Cuevas. Listen to me.' Cassián's reply was half-drowned by the engine and slipstream roar. Cuevas wound the canopy shut as Cassián continued. 'The Skyhawk is the police. I order you to land. Now! Bring back that Corsair – it is government property!'

'And if I don't?'

'He will shoot you down.'

'Ha! You think that is easy? Hey! You see those gringos run away! You see them run? How many now? Five?'

'Six, Cuevas. You killed Corporal Vargas from Air Traffic Control. I hope you feel good!'

'Bastard!' Cuevas screamed, his left thumb pressing the transmit button with vicious force as he swivelled his head, looking for the Skyhawk. 'Bastard! I wanted gringos – I said gringos – not – this is your fault, Contraalmirante! Now I tell you what I do. I climb to ten thousand feet and you better get out of that tower because now I do what I said.' Cuevas paused, struck by a thought. 'Eh, Contraalmirante – who is in the Skyhawk?'

'Captain Tracey.'

The words lowered the temperature in Cuevas's cockpit and did something inside his guts. He went to full power, reversed his turn in a snap roll and pulled hard to the right, squirming in his seat to see behind.

'Cuevas?' The Commodore was calling. The Skyhawk was

nowhere to be seen. Cuevas climbed in the turn, throttle in War Emerg.

'Yeah – what you want?'

'You should not to do this. It makes no sense. There is no honour in it for you. No respect – nothing! I ask you again – bring the plane back!'

But Cuevas by now was incapable of handling ideas.

'Shut up! *Bastard!* Just *shut up!*' he yelled into his sweaty face-mask.

'What will they think of you at home – when they hear you die like a girl, in a fit of temper? Big hero, eh?' Cuevas didn't answer. He had just spotted the Skyhawk, several thousand feet above, wheeling like a buzzard. 'You think they will write stories about this, Cuevas? Make you a hero? I tell you what they will do – they will laugh! They will tell the story of Cuevas, but only to laugh. The gaucho who died like a girl!'

Cuevas was no longer hearing Cassián. His head strained back, his eyes fixed on the Skyhawk, his brain had changed gear. The tower was forgotten. No ranting paranoic now. A mean, predatory Buenos Aires street-kid, tight-faced, adrenalin pumping, Cuevas checked his switches again, opened up his cowl gills and eased up the Corsair's nose to combat climb speed. His Sidewinders growled as they went through the sun. He was too excited to notice the increasing vibration that went through the airframe.

Tracey had half-looped after take-off, back overhead the field at 8,000 feet, talking to Cassián on a discrete frequency. He was told to keep Cuevas in sight but not attack until instructed.

He gave a laconic 'OK', set up his switches, fired a short burst to prove the cannon and settled down to wait, conserving fuel.

The Commodore came back after a few minutes. 'Cuevas does not reply any more. I think he still intends to dive on the tower. Are you still contact?'

'Affirmative. He's climbing in your overhead.'

'OK. It he starts a dive, attack and shoot him down. We are leaving the tower. Stand by for me on portable radio.'

'Understood.' No problem. The Skyhawk could out-accelerate the Corsair in the dive. Easy. Tracey adjusted his turn to stay wide and behind Cuevas as he spiralled up. He had no intention of getting out in front of the two black-eyed Sidewinders under Cuevas's wings. Like turning your back on a dago with a knife. He eased on some throttle to match the Corsair's climb.

Five minutes later, as Tracey was reporting through 20,000 feet, the Corsair flipped over into a dive.

'Stand by! He's on the way down!' Tracey called and rolled over into a near-vertical dive.

He got the aiming marker on the Corsair, tracked it, larger and larger in the sight-glass, throttle shut, airbrakes out, finger on the trigger . . . Vapour streamed from the Corsair's wingtips. Cuevas was pulling out! Tracey swore, flipped airbrakes in, gave the Skyhawk full throttle and pulled.

He clenched his teeth and strained to keep his vision open against the 7g pull. It was a huge effort, but Cuevas's plane was stressed to 9g and he wouldn't worry about bending it. If Tracey didn't keep the pull-out tight Cuevas would barrel in behind and let off a 'Winder. Power and energy were the only things Tracey had against the agile Corsair.

With the Skyhawk going vertically up he relaxed the pull, gasping with effort, senses reeling as blood flowed back into his brain. At 250 knots he pulled over onto his back, looking below for the Corsair. There it was, as before, spiralling up towards him, a few thousand feet below.

Not bad for a kid, thought Tracey. Nearly sucked me out ahead on that one! Neat! And he's got four hours' fuel to my one. Right. My move. He loosened his straps.

Tracey could never explain his phenomenal success in air combat. It was a gift. He allowed Cuevas to close the vertical gap again to about 3,000 feet and eased him across to the opposite side of their left-hand spiral. Without warning he slammed into a reverse turn to the right, out of the circle and away from Cuevas – as if to break and run. When he judged Cuevas to be in his six o'clock, he rolled inverted, put out 20° flap and pulled the Skyhawk to the buffet, throttle closed, airbrakes out, 200 knots. Looking up through the canopy, he could see Cuevas rolling towards him in a classic counter. They passed in the centre of the loop. Tracey bottomed out, power back on, airbrakes and flaps in, speed 250 and rising.

Vertical scissors. Tracey went on up at full power and pulled over until he hung inverted and almost stationary, about a thousand feet above the Corsair. Cuevas too had run out of speed, but more quickly, and had to drop the Corsair's nose first. Checkmate! The Corsair was too slow to fight. Tracey came down on Cuevas like a plunging hawk before he could pull clear, and fired.

A one-second burst sent metal flying from the Corsair's left wing, then Tracey's guns stopped firing. Swearing foully, he had to pull away and take the defenceless Skyhawk back up to safety. Circling, he watched Cuevas who seemed to have lost interest in both him and the airfield.

Cuevas had a runaway propeller. The vibrating damaged blade had loosened and cracked one of the oil feed lines to the pitch control. Cuevas was recovering from the shock of three hammer-blow explosions in his left wing, still in a full-power dive when his engine set up a rising catatonic wail that paralysed him with fear. He looked at his RPM gauge and saw instead of the 2,700 he had set for combat a horrifying 3,400, and rising.

Wild-eyed, Cuevas slammed the throttle shut and the rising engine speed slowed. If he had pulled up and killed his speed, he might have lived longer, but it was too late. Valves jumped their collets and fell into cylinders. Pistons broke and jammed, conrods snapped and thrashed the crankcase apart. When the crankshaft seized the propeller twisted free of its shaft and spun away into space and the whole shattered overheated mass of engine burst into flames with an orgasmic roar.

Cuevas died in a comet that streaked to earth with a solid thump two miles inland from Roca. He never knew it was Corporal Vargas that killed him. But nobody laughed.

Chapter 7

'I will *not, not* have the operational integrity of this unit compromised by *any* individual, for *any* reason!'

Cassián worked fast. With Hicks and a small team of provosts, he located the focus of anti-British sentiment in Cuevas's squadron and discovered a clique of which Funk, the blond German cadet and Blount's tormentor, was leader. Their activities had been quite open.

Asked why he had done nothing about it, Capitán Soto, OC4, had replied, 'With respect, sir, here at Roca are several hundred of the best of Argentine youth. I suggest it would be naive to expect these not to form factions. I would go further and say, if they did not, we should suspect something is wrong with them!'

Cassián's storming reply had taken Hicks aback. The Commodore had lost his temper. With a voice like a knife he went on: 'So you think it's all right. Capitán Soto? Three men dead! One aircraft lost and another damaged in the equivalent of a bar-room brawl!' He pointed a finger up at the tall, aristocratic Soto. 'I will hold *you* personally responsible, in future, if anything like this happens again!'

Cassián next paraded the Grupo on the concrete apron and against the cold malignant wind made a speech that finished, 'Cuevas? He put his ego, his small and imagined grievance, above the interests of the Grupo, above the interests of his country. What he did was small, selfish, and dishonourable. He was a *traitor!*'

The bullhorns wafted the word over the silent audience among the williwaws of wind. It felt as if it ought to rain. A

69

clap of thunder would fill the bill nicely, thought Hicks, hoping Cassián would stop now, anyway. But the Commodore was not quite finished.

'The penalty for treason,' he said, 'is death.'

He made them attend the funeral of Munro and Vargas. In a small enclosure on the clifftop south of the field two graves lay open at the end of a neat row of seven crosses. There was no Anglican priest, but Hicks imagined Munro would not have been much put out. He tried to recall how many funerals he had attended in uniform, like this. That's the saddest thing, he thought, that you don't even remember them.

Soto was there. Hicks watched him during the prayers. A *hidalgo*, a Spanish gentleman with nothing to learn from foreigners, or upstart admirals. He'd never been as easy with the *consejeros* as the other Argentines. He hadn't said he sympathised with Cuevas, but neither had he in any way condemned him. He would bear watching.

And that evening, Hicks got an opportunity to watch them all, hair down, when Cassián entertained all the base senior officers. Bridge-building, damage-limitation, whatever, it was a remarkably valuable exercise, he thought. Very good generalship. Good food, wine, and talk. And the longer they talked the deeper they got into *argentinidad* – Argentity, and what lay behind Cuevas. The Argentines seemed eager to bare their souls and expose their uncertainties. The country is too big, said one, and we are too few: it makes us nervous. We don't know what we are, said another: you read our books, you see they try to build a country of words, they invent a folklore of *caudillismo, caciquismo, gauchismo*. Anglo-Saxons don't need all these *ismos* – you are lucky. Don't try to understand Argentina! Can you imagine an Argentine cricket team? They laughed together and clapped each other's backs and sang songs. Tracey got drunk and fell asleep. LeStrange was in his element. Only Soto kept his distance. But Hicks could see the steel under all this: a fierce positive national pride that he found himself envying.

Carla was waiting up when Hicks got back to his rooms, the orientality of her small pale face heightened by a white bathrobe. An altogether feminine thing. He didn't kiss her. That would have been husbandly.

'So, what did he say, our *Contraalmirante*?' Her usually lilting, musical voice was serious. Munro's poor death and Cuevas's fiery plunge still hung in the air of the place.

'The thing is not finished,' she said after he had told her. Cassián had said the same, at the end, urging precautions like locked doors.

'You have seen it then?'

'Of course! *Indigenistas!* Like the *Contraalmirante* says, this is Argentina!'

'*Indigenistas!*' More istas! 'What are *indigenistas*?'

'The people who think it wrong to bring English here. What they say is, if GEA is going to make Argentina great, it is wrong to have help from outside. Especially Anglo-Saxons. Gringos. It will be said that Argentina was not capable to do it alone.'

'It is only technical assistance. Every country uses technical experts.'

'Eeks, you don't understand. In Argentina we need – how you say? – flatter, to feel proud, to have our own success. Just one time. Just once!'

'This is very feminine – for a nation of gauchos!'

She smiled. 'You are right! This perhaps makes Argentina so interesting country?'

The smile stirred him. She knew it would. He wanted to talk, to find out how Carla was able so easily to distance herself emotionally from Argentina's nationalism, while accepting it intellectually wholesale. He suspected it would be a waste of time. She would see no paradox. Her white things were white because they were white and her black things were black because they were black, and the absurdity lay in attempting explanations.

But he would talk no more for now. Her small smile closed a door, opened another: he sat quiet, looking through it. She was still spending only about half her time with him and the other half of her private life was as obscure as the far side of the moon. But this girl with her long body, her primitive hair, her high voice and her powerful fragility, had already grooved his soul. Impossible, now, to imagine life without her. He still knew very little about her: daughter of a wine merchant; Córdoba University, history and economics; worked for her father; travelled to the US for six months with 'a friend'. That was all, she insisted. 'Very ordinary girl, Eeks, you see?'

She was, certainly, completely unpretentious, both physically and intellectually. She took no more than decent trouble with her appearance and was incapable of intellectual or moral cosmetics to a degree that bordered upon arrogance. She was as implacably independent as a cat: Hicks has sensed, early on, the danger in trying to confine her. He often wondered why she had chosen to walk in on him that first night. He could see now, in that extraordinary act, in its untrammelled decisiveness and unreserved honesty, the essence of Carla. But why? Why him? He would never know that either, because he would never ask.

She was not sexually demanding, rather given to cautious indications of an availability of passion. As now. As if not sure of the quality of what she was offering. Naked, she was thin; tiny breasts and bony shoulders and a surprisingly small black triangle. Naked too, she had always seemed to take on, in place of clothes, a solemn, self-contained, inaccessible, mysterious intensity – suggestive of an ordeal. Carla naked and demure in private, and Carla in public, the contrast was arresting; and here was another mystery – neither was a pose. Of that he was sure. Each was natural, tap-rooted into her personality. Equally, her unaffected liking, even affection, for him. Like now. She was looking steadily back at him, offering. The public smile had gone. Her eyes carried a private rhetoric of intimate request and vulnerability. It was especially in these moments of privileged intimacy, when he could see her like this, that Hicks was made aware of the magnitude of his feelings for Carla, and of the hurt that would come of them, one day.

He stood, opened his arms. She came, stood close, arms by her side, he a little taller of the two. A long stray spiral of her hair was trapped inside the collar of her soft bathrobe. Hicks delicately attended to it, tidying it. Then the other side. She closed her eyes and raised her face as his hands slid around her neck and raised the heavy bush of her hair, but she made no other move.

They kissed, lightly, her lips a tender petition. He slid the bathrobe off her shoulders and let it fall to the floor. Carla had never done this for herself: she seemed to find the last step into nakedness too difficult to accomplish alone, and it was for Hicks the most delicious of the little duties of their relationship. Carla opened her eyes and smiled, and Hicks found himself in a maelstrom of pleasure and pain. The view from the summit. From the peak all ways were down. The ecstasy was unsustainable. To break the tension, he reached forward and taking her gently by the upper arms, said, 'These arms are ridiculous, for a pilot. Too thin! How can you fly a Corsair with arms like this!'

She turned her back against him and hugged his hands to her little breasts. 'You know what Chinese say, Eeks?'

'No.' His face was buried in her hair.

'In time of war, find a strong leader.'

'And in time of peace?' he mumbled.

'In time of peace, find a strong woman!'

Ten hours later Carla had two fat green 1,000-lb bombs under the wings of her Corsair, one of an echelon of six led by Finch to show Cassián the laydown profile.

Cassián was behind Hicks in a two-seater, his first flight with the Grupo. It was a diamond spring morning, the sea royal blue and white, and after an exhilarating half-hour at wavetop height Hicks pulled out to one side to watch. The unfused bombs fell gracefully away from the Corsairs' wings into the ocean close around the fast-moving target. One bounced in a high tumbling parabola, close to a following Corsair. Hicks winced.

'Fifteen seconds.' He had stopwatched the attack.

'Pretty good, Eeks! Eh? Pretty good for first time! I would not like to be down there! – er – we go back now, OK?' The Commodore was no flier.

He showed up after lunch, only slightly pale, to take the chair at the de-briefing. Finch took them through the operation and summed up: 'A success then. Five first-timers on lay-down and from the reports it seems we would have put several holes in a normal-sized vessel. No training. No practice. Says a lot for the standard of flying in the Grupo.' Hicks smiled at the plug.

'But six *is* too many!' Finch had wanted three, but none of the squadrons would be left out, recalling the joke about the Argentine cricket team. He went on to argue the case for smaller formations, and finished, 'And of course we still don't have the bomb fuses, as you know.'

Bombs they used in prodigous numbers. Anywhere else, they would have been small cheap practice bombs. But from Roca three hundred tons of live HE went into the Atlantic every week. Trucks hauled bombs in along the supply road from the north. The bombs themselves had US and British markings: surplus strategic stock, bought cheap. Extravagant, but there were certainly no pilots anywhere in the world so familiar with the carriage and delivery of the 1000-lb iron bomb, and nowhere had its ungainly ballistics been so assiduously refined. But the bomb-fusing manual remained on the US Strategic Prohibited List.

'However,' Finch went on, 'we can see from this how our operation is beginning to look. As Martinez suggested,' he indicated Martinez Soler, OC2, 'coordinated high and low attacks. Assume the target here,' He put some models on the floor. 'Six ships. Assume two hundred aircraft. Two wings. Each wing, eighty bombers in twenty divisions of four, split, half high, half low. Twenty Sierras with 'Winders, and four Echoes.

'We locate. We identify. We form up for the attack. Dive-bombers up there –' he pointed at the ceiling; 'Laydowns at a thousand feet or so, out here –' he drew a wide circle on the floor, 'all around like numbers on a clock.' He put his pointer on the centre ship. 'The captain here will see one division of Corsairs about every thirty degress, all round the horizon. And if he thinks to look up, the same at fifteen thousand feet. The fighters, meanwhile, deal with any opposition. The Echoes go in first with ECM, and Anti-Radar missiles to take out the fire-control radars. The Wing Leader calls the attack sequence, going for weak points, alternating high and low. In this case,' he indicated one of the ships, 'this one could probably expect two laydown attacks from this side, and one or two dive-bomber divisions, depending on his luck. Mathematically, four of these ships will be attacked by eight lows and eight highs; two of them get away with only four lows and four highs. Only sixteen bombs! I would not like to be in any of them!'

Carnage. Absolute carnage, thought Hicks. Sudden, violent death in the South Atlantic for hundreds of men who, literally, would not know what hit them; even those lucky enough to see the Corsairs before they died wouldn't know what they were. If they did, would not believe their eyes. And who would rescue the survivors? Six ships! Would it be that many? Might there be more?

'Thank you, Commander.' Cassián rose from his chair. 'I like the new low attack, and I like this plan.' Finch put his pointer down and took a seat as the Commodore asked, 'Now, what are the problems?'

'Contraalmirante.' It was Soto, speaking as one who has a lot to say. 'First. Four planes each division is not enough. Perhaps Capitán Finch forgets what everybody knows; accuracy in operations is only five, ten percent of practice scores. So four planes, eight bombs, maybe one hit only. Maybe none. We carry our bombs five hundred miles for nothing.' He spoke flatly, as if it hardly needed saying. 'Second –'

'Wait, please.' Cassián interrupted. 'We take this first.' He pulled his chair into the centre of the floor and sat down. 'Commander Finch, please?'

Finch replied easily: 'You can't argue with statistics. The percentage score is constant. You get the same number of hits either way. But concentrating the attack leaves untargeted ships free to manoeuvre and interfere. We lose more aircraft. This plan will sink or disable most ships in the first wave. The second wave will finish the job.' He looked directly at Soto. 'If my arithmetic is correct, eighty aircraft, one hundred and sixty bombs at five percent accuracy is eight hits. Agreed?'

'Statistics do not win wars!' Soto shook his head.

'I totally disagree. Statistics and analysis are indispensable. If you want to win, that is!'

'It is easy for you to make jokes. It is not your war!'

'That also is untrue.'

The Commodore, after the briefest of pauses, said 'This question obviously needs more discussion. Capitán Soto, you had another point?'

'Fuses, Contraalmirante.' Soto was still angry. 'We were told our English experts would soon make a solution to this problem. For dive-bombing, it is not critical. But this, this new laydown –' he pronounced the English term with distaste, 'needs delay fuse and reduced arming time. I understand we still do not have the solution to this.'

Cassián thought for a moment, then: 'Perhaps it would help if Capitán Blount explains again the problem, and the progress of the work. Please?'

Blount took the floor. 'This is all very basic,' he began. 'Bomb fuses have been around a long time, and they haven't changed much. I'll draw it.' He did. A large coloured diagram appeared on the blackboard and Blount made it sound childishly simple. Soto looked studiously bored as he went on to describe the work being done to produce a rapid-arming delayed-action fuse.

When Blount finished Soto ignored him and said to Cassián, 'It seems we are more concerned here with problems than with solutions. This does not answer my question about the arming time.'

Blount said patiently, 'I have explained, as best I can.' He dusted the chalk off his hands and sat down.

Cassián said, 'Thank you, Capitán. My understanding is that production of a fixed delay fuse can begin now, but time does not allow development of a variable fuse. The delay will be set between ten seconds and three minutes, all bombs the same. You must decide, soon, the best time delay for your tactics, and that will be the delay for all fuses.'

Soto stood up. 'Contraalmirante,' he began belligerently, 'I would like to place on record, now, that I, Capitán de Corbeta Soto, am not satisfied with the service our Navy has received from these *consejeros*!' Cassián sat up and fixed Soto with a slightly puzzled look as he went on. 'First, they advise on choice of weapons. Bombs and Sidewinders. But they cannot make fuses for the bombs. And as for Sidewinder, they tell us Corsair with Sidewinder will always beat a jet – but what about Cuevas? A few seconds combat and *poof*! The Corsair is in flames! Is this what they told us? Then they advise high-level dive-bombing – on ships in winter when it is plainly impossible. So they invent "lay-down". But if this "lay-down" is so good now, why not at the beginning? Finally we have seen the disruptive effect of foreigners on at least one student. I mean Guardiamarina Cuevas. How many more? These advisors have brought nothing to Roca we could not do ourselves!' Soto remained stiffly standing, glaring at Cassián.

'Thank you, Capitán Soto. Will you please sit down?' said the Commodore after a long silence. He got up from his chair.

'I will say two things now. Then the meeting is closed.' Looking at Soto he continued, 'First, there is no record for your opinion to be placed on. I welcome advice and opinions. I need not act on them. Your comments are noted, thank you. Secondly –' and he addressed the row of junior officers at the back '– You know why this base is called Roca? I hope you do. After General Roca, founder with Sarmiento of the Collegio Militar, the man who professionalised our army. Before Roca, all was rabble. And how did General Roca do this? He brought military instructors from Europe. Without these, all would still be rabble!'

Soto stirred, as if to protest. Cassián fixed him with a stare that made Hicks think of obsidian. 'That is *my* opinion, as a good Argentine!' He spat the words at Soto. 'The meeting is closed. Enough talk – there is much to do!' Cassián put his chair aside, took up his cap. All stood.

'Contraalmirante?' A voice from the back row.

'What is it?' Cassián's voice carried unwelcome.

'Would you say who will lead the second wing, sir?' It was Funk, blond and haughty; standing, Hicks was pleased to note, not next to Carla.

The question had an impertinent cheeky ring. But the little Commodore set his gold-crusted cap on his head and smiled.

'I don't know, yet. Why? You think it should be Teniente Funk?'

Everybody laughed, except Funk.

Chapter 8

Cassián went straight to his office, told his PA not to disturb him, closed the door and sat down.

The room was sparsely furnished and uncarpeted. There was no paper: books in abundance, on shelves, a bookcase, at random on filing cabinets, half a dozen on the big metal desk, but of paper and files, none. On the wall opposite the desk, a picture of a Corsair F4U-7 in US Marine colours, used-looking with dirty exhaust streaks, chipped paint, underslung bombs. The picture was in glossy, travel-poster style, big, stark, unignorable.

Cassián swung his chair and sat for a few minutes staring across the sprawling airfield. Spring showed in the quality of the sky, a less aggressive weight of cloud and wind, a feeling of release. October. But the brooding brown eyes went far beyond the Santa Cruz landscape. Cassián's thoughts were hundreds of miles north, in the marbled corridors of the Casa Rosada, Buenos Aires. There, last week, he had felt an atmosphere that, compared with the scene beyond the window, was a photographic negative, an adumbration of approaching political winter. Gloom, tight faces, desperation. He had seen Galtieri, the chairman of the Junta, who smelled of whisky, and Admiral Anaya, hard-line politician and author and tireless proponent of 'the Goa option'. They had pressed him on the state of readiness of the Grupo. Lami Dozo, the Air Force chief, had absented himself, as usual.

Cassián's report, that the Grupo had completed what he called its academic training phase, had not cheered the Junta. How long? they wanted to know. Eight weeks, he told them.

Less if they could accept a reduction in the number of pilots being given full operational training. He had been told to proceed with the full training programme, with all haste, until advised otherwise.

'I want to see Capitán Soto,' Cassián said on the intercom to his PA, and swung back to the window. This time, he examined the scene beyond the airfield, the unattractive, barren old Patagonian plain. Argentina! He realised, with some surprise, he did not even know who owned the surrounding land. Not that the owner was likely to be any nearer than Buenos Aires. He might be in Europe. The officer he had sent for was, he knew, a younger son of a land-owner, *hacendado*, *estanciero*, what you called them depended on what you thought of them, what they thought of themselves. Powerful, rich men set in the bedrock of Argentine history from the time of the *Conquista*, resistant to the acids of democracy. A *porteño* himself, from a merchant family in Buenos Aires, Cassián disliked these aristocrats but had to respect them for their power. And anyway his rank, his uniform, aligned him with their interests.

Soto came in. 'You wish to see me, Contraalmirante?' he said, saluting.

'Yes,' replied the Commodore. 'I do.' He left Soto standing.

Soto took off his cap, looked around for somewhere to put it, then held it behind his back. 'Sir, I regret to cause trouble with the English. But I think you will understand it is a question of –'

'I understand very well!' Cassián's hard voice stopped Soto rudely. The Commodore's chair looked too large for him. 'Your regret means nothing and I have no interest in explanations! Your attitude to the English is not acceptable. It places you, in relation to this Grupo, in the position of a renegade. You understand?'

Soto, the *estanciero*'s son, stood erect, face blank. He raised his eyes to look over Cassián's head, through the window, seemed about to speak, but the quiet steely voice cut in again.

'You have three choices, now. You can alter your attitude to the English, acknowledge their value to the Grupo, and co-operate with them, like the other *comandantes*, to finish their work. Or you can resign your command. In this case I will assign you other duties which will effectively remove you from all contact with the British. Or I will dismiss you. There are no other alternatives. And I want your decision now!'

Soto's incredulity showed on his long Spanish face. He was thirty-four, a loyal Argentine of impeccable background. Not a brilliant officer nor any longer a man of high expectations, he was nevertheless comfortable in his role, knew no other. But his attitude to the English was fundamental. He disliked them and their country, could not stomach the flavour of their arrogance. And equally strong was his conviction that in standing against them he was doing his duty as an Argentine, as an officer. Their presence tainted the Grupo, would debase its achievements.

What should he do? His indecision showed now: he knew it and was ashamed, hated Cassián for it. If he resigned his command, or for that matter if he were dismissed, it would be the end of his naval career. He would become a despised civilian, looking for a job. Work! With a name like his he would prefer beggary! And he would take nothing from the elder brother who had inherited the *estancia* in Missiones. He could not conceive an existence out of uniform; not flying; not being an officer, among officers. What of his wife Emelda, another high-born Argentine! If he left or was sacked, would it make any difference? The English would stay. With a little spurt of excitement he realised that his departure, now, would reinforce their position even. While he, a true Argentine, would be neutralised, of no account. He would not be allowed to leave Roca, of course. He would be here, humiliated for all to see. Probably for many months. But as a squadron *comandante*. . . . His face stiffened.

'Contraalmirante, if –'

'No ifs, Capitán!' Their eyes locked in a long hard silence.

Soto swallowed. 'Very well. I accept that the English have made a contribution to our Grupo. The training organisation is good. They have experience we do not. I will continue in command of Number Four Squadron and work with these people – for my country!'

'Good! Very good!' Cassián looked genuinely pleased. He

smiled and came upright in his chair. 'You are a good *coman-dante* and I do not want to lose you. We are on the same side, you and I!' They drank small glasses of brandy, to Argentina, to GEA. When Soto left, he looked less tall.

At about the same time, eight thousand miles away in London, another door closed behind another long-serving lieutenant-commander. It was 7.30 in the evening, not unusually late for service officers in MOD Whitehall to be finishing – certainly not for Lieutenant-Commander Bagshaw in Room 616. Bagshaw was a pilot, or had been many years ago, before moving into Intelligence. Short, fat and loquacious, he enjoyed his work, and as he set off in his tired London pinstripe for The Clarence, he was thinking about the last piece of paper he had placed in his Out tray before locking up.

Contained in a file marked ARG/N/130/1, it was a Foreign Office memo headed 'South Atlantic – unidentified aircraft sighting'. The text read:

Following report passed for information NI16 from BNA Montevideo. Yacht *Maudelayne* (Mr D.F. Clark) sighted eight unidentified single-engine piston aircraft position 4830S 6529W a.m. 3 October 1981. Aircraft were quote single-seat radial-engine, long nose, bent wing. No markings. No dimensions unquote. Attention NI16 drawn to BNA report dated 13 December 1980 of new overflight prohibition of 200km radius area centred on 4820S 6630W.

Bagshaw had sent the file to his boss, Naval Director Intelligence, minuted:

By NI16
Recommend a. Sat phot review of 4820S 6630W
            b. SSN recce if opportunity presents
and/or   c. BNA Buenos Aires get down there and
            look.

Reason – Falklands. DPB Lt Cdr

He had thought of tagging it *Urgent*, but decided against it. He had a bit of a reputation for getting over-excited.

In the same building that evening, there were several other

81

pieces of paper, any two of which, brought together, would have kept Bagshaw and many others at their desks all night.

In NavPers, a file marked 'CDR J W HICKS RN' carried a note:

'Resigned employment Anglo-Continental Airlines Nov 1980. Observed around this time, in Rotterdam and London, in company of Cdre. Cassián. Arg. Navy. Dep LHR Jan 1981 to Luxembourg. NFT.

Similar notes could have been found on files for the other six Britons now in Roca.

RAF Intelligence (SA) had on file a noted dated 1979 from its Air Attache Buenos Aires:

Argentine government or military have acquired large numbers (est. 300) light training aircraft from unknown sources. Aim is obscure – Argentine officers in the dark. Query funding. Will report further.

But there were no more reports.

In another file marked AI/SA/ARG/INDUST, AirInt (SA) had a photostat of an article from *Banking International*, dated 1978, on a visit by banking officials to Argentina. Under AIRCRAFT, was the following paragraph:

At the Cordoba factory of the AGA the delegation was shown new plant for large-scale production of airframe components, evidently for assembly elsewhere. The aircraft was not identified but was of fighter dimensions.

In the same drawer in a file marked AI/SA/ARG/MIL a photostat from *International Defence Review*, September 1979, under Market Notes:

Traders report urgent enquiries worldwide, believed to be emanating from South American Embassies and in at least one case (Karachi) Argentina's, for surplus Hamilton Standard Hydromatic 54H60 propellers, 'any condition!'

And in AI/SA/GEN, the earliest clue, a scissor-and-paste job from *The Engineer*, 16.7.76:

Mystery recruitment: In an intriguing recent phenomenon, covert but very determined approaches have been made to airframe and propulsion engineers throughout Britain and Europe with offers of lucrative contract work in South America. Qualifications required are, oddly, experience of reciprocating engines, and pre-jet airframes. Senior men have left Hawker Siddeley, British Aerospace, Fiat, Messerschmitt-Bolkow and Fokker at short notice, having apparently received offers they could not refuse. . . . all that can be said, at this stage, on this very interesting little matter is that whatever is afoot in South America is extremely well funded, probably military, and clandestine.

There was nothing to indicate that anybody had ever read the item.

And anyway, Dave Bagshaw did not even know of its existence. He breezed, as he always did, cheerily out of the MOD main door with a goodnight to Security. Sadly, since he liked nothing better than a good jaw at the end of the day – his office was small, with a high tiny window and a view of bricks and drainpipes – The Clarence was empty. That is, no one from MOD. So Bagshaw stood alone, foot on the rail, took a long pull at his Worthington. He set the glass down, idly thinking . . . long nose . . . bent wing . . .

And suddenly he was back in the early 60's in hot sun, at the French Aero-Navale base at Toulon, watching their Corsairs. 'Hose-nose' they called them. They were almost curios then, cranked wings, like nothing else on earth. He'd never flown them but they said they went like shit off a shovel and carried a fantastic load. Eight Corsairs, eh? Just eight? Well, remember the first rule of the fighter-pilot – never mind the ones you can see, look for the other bastards! Might be dozens of them, if somebody saw eight all at once. Don't suppose he thought to take a photograph. They never do. So – very interesting! He seemed to remember the French were last to operate Corsairs, had them in Indo-China, definitely. Algeria? Couldn't remember. But how did the Argies get hold of the French Navy's Corsairs without anybody knowing? You can't just quietly sell off aircraft like that – though it would be typical of the bloody French!

Suppose they are the French Corsairs, though. What then? Bagshaw had been in Naval Intelligence over ten years. He

83

thought he had a good feel for it, liked it even if it was easy to get stale at his level. He didn't think he was stale. There was always the chance of something big. Pearl Harbour wouldn't have happened if his equivalent at Oahu had been on the ball. He looked forward to chasing up these French Corsairs, as he was now convinced they were. But not now.

'Poppy! Thank god!' He had had his eye on the door and got an instant lock-on on his friend Lieutenant-Commander Popham as the latter shoved it open with his briefcase. 'Bloody place is like a morgue. What'll you have?'

''E please. Pint. No. Six pints. I'm going to drown myself. I'm sick to fucking death and beyond of being a civil servant!' Popham's chalk-stripe looked as if it had just come out of a kit-bag.

'Cheer up, Poppy! Only another eighteen months! Think of the money!'

'Piss off and get the bloody beer in!'

Bagshaw grinned. Popham would stay an hour at least. They would talk. Old friends, old ships, personalities, runs ashore. Folklore. And some work. But not the Corsair. Popham, a 'fish-head', wouldn't be interested. But Bagshaw made a mental note, before letting go the day's work, to put an urgent tag on that file first thing in the morning, and, equally important, to add a note to show that he, NI16, had made the connection between 'long nose, bent wing' and the French Corsairs. 'The French Connection?' Eat your heart out, le Carré – this one's mine!

File ARG/N/130/1, red-tagged and duly annotated, was collected from Room 616 at 0930, passed through registry and logged to NDI, to whom it was delivered an hour later. The Director, Captain Pollard, a squat, pugnacious man with crinkly grey hair, opened it immediately, read the latest insertion, re-read it, leafed through the rest of the file and then sat a moment with his eyes closed. Then he got up, taking the file, and went out, locking the door behind him.

He went into an office like his own, marked NAVAL DIRECTOR SURFACE. NDS, Captain Laski, MA, was at his desk. He would have been more at home, from his appearance, directing a city art gallery; and to those who knew him, the elegance was more than skin-deep. An Oxford double first, his short and apparently effortless Naval career had included command of a carrier-born Buccaneer squadron, and a destroyer. After NDS would come big-ship command and flag rank. After one look at Pollard, Laski dismissed the WRNS officer with whom he had been discussing a file. He took and read the one Pollard handed him.

'They're off, then, Jack!' There was satisfaction, and some relief, in the tone.

'Aye. This, as they say, is it. What do we do now?'

'Absolutely nothing, old boy! Except our bounden duty.'

'We couldn't delay this? Mislay it?'

'Good Lord no! Why? We've wound this thing up; now we just let it run.'

'Yes.' Pollard was less enthusiastic.

'But remember, Jack. For us, now, it's a clean sheet. We've given history a nudge, that's all. We want a small dust-up between one of our so-called warships and some basic air to bring people to their senses. From now on, we do our jobs. Otherwise, the exercise loses its point!'

Pollard pointed at the file. 'So what's NDS's reaction to that?'

'Mild interest. But it's a bit far away. What's NDI think?'

'Ditto. I'll go along with Bagshaw. Get him to do a search on Argentina's aircraft industry.'

'Very reasonable. I suppose the Commodore must know his slip is showing?'

'By now? I'm pretty sure he will have anticipated the eventuality.'

'I'm sure you're right, James!' smiled the elegant Captain Laski.

Chapter 9

Cassián introduced what became known as the Saturday War. At a dawn briefing two hundred pilots were allocated formation positions and callsigns. They took off in two waves to find and attack *Sylvestre* five hundred miles out in the Atlantic. *Sylvestre*'s SatNav position was relayed to the Kondor Boeing who set up the *Tacan-Hayrake* bearing for the Corsairs.

As long oversea flights became a commonplace and the pilots lost their awe of distance, confidence improved. And these massive exercises bred a discipline in the Grupo that gave the British new regard for the Latin.

When the target was located, the wing would form 'Carousel' for the attack plan Finch had outlined on the Tactical Floor. Twelve four-plane laydown divisions, callsigns Cormorán One to Twelve, took station at about five miles range, like the numbers on a clock-face, Cormorán 12 due north of the target. These were at a thousand feet. Above, at about 17,000 feet, the dive-bomber divisions – christened Págalo One to Twelve, after the Argentine Skua – took up the same stations. The wing leader – Monegario called himself Aguila – ordered the sequence of attack and gave the order to commence. At ten-second intervals, Págalo leaders began their dives and Cormoráns their run-in at wave-top height in a co-ordinated attack that was calculated to confuse, overwhelm and destroy. A hundred tons of HE was delivered in a continuous attack over about twelve minutes.

'Bloody spectacular!' was Tracey's verdict. 'But what about the poor bleeding ships! They're going to get blown out of the water!'

'Don't worry, Trix,' LeStrange told him. 'It'll never happen. Will it, Jeff?'

Hicks puzzled over this. Was Pierre up to something? Odd bugger! You could never really talk to him!

New bomb-racks reduced hang-ups from around eight percent to one, but the new centreline drop-tank increased fuel transfer problems. Fuel failures were a source of great tension. Most became apparent before the point of no return. But at least two of the less prudent young pilots pressed on too far and failed to make it home. The Wasp engines were very dependable and would run for hours with a cracked ring or valve, even cylinder head, and the 23-gallon oil reserve was insurance against minor leaks.

But if the statistics of mechanical failure were comforting, it was the weather that gave the Grupo starkest evidence of its vulnerability.

Thirty-four aircraft were caught out when freak conditions of wind, temperature and humidity brought a bank of sea-fog in over the field one late afternoon. Hicks, in his office, became aware of a sudden chill and quiet. The airfield outside had disappeared. Sea fog! He knew it would happen some day! Carla was airborne.

There was a thick frightening smell of sea as Hicks hurried to the control-tower, where Monegario was already in charge, listening to a report from a Corsair overhead.

'Three, four hundred feet thick over the field. Getting thicker.'

'How far inland?' Monegario asked on the controller's mike.

'Two, three miles now. But soon will be more I think. It is moving in.'

'Are there any breaks over the sea?' It was Figari, OC1.

'Nothing. Not from here. You want I look out there? I have plenty fuel.'

'No. Wait please, Pedro. Stay overhead.'

Monegario put down the microphone and spoke to the controller. 'Get fuel states.'

There was a clatter on the stairs. The senior controller came up fast. Bright-eyed and breathless, he reported to Monegario: 'All off-duty controllers are coming to the tower, sir. All radio and radar equipment is being checked and maintenance crews on standby. Emergency services are on alert!'

'Thank you, Christos. Stack overhead, in order of fuel state.'

Someone brought the list to Monegario. Hicks looked over his shoulder. The lowest figure was 65 gallons. Carla was leading Violet Division. She had told him she liked the colour. 'Violet-L' had eighty gallons left in her tanks. An hour and a half. It would be dark by then.

A phone buzzed. The controller relayed to Monegario, 'From Meteo, sir. Rio Gallegos is open. CAVOK.'

'Thank you.'

Cassián arrived, peered around at the fog-blanked windows and asked Monegario, 'Can they land in this?'

'Not safely, sir,'

'What will happen if they try?'

'Some will succeed. Some will crash.'

'And the alternative?'

'The lowest aircraft can still make Rio Gallegos. There is also San Julian, or even the civil field at Punta Deseada. Otherwise, there is the supply road. Some could land on it. Or they land here. Or they bale out.'

Cassián said grimly, after only the slightest hesitation, 'Get them down, here. Or on the road. Now!'

Carla was eighth in the pattern and very glad to be going down so soon. Already the photochromic evening had drained away west. The east was black. She saw a Corsair sink into the smooth tops of the fog-bank and vanish. Despite the warmth of the cockpit, she shivered.

Her call came: 'Violet Leader, roll out heading three six zero degrees, set QFE one zero one two millibars, descend to one thousand five hundred feet and report landing checks complete.' She started down. Latest runway visibility was less than fifty metres.

The approach culminated with four hundred feet of flying the needles in the thick dark mist with the ground getting closer. Eighty-four knots. The droning talkdown: *glidepath centreline, glidepath centreline*, then *Touchdown . . . touchdown . . . Now!* Carla looked up from the green

needles. She peered sideways and down through the streaming perspex, saw a blur of ground, hesitated a long instant,
and pulled the throttle fully back.

Five tons of Corsair fell out of the air and hit the runway
with a crash that rattled the instrument panel. Carla pulled
the stick hard back and began braking. A light went past,
close to the left wingtip, another, closer. Another whipped
past under the wing. She braked harder, as hard as she dared.
A wheel thumped something as the next light passed. She was
leaving the runway. Carla sensed yaw left, corrected, first one
way then the other until realising she had lost all sense of
direction she put the pedals central and braked both wheels
harder and harder until her long body was bar-rigid with the
effort.

It took a while to realise she was stopped. Alone in the fog
with her Corsair, the Pratt & Whitney idling contentedly, she
opened the canopy and smelled at the same time effluent of
hot sweat, fuel, oil, electrics and fear, and the blessed inswirl
of cold, damp, ocean mist, earth, dust, and relief.

'Violet Leader, are you down? Check in please!'

Carla collected her wits. '*Si*. Violet Leader is on the field!'

'*Excelente! Excelente!*' Talkdown sounded just as relieved.
'Violet Leader has landed! Now call Ground Control Channel 4, Out.'

She changed frequency and checked in. 'Turn north and
taxi until you come to the north taxiway. Then stop and
report. And caution! There is another aircraft in that sector
also taxying, and maybe others not on radio!'

Carla checked her compass, eased up the throttle and
started turning left. But now a new difficulty – her legs!
Astonished, she looked down at them. They were shaking,
uncontrollably! Furiously as she tried, she couldn't stop the
quivering and had to taxi with legs that felt as if they didn't
belong to her. When she reached the taxiway edge, marked
by blue lights, she checked in.

'Roger, Violet Leader. Shut down. You can walk on the
taxiway round to the tower.'

Carla stopped the engine, got out carefully, sat down on the
dusty ground beside the fuselage. She lay back and dug her
nails into the poor Patagonian earth. Her whole body

trembled violently. Her small face screwed up tight against them, but the big tears forced themselves from her eyes and ran back into her hair. Presently, she got up and began to walk.

Hicks watched Carla's talkdown on a remote monitor tube in the tower. Of the first seven Corsairs to land, only three had answered the radio after touchdown. There was no telling what had happened to the others after they had gone off the screen.

'*Si*. Violet Leader is on the field!' Her voice had been higher than usual. It rang frail in the loudspeaker. Hicks was astonished at the monsoon of relief these words let through him. Monegario, who had been listening alongside, put his hand on his shoulder. Hicks turned his face away.

After a little while, when it was evident he could do nothing to help, Hicks left the tower and started walking slowly in the mist out along the northern taxiway. By keeping to the yellow centreline, he could just see both edges, blue lights to the right, ambers on his left, dim pools. A Pratt & Whitney was running, somewhere, idling on the ground. Another higher note told of a Corsair still in the air, coming closer. Hicks walked slowly on. He heard, muffled and non-directional, the tweek-tweek of tyres hitting concrete, the engine throttled back, then more tyre noises, a high shriek of skidding rubber and a muffled, metallic bang. The fog around lit up dull pink with fire. Surreal. He walked on. Other Corsairs came in, sound-pictures in the lurid fog. He heard one taxying to his right, getting closer. It went behind him and stopped its engine with a puffing rattle of dying machinery. On in the Dantéan scene he walked, peering left and right until, when he was about to give up, thinking he must have come too far, he saw her.

He stood still. Only a silent black silhouette, walking slowly, head down, helmet swinging in one hand. But unmistakably Carla, tall, slim, too much hair, and that awkward walk. A shade. Back from the dead. Out of the inferno.

'Carla?' Softly.

She stopped, turned vaguely towards him, searching the blank mist. Away from the fireglow, he was invisible to her. 'Eeks! Is that you?'

90

He walked towards her out of the mist. They held each other tight for a long time, he stroking her hair, pressing his cheek to hers, before they began to walk back. No word was said. They just held hands.

Of the thirty-four Corsairs, seven landed on the supply road, one crashing. Twelve landed successfully at Roca. Two pilots, among the last in the pattern, and unnerved by the pall of black smoke coming up out of the fogbank and the fireglow at its root, overshot their landings, climbed and baled out. Six aircraft were total losses, including the bale-outs and the collision Hicks had heard. Three others suffered heavy damage. Four pilots died and five were injured.

Before the recovery was complete, Cassián had sacked the senior forecaster, consigning him to menial duties in barrack catering, after pointing out to him, in a blistering interview, the order requiring him to issue a formal fog warning whenever conditions were pre-disposed to fog, as they were, by his own testimony, that afternoon.

Monegario he congratulated, on the performance of his pilots. Himself he castigated quite publicly for not anticipating the disaster and ordering a relief landing-strip, however primitive, to be constructed inland, beyond the menace of sea-fog.

When it was all over, after a subdued meal in the Rancho, Hicks took Carla home. She was still tense. He wanted her to talk. He poured a tiny glass of her favourite liqueur.

'When did you first see the runway?' he prompted. She slumped, uncharacteristically, in an armchair. He had, he realised, never seen her unhappy before. She was avoiding his eyes.

She spoke listlessly: 'Just before – I don't know. Maybe a metre below – or ten. I don't know.'

'Any lights?'

'Before I land? No. Only after.' She took a sip of liqueur. She was looking at her legs.

'So – how did you land?' He genuinely wanted to know. She seemed not to hear. 'Carla?' Softly. 'Carla?'

She lowered her head. He waited. Then he got up, went across to her, knelt beside her chair. Took her hand.

She turned her head away.

He waited, gently stroking the limp hand. Presently, she sniffed. She put her glass down, fished out a little handkerchief and blew her nose, all with one hand. The other squeezed Hicks's as she turned her face towards him: defiance and distress, wet cheeks, red nose, brimming eyes.

'Some beeg pilot, eh?' She tried to smile, sniffed.

God, how he wanted to kiss her. But it was not the time. He just folded her hands tight in his. And hesitantly, she began to talk. The worst had been waiting. Trying not to think. Not so much of crashing, even dying, but fire. The quarter-full tank just in front. Being trapped. She covered her eyes, wiped them, put her damp hand and the wet hanky back between his, sniffed, and talked on. Once on the way down, it was better! She flew a beautiful pattern. Beautiful, Eeks! And the talkdown. She was very pleased with that part. Hardly any corrections! And the landing. Probably not much worse than in training. Well, perhaps a bit! She hoped the Corsair was OK, her Corsair. She must go and see it, in the morning. Yes, the landing, not too bad . . . not too bad . . .

He waited. 'And then?'

The head was down again. 'Carla? Why so sad? This was a magnificent thing you did! A big, impossible thing! And you did it perfectly!'

She took her hands away, grasped her knees. 'You see these legs, Eeks? After the landing they were like this!' She shook them angrily. 'Like *this*! I could not taxi proper! My legs – like jelly! What good is a pilot with legs like that when there is a little trouble! They are right to say women should not fly!'

'Ha! So! Now I see! Now I understand!' Hicks lifted the wet bundle of hands and fingers, kissed them all, and put them down. He stood, went to another chair facing Carla, and sat down again. 'Now let me tell you a story.'

He told her of a night years ago. Indian Ocean, dark and moonless. He was in a 20-ton twin-jet fighter, flying from a small carrier. He had an electrical failure that was going to make the deck-landing even more difficult and dangerous than usual. He explained how the Navy had made the mistake of assuming that the mirror landing sight, which they had invented, solved all the pilot's problems, and had dispensed with the landing safety officer whose job it was to prevent pilots making fatal errors. And how as a result the fatal-accident rate for night deck-landings had become, by peacetime standards, grotesque.

With no land within a thousand miles and the carrier pitching through the long ocean swell, he, like her, had began his let-down, flown the recovery pattern, and been lucky enough to catch a reasonably level deck for a successful wire-trap at the second attempt. He told Carla of his own morbid thoughts as he looked down from the wait, at 20,000 feet, at the ship's tiny lights: the awful depth of water down to the black-ooze ocean bed. He told her of the near-blind 130-knot thumping arrival on the deck, the wonderful fierce snatch of the cable, the huge relief at being stopped, alive, and the sweetness of the warm salty sea air that galed in when he opened the canopy. And he told her of his own astonishment at finding, when he had taxied and parked, that his legs were shaking. Just like hers.

'You?' Carla looked unbelieving.

'I never told anybody, until you. There were plenty of other times I was probably more frightened. But that was the only time I got the shakes!'

'Shakes? What is shakes?'

He went and shook her knees playfully. 'This is shakes!' He knelt, hands on her knees. 'And if Eeks gets shakes, and Carla gets shakes, I think probably most pilots do, some time. They just don't advertise it. Not the sort of thing you yell out to all your friends – "Hey fellas, guess what! I've just had an attack of the shakes!" Eh?'

'Is shakes like ibby-jibbies? And willies?'

'Heeby-jeebies. Sort of. Yes.' Hicks stood up, paced the floor. 'The genus Fright.' He ticked off on his fingers. 'Shakes, Heeby-jeebies, Willies, Jitters, Creeps, Butterflies, Cold feet – and Twitch. These are some of the common European species. With the native species of South America I am less familiar – yet. But your description suggests little significant difference. Much work remains to be done, of course, but it is well known that all are amenable to one certain cure.' He stopped pacing.

Carla looked up, a puzzled half-smile. 'What you say, Eeks?'

He held out his arms. She stood, and he drew her to him, folded her close. 'The Hug. Guaranteed remedy for all known varieties of genus Fright. Never been known to fail.' His face was in her hair, the cockpit smell.

'Mmmm.' Face against his shoulder. 'I like this 'ug very much.'

'It was invented by the English, in the eighteenth century.'

'I thought English are cold. Always, in books.'

'That is why we need hugs. But only in private, between consenting adults. And it is well known that the most effective variety of hug is one, like the present example, between people of opposite gender.'

'Eeks.'

'Umm?'

'Shut up!'

Later, before she went into deep twitching sleep beside him, Carla said to Hicks in the dark, 'You know, first time I see Commander Eeks, he did not look a man who 'aves ibby-jibbies and 'ugs.'

'You're disappointed?'

She squeezed his hand and fell asleep.

Chapter 10

'Absolutely incredible!' was LeStrange's reaction when they viewed the wreckage from the tower next morning. A mobile crane was trying to pick apart the fused carcasses of two burnt-out Corsairs. Elsewhere other relics of 'the Black Night': an up-ended Corsair, propeller wrapped around its cowling; one on its belly; one askew on a broken oleo; others being tractored back to hangars. Hicks fancied he could see Carla on the north taxiway – she had wanted to go and 'see' her aircraft. 'Two or three years ago most of those pilots were boys and girls on the streets. In school, for God's sake!'

'Well, if you had any hope Cassián wasn't in deadly earnest,' Finch told him, 'I reckon after this you can forget it!'

'You know these kids are just too good. When I see the way they play that Carousel, one word keeps going through my head – Massacre!'

Hicks for once found himself agreeing with LeStrange. Cassián's decision last night had shaken him. And he too found the Carousel a frighteningly savage spectacle of destruction.

'Well, we've been over all that,' Finch said. They had. Over and over. But without, so far as Hicks was concerned, much benefit. He felt the moral ground getting softer all the time.

There was more gloomy news for Hicks. The ECM electronic countermeasures equipment had arrived and twenty Corsairs were fited out as -E 'Echo' ECM versions with jammers, PWR passive warning radar, chaff rockets and Sidearm anti-radar missiles, the latter a Motorola conversion of Sidewinder.

This formidable outfit would neutralise ship radars and fire-control and guidance systems and allow the horrifying Carousel free play with the defenceless ships.

But Hicks and indeed all the *consejeros* would have taken some comfort from the fact that it was ECM, the tool of concealment, that first revealed to London that all was not as it seemed in the South Atlantic. An Echo was included in each wing of the Saturday wars, and wing leaders instructed not to proceed without serviceable PWR. This auto-scanned the entire radar waveband and warned off if anything was detected, the signals then being used to avoid the radar lobe and escape detection. Cassián didn't want these large formations showing themselves to warships. Unfortunately for Cassián, although PWRs were BIT-tested before take-off, an in-flight failure could go undetected.

HMS *Warhawk* was on passage south to the Falklands with a relief party of Marines, stores for the Governor; then on to Antarctica with a scientific party. The ship was relaxed, Saturday forenoon Sea Routine. In the ops room Petty Officer Green occupied the captain's chair while minions cleaned and polished around him, the room reeling lazily in the long swell. 965 tube looks a bit shitty, he thought! 965 was the 200-mile air-warning radar, aerial the size of a tennis net. It didn't like heavy seas, but this little swell was nothing. Yet there was a rash of contacts in the top left of the tube. Well, he'd wait till this lot had finished – it was only ten minutes to stand-easy – then he'd ring the WE office and tell them to fix it.

'Hey, PO! Look at this lot!' One of the youngsters, polish and rag in hand. 'Looks like one of them thousand-bomber raids on 'ere!'

'Yeah? Well you just polish it! I want you finished this lot by stand-easy.' Green pointed at the bulkhead clock. It was set to GMT.

'Tea-time, you mean!' The lad went on polishing.

'Hey, PO – this lot's moving! Look!'

'Don't be bloody daft, lad! We are, in case you had forgot, in the precise middle of the South At-bleeding-lantic.' Green didn't even look. The sailor put down his rag, swung the cursor onto the leading green blip of the shoal and made a mark. He watched for two sweeps of the aerial, then made another mark, then another. The ghostly formation step-stepped down the screen. The young sailor's scalp was just beginning to prickle when Green yelled: 'Anstey! Will you stop playing with that and –' He felt himself pushed aside. Green, abruptly silent, stared at the tube.

'Jesus!' Green pressed a switch and spoke into the desk mike: 'Bridge, Operations!'

'Bridge?' The officer of the watch, bored.

'Multiple aircraft contacts on 965, sir, bearing 340 degrees, range now one six zero and closing.'

In seconds, the captain was in the ops room. Two and a half hours later the duty staff officer at the underground head-quarters of CINCFLEET, Northwood, was reading his signal.

IMMEDIATE   SECRET

231742Z

FROM WARHAWK

TO CINCFLEET

INFO FOF2

= IN POSITION 4712S 5501W AT 231600Z RADAR CONTACT ESTI-MATED ONE HUNDRED AIRCRAFT BEARING 340 RANGE 160. AIRCRAFT IN FORMATION ON COURSE 135 SPEED ESTIMATED 200. FORMATION REACHED LONGITUDE 5645W, HELD FOR FIFTEEN MINUTES, THEN WITHDREW WNW. LOST CONTACT IN POSITION 4725S 5900W TRACKING 285 DEGREES. CLOSED TO WITHIN 60 MILES BUT REGRET NO VISUAL. NO ELECTRONIC EMISSIONS DETECTED. 2. REVISED ETA PORT STANLEY 231400Z. GOVERNOR INFORMED =

Captain Pollard, NDI, saw it on Monday morning. He sent for Bagshaw who behind his door marked NI16 had already as-sembled a strong circumstantial case for clandestine warplane manufacture in Argentina. 'Drop everything, Dave,' he said. 'I want this taken seriously!' He had already seen Laski.

*

After Black Night Carla stayed with Hicks, and brought him to a new high happiness. It had all the vulnerable intensity of a

97

tropical bloom. He tried to suppress it, to conserve it, to hide it from others, to protect it. The certain knowledge that it would have to end, in pain, assuaged his guilt. A thing like this embodied its own exact measure of chastisement: there would be no net gain, or loss. Just footprints on his soul.

They took to jogging, in the summer evenings, out along the high cliffs and down a rocky gully to a small beach where the sea-life was relief from the sterility of the land around Roca. They would watch the teeming birds, cormorants and *págalo*-skuas among them, seals, and the cruising orcs or killer-whales that preyed upon their young. After work, before dinner, these runs became a routine, until one evening, climbing back up the gully, they were nearly killed by a rock fall. At the top of the cliff Hicks found evidence that somebody had deliberately dislodged a boulder.

The ghost of Cuevas, Carla called it. Blount was next. Stung by Munro's murder, nourished by the aggressive affection of the redoubtable Conchita, he had healed. With her forceful help he cut his drinking, got himself back into physical shape, and one day in November he flew again. A few days later on an ACM flight his engine began cutting out. He just made the runway with a coughing engine and landed safely. The engine stopped during the taxi-in and would not re-start. His fuel tank was found to contain several gallons of water. Had the aircraft been lost, crime would never have been suspected.

Blount needed all Conchita's care and firmness to keep him out of relapse. Hicks watched her work and marvelled; shipyard worker, bomber pilot, mental nurse! An odd couple; the quaint chemistry of their relationship intrigued Hicks.

The attempted murder of Finch was more elegant. He and an Argentine, Teniente Delgado, in Skyhawks, intercepted four Cobra Corsairs coming in at 15,000 feet west of Roca. The jets came up from behind, a mile abreast, throttled down to a slow overtake, one on each side of the loose formation of Corsairs. Finch had briefed Delgado: he wanted them to come up on the Corsairs slowly, get as close as possible without being seen, force them to turn. Whichever way the Corsairs turned, one of the Skyhawks should be able to accelerate in behind for a cannon pass. That was the theory. And in the early days, it worked. Not now. The Cobra pilots were old hands.

'Gold Four. Two bandits, right four o'clock low. Six miles.'

'Gold Leader contact.' Teniente Videla let the jets get in to about a mile then called, 'Gold Three and Four break right. Gold Leader and Two breaking left. *Go!*'

The Corsairs split outwards.

'Black, Crossover – *Go!*' Finch went left and the Skyhawks crossed a few hundred feet apart. The combat split in two, each gun-armed jet engaged with two missile-armed Corsairs. The Cobra pilots would look for an opportunity kill on any jet within a mile: Sidewinders were only interested in the jets, so the Corsairs were safe. Finch, enjoying the solid little Skyhawk, was thrilled to see how neatly the young Cobras flew the sequence.

'Black Leader! Missile break left! *Break left!*' Delgado! That wasn't right! Finch craned back over his left shoulder, saw two Corsairs, one Skyhawk – and something else. Against the landscape far below, a thin smoke-trail, from somewhere behind one of the Corsairs, was streaking incredibly fast, towards him! A live missile, doing Mach 2.2 with its black eye fastened on his tailpipe! Options! Three: Flame-out, kill the heat-source; try to out-turn it; or eject. He couldn't see the missile and didn't know how close it was. He ejected.

After the colossal bang of the exploding canopy, the huge acceleration and a solid blast of freezing air, tumbling and spinning, Finch heard another explosion, and a few seconds later, safe in his parachute, he saw the largest remaining part of his Skyhawk, the front fuselage and one and a half wings, tumbled away and down towards the drab Patagonian plain.

He was back at Roca, none the worse except for a stiff back, in three quarters of an hour. The others had landed; aircraft impounded; crews effectively under arrest: Cassián, Perez and Monegario at No. 4 Squadron: an inquisition.

Soto's squadron again. The pilot who had shot Finch down was either distraught or a very good actress. Guardiamarina Francesca Verdo had, she said, like the other three, assumed she was carrying a dummy missile. She pulled the trigger when it growled at Finch's Skyhawk, and had been horrified when it fired. She was allowed to see Finch, to see that he was all right, and to protest her innocence.

There was no longer any doubt about the water in Blount's tank, or the rock-fall. Corridors echoed to the crash of police boots. Whistles blew. Rooms were ransacked at random, documents were impounded. The Sidewinder incident ramified the anti-gringo movement into support services, stores, hangars and workshops. Late in the day Cassián assembled the entire senior echelon of the base and the British were spectators to a parabola of discussion rising from hesitant beginnings to a crescendo of argument, then tailing away, spent, as if some sort of consensus had been achieved, or imposed. It was all in Spanish. Hicks caught less than half of it and said nothing himself. Finally Cassián turned to him with an apologetic smile.

'Commander Eeks. Please forgive our impoliteness! We run away like wild horses at this problem! Did you understand?'

'A little, *Poco*.' Hicks had been watching Soto, who had had less to say than any of his fellows.

'It will be good then if I summarise the feelings of the meeting,' said Cassián, sitting at the head of the big oblong table.

'First, there is complete condemnation of these acts, as there was of the murder of Commander Munro.' Not quite true: Hicks had never heard Soto condemn anything. But he smiled his acknowledgement. Cassián went on: 'We also agree this is not a thing to surprise. These feelings lie too deep to be affected by anything we do here. But you should not feel you and your colleagues are personal targets: if you were not here it would be something else – Peronístas versus anti-Peronístas probably, even if nobody knows what these words mean any more. But we are surprised at the energy of this Cuevas faction. The important question is: what do we do? What do our *consejeros* think?' He put the question to Hicks.

Hicks made them wait while he looked at all the Argentines in the room, particularly their eyes. The concern in the faces was genuine. He was sure of this. Colleagues, friends, he had long ago stopped thinking of them as foreigners. With the exception of Soto they were good guys, the sort of men he liked. Even Soto, a good CO. Absurdly he found himself feeling sorry for them. They were ashamed of this undercurrent of craziness that kept poking though all their lives; it had certainly added stature to the *consejeros*.

After the long pause he said, 'As you can imagine, this is a very unpleasant situation for us, and not of our making,' he made another dramatic pause and went on, 'but we don't want purges. That would destroy everything we've worked for. We think, we hope, the problem may solve itself. When we get operational, GEA's energy will have a new focus. The Cuevas faction will be pushed off-stage: if they persist, they will look ridiculous. We all agree the best thing is, let it ride for now.'

Cassián turned to the Argentines. 'You see? Alberdi it was who said a country without Anglo-Saxons is like a wood without birds! This is why –'

'One proviso!' Hicks interrupted the Commodore. 'Bring the principals, at least, to justice.' They owed Munro this much.

'Of course! Of course!' Cassián smiled and rubbed his hands. Relieved. 'It will be done! And maximum security! You must all be most careful. These people are snakes in the grass. We will try to eliminate them, but –'

Hicks was looking at Soto. The *hidalgo* raised his eyes, expressionless, for a long moment, from the glittering silver pencil he had been toying with throughout the meeting.

'It is regrettable,' Hicks said to Cassián, 'but understandable, that snakes in the grass are often killed.'

'There will be no regret, by me,' the Commodore replied steadily.

101

Chapter 11

If the even tenor of MOD Whitehall was little disturbed by Lieutenant-Commander Bagshaw's pursuit of the South Atlantic UFO's, it was not for want of trying on his part.

He fired salvoes of red-tabbed minute-sheets and search notes around inside the ministry and followed tendrils of information deep into the filing system. He was good at this. It excited him. He wrote engagingly naive letters, signed with a flourish, on bland paper not to advertise their real origin, to Standard-Hamilton Propellers Inc, Vought Aircraft, Pratt & Whitney Aero-Engines, the US Navy Historical Branch, the Musée Aero-Navale Française, Toulon. And he tapped into a network of ex-service friends making a lot of money in arms consultancy posts all over the world.

Just before Christmas 1981, Bagshaw presented his boss, Captain Pollard, with an elegant staff paper outlining his case for the Corsair. Attached and forming Annexes A to W were photostats of his evidence. Annexe X contained Operating Data on the F4U-4 as supplied to the Royal Navy in 1944: speeds, range, armament, payload. A note was added that the ultimate US Corsair, the -6 used by the Marine Corps in Korea, had lifted bombloads up to 5000 lb. Annex S was a sheaf of satellite photographs obtained from the CIA showing the new airfield south of Punta Deseada. Bagshaw was especially proud of his discovery that a small black swept-wing aircraft on one photograph, apparently having just lifted off the runway on take-off, cast a shadow of blunt, straight wings.

Pollard's reaction was disappointing. He read the paper

quickly, initialled it and put it in his out tray. 'Well done, Dave. I'll send it down to NDA.' Naval Director Air was down the passage, past Ships.

'Is that all, sir?' Bagshaw was surprised to hear himself ask.

The Director looked up. 'How do you mean? What else do you want?'

Bagshaw hesitated. He didn't know. He just felt his discovery was more important that that. 'What about the cousins, sir?' he liked the arcane parlance of his little world.

'I'll buy that. They do think it's their hemisphere.' NDI retrieved the file, pinned on a tag and wrote 'Action – NDA. Copy to D of I, US Navy Department. (Draft covering letter)' and put it back. 'That do?'

'Thank you, sir.' What for?

NDA was Captain 'Ozzy' Baldwin. Nature had cast him for the role of Shelley's Ozymandias, full wrinkled lip and sneer of cold command, and he had lived with the soubriquet for most of his twenty-nine years in the navy and had come to enjoy it. A shrewd and kind man, he too had a solid career in naval aviation behind him and more than an even chance of flag rank.

He read Bagshaw's paper twice through and rang for his Deputy. 'Take that away, John, have a good look at it and tell me what you think.'

Half an hour later, Commander John Ward was back.

'Well?' Baldwin sneered at his coffee, his cigarette, and Ward.

'Fishy – in a word.' Ward put the file on Baldwin's desk, none too reverentially, and sat down uninvited. Baldwin regarded him stonily, head back, lip raised and several teeth on display, cigarette awkwardly poised. There might have been a bad smell somewhere. Ward always enjoyed this bit.

'I know,' said Baldwin stiffly, 'that we live in austere times; that we drink ersatz coffee;' he pushed contemptuously at his empty cup, 'that our ships steam at half speed to save coal or whatever it is they use nowadays; that we don't have enough paper to wipe our backsides. But a verbal economy pro-gramme now, is it? "Fishy". A choice word though. Summ-arises my own view most elegantly.' Ward examined his nails.

Baldwin inhaled smoke with an expression of utter disgust. 'Dare we hope you have some others to go with it?'

Ward smiled appreciatively. 'I find it hard to resist Bagshaw's conclusions, sir. The sighting, the sat pictures, the prohibited area. Then *Warhawk*'s signal, on top of all his background stuff. Corsair clones, in fairly large numbers. And the position of this new base seems to allow only one rationale, namely the Falklands. And I think the camouflage of the aircraft is significant.'

'So?' The histrionics were over.

'It's eight thousand miles down there – a long way off our patch these days. But here's a large build-up of potentially hostile air within range of Crown territory. Response, if any, would have to be Naval Air. I would take the problem in isolation, ignoring distance and logistics – for a start anyway – model it up and see what comes out.'

'Anything else?' Baldwin wouldn't have asked unless there was. This was typical of the way he had been schooling Ward for years.

'In your place, sir, I would waste no time in shoving this up the appropriate political nostril – as high as I could get it!'

The crudity, as expected, raised the lip. 'Just like that? Your simple military mind is showing, John.' Baldwin pointed to the file. 'Take it away. Get a team on it. Report in . . .' he consulted his desk diary, 'damn it's Christmas! . . . say Jan 12.'

Captain Baldwin went down the corridor and into the office marked NDI.

'Are the Argies about to invade the Falklands?'

Pollard's pen stopped, mid-word. He recovered, went on writing. 'Sam, I thought you knew better than to ask straight questions down here. What's the problem?'

'This Corsair resurrection of yours. You don't believe it?'

'Oh that!' Pollard was still writing.

'You don't believe it?'

'Do you?'

'We think we do.' Baldwin sat down. Pollard put away his paper. 'And there are two ifs about it that bother me. If they've got Corsairs, or anything like them, in any numbers, and if we get involved, we might not be able to handle them. Nobody thinks in those sort of numbers nowadays. So what about a credibility rating on this?'

Baldwin often wondered but never did know why the Naval Director Intelligence should look so relieved just then, nor why he should speak so fervently when he answered. 'You've seen the evidence, Ozzy. There's no doubt about the aircraft. They've got a lot of them, and they're on a new base about as close as they can get to the Falklands.'

'And the politics?'

NDI gave NDA a resumé of the history and present status of Argentina's claim to the islands. 'It's an obsession with them,' he concluded. 'They take it out and wave it at us from time to time – usually when they're having problems elsewhere.'

'And have they got problems now?'

'Perennial. You name it. Two hundred percent inflation. Foreign debt. Balance of payments. Labour troubles and a lot of general nastiness held down by an equally nasty military Junta. They could do with a diversion.'

Baldwin looked at Pollard long and hard, sniffed and stood up. He stood, hands behind his back, examining a *Daily Telegraph* Map of the World sellotaped inefficiently to the wall.

'Eight thousand miles. Seventeen days at twenty knots,' Pollard told him.

'Do you think they would, Jack?' Baldwin asked eventually.

'I don't know, Ozzy. But what counts is that they sure as hell could. That is not new. But these Corsairs, or whatever, are – and the base.'

'How would we respond?'

'Ask Plans.'

In Plans the Director, Captain Cuthbert, handed Baldwin a file marked NDP/FALK/73/1, a thin floppy document. 'Is this all?' asked Baldwin incredulously, quickly leafing through it.

'They've all been weeded,' Cuthbert explained.

'If Argentina invaded, what would we do?'

'Doesn't that tell you?'

'No.'

'Then we have no plans. After all it's –'

'I know. Eight thousand miles. But haven't you *any* idea what our response would be?'

'Ozzy, in this office we deal with the real world. The fifty-frigate navy in NATO.'

Baldwin smiled evilly, an exercise for which his features were well designed. 'That's all right then, Bertie. When the bedside telephone in Number Ten rings in the small hours, one of these days, with the news of an invasion fleet anchored off Port Stanley, you'll be able to show her this!'

He dropped NDP/FALK/73/1 on the Naval Director Planning's desk. 'Seriously, Bertie, I'd have a word with Jack Pollard about that.'

Before the Ministry of Defence thinned down to a skeleton for the Christmas holiday, Captain Pollard pursued the hare put up by Bagshaw with such energy as to draw comments about bees in bonnets; very few in the MOD shared his interest, but no one afterwards could doubt NDI's commitment to exposing the threat in the South Atlantic. Three days before Christmas he got Laski and Captain Frank Sargent, then commanding one of the Navy's air bases in the southwest, to meet him at home. They were given lunch by Pollard's wife before retiring to his study. In a cosy atmosphere of books, warm fire and coffee the men settled into chairs. Cold Somerset rain pattered down the mullioned window and a black cat called Burberry sat hunched up before the fire.

Pollard put a couple of logs on the fire, poked them down, stroked the cat and said, 'Sitrep then, Frank.' Situation report.

Sargent, a small wise-looking man, listened without comment while NDI briefed him on the contents of the Bagshaw file.

'Well this sounds a right bag o' nails! What are the bastards up to? Are they going to invade?' Sargent sounded both surprised and indignant.

'No way of telling. We know now they nearly did after the coup in '76, and when they won the World Cup in '78. Callaghan slipped a nuke down that way to warn them off.

106

But now, HMG is pulling out of South Georgia and scrapping *Endurance*, and if I were standing in Argentina I'd probably read that as an invitation.'

'Bloody hell! Looks like our little scheme's gone over the top then!'

'Not yet, Frank,' put in Laski, 'it may never happen. And if it does, we've nothing to feel guilty about. All we did was give Cassián some names.'

'George, this could be a bloody massacre! Are you going to explain to the relatives, afterwards? We only gave them names!'

'Steady, Frank!' Pollard intruded. 'Cassián would have had his Corsairs anyway!'

'Well I don't know how you can just sit there!' said Sargent angrily. 'OK, all we gave Cassián was names. And we did it for a good reason, namely in the hope of a little confrontation between one of our modern pathetic toothless so-called warships and a handful of antique aircraft, to prove a point and wake people up. Let's get back to numbers, we said, remember? But not these sort of numbers! George, you're the expert: what odds say three of your frigates against a hundred Corsairs with bombs? You shoot down the first ten with your space-age gadgets, if you're lucky, whoopee! you say . . . but there's still ninety more of the bastards to come! Eh?'

'It need never happen, Frank,' insisted Laski. 'Now we know about the threat. If there's a little dust-up around the Falklands, as we hoped, we just keep out of their way. We don't have to play their game.'

'And what would HMG do if they were to invade? The full thing.'

'Ah! That's different! Jack?'

'In my opinion,' said Pollard, 'if they were to invade tomorrow, the basking seals of Westminster would just bark and roll over, the way they do. But I have a strong suspicion the PM would reach for the big stick. Marines. Paras. The works.'

'A task force eight thousand miles, and God knows how many of these Corsairs down there!'

'Look, Frank,' put in Laski, 'there's absolutely no point agonising over this. George got us here to establish our position.'

'Which is?'

'No different from anybody else,' stated Pollard, 'except we're better placed to read the threat. The big problem is to get anybody to take this seriously. George will tell you, the Falklands is a big yawn. So – just talk it up as much as you can, everywhere.'

'Meanwhile,' said Laski, 'Ozzy's got the bit between his teeth and he's off and running. It couldn't be in better hands.'

'God bless Ozzy!' said Sargent with feeling. 'And this chap Bagshaw – he's done a pretty good job, Jack?'

'Bloody good! Ferret with his ass on fire ever since that first signal!'

They sat with their thoughts for a while in the darkening room, three men and a cat. 'Heard something amusing the other day,' said Sargent with a grin. 'From the RAF. One of Their Airships worked out the way things are going, by 2020 they'll need the whole RAF budget to buy one fighter! That was our point, wasn't it?'

Laski said thoughtfully, 'But these sort of numbers spoil the argument. People would say, quite rightly, there's no answer to a hundred-aircraft attack. It's a one-off. It doesn't change anything.'

'Aye, but think on, George,' answered Sargent. 'Say a hundred Corsairs for the price of ten Backfires. We could handle the Backfires. It's the same argument.'

As they were leaving to go home for the holiday, Laski observed, 'Hicks of course, doesn't even know why he's down there!'

'Jeff'll know what to do,' Sargent told him confidently.

Burberry was left alone, unblinking in front of the burning logs.

Ward reported to Baldwin that British Aerospace would programme the Corsair into their Air Combat Simulator at Warton in Lancashire and fly it off against any of the standard jets. On an old-boy basis, since MOD had no money for such skylarking. That would take three weeks. Some squalid little sod who wanted to know who was paying was led away by 'a friend'. A parallel plan to fit one of the Navy's 'historic' Sea Furies – Corsair equivalents – with Sidewinder and fly it against the Sea Harrier got the condescending consent of Flag

Officer (Air) – 'all right, so long as it doesn't cost anything!' –
and the enthusiastic support of everyone else at Yeovilton.
'Very keen, sir. Bob Oakes has started a book. Three to one
on the Fury!'

'He would!' Baldwin actually grinned. 'You know, you
have to admire our national talent for insecurity. Local paper
in on it? Sports page?'

Ward smiled. 'The attitude seems to be, since it's unofficial
it can't be anything serious. I didn't enlighten them.'

'What about LeStrange? Anybody manage to find him
yet?' Baldwin asked.

'No.' LeStrange would have been their first choice to evalu-
ate the Fury-Sidewinder combination against the Sea Harrier. 'He didn't have a job. Camilla – his third wife, did you
know? – just says he's abroad and not available. But here's a
funny thing. I thought Camilla might be covering – it wouldn't
be the first time Pierre's walked out on a woman – so I phoned
to ask Jeff Hicks if he knew where he was. Pauline says, guess
what, Jeff is 'abroad and not available'! Checked Anglo–
Continental. He left them a year ago, very short notice, and –
they say shortly before he left he was contacted in their
Rotterdam hotel by a commodore of the Argentine Navy!'

Baldwin took a deep drag on his cigarette and inhaled
noisily through clenched teeth. Two minutes later he was in
Pollard's room.

'Jack. That ferret of yours – what's his name, Bagwash? – can
you get him on to this?' He put a paper on the desk. 'Hicks and
LeStrange. And if his nose is in good form, other recently retired
fixed-wing pilots. Argentina!' Baldwin snarled the last word.

Without looking up, Pollard groped for Baldwin's memo,
pressed a buzzer, gave the paper to a secretary and said,
'NavSec Group Update.'

Baldwin sniffed, said 'Thanks,' and left.

The print-out came back almost immediately, a long list of
pilots' names, addresses, occupations, abstracted from the
Emergency Reserve List. Pollard underlined seven before
sending the sheet down to Baldwin's office: Hicks, LeStrange
and five others were shown as having left the country on the
same date in January 1981, via Gatwick for Luxembourg. All
bore the final abbreviation *NFT. No Further Trace.*

Chapter 12

January, Patagonia's August. Less cold, more dust on the williwaws bounding energetically oceanwards from the high Andes. The British, like the sparse vegetation, absorbed high summer gratefully into their life-cycle. The Argentines appeared to notice it hardly at all.

Hicks introduced Carla to the country walk, sandwiches, silly hats, wild flowers. They laughed at each other's bare legs, held hands, embraced and kissed in the mild sun. She was happy and relaxed. He was intoxicated. Her long thin legs, pallid, were by any standards unlovely, even gaunt; yet to him they spoke a vulnerability, made him feel privileged and protective – no matter he knew they could control the Corsair's swing as well as his.

Indeed she was altogether a creature of angles and bones, a configuration matching the awkwardness of her agile personality. There was nothing either straight or round or static about her. No mould she might fit into – she shrugged them off as soon as they began to form, a bird shaking raindrops.

She moved in permanently with Hicks after Black Night, any stir of unease he felt at the unwonted connubiality of the new arrangement smothered by something else he didn't want to name. He had never, in his whole life, known such happiness as he felt in having her, her hair, her high voice, gay little laugh, her smell, her things, with him behind the closed door of his room. Thus Hicks walked, open-eyed, his precipice of happiness.

Blount had Conchita. She fussed, ministered, bullied, excited and loved him. He accepted her with bewildered gratitude, and they became as man and wife.

110

LeStrange found himself unaccountably comfortless amid a busy swirl of femininity. Never before had he had such ready access to so much young womanhood, been in such close and tantalizing proximity to it, and yet never had he been so lonely. Such self-analysis as he was capable of led only to the unsatisfactory conclusion that he had lost his touch. He redoubled his efforts, raising his already high profile with new subtleties of preening and display – without suspecting for a moment that he was being laughed at.

What LeStrange had failed to appreciate was that among all the ostensible femininity around him there was no single example of his conception of an ordinary woman. GEA females worked and lived in a way that took no account of and made no concessions to gender. To the inescapable corollary of this sexual equivalence, they adjusted as individuals. Girls from widely various Catholic backgrounds pitched into confrontation with the soulless sexuality of the young Latin male recoiled, or emerged either diminished, bruised, damaged, hurt and wary, or enhanced, aware, and powerful – brokers of male vulnerability. With neither of these categories of women were the British, and especially LeStrange, attuned. And besides, the omnicompetent woman made them all, willy-nilly, uncomfortable.

Finch, a man who had never asked anybody for anything, attracted the curious with his putative virility. None of the resultant attachments was satisfying either way, the women usually retreating, baffled by his needs.

Those whom Channing attracted were the casualties. His low, unexciting profile, product of a long and stable marriage, advertised an availability of affection, an emotional dressing-station for the hurt. He, realising this, nevertheless found himself awakened and excited by each tentative approach, and his avuncular defence was cunningly contrived – he would never have admitted it, especially to himself – to invite. On the small number who responded, interest and affection were lavished.

Tracey was never short of female company, which he seemed to regard as an agreeable nuisance. He was never known to do or say anything that could be interpreted as an initiative – indeed succeeded in giving the impression he

111

wished 'the one with the squeaky voices', or 'the ones with the bumps on their chests', would behave more like men – but his fair hair, blue eyes, boyish grin and candid amorality could hardly but make him something of a cult figure. Downing Cuevas had given him a special stature, but his main attraction was intrigue: women could never know if his indifference was feigned, or not, and none was prepared to take another's word for it.

In their short periods of leisure, a beach barbecue, gaucho style with the meat hanging on iron frames around the fire, became a social focus on weekend evenings, replacing the films that had helped pass the winter. Out of uniform, away from the confines of the base, irrepressible femininity blossomed.

But the weather was never reliable. One Saturday evening a blustery sou'easter brought cold mist and a noisy swell into the little beach cove. Heavy showers threatened. A film was announced – *The Battle of Britain*, with Spanish sub-titles, and drew a packed audience after supper.

When the film was over, Blount joined the bar throng just behind the tall, blond Teniente Funk. They waited their turn to be served amid a chatter of talk about the film.

Looking about him, Funk saw Blount, gave him a hostile stare and turned his back. To a young man beside him, he said, very loudly, 'Of course Germany would have won this battle if it had not been for Hermann Goering. It is well known the British pilots were beaten by the Luftwaffe, except Goering stopped them. This film is typical British propaganda.' Funk turned again, pretended to notice Blount, smiled down condescendingly. 'Oh, good evening, Capitán Blount! Did you enjoy the film?'

'Yes I did,' Blount replied, Funk sickened him. Conversation around them had died away.

'You did not think it exaggerated?'

'Most of it is historically true.'

'Ah!' Funk smiled wisely. 'But history is always written by the victors, I think! Excuse me.' He turned his back on Blount again and moved forward into a space at the bar.

Conchita noted Blount's tight expression as he set down the drinks. She said nothing, but there was worry on her broad, high-cheeked face. The others talked about the film. There was some argument when it came to comparing the aircraft in it with the Corsair.

'What you think, Teem, eh?' Conchita squeezed Blount's hand. 'Teem?'

But it was obvious Blount had not heard a word. He looked up, unseeing, at LeStrange, then said to Conchita, 'Excuse me,' and stood up. Conchita stood too, holding his right hand.

'Teem – watsa matter, eh?'

'Got to talk to somebody.' Blount turned abruptly and walked across the room, Conchita trailing. He made for a big noisy group of pilots containing Teniente Funk, stopping on the edge of the seated circle.

'Funk!' he called loudly, voice coarse with anger.

Funk looked up. Again, the talk died away around them. 'Capitán Blount!' Funk smiled. 'You would like to join us? Here? – sit down please!' He made a place.

Blount waited long enough to ensure he could be heard around the room. When he spoke, his voice was clear and tight. 'You want to know why Germany lost the Battle of Britain? I will tell you. It was not your stupid Field Marshal – it was your stupid arrogance! You could not admit to yourselves the English might be as good as Germans in the air!' Blount's face flushed with anger. Funk looked at his friends, smiling apologetically. He made to speak. Blount transfixed him with a pointed finger and went on in a tone that rang like bare steel: 'Arrogance! And you lost the war for the same reason. Arrogance! Like arrogant ridiculous sheep you followed a man who told you you could rule the world; with your blitzkrieg and your panzers and your SS! All shouting Heil Hitler! in your stupid arrogant millions!'

Blount had a glass of beer in his hand. He was six feet from the seated Funk. He stepped closer, unconscious of Conchita's grip on his arm. He swung the glass, cried, *'Achtung!'* Funk flinched, put up both hands to protect his face. Blount cleverly converted the swing to bring the glass to his mouth. He took a long draught of the beer and grinned at the German.

Conchita's uninhibited giggle echoed around the big crowded room.

Funk was no longer smiling. He looked long and venomously at Conchita. Then he stood up. 'Arrogant! Germans are arrogant! Ha!' Tall, he addressed the silent onlookers over Blount's head. 'This is a joke! The English for their national anthem sing "Britannia rules the Waves" – but it is the Germans who are arrogant!'

'Unlike you, *we win our wars!*' Blount said the words up into Funk's face like four blows of a hammer. He turned away.

'And take your slut with you!' Funk called.

Blount whirled, used the impetus of the turn to project the contents of his glass with tremendous force into Funk's face. Funk staggered back, half-blind and choking. In a rush, Hicks and LeStrange were at Blount's side. He was in a tense, menacing crouch, holding the empty glass like a weapon. Funk mopped his eyes. Three or four young men were grouped around him.

'Leave it, Tim,' Hicks said quietly, taking Blount's arm.

'I'll kill the bastard,' Blount stated.

'Teem – come!' Conchita went and stood in front of him, took the glass and set it on a table. He relaxed, seemed to start breathing again, curled his lip as though to spit at Funk's feet, turned away again.

Hicks would have liked to take Blount out of the public room, but thought it better to try to normalize the atmosphere as soon as possible. So despite Conchita's impatience Blount was persuaded to stay. He needed, as he said, another drink anyway, having wasted that one.

The room relaxed. Hicks asked, 'What was all that about, Tim?'

Blount told him. It sounded petty without the background, all the other sneers and taunts. 'I know!' Blount finished. 'Old enough to know better! But Jeff, that Prussian bastard really gets to me!'

'Me too, Tim. We've just got to live with it.'

'Unfortunately! It'd almost be worth swinging for!'

Carla said: 'Teem, you should be very careful of Rudi Funk. He is dangerous.'

Snakes in the grass. Hicks remembered Cassián's warning. It was a month since Blount and Finch's narrow escapes, and

114

since then they worn loaded Colt automatics at work. 'Take care, Tim,' he said to Blount when the two couples parted a little later.

Blount did take care. But not enough.

He was at that time often working late in the Weapons Lab on the final stages of the new bomb fuse. Conchita used such evenings to indulge her passion for embroidery, secure behind the double-locked door of Blount's suite. Blount enjoyed coming 'home' to this domestic scene, being shown the latest piece – Spanish Blackwork was her special interest – spread and smoothed on her plump thigh after he had kissed her: 'See? You like eet?' – making grumpy noises about bits of thread in everything. He found it hard to believe, and often said so, that this militantly feminine little person had actually been a shipyard welder. 'Why not?' she would reply. It was a good job! She had been content – he could not imagine her otherwise – with the work, the pay was good, and important in a poor family. She had a good time, she always insisted. Then somebody told her about 'tests' for a special job, and she thought again, 'Why not?' She found all the tests very easy. And here she was!

Dead. Someone had tricked her into opening the door, overpowered her quickly it seemed since the place was not much disturbed, and stabbed her to the heart with a gaucho knife, a *facon*. She lay on her back. There was a lot of blood, though the knife was still in the wound.

Blount froze. He held onto the door, keys still in his hand. Conchita was very obviously past help. For a short eternity the activity of his brain was suspended. Only his eyes moved; and the film they made was permanent: the familiar room that had become, with its flowers and Spanish wall-hangings and comfortable untidiness, an expression of the personality of the pathetic figure on the floor. Her favourite chair, still the imprint of her body, bits of thread all around it. Her, there. Her smell – No! That was gone! Instead, the ghastly coppery reek of oxidizing blood.

Quietly he closed the door and went and knelt beside his sweetheart.

The last spasm of her dying agony had left its mark on her face; the eyes were closed, but the expression was that of one who has tasted something sour. Her hands were bloody as though she had tried to pull the knife from her breast before the strength left her. Not far from her head, on the floor, lay her embroidery, a square of linen with a near-complete Blackwork fleur-de-lys, the needle tucked neatly into the material: she had carried it to the door.

Blount picked up a limp hand, not cold, not warm, held it between his, looking down on Conchita's face. He'd been here before: another hand, very thin; another face; another chasm of black loss. He kissed Conchita's cheek, tidied her thick, straight, raven hair, stayed there on his knees beside her for he knew not how long. Long enough for his shock and sorrow to catalyse into hard, white-hot, murderous anger.

He stood up, hesitated, and with some difficulty extracted the big broad-bladed knife from Conchita's chest. He took it into the bathroom, placing it in the washbasin while he retched down the lavatory pan. Then he washed the knife and hit it in the cistern, cleaned away all traces of blood from the bathroom, and went to the telephone.

Funk lived with the other *tenientes* in barracks a short distance from the Rancho. On the night of Conchita's funeral, two days after her death, Funk and four of his friends were making their way to their beds. It was nearly midnight, but the path was lighted from several ground-floor windows. Funk was in the lead when turning a bend in the path he came face to face with Blount standing squarely in his way. He halted abruptly, as if he had come upon a dangerous animal. They stood in silence, regarding each other; the short, balding Britisher, the tall German Argentine and his shadowy cohorts.

Blount stood square in the middle of the path, arms akimbo, fists on hips. The light was good enough for Funk to see the holster on Blount's right hip. Blount said nothing, didn't look as if he had anything to say.

'What do you want?' Funk's voice a mixture of surprise and truculent unease. He and his friends had shared a couple of bottles of wine in the subdued atmosphere of the Rancho bar, at a table by themselves in a corner.

Blount made no reply. He blinked regularly, as it were mechanically. Otherwise he might have been made of stone.

'Well, what do you *want*?' Funk repeated, unease in his tone this time. He might not have spoken, for any effect it had on Blount. Just the occulting wet eyes from which issued nothing but cold, viperish malevolence.

Funk could by now see well enough to be fairly sure that the flap on Blount's holster was in place and fastened. He said, 'Look, I'm coming past. You had better get out of my way!'

Funk made a deliberate move forward to Blount's left, as though to squeeze past, but had hardly began to move when he froze. For although Blount remained stock still, the eyes tightened and Funk sensed danger. But with another careful look to confirm that the holster really was fastened, he over-rode his indefinable unease that there was something wrong, something he had missed. He stepped forward and put his hands on Blount's shoulders, as if to move him out of the way. At that moment, he knew he had made a mistake.

Too late, Funk realised he was handling a hamadryad. And not only that, as a last irony, the difference in their heights had obliged him to lean forward and present his belly unguarded for what, in that last instant, he knew was coming.

So swiftly that all the onlookers saw was a flash of steel, Blount's right arm swung in a short powerful arc that carried every erg of his coiled energy. They heard, from Blount, a short grunt of effort. Funk's explosive gasp carried astonishment and sharp agony and tailed into a long, hoarse, despairing exhalation as he staggered back under the force of the blow, knees buckling. His hands clutched the hilt of the *facon* that had passed up under his breastbone and into his heart. He crashed into the tight group. They scattered, and Funk's body fell to the ground, his head striking the concrete with a heavy thud.

Such is the power of the human mind that in the three seconds it took Funk to die after the point of his own knife severed his aorta and shut off the blood supply to his brain he reviewed, almost lazily, the events that had brought him here. He went over it all and died wondering why? Why had he hated Blount? It was desperately important, suddenly, to know; because now, dying, Funk respected him for his hard cunning and his ability to kill in cold blood, to use a knife. This was not one of his father's English. So why had he . . . why . . . ?

Fighting for survival, Funk's drowning mind synthesised frantically from its racks of memories and in its final instants with the penetration of genius it presented him with the stark irony of his downfall – a fatal trap whose mainspring had been his own arrogance! He heard Blount say, 'And in case you wondered, it *is* his own knife,' but the words neither registered nor needed to. In his heart of hearts, Funk knew. His half-open eyes, for a moment, showed a gloomy, vitreous clarity of understanding. Then they closed. The burning ball in his chest expanded, lost its fierce intensity and glowed warm, suffused and died away, leaving him ice-cold as he slipped from life into death.

Blount looked long upon the prostrate form of Conchita's killer. For there was no doubt in his mind. He turned, finally, and began to walk away. Bushes crackled behind him. He checked momentarily, then walked on, more briskly, out of sight of the stunned group around Funk's body.

When Cassián came, with Hicks, Blount was showered and changed. He sat amid the untidied relics of Conchita: her sewing-bag, scissors, bits and pieces of thread and material lay about him. No greetings were exchanged. Cassián took off his cap, set it on the small dining table, sat himself deliberately on a small upright chair and said to Blount, 'Funk is dead.'

'Yes?' Polite interest. Blount might have been told it had just stopped raining.

'Stabbed.'

'Oh?'

'Just behind the Rancho block. They believe it was his own knife.'

'Uh huh?'

Cassián took out a cigar, prepared and lit it in silence. 'There were witnesses. His friends.'

'Oh yes?'

'They say –' the little Commodore paused, puffed, blew smoke, brushed off his trouser-leg with his free hand, '– they say they cannot identify the killer.'

118

'Oh!' For the first time, there was more than casual interest in Blount's voice. He examined the nails on his right hand carefully.

'They say a man jumped from the bushes, stabbed him and ran off. They did not see him properly. None can give any clue to the murderer's identity.'

'Murderer, you say?' Blount thought about the word. 'Murderer?'

Cassián looked about the room. Hicks became aware of a smell of soap and talcum.

'You have just had a shower, Commander Blount?' Cassián asked.

'Yes.'

'And changed your clothes?'

'Yes.'

'May I see the clothes you have take off?'

'In the bathroom.'

Cassián didn't move. Hicks felt the tension rise as Blount met the Commodore's coal-black eyes. Presently, Cassián said, 'Funk's companions – people I would expect to feel anger and revenge – say they remember nothing, absolutely nothing about the man who killed him. Not if he was tall or short; not if he was wearing white or black. Nothing.'

'Very strange!'

'And of course without witnesses, unless other evidence can be found, the killer may never be discovered.'

'Just so.'

Cassián smoked in silence for a long while. Hicks would have liked a drink. Presently the Commodore got up, thoughtful, brushed down his trousers, went to the door of the bathroom, took the handle and pulled it elaborately shut. He resumed his seat.

'I want you to tell me,' he said to Blount, 'did you kill Funk?'

Blount picked up the limp little square of material that had been lying beside Conchita's body, looked at it critically this way and that. He seemed far away.

Cassián sighed. Taking up Blount's gun, he said, 'You will have no need for this now.' He made a little gesture with his eyes to Hicks which said 'Stay with him'. His hand was on the door-handle when Blount spoke at last:

119

'Commodore.'

'Yes.' Without turning.

'Murder, you said?'

Cassián turned then, his face softer than Hicks remembered seeing it before. Looking down at the seated Blount, he said quietly, 'No. You have to excuse my English. This is not the right word for what you did.'

Hicks shut the door after him. The silent room was acrid with spent tension and acute sorrow.

In the small hours when he got back, Carla was soon awake. He related the night's events. 'Do you think the Commodore is right?' he finished. 'Will it be the end of the trouble with these *indigenistas*?'

'Of course!' dismissively, as if the question were ridiculous. 'But Teem! Oh, poor Teem!'

Chapter 13

'So it works!' Ward summarised, back in Baldwin's office after a busy month. 'Big piston plus Sidewinder equals trouble.' He'd seen it proved in the combat simulator and in the air.

Baldwin had been pacing his office. He sat down. 'What I want to know is how a bunch of dagoes down near Cape Horn – last I heard they were standing round bonfires dressed in skins for God's sake – can come up with something like this –' he gestured at the files on his desk, 'that pulls the rug from under everything we've been doing since World War Two. I am Naval Director Air. I have a large staff of experts, all highly trained and very highly paid –' Ward almost laughed: he, two lieutenant-commanders, a Wren officer and two female civil servants comprised the staff of NDA; the 'team' that Baldwin had appointed to tackle the Corsair project, himself and his number two, had worked six and a half days a week for the past month on it, while other work piled up on their desks; – 'but if these people are right it seems I and my predecessors have been directing Naval Air up the garden path! What do you say to that?' Looks angry, thought Ward. Difficult to tell. And who with, anyway?

'Small, cheap, simple, lo-tech, larger numbers. The austere alternative.'

'Eh?' Baldwin lifted the lip, cocked his ear.

'I'm quoting, sir. Somebody called Kaldor. Too much elaboration, everything too expensive, too fragile, not enough of it. The Baroque Arsenal, it's called.'

'Read it. Agree,' said Baldwin briskly. 'But we're stuck

with what we've got. Right, what do we do, then, about these primitive savages with their bow-and-arrow aeroplanes?'

Ward had his answers ready: 'As I see it, sir, the first problem is credibility. We both know that if the Argentines have any appreciable number of these things then we daren't go within range of them with out ships. But how do you tell the politicians, even some of our own Lordships, that our much-vaunted small-but-professional all-volunteer best-in-the-world armed forces, equipped to the highest standards at huge expense to the taxpayer, is impotent in face of the antique weapons of a third-world country? They wouldn't just laugh, in the House. They'd bray and fall about! And nobody above your level in the Service could afford to acknowledge the problem. Not publicly. It follows we are on our own.'

Ward's tone implied an interval. 'Go on.' His Director had swivelled his chair and now, feet on desk, looked away from Ward, out through the high window at other windows beyond.

'But: neither will our Lordships and High Admirals relish the prospect of a massacre in the South Atlantic at the hands of these primitives if we should get involved. Heads would roll. Therefore, you could expect a degree of unofficial interest, and help. At no cost, of course!'

'Cynicism does not become the serving officer.'

'Ah! But how does the serving officer not become cynical?'

'Touché. Proceed.'

But they were interrupted. MOD coffee and MOD biscuits, two each, were brought in by a tired MOD female with thick legs. The Director exclaimed, 'Gingersnaps – good-oh!' and dunked vigorously. 'Go on.'

'Our second main effort should be on intelligence. Numbers. And range with bombs. On the practical side, sir, I can't do any more. As you see, they've broken the Fury.' A jet pilot had been flying the old Sea Fury for air combat evaluation and had ground-looped it landing in a crosswind. The starboard undercarriage leg collapsed. The propeller was damaged and the engine shock-loaded and the Sea Fury would be grounded for months. Flag Officer (Air) was apoplectic; the Sea Fury was the star of the Navy's Historic

Aircraft display, and now it would probably miss the season.

'Stupid bugger!' Baldwin lit an elaborate cigarette and took to pacing again. 'That's all then, is it? Well I'm disappointed, John. It's been left to me to do the real thinking. No time, you say? You ever hear of Churchill complaining of lack of sleep? Or Napoleon? No. The foundations of empires are laid in the small hours, while small men sleep!' Very Ozymandias, now, except the cigarette. Ward settled back to listen.

'While you have been playing arcade games and amusing yourself in Her Majesty's aeroplanes, I, with the onerous burden of the nation's security on my shoulders, have been sitting here giving deep and knotty thought to the problems posed by this resurrection of Corsairs.' NDA paced the length of his office like a quarterdeck; six moderate steps each way. 'First, to have Corsairs in the numbers we've been led to believe, they must be manufacturing them. But the Corsair itself, however many, is only the face, the manifestation of an underlying strategy. Somebody down there has been clever enough to spot the weakness in modern so-called weapon systems – namely, vulnerability to numbers. Cunning.'

'Or commonsense?'

'Eh?' Baldwin stopped and peered at Ward as at some sort of imbecile.

'Well, it is common sense. And the Argentine military aren't under political pressure to buy things they don't want, like us.'

'Political! Let's stick to the agenda.' Baldwin paced on. 'Now my hypothesis requires he apply this doctrine of simplicity across the board. For example, the mind that produced the Corsair would not consider it necessary to have modern airfield defences, hardened shelters and the like. He will be thinking in World War Two terms – dispersal and camouflage. The photographs bear this out. And this gives us our chance. Consider –' Halting, NDA indicated, with both hands, a corner of the room; 'A hornet's nest. A concentration of any objectionable flying creatures. How best deal with them if you don't want to get stung?' Ward let the rhetorical question hang. 'Catch the bastards on the ground, in their nest, out of their element. Preferable asleep!'

123

'Counter Air!' Ward offered: no harm in reminding his Director he had been to Staff College.

'Exactly!' with a touch of chagrin.

'But – eight thousand miles!'

'Do not,' said Baldwin, with tremendous severity, 'make difficulties.' He sat down. They talked the morning out, with interruptions. After lunch, which Baldwin didn't believe in, he was in the office of Director Plans, looking at the Falklands file. It was, like a pregnant woman, thicker now, though the apt simile did not occur to Baldwin as he studied a paper entitled 'Ascension Island – Harbour and Airfield Facilities'. From here he swirled through passages and lifts to another part of the MOD building, noticing again the nuance of change, different sorts of people doing different sorts of things. He could never suppress a twisted smile as he crossed the invisible frontier between Navy and Air Force: for some inscrutable, distant reason RAF personnel had always been known in the navy as 'crabs', and even Captain Baldwin AFC Royal Navy really wanted to come here one day and find them all walking sideways.

Entering without ceremony through a door marked GSO2 he was greeted: 'Aar! Cap'n Sam! Shiver y'r timbers!' Group Captain Williams was an old friend. Baldwin had telephoned ahead. Twenty minutes later the General Staff Officer got up to open his window. The air was blue with smoke.

Resuming his seat, Williams said, 'No problem, in theory. Given the Ascension base we could get tankers down to forty-five south with enough give-away for Harriers to get in to this Newfield place from six hundred miles. Probably hang about and refuel them on the way out too, if necessary. I would need to check the figures.'

'Just like that?' Baldwin sounded amazed.

'I said in theory, Sam!' Williams held up his hand. 'Don't get carried away. To get two full tankers that distance would take, by rule of thumb –' he finger-spanned the map Baldwin had put on his desk – 'ten Victor tankers, launching from Ascension, passing on fuel in relays down to the last two. Ten tankers. And the Harriers would have to be ours, not yours.'

'Eh?' NDA looked as if he had been stung. He fixed the Royal Air Force's GSO2 with an intimidating glare.

'You want air-to-ground with special weapons. JP233, Durandel, smarts, etc. Correct me if I'm wrong, but your Sea Harriers can't carry these. Ours do, all the time. It's their business.'

'Hm.' Baldwin looked shaken. He recovered. 'But it *could* be done?'

'No question. And with some of the gear we've got we could guarantee the results if we can get ten or a dozen Harriers in there.'

Baldwin nodded. There was something of the relief and gratitude of a doctor's consulting-room about the gesture. He got up to go.

'Classification, Sam?' Williams asked.

'Top Secret, Willie. And I mean it!' said the Director of Naval Air.

Back in his own office, he buzzed Ward. 'John, drop everything and get on to this.' He held up his hand to check the unvoiced protest. 'Forget your in-tray. I'll get somebody else to deal with it. Sit down.' Ward sat, sensing his Director's excitement. 'Pre-emptive strike on this place.' Baldwin spread the map and jabbed down with his finger on the red cross marked 'Newfield'. 'Operation Barbary Coast', he announced with fatherly pride. Ward pulled up his chair. 'Get together with the RAF – Tactics and Weapons Division, I think it is. Aim: destroy these Corsairs on the ground; Method: carrier-borne fixed-wing ground-attack; Execution? The carrier, or carriers, stay at least fifty miles outside our best estimate of the Corsair's radius. It will involve in-flight refuelling.' Ward raised his eyebrows. 'Yes, and furthermore the Harriers will probably have to be RAF GR3's. Get the best target-analysis you can, from the pictures we have. I'll try for some better ones. And when you come to choice of weapons, go for the best now available. There are some new cluster-bombs on the market with baby bombs that recognise shapes: you just tell them what a Corsair looks like, sprinkle hundreds of the little dears out over the airfield, and each one obligingly homes in on a Corsair. Perfect. But I don't know if they're in the shops yet.'

'What about the runway?'

'Don't bother. They're not runway-critical. Go for aircraft,

125

and hangars. Now . . .' Baldwin looked at the wall-chart.
'Feb 2. Report in a week. Sooner if you run into difficulty.'
   'Do the Air Force know about this?'
   'They will, soon.'
   'And the Classification?'
   'Operation Barbary Coast,' pronounced Ozymandias, 'is
Top Secret.'

Friday. Struggling against the ebb-tide of weekending
commuters draining from the building, Baldwin got half an
hour with Pollard in Intelligence, a brief meeting with Laski,
NDS – who was clearing his office after receiving a crash
appointment to sea in command of HMS *Antares* and the 7th
Frigate Flotilla – and finally, before himself making for
Waterloo and Somerset, he bled Bagshaw dry, in his own tiny
office, of everything he had picked up on the Corsair since his
first seminal report.
   One item stood out. Bagshaw had traced and grilled the
author of a report on a visit to the Fábrica Militar de Aviones
(FMA) at Córdoba. He had coaxed from the man a recollec-
tion – a single cranked wing, damaged and awaiting repair,
oddly painted diagonally half black and grey, had lain outside
a workshop. Intrigued by the unusual shape, the visitor had
examined it closely.
   'A Corsair wing, sir,' Bagshaw told Baldwin, 'from what he
said. No doubt about it. And – he's absolutely sure there was
a fuel filler-cap in it. Now I've worked out roughly that
without cannon or wingfold gear inside the stub-wings there's
room for about a hundred gallons of fuel a side. It nearly
doubles internal fuel capacity.'
   'Giving a range of?'
   'Say sixteen hundred miles clean. Twelve hundred with
bombs. Rough figures again, sir.'
   'Why do you say no cannon?'
   'I know they're not dealing with Hispano or Mauser, and
nobody else in the West supplies now.' This was good enough
for Baldwin: Bagshaw knew people in most reaches of the
arms industry.
   Baldwin's face tightened as he considered this new
information. Twelve hundred miles. Hang on some bombs,

126

and the Argentines had an iron umbrella, radius say six hundred miles, centred on the new mainland base. We wouldn't be able to get within a hundred and fifty miles of the Falklands – even if they didn't base Corsairs on the islands, which was highly likely.

'That's my appreciation, then, sir. If they have large numbers of Corsairs, based there . . .' Baldwin put his pen on the map, 'then their only application is the Falklands. If they invade, and if we respond, we will lose any ships that come within range of them. We have no defence against these sort of numbers.'

Flag Officer Air walked to his window. '*If* they invade. *If* we respond,' he mused doubtfully, regarding the wet garden outside. 'But you're right, Sam. Either way, we come out of it badly: we go in under your iron umbrella and get sunk, or we hang about outside looking sheepish, in the face of a resurrection of World War Two technology by a third-world country!' In slacks and sweater, the Admiral came back to look again at the map. 'Could be that's the aim!' The Admiral swung away again to the window. 'The Falklands are no bloody good to them – not a lot of mileage in an unopposed invasion to conquer a few thousand sheep. But a victory over the Royal Navy on the high seas – an Armada – a Trafalgar – priceless! Oh yes!' He swung around. 'Well, Sam, it better not happen. What's the plan?'

This was all highly irregular. NDA had no business coming direct to the Flag with a problem like this. The Admiral understood Baldwin's token hesitation: 'Come on, Sam. You wouldn't be here if you weren't trying to sell something!' Baldwin outlined Operation Barbary Coast.

The Admiral groaned. 'RAF! You know how hard it is to get them to take an interest in anything maritime! This would take a directive from Number Ten!'

Crunching down the official gravel a little later, Baldwin drew deeply on his first cigarette for an hour and a half. An observer would not have guessed that inwardly he was rejoicing, confident that at least one influential person was now alert to the danger in the South Atlantic, a missionary in the corridors of power. FO Air was unique among the Flags in having direct access to the Admiralty Board. That the Admiral's zeal was political – rather than military – bothered Baldwin not at all. The effect would be the same. Things would happen. Locks would ease; doors would open; and funds would seep through cracks in hitherto watertight compartments.

Out on the A30, heading west for home, Baldwin discovered he was singing. He caught himself and grinned, an affair not easily distinguishable among his much-used features. But his wife, with unique skill, discerned the triumph in the stern visage of her returning warrior, and poured sherry to celebrate she knew not what.

Admiral Hext, First Sea Lord, and the other nine permanent members of the Board of Admiralty, heard FO Air's extraordinary disquisition in silence. It was delivered, at his urgent request, at their weekly Tuesday meeting on 9th February. He had used the three days since Baldwin's visit to fashion and hone it. It was, for him, as for Baldwin, a gamble: if nothing came of the thing, he might appear a crank; but he hoped to limit the damage to his career by playing down his own part. If on the other hand the Argentines obliged, and invaded the Falklands, and he were proved right – well, the chance was too good to miss.

Their Lordships, none of them aviators, looked at each other blankly. Whitehall traffic noise came faintly into the room of mahogany and blue leather. The First Sea Lord then asked, rather coolly, 'Can you explain, first, for the board, why it is that a supersonic jet can't match a World War Two fighter in air combat?'

'I'll try,' said FO Air, and he did. The Corsair couldn't catch a jet, but that wasn't the point. If it was engaged by a jet it could fly slower and manoeuvre better and it gave off no exhaust heat for IR missiles to home on. It was virtually impossible to shoot down in a dog-fight. From the ground, guns or active-homing missiles would be needed. On the other hand, the Corsair itself could carry most modern weapons and would be lethal to jets. And he reminded Their Lordships of the numbers believed to be involved. Hundreds.

'Where's the flaw?' The Third Sea Lord, 3SL, broke the silence.

'In what?'

'Oh come on, Ned! A Latin American republic, extinct aircraft, and we can't handle it? There's got to be a flaw in this Corsair thing – what you're saying makes a nonsense of current weapon thinking!'

'That's rather what I thought. But I haven't spotted the flaw yet.'

The Comptroller of the Navy, 5SL, a lawyer by training, spoke: 'There seems to be strong circumstantial evidence here of a radical departure, in Argentina, from established trends in weapon-system development. The brain behind this has seen a weakness and aims to exploit it. Remember the Indian wars? The gun was better than a bow and arrow, but it wasn't until they got repeating rifles that the whites had a clear edge over large numbers of Indians with stone-age weapons. We seem to have thrown away our equivalent of the repeating rifle – and the Injuns are back! The flaw is not in the Corsair!' 5SL, a small bespectacled Chekhovian man, sat back.

Personnel and Manning – 2SL – a sailor largely unencumbered by intellect whose rise to Flag rank had been by intuition and luck, a short man with a broad face and crinkly hair, leaned forward and spoke: 'Injuns is right! This is an ambush if ever there was one! If they *did* go for the Falklands, we should have to pre-empt this lot before we did anything else!'

'That would be a direct act of war – an attack on the Argentine mainland – with very wide implications,' said 5SL, primly.

'If they complained, they'd have to explain the base. From what we've heard of their security, I imagine they'd rather not,' retorted 2SL. 'More to the point – could it be done?' He directed the question to the First Sea Lord, who looked in turn to FO Air.

He told them. Operation Barbary Coast was received coolly. 'RAF!' they protested. He insisted. After some while, in a pause, he said, 'Of course all this is speculation. It may never come about. The Board will make its own assessment of

129

the likelihood of armed conflict over the Falklands and how the Royal Navy would stand in that event. With your permission?' He received leave to go, and passed out of the Old Admiralty Building into Whitehall feeling that, without over-selling, he had awakened just the right amount of anxiety: he was reasonably sure that at least two of Their Lordships would, for entirely different reasons, keep the issue alive and moving, and that would be enough to open doors.

Chapter 14

Hicks said to Carla, 'So now you have *Las Malvinas!* A big day for Argentina, eh?' His overriding emotion on hearing the news of the invasion was relief. Goa had become Rosario. At last the dice were on the table and everybody could see the numbers.

It had been a day of suppressed rejoicing. Unusually, Cassián had been on the base all weekend, and had instructed that Monday's training should not be interrupted. That evening Hicks poured a celebratory drink for himself and Carla in his suite.

She took the glass and shook her head in the horse-like way that he had noticed served two purposes: it extracted the tendrils of dark hair that persistently strayed inside her collar, against her neck, and it was a warning signal.

'*Si.* For my country, this is historic day!'

They stood apart, both in uniform, her face tired, dirty with the marks of oxygen mask. Her trousers were creased and she smelled of aeroplane. Hicks had time to respond, as ever, to her vibrant femininity before replying, 'Then let us drink a toast. To Argentina!' He raised his glass.

Carla searched his face, a little wary, then replied, 'To Argentina!'

'Is it allowed to kiss a member of the conquering nation?' Hicks asked quietly with a smile. There was a minefield here.

Again the long stern scrutiny. Then the corner of the small mouth moved, a little smile. The eyelids dropped, the head lifted and the thin shoulders went back to draw the shirt tight across her breasts.

They kissed. And when he had tenderly undressed her, they loved each other to exhaustion.

For Hicks was indeed sincere. Distrust – of the Junta as employers – and disgust at the casual murders of Munro and Conchita, had given way recently to a fondness for Argentina and its awkward people. Post-Funk, as *indigenismo* melted away and the British were accepted as friends and allies, it became possible to appreciate the personal qualities of the now unguarded young: their patriotism, sincere to the point of spirituality, and the more touching for being open-eyed to the failings of their government; their naivete and their fervour. They lived in a mould they had not cast: not their fault Catholic Spain never had a Magna Carta! Yet in that mould, he judged, they lived their lives more honestly, less greedily than their counterparts at home. They *were* awkward though! He grinned to himself, pulled aside a handful of springy black hair, kissed Carla's forehead. She was asleep, head on his shoulder. Irritating before, the Argentines' love of melodrama, tragedy, life on the bass clef – and a minor key at that! – now seemed endearing. Their tango, two people trying to pull each other apart! All charming, like children! Like children too, they expected the Malvinas would make them happy ever after. He wished it could be so, sincerely.

'Eeks?' His kiss had awakened her.

'Mm?' He could still smell aeroplane on her hair.

'You think the British will come?' Her voice was very small.

'Yes.' He was convinced of it.

She seemed to fall asleep again, breath warm on his flesh. But then, after a minute or so: 'And you go out with us?' They were in the minefield.

'Yes. If I am asked.'

She pushed suddenly away, propped herself up on two straight, thin arms and looked down at him. The bed bounced with the movement. 'But why, Eeks? I do not understand how you can fight against your own country! I know you explain before, but – please – why you do this?'

Long. Lean. Languid. Leonine. Lovely. Carla's total frontality, so close, distracted Hicks. She pulled the sheet around her, turned and sat with arms around her drawn-up knees. 'I would *never* fight against Argentina! Nobody here would do this!'

Of course they'd talked about it before. Now she wanted an answer. But how to explain? There was no language between a Latin-American republic and an Anglo-Saxon democracy to express the difference, why the one always flies to defend its nationality simply because it is so sickly and fragile, while the other needs all the time to rebel because rebellion is the irritant that keeps democracy awake.

He hadn't always been so clear about this. Not until a few days post-Funk. Pre-Funk, attitudes among the British had been confused. But relieved of threat, respected and accepted, the fresh benignity of the atmosphere stimulated soul-searching. The prospect of action against British ships was not a difficulty. Well-paid professionals like themselves, their crews should not have imagined, as Channing put it, that the RN was an ornament of state. You don't chose to be a professional boxer and hope never to go in the ring. But as the Grupo trained and trained to new peaks of efficiency in the deadly business of bombing it became increasingly plain that no group of ships the Royal Navy could assemble and send to the South Atlantic, however large and well-equipped, stood any chance if it came within range of Cassián's Grupo. They would be smashed and sunk in deep lonely waters beyond hope of help.

They recognised that the massive overkill potential of the Grupo had a certain consonance with the savagery of South American politics, but it stuck in the British throat.

Hicks had expressed their doubts to Cassián. The Commodore had of course expected misgivings about attacking British ships, but could not understand why, having accepted the principle, Hicks and the others should question the degree of force to be used.

'I have the aircraft,' he protested, 'I have the numbers – why not use them? You think one hundred too much? How many then? Fifty? Or forty? Twenty-five? How do I measure the force to be used? What is your criterion? Should I risk to lose more Corsairs because ships have time to reload?'

Hicks tried an argument his friend Frank Sargent would have recognised: the prestige value of a victory over the

Royal Navy would be reduced when it became known it had been achieved by overwhelming numbers.

Cassián had rounded on him: 'This is not so, Eeks! You don't understand South America yet. Here, we don't play cricket. We go for victory! To win! How, is no matter, but most important is to win well!' and he slammed a podgy fist into his palm.

For the first time since they met, Hicks had felt a gulf between himself and the little Argentine. He understood his argument and its origins in the culture of the country he had come to respect and like. But he understood now that for all the same reasons Cassián would never see the British view.

Cassián though, acute as ever, could at least sense the gulf. He had looked searchingly at Hicks. 'Is there a difficulty?'

'Maybe,' Hicks answered. He explained their reservations and finished by saying, 'What you are planning would probably go down in the history books as infamous.' The Commodore looked puzzled. Hicks consulted his dictionary.

'*Infame?* Infamous. Not because you ambushed the Royal Navy and inflicted a defeat, but because excessive force was used, causing unnecessary casualties.'

Cassián went and sat down, spun his chair, looked out across the base. Hicks felt he was making an effort to understand: an intellectually hungry man, he would have seized upon this new disharmony between them and be looking for its roots. After a while, without turning round, he said to Hicks: 'You know what I am trying to do, Eeks? I don't think you do. I tell you. It is to put Argentina on the map. This will not be done by small things. This must be *beeg*, Eeks!' He swung his chair round and emphasised the word with a thump on his desk. 'And it will not be *infame* in our history books!' he added.

Hicks knew it was hopeless. He tried his last card. 'Is South America really so backward? You want to put Argentina on the world map? You will certainly do that! Everybody will know that the Black Legend lives on, south of the Rio Plata!'

Cassián didn't like this. The eyebrows came down. He shot out his disorderly lips and glowered at Hicks. 'It is no matter what you think! It is no matter what I think! I serve my country, and this is what my government wants.' But as a

134

sweet-running engine suddenly falters, so at this point did Cassián. Hicks saw the question in his face. The eyes dropped, a passing frown. Then he picked up. 'You too serve Argentina by your contract. Now, I must know if there is a difficulty.'

Hicks considered awhile, then he said, 'I cannot speak for the others.'

The Commodore stood up abruptly. 'Very well. We will meet, and discuss. Today. As soon as possible.' He looked at his watch, coming around the desk and reaching for his cap. 'You will arrange, please?' He stopped with his hand on the door, turned. Hicks had risen. 'You cannot speak for the others. But what about Commander Eeks? Does he have a difficulty?'

'Yes,' Hicks replied flatly. 'It remains to see if it can be overcome.'

That was mid-morning. Finch was airborne on a trial of the latest batch of fuses for the laydown bombs, which were giving good results at last, and Tracey was up in one of the Skyhawks with a four-ship of Corsairs on air combat drill, so it was early afternoon before Hicks could get them all together. They met in the conference room. The long table as familiar by now as a school desk, but the mood was uneasy.

The Commodore bustled in. They stood. He started speaking as he threw his cap on the table. 'Sit down, gentlemen. I will do you the courtesy to speak plainly. You come to Argentina with a contract whose terms are very clear. You accept these terms and to now you have more than satisfied them, as I expected of British officers. I am aware that for GEA's proficiency in operations – which I will admit is above anything I had hoped – I have to thank your skill and commitment.'

The next word hung like expected rain. They waited: Tracey laid-back in his chair, as usual, nearly horizontal; LeStrange avuncularly attentive; Finch impatient, upright, probably foot-tapping; Blount stolid, detached; Channing ruminative. Hicks felt a sudden wave of unsentimental affection for his diverse band of exiles: fair play was all they wanted, but in this place, in this room, the idea was as foreign as a union jack.

'But now, it seems,' Cassián continued, 'you have done your work too well! And you have worry about the British Navy. Let me tell you what I think Commander Eeks says. You think that to work with GEA, to attack, to fight, to defeat, the British Navy is honourable and acceptable. This must be so. You know I get your names from officers of the British Navy who believe it needs a lesson. You know why. You agree. So. This is no problem. Your difficulty is that GEA is now too good and the defeat will be too big. Yes?' The Commodore spoke as one delivering a simple truth. He really does not understand, thought Hicks.

'No, Contraalmirante.' Finch's tone was flat and brusque. 'It's nothing to do with the size of the defeat. It's what happens *after* the defeat. I don't want to be involved in chopping a lot of defenceless sailors up into small pieces, and their nationality is nothing to do with it.'

'I think we all agree on that,' Hicks put in. 'It makes no difference who the sailors are.'

'Precisely!' LeStrange boomed. 'Rules of war and all that! Got to give people a decent chance! You don't kick a man when he's down!' Blazer and cravat, Hicks realised just then, was how he always thought of LeStrange.

'Yes,' said Blount. 'What's the point of pounding people to pulp when you've already won the battle. That's what's wrong!' He put his fist on the table for emphasis. 'Overkill! And what about the Geneva Convention?'

'I think,' said Channing reasonably, 'the problem is one of definition?' Hicks had heard this before. 'A victory, to us, is a battle won. Two forces meet and fight. When one is no longer in a position to achieve its aim – at that moment – it is defeated. It surrenders or retreats. The other is the victor, and he has no need or moral right to destroy the defeated.'

'Ah, so the Russians had no need or right to pursue and destroy the Germans, after the defeat of Moscow?' Cassián made it sound ridiculous.

'With respect, sir, a very different case,' Channing answered easily. 'That was one battle in a global war. Yours will be in the context of a limited war with the strictly limited aim of taking and holding the Falklands and giving the British a bloody nose. If our business is to deal with a relieving task

136

force, our aim, and your victory, is achieved at the moment the Task Force Commander abandons his mission and retreats north.'

'If we do not sink the ships, he comes again!'

'So? Then you have two victories!'

Cassián grinned. 'You English, you talk too technical. You make this sound cold, surgical. For us, victory is not like this, like something to be measured. It is here –' he thumped his chest, 'that we understand and feel these things. Feel! Not in the brain like something technical!'

Channing had him now. Hicks watched the Commodore's face carefully. 'Then you confirm my point, Contraalmirante. The problem is one of definition,' Channing went on. 'If the interpretation of victory in Argentina is emotive rather than rational and requires the use of force beyond victory, then such action goes beyond our obligations under the contract – as *we* read it.'

Cassián had listened intently, deep brown eyes fixed upon Channing. When Channing finished, he looked from one to the other of the British, coming last to Tracey whose eyes were closed. He nodded slowly, a gesture of reluctant, and probably only partial, understanding. 'So?' he asked.

'Zap 'em!' said Tracey, opening his eyes. 'Put 'em out of action. Then leave 'em alone.'

Cassián's eyebrows went up. He looked enquiringly to Hicks.

'That sums it up,' Hicks interpreted. 'We're contracted for military operations. Extra action, 'beyond victory', as Miles puts it, doesn't in our language fit into the category of military operations.'

Cassián's brooding eyes roved the room. It seemed to Hicks he was seeing beyond the walls, seeing the base, Roca, his Corsairs, his creation; seeing Buenos Aires, his bosses.

He came to a decision. 'This *is* South America!' he exclaimed. 'Latin America! This is *not* a place of technical definitions! The policy of this Grupo remains as I stated. I regret you cannot support it – but you are honourable men and I respect your reasons even if I do not understand them. So,' he paused, 'I will release you from obligation to take part in the attack on British forces. I will expect you continue your

137

work as before and do nothing to interfere with the operation which is now, as you say, none of your business. Is this agreed?'

Much relieved and not a little surprised, Hicks had thanked the Commodore. 'There will be no interference,' he added. 'We are technical advisors.'

'Thank you,' said Cassián. 'And the others?' He looked around the table.

'Agree,' snapped Finch.

'Agree,' nodded Blount.

'Suppose we'd been civil engineers,' said Tracey, sitting up, head on one side, thinking hard, 'and we'd helped you build a skyscraper. Then you round up all the political opposition, tie their hands behind their backs and push them off the top. Nobody could blame us, could they? Saw it happen in Africa. I mean, we just helped *build* the Grupo, didn't we? What you do with it's up to you!' Tracey delivered this, for him, astonishingly long judgement directly to Cassián, on whose left he was sitting. Then he glanced quickly around at the others. 'That's what I think, anyway,' he finished, and lay back, adding as an afterthought, 'and nobody gives a shit about the Falklands, Malvinas.'

LeStrange after a deep throat-clearing 'H-hmmm' spoke, very public-school: 'Well. I can't say I like it, but I'm dashed if I can deny the logic of that!'

'So you agree?' Cassián pressed him.

'I have to agree,' said LeStrange heavily.

'And Commander Channing?'

'Yes. I agree.'

The Commodore sighed and shook his head. 'You Anglo-Saxons are a puzzle. But I do not complain –' he held up his hands. 'The qualities that bring you here to do such good work are the same that make this difficulty. I know too these qualities will make sure you continue your contract. Good! Thank you, gentlemen.' He stood up. They did likewise. 'There is no need,' he said, 'that anybody else knows about this new arrangement.'

The ground had felt more solid as Hicks left the meeting. They had come to this only after agonies of self-inquisition.

Many long discussions, particularly with Channing, on the morality of war and of their position as mercenaries lay behind it, rationalizing their own inclinations around war as a profession, surrounding themselves with concentric ramparts of moral arguments: war was a business like any other and more decent than some; all modern fighting men were mercenaries and the mercenary ethic had become institutionalised into all professions without exception; patriotism is a tool of politicians who live by consuming little bits of other people's lives, else why pay private soldiers more than nurses and teachers? And the British at Roca differed from other soldiers only in wanting to stand on their own feet; what they were doing in Argentina constituted no threat to their own country, for which they had long stood uniformed and ready to die and would again if need be; it was in fact no more a violation of the terms of their citizenship, even if they did drop bombs on British ships, than was the selling and financing of arms to potential enemies that provided so much private and public profit in Britain. This moral laundering had been an ongoing process for all of them, essential to health.

Even to Tracey. 'Never mind all that guff!' he had once said. 'I'll do whatever they want, so long as it doesn't feel wrong. If it feels wrong, they can stuff it! Simple as that!'

Only LeStrange hung back, so cluttered about with miscellaneous attitudes that he could not avoid the role of bastion, patriot. He exercised his powerful voice in singing 'Land of Hope and Glory' loud and often. None of the Argentines knew the significance of this except Cassián, who also knew enough about the English to recognise a crank. But even LeStrange could not escape the fact that had most influenced everybody else, that they were in Argentina by design of somebody with the Navy's and the country's interests at heart and with whom they saw eye to eye. Nevertheless, Hicks had never been sure of LeStrange: that he might not, one day, peel off from a 'Saturday War' and make for the Port Stanley airstrip – or simply make the three-hour trip direct from Roca in a stolen Corsair. Such a flamboyant gesture would have suited him perfectly and undone all of Cassián's elaborate security. But besides there being in the contract a clause causing it to be cancelled and annulled, for all of them, in the event of a defection, Hicks had felt, after this final talk-out, that LeStrange had probably crossed his Rubicon and would see the thing through.

This had been a month ago, a month before this morning's invasion. Now he lay with this woman beside him, rangy and militant, wanting it all explained. Baulking at the task, he decided on a little militancy of his own.

'Is anything all right then, Carla, if you do it for Argentina?' He spoke to her long, curved back.

'Of course! The country is the most important thing!'

'Do you like your government? The Junta?'

'No so much. I don't like the men. But they are the government.'

'Do you like what they do?'

'What do you mean?'

'*Los desaparecidos?*'

There was a very long silence.

'Eeks . . . this is a bad question. Nobody likes to talk about *los desaparecidos*. Why you ask me this?' The hard edge to Carla's voice contrasted with the soft roundness of her shoulder.

'Because sometimes, people have to stand against governments,' he said, carefully.

'Is that what you do?'

'Yes.' It was the truth – even if it had been uneasily subsumed by other things. Like Carla.

Carla said nothing for a while. Her body began to rock, to and fro, to and fro. Hicks could only watch, puzzled. Finally she fell back and lay prone and naked beside him, arms limp, staring at the ceiling. She spoke, slowly and deliberately, her voice small with emotion: 'Three years ago, in Córdoba, they take my brother, Horatio. He is seventeen. In the night they come, the soldiers. Six soldiers for one boy. They break the door. They hit my father when he speak to them. Then they take Horatio. He look so young, so small. He had no clothes. He was frightened. My mother screams. My father is on the floor, bleeding. We watch him go, to the van. When he look back, they hit him.'

Hicks lay very still. Watching her profile; her eye searching

140

the ceiling; her mouth, a little open, the jaw slack; her cheek, still a small smudge of black.

'He came back. He was lucky. After five months, he came back. But not the same boy. He did not laugh any more – never. And he could not – how you say, *oír*?'

'To hear. He was deaf?'

'Daff. *Si*. He could not to hear.'

'Oh, Carla!' Hicks put his hand over hers, limp on the bed. 'I am sorry.'

'Ha! We were lucky – he came back. Not like the others.'

'Why was he taken?'

'He made a letter, in the school paper, to complain that poor children must pay for their lessons.'

Hicks was at a loss. Even and perhaps especially, at this moment, to criticize anything Argentine would be dangerous.

'This would not happen in England?' Carla asked, though more a statement than a question.

'No.'

'Well, Eeks, this is Argentina. These things the government do. We do not like it, but we must have *some* government. I help the government so one day Argentina is rich, and powerful, a good place to live and have my bebbies, and the government not has to do these things.'

She turned her long nakedness towards him and lay for a while examining his face. Then she reached out, and he gathered her into his arms. With his face in her wiry black hair, he asked, 'Where is Horatio, now?'

'He mends shoes,' came the muffled reply, in his ear.

The tango! The endless, stamping, tearing tango these people live! A thought struck Hicks – was he a refuge? A sanctuary? Carla a refugee, from the tango? It was a disturbing idea. He was more than willing to allow it to be submerged by a rising tide of carnal contentment as he folded Carla tighter to him.

Chapter 15

Blount died that week. For him, life ended in the small hours of Sunday, 4th April, in position 48°57'S 59°56'W.

He need not have died. But it was a long time since he had flown a Saturday War, and he had felt an obligation. Cassián had intimated this might be the last, now that the prospect of real action was so close.

'It scares me fartless,' Blount had admitted before, to Hicks, 'Seven hours over the water on one engine. No SAR. But not going is worse!'

Hicks knew exactly how he felt. Each Saturday attack, two waves of a hundred aircraft each, meant nearly one thousand five hundred flying hours over water. The risk in these long-range missions was statistical: major propulsion failures per thousand hours, minor propulsion failures, major other failures, minor other – the figures were public knowledge at Roca and boiled down to a one and half percent chance of ending up in the water for every pilot setting out. There were twenty-three graves or memorials in the cemetery. A palpable tension began, for those listed, on Friday evening, built up from the dawn breakfast, through the briefing and the long outward flight. It drained slowly from the cramped, comfortless cockpits on the return leg. It was said you could recognise those who had flown – by the 'thousand-mile stare'.

But not to go was to feel exclusion, deprivation, eventually frustration: one hundred Corsairs to five hundred miles was after all the peak and summit of their joint endeavour. To be of the company, you went.

So Blount had himself programmed in as #4 of a division of

bombers led by a Teniente Sevilla and set off into the low morning sun on 3rd April, Saturday morning. A spanking tailwind got them to the target area – with the help of a Kondor Boeing – in just under three hours. The weather was bright and clear. Monegario was Air Group Commander and leading the first wing. Taking his turn as Second Wing Leader was Capitán Soto, OC4. Sevilla's four dive-bombers formed Págalo 8 Division in this second wave

As soon as Soto brought them in sight of the tiny *Sylvestre*, twenty-five minutes after passing the homeward-bound first wave, his division leaders formed Carousel, moving with chorus-like precision into their high and low wait circles, three miles out, each on his briefed line of bearing. Soto slowly and deliberately read out the attack sequence.

Then: 'Cormorán 12, Commence!' And the due-north division of laydown bombers steadied up in deep echelon for their wave-top run-in. Automatically thirty seconds later, Comorán 5 on a bearing of 150° – 5 o'clock from the target – rolled out on attack heading, followed by Cormorán 9, due west at 9 o'clock, and so on in the ordered sequence.

After six laydown divisions, the attack switched to dive-bombing. Again automatically, Págalo 12 took his division down from 18,000 feet, followed by four more divisions of Págalos. The pattern looked random. It was calculated to confuse fleet air defences.

Sevilla lowered his undercarriage. Blount did likewise. Sevilla tightened the left turn, manoeuvring for the roll-in. Blount on the outside of the loose four, increased power to hold station, put his windscreen de-fog 'On', set his propeller to 2,700 rpm, rudder trim ten degrees left, Armament Master 'On', 'Bombs' on the rotary selector. The bomb pickle-switch, on top of the stick grip, was protected by a spring flap. Blount made a final inspection of his engine gauges. So far, so good. His mouth was dry.

Sevilla's Corsair reared up, stark, close and dirty against the deep-blue western sky, rolled over left and plunged out of sight. Pause, two, three – #2 up, over and down. Pause, two, three – #3. Pause, two, three – Blount pulled up, rolled inverted, adjusted his throttle carefully to 15″ on the Manifold Pressure gauge as *Sylvestre* came into view three miles below,

143

through the top of his canopy, trailing a ragged line of white bomb-circles. He allowed the Corsair's nose to drop, rolling to bring the tiny ship into the sight graticule. The dive, only sixty degrees, always felt vertical.

There was less drift than he had allowed for. The target, just discernible now from ten thousand feet, was not moving up the sight-glass as expected. Blount adjusted nose-down and right, resettled in the dive.

The Corsair's speed stabilised at 360 knots – five knots below the red line. Tension was in the airframe; tension was in the bomb and tank fittings, nearing structural limits; tension was in the high roaring slipstream over the canopy, in the near-solid flying controls, in the bar-taut muscles of Blount's small frame. And most dangerously, tension was in the propeller whose natural inclination to rotate ever faster was restrained by a hydraulic ram in its hub, the Pitch Control Unit.

Blount's eyes were momentarily on his altimeter at seven thousand feet when there came a bang and a wailing scream from his engine. It took only milliseconds to switch to the RPM gauge and register its message. Fear crawled over him and adrenalin spurted through his body. His reactions were almost immediate.

He jerked throttle and propeller levers fully aft. He pulled. As many g's as he knew how without breaking the aircraft or blacking himself out. He half-said, half-thought, half-grunted through clenched teeth, 'Oh Jesus!'

RPM had been 3,300 and rising. PCU failure. As the 'g' hit him Blount greyed-out. He couldn't see the gauge. But he could hear. The note went on rising, no longer recognisably mechanical but the scream of a tortured metal organism twisted way up and beyond its design limits. Blount kept pulling. It was all he could do. Reduce speed. Virtually blind, his nose twitched for smoke, fire. None, yet.

The 'g' eased. Blood returned to Blount's head, oxygen to his retinae, daylight flooded his brain, disorientating. He could see nothing but sky. He shook his head, found the horizon. The Corsair was fifty degrees nose-up, airspeed dropping rapidly. RPM? . . . RPM? – down. Mercifully, about 1,800 and falling. Blount eased over into a right side-

144

slip, regained control and levelled off. Gingerly, he advanced the throttle so that with about 30″Hg he was flying at 155 knots with an RPM of 2,450. It should have been about 1,500. As he examined the other engine instruments for signs of damage he instinctively turned to put the sun behind him, heading for the distant coast of Patagonia.

Oil temperature – low, normal post-dive. Cylinder head – only a little higher than Blount would have expected. Only the oil pressure told the engine's internal injuries: from a steady 70psi on the outward flight the needle hovered now erratically around the '30' mark. He tried the propeller control lever. It felt amputated.

But there was no fire. Blount was shaking. Taking a grip, wriggling upright in his straps, he looked around.

'Págalo 3–4,' he transmitted. 'Broken off. PCU failure in the dive. Overspeed. I'm heading west at six thousand feet with low oil pressure.' Blount didn't bother to mention the vibration he now felt. He had just noticed it. As he spoke, another Págalo division hurtled down in front of him, half a mile away, possible P-9 on the west side of the Carousel. It had all happened that quickly! Bombs! He looked quickly at his wings. The left bomb had gone, torn off. He pulled the jettison handle and the other one fell away. He had also forgotten the undercarriage. It retracted normally and locked up.

Lame-duck drill. Wing Leader acknowledged his call, Págalo 3–3 formed up on him as escort, and they left the ring together, heading west.

But Blount knew his position was hopeless. It was unreasonable to expect the sick engine to last for the long return flight against the wind; and even if it did, at 2,450 rpm it was grossly inefficient. The fuel wouldn't last. He looked down at the sea. Hardly moving. He remembered, on the way out, not looking forward to the grind back against this headwind. He felt tired. Cold. He had stopped trying to decide if the vibration was getting worse.

After half an hour or so, Soto enquired: 'Págalo 3–4. How is the engine?' Blount told him. 'P3–4, roger,' replied Soto. 'You may divert to *Las Malvinas*. It is my authority.'

Blount smiled to himself. A wan smile. Port Stanley airstrip was less than 150 miles south. An hour. Just possible. Roca, 400 miles ahead, might as well be on the moon. *Sylvestre* already fifty or sixty miles astern. But he didn't have to think.

'Negative,' he replied, and flew on.

He ditched forty minutes later, reporting first that his oil pressure was down to 20 and he wanted to land before the engine quit. He feared the deep water, but the fear of fire was greater. Canopy gone, flaps full down, wheels up, engine at a low tick-over, Blount put the Corsair onto the water crosswind, along the swell. The cockpit instantly filled with ice-cold water. It came in with great force, foaming, and fiercely salty. The aircraft settled nose-down, tail high. Blount, uninjured, threw off his safety harness, stood up, hauled out the seat-pack dinghy, jumped into the sea and struck away from the sinking Corsair. He needn't have hurried, for it floated well. From twenty yards he watched, mesmerized, as it gradually tipped towards the vertical and slid unceremoniously under the surface, to begin its long glide down into the lightless depths of the ocean. The cold gripped his body like a vice.

Guardiamarina Tomba, Págalo 3–3, escorting Blount, saw him inflate his dinghy and climb aboard, apparently well, his locator beacon bleeping on distress channel. Fixes were taken. *Sylvestre* abandoned her target and set course westward at best speed, hoping to reach Blount's position before dark. Unable to linger, Tomba made a low pass, rocking his wings in a cheering gesture, and climbed away. Blount heard his engine sobbing westward into silence.

Unaccountably, *Sylvestre* was unable to pick up Blount's locator beacon. She reached the datum position an hour or so before sunset and began a standard search pattern. The search continued through the night. Hicks, Finch, Tracey and Channing took off three hours before dawn with twenty other volunteers, were homed by *Sylvestre* to arrive overhead search datum as the sun cracked the eastern horizon. They found him, a good way north of where he should have been according to calculations of wind and current. *Sylvestre*, homed by the circling aircraft, picked up the cold body and brought it back.

Hicks and Cassián went to see it together, in the base

146

hospital. It was unmarked, just very pale, the face bland. Hicks couldn't avoid the thought – death suited Tim. His life had been a series of painful miscarriages, and there was that about him that proclaimed a familiarity with the notion of death. Now here he was, bills paid and clean gone.

'He paid his bills,' Hicks said to Cassián.

The Commodore glanced up enquiringly.

'The Malvinas option.' They had already discussed Blount's last decision. Everybody had. He might have made it to the Stanley strip. It was accepted that he had wished to avoid compromising the security of the Grupo.

'Ah, yes. Yes. His account is clear. You are right.' The Commodore nodded.

Blount was buried on Monday evening. Unbidden, every pilot in the Grupo who was not sick or on essential duty – and some who were – walked behind the jeep-drawn coffin, braving a gale of wind and dust out along the track to the cliff-top cemetery.

Half a thousand stood bareheaded as Blount's body was lowered into the dry earth. Cuevas had drawn a score of mourners, Funk none.

Hicks, standing close, could barely hear the trite words of the burial service, whipped away by the hooligan wind; but he was aware around him of a construct of feeling the like of which he had never known. Sorrow was there, grief, loss, affection, yet buttressed with a sense of gain, and towered with pride – a veritable cathedral of emotion. If history were still being written, he thought illogically, then Blount would surely by his death if not his life accrue to that of Argentina – notwithstanding the unmanageable diphthong. But there was no history in this desolate place. No future either. Hicks looked from the white-capped ocean on his right to the barren scrubby semi-desert stretching away inland, as they walked back. It smelled of desolation. Tim would stay here for ever, after they had all gone and the salty, dusty wind-torn wilderness reclaimed the place until the next ice-age. The thought suddenly turned his stomach with – sadness? Fear? Hicks overcame an urge to turn back, to go to the grave again with comforts. Instead, he was determining how he was going to

147

make, with his own hands, a permanent memorial stone, one that would last those ten thousand years, when he found Soto at his elbow.

'Commander Eeks, Permit me to say, this Plont is a very good man.'

'Yes, Herado. He was.'

The tall Argentine, surprised at the use of his Christian name, smiled. 'I am – how you say, *urgulloso?* – to know him.' Proud. He gestured around him at the walking crowd. 'So too, everybody! Will you shake my hand and thank you for his life?'

They joined the airfield perimeter track for part of the way back to the living site. Across the airfield, a mile away north-west, they could see the control tower, the five hangars and in front of these the aircraft, maybe a hundred and fifty, on the concrete. Serviceable aircraft were always parked out. Hicks examined the sky, trying to penetrate the dust-haze, trying to visualise Roca with a satellite's eye, or a high-flying TR-1. The Corsairs, viewed from where he stood, presented a solid mass.

Walking beside him, Channing too must have had his mind on the Falklands invasion. He pointed covertly at the parked Corsairs and said quietly, 'Do you suppose they've heard of cluster-bombs?'

In Whitehall, Commander Ward, Deputy NDA, pored over a table-sized plan of 'Newfield' not at all interested in the tiny, one-millimetre blurred square that was Roca's cemetery on the glossy TR-1 photoplates littering his office. These had been analysed and used to construct a blow-up of Roca's main operating area – the Control Tower, the five hangars in their shallow arc, the concrete pan. The model hangars were the size of books. The six-hundred metre parking apron with its untidy rows of Corsars – the same that Hicks was looking at just then with the eye of a professional destroyer, and from which was coming to him on the wind the attenuated roar of a full-power run – this area was scale-modelled in detail on Ward's table, gridded with GeoRef lines and complete with one-inch cardboard Corsairs. Oil-stains on the concrete

148

showed that Argentine engineers, like anywhere else in the world, walked no further than they had to; the outer concrete was quite clean.

It was nearly eleven o'clock in London. The Advance Task Force had sailed that day with two carriers, *Hermes* and *Invincible*, a declaration of Britain's intention to recover the Falklands. Operation Corporate was under way. But another carrier of the same class, HMS *Eagle*, lay at Gibraltar awaiting orders that were too secret to be entrusted to radio. Ward's office smelled of stale smoke, three days of Baldwin's cigarettes. Red-eyed, unshaven, unwashed people came and went. Phones rang. They had had to wait, first for the photographs, then for the analysis, before they could start the precision planning for Roca's destruction.

In another room marked 'Target Planning', deep underground in the RAF's Strike Command HQ at Bentley Priory, electronic equivalents of Ward's perspex sheets and cardboard models had confirmed the choice of BL755 cluster-bombs for the parked-out Corsairs, and offered a close option, for Roca's hangars, between two French weapons: Thomson-Brandt BAP 100mm Tactical Support Bomb – an outfit of twelve 34kg fragmentation bombs; and the SNEB 47mm Unguided Rocket Projectile in pods of twenty-four with choice of HE or incendiary heads.

In the end, availability dictated the choice. 'BL755' and 'SNEB 47mm mix HE/Incend' were inserted into blank spaces in orders that had been written for days. After the briefest of discussions between Admiralty and Air Ministry – so well had the political undergrowth been cleared – Commander Ward, Lieutenant-Commander Bagshaw and a Wing Commander Tillman lifted off the Horse-Guards Parade shortly after midnight in an Army Puma. They flew west to the Naval air base at Yeovilton where they transferred to a Naval Canberra – a utility model used for target-towing whose pilot had one engine running as they got in and was taxying while they fumbled with their straps. There were only three ejection seats. Ward and Tillman were asleep in theirs soon after take-off. Bagshaw crouched uncomfortably but uncomplaining in the nose, clutching a locked black leather case marked EIIR.

At Gibraltar at 0410GMT, still just dark, a Navy Sea King, rotors running, awaited them. It went east around the Rock, then turned west, flying very low and showing no lights. Bagshaw talked, to everybody, enjoying himself, excited. They caught up with *Eagle*, after an hour and a half, lifted, slowed, hovered in a crescendo of noise and vibration and landed on. As the rotors ran down they got out, to a heavy tremble of steel plate underfoot, and a warm salty gale down the flight deck. The sky was light behind the ship, the sun overhanging her wake.

She had sailed from Gibraltar, on a scheduled departure for a short Mediterranean deployment, the previous afternoon, turning left around the Rock and heading away east. Forty miles into the Mediterranean she had stopped, exercising her boats until sunset. At midnight, fully darkened, she had passed westward through the Straits at twenty-five knots. *Eagle* was now steering a course of 260°, to clear Madeira before turning south for her destination, Ascension.

The three new arrivals were taken straight to the bridge to meet the captain who accompanied them to the operations room on the deck below. There the Executive Officer, Commander (Air), and the Operations Officer were waiting. Bagshaw unlocked his despatch case and handed over the orders for Operation Barbary Coast.

An hour or so later Ward, Tillman and Bagshaw were eating bacon and egg off a rattling table in the Bridge Mess when reveille sounded. Bagshaw was still talking, tireless. Ward felt that first bugle call of Tuesday, 6th April was likely to be a marker in his life.

The RAF Harrier pilots, or those who thought about it, could have said the same of the phone calls that had summoned them that night to their squadrons in Germany and Eastern England. Twenty of the most experienced had been selected – including all those pilots who had flown from carriers on exchange tours with the Navy. They left warm beds that they would not see again for weeks, some never. They were isolated, and after heavy security warnings, briefed on Barbary Coast and given two days to prepare the mission. Various squadrons were milked of sixteen harrier GR3's and

150

a nucleus of engineering expertise and critical spares. All unobtrusively, on 8th April, in a stripped-out Transport VC-10, with a cargo of cluster-bombs, spare parts and missiles, the engineers and four spare pilots flew to Ascension. On that and the following day the Tanker Force mounted a huge operation to take the sixteen Harriers to Ascension, the second group coming close to *Eagle* as she refuelled from the auxiliary oiler *Orangeleaf* in latitude 20°S.

Late on Sunday, 11th April, two of the three elements of Barbary Coast came together. *Eagle*'s engines slowed, then stopped. Her anchor went down in the deep warm waters of South East Bay, Ascension Island. A balmy quiet, for a brief period, replaced the thunder of the past five days at twenty-five knots. Then an oiler – *Cherryleaf* this time – came alongside to starboard, an ammunition barge to port, small boats to the gangways: few in the crew slept that night. One by one, *Eagle*'s Sea King helicopters were ranged, started up and departed ashore, laden with squadron stores and personnel, making space. When they had finished ferrying personnel, stores and ordnance, only two, stripped for SAR, were retained onboard.

Squadron Leader Bill Pothecary, commander of the six-day-old Barbary Coast Harrier Squadron, came off by launch. Taken to meet the captain on the darkened bridge he gave him, to his lasting embarrassment, a crisp RAF salute. Shown his cabin, he said, 'Bloody Hell!' He did not stay long. Having received painful knocks to head and shin from door sills and hatch covers, and a very poor impression of the manners of the British tar after clashing with a gang of stokers manhandling refuelling hoses in the dark, he boarded his launch, thankfully, for a last few hours ashore. He saw what he came to see, the flight deck, in the dark.

Refuelling hoses were uncoupled at 0545. With full tanks, *Eagle* sailed and picked up speed to the south. Her crew's only glimpse of Ascension was the cloud-capped peak of Green Mountain astern, lit by the rising sun. Few were interested.

At the base of the mountain, Bill Pothecary and his fifteen pilots manned their planes, some a little disconcerted at the novel experience of seeing their destination vanish over the horizon. They roared off Ascension's 12,000-foot runway in staggered threes, five minutes apart, and headed south over the sea. They landed without mishap, though gingerly for the most part, *Eagle* a mere thirty miles out and pitching hardly at all.

Then, with all aboard and well lashed down, the carrier swung starboard out of wind and settled on course 218°, twenty knots now to accommodate *Cherryleaf*, two frigates out ahead on either bow.

Said one Harrier pilot to another as they surveyed the tiny – and by naval standards luxuriously modern – cabin they were to share for the foreseeable future: 'I don't believe it!'

Chapter 16

After the invasion, and especially after Blount's funeral, the possibility of a pre-emptive strike was much in the minds of the British at Roca. Blount had died for Argentina. The manner of his death sharpened all their perceptions about their positions as individuals. They felt it weighed heavily in the balance of obligations. Now the gut-feeling was for a fairer balance of power, to thwart what they saw as Cassián's vindictive aim.

Hicks was very thankful that at their very first operational meeting at Roca he had raised the question of airfield protection. He had been surprised then at the Commodore's uncharacteristic complacency. Hicks had also, long before this, speculated on the number of Corsairs – there were often more than a hundred and fifty parked out – that might be destroyed in a single attack. He had never seen so many aircraft close-parked in the open before; though there was a photograph in Roca's library of a US Marine Air Corps base showing over a hundred Corsairs on a huge concrete pan like Roca's. That was El Toro, California. To Cassián, then, Patagonia was as safe as California.

And it might well be. The *consejeros* hoped against hope. The distances seemed insurmountable, and at the slightest breath of suspicion of a threat, an hour's work would disperse the Corsairs all over the field in such a way that conventional weapons could destroy or damage only a few. Hicks dreaded Cassián raising the subject, but he never did. The Commodore was very surprised, but equally pleased, when the British task force sailed three days after the invasion with the carriers *Hermes* and *Invincible*. But they would take, at best speed, eight days to Ascension and another eight from there before coming within striking range of either Roca or the Falklands. Say 21st April. The BBC Overseas Service reported the frantic diplomatic activity stirred up by the invasion. *Eagle* was never mentioned.

Cassián ordered a battle-trial of the Group's ECM policy. The -E 'Echo' Corsairs, fitted with the latest radar-suppression equipment, had never been tested operationally. He obtained from Armada High Command a frigate, the *Hercules*, a British-built Type 42 with the same 997/998 Doppler radars and Sea Dart and Sea Wolf surface-to-air missiles, had himself helicoptered aboard, took the ship 150 miles east of Roca, ordered the captain to stream his splash target and go to Battle Stations, and then retired to the operations room. All the ship's active and passive warning devices were on full alert status. Within an hour, radar operators began reporting spoking and snow-flaking on their screens. This got rapidly worse. Passive-warning radars were double-checked: there was no 'hostile' radar activity. A Klaxon sounded 'Air Raid Warning Red'. Cassián bustled up the bridge ladder and out onto the port bridge wing, looking up. Already, with the naked eye, they could be seen. He raised his binoculars and could see Monegario's Corsair quite plainly. He grinned with pleasure: what would the British lookouts make of that! The frigate's captain joined him, looking baffled.

'Hold your course,' the Commodore ordered.

A bright day, very little cloud, wind north-west Force Four, the ship steering north, 22 knots, corkscrewing across the swell. The cold wind moaned through the mass of aerials above, and spray curled up from the bow. Too much wind to talk. Half a mile astern, a twenty-foot plume of spray, the splash target.

'Watch!' shouted the Commodore. 'I will explain after.'

The officer of the watch yelled from the bridge door: 'Sea Dart controllers reporting, sir! They cannot lock on! Radars are swamped!'

The captain acknowledged, looked from the slowly-enlarging dots in the western sky to Cassián who grinned widely, nodding as he raised his binoculars again. The dots began to diverge. Cassián nodded again and began searching the sea horizon. There, in the salt-laden lower air, it was a little while before he picked up the first of the Cormorán divisions, just above the waves and moving right. He checked left, and there were more, setting up the Carousel. The look-outs didn't pick them up until they were in to about seven kilometres. Then there was much excitement: 'They are all around – all around!'

They were: Págalos and Cormoráns every thirty degrees around the compass. And this 'British' frigate had so far been able to do nothing about it! Absolutely nothing! The reports filled Cassián with unholy joy. 909 and 910 Radars, GWS 30 and 25, the missile fire-control systems, had, like the long-range air-warning radars, been blinded by jamming. Sea Dart, the medium-range anti-aircraft missile, was known to be confused by multiple targets; the attack was about to start and *Hercules* was reduced to manually-aimed Sea Wolf, the short-range missile, and her gun. Grinning, Cassián started his stop-watch.

'Aircraft! Bearing Green six zero! Closing, low-level! Four aircraft on the bearing!' The starboard look-out's call came over the bridge intercom.

'Engage Sea-Wolf! For Exercise, For Exercise – Engage Sea-Wolf starboard!'

'Aircraft Red three zero! Closing, low-level! Four aircraft on bearing!'

'Engage, engage! For Exercise, for Exercise. Guns engage port!' The twin barrels of the three-inch automatic gun swung left.

'Aircraft bearing Red one five zero, closing. Low-level. Four aircraft on bearing!' Port look-out again, the voice higher.

'Engage! Engage! For Exercise. For Exercise. Guns engage port!'

'Aircraft bearing Green nine zero! Low-level, closing! Four aircraft!'

'Aircraft bearing Green one two zero! High-level! High-level! Four aircraft attacking!'

'Engage! Engage! Sea-Wolf engage!'

'Aircraft bearing Red six zero! High-level, attacking. Four aircraft!'

155

'Engage! Engage! Guns for Exercise engage port!'

'Bridge, this is Gunnery Control. Fire-control radar failed! Request local control?'

'You have local control!'

'Aircraft bearing Green six zero! High-level, attacking. Four aircraft!'

'Aircraft bearing Green one two zero! High-level!'

'Aircraft bearing Green one two zero! Low-level!'

The bridge loudspeakers barked alternately, sometimes together. The officer of the watched dashed from side to side, cursing, craning through the overhanging windows, pausing now and then to look helplessly at the captain.

'Hold your course!' the Commodore shouted. The operations officer, all his sensors disabled, appeared from below to see what was going on. The ship struck a curling wave that sent a streamer of heavy, cold spray over the bridge, drenching Cassián and the captain. Neither appeared to notice, Cassián's eyes were on his stop-watch.

Boom-boom! All eyes swung aft. Two white geysers erupted from the ocean to the right of the splash target, and right of those, a Corsair going fast away. The fat towers of spray were beginning to subside when another Corsair came into view from behind the superstructure with two black bombs keeping perfect station on it below, but descending. *Boom-boom!* A slightly shorter aim this time. *Boom-boom!* Shorter still, nearly on the target. *Boom-boom!* Well over. Cormorán 2 Division cleared, very low, going south-west. The aircraft themselves, half a mile downwind, had been barely audible, mainly supercharger whine.

Cassián swung round as the noise of Cormorán 11 reached him. They came in thirty degrees on the port bow, in ragged echelon at two hundred feet. Very close already – and fast, with thirty knots of relative wind behind them. Not yet abeam the bridge, the leader pickled his bombs. They left their racks and curved down to pass apparently through the splash plume just above the water. Only one exploded, by which time the fading roar of Leader's engine was being supplanted by the rising whistle of his #2, then #3, #4. Then Cormorán 7 Division from the port quarter. And 3 from the starboard beam.

Hercules's sailors crowded onto the upper decks, abandoning their pretence at Battle Stations. Metronomically, the cracking thud of the exploding bombs came through the water and slammed into the ship's hull. When they saw the markings on the Corsairs, the ship's company began to cheer – the dive-bombers most of all. These looked, and sounded, most heroic. The greatest cheer of all, towards the end, was for the dive-bomber who took off the target – only about six feet square – with a direct hit.

It was not a long show, the finale a low fly-past and victory roll by Monegario. Cassián told *Hercules*'s captain: 'It is finished. Thank you, Captain. Now please set course for Punta Deseada where I will disembark by helicopter.' In borrowed shirt and sweater he retired to the tranquillity of the captain's day cabin whose owner soon joined him. The ship, on her new course, pitched heavily.

'Commodore, that was magnificent! Magnificent! I have never seen such bombing!' The captain was full of questions. But so was the Commodore, and time was short.

'Tell me, Captain: how did your weapons perform?'

'Not good, Commodore! I think these planes – what are they, anyway?'

'Corsairs.'

'These Corsairs, they must have pretty good ECM. First, I lose the 997, even with antiference on. Then Sea-Cat – well everybody knows Sea-Cat is very good with one or two targets; but these – how many? – Sea-Cat lost discrimination and could not lock. It has no manual fire-control, so it was useless. Sea-Wolf fire-control radar was jammed out: in local control, with manual reloading, I estimate perhaps four, maybe six rounds in this attack. The gun is best – though as you saw its director too was jammed: even without this, in local control, the gun would have shot down several.'

'Several. Hm. Maybe not if you take a bomb on the fo'cstle! Do you know how many there were?'

'No.'

'Eighty. Eighty bombers. So, in real life, in this situation, what would you do?'

The captain spread his hands, said nothing.

'You would manoeuvre?' Cassián pressed him.

'Of course! But . . . ? Which way?'

Before he was winched off by Roca's Sea King, Cassián told *Hercules*'s captain his ship would be remaining at sea until further notice. Under no circumstances was any member of his crew to be allowed ashore. These orders were confirmed, later in the day, by the Commander-in-Chief, Admiral Anaya.

Returning to Roca in high good humour, the Commodore declared the next day a holiday and laid on a dinner for his staff. It was Friday, 9th April. The Falklands had been *Las Malvinas* for a week. Knowing it was still much too soon to expect anything did not stop Hicks, before he left his office at six o'clock, counting the Corsairs on the pan: one hundred and sixteen. At the Commodore's table, he tried to keep from his mind all thoughts of the pre-emptive strike he desperately hoped for, as if such thoughts might be communicated.

Their host, of course, was full of what he had seen that morning, and delighted with everything including himself. This was a safe track, thought Hicks. The others too, and they led him on as far as it went. Hicks chose his moment to throw the points down another safe track.

'Commodore, you haven't yet told us the story of the Corsair. Are we allowed to know?'

'Why not!' Cassián smiled expansively. 'Why not indeed! I tell you. It is very interesting. Only my modesty has prevented me so far from telling you!' The company settled to listen.

'Nineteen forty-five: my ship was in Panama. I was *Guardiamarina*, seventeen; and my uncle was the captain. Panama is full of ships, many with cargo for the West Pacific, when the war ends and they are told to wait. All is confusion. We too wait – I don't know why. I begin to find out about the ships. One has six hundred aero-engines. My family were shipping agents, in Buenos Aires.'

'So!' A new cigar. Captain Perez, on his right, poured brandy for the Commodore who clapped him on the shoulder. '*Gracias*, Rinaldo. What –' he waved away the smoke and resumed, '– what do you do with six hundred Pratt and Whitney R-2800 engines? We build a warehouse and put them in.'

158

'Next I meet this Bugatti in New York, 1952. Italian. Like me he is crazy on aeroplanes, used to work in the US for Vought, making Corsairs. At the end of the war he took the drawings – nobody was interested. He was very enthusiastic about the Corsair, and we had a very good talk. I asked him about its engine. Pratt and Whitney R-2800, he said!

'This was the moment of conception! The idea was in my mind. As I got more senior, I could see Argentina, like everybody else, buying expensive foreign planes. Expensive. We could afford so few it was ridiculous. I thought of those engines, and those Corsair plans. I was able to get Bugatti traced, and the drawings. And then – and then! The long battle to sell the idea! You will all understand the difficulty: the military has an immune system to protect it from the radical!'

'But in 1976, we have a military government! Now the priorities are different! I make great emphasis that Project Corsair, more than anything else, will bring *Las Malvinas* back to Argentina, and you see the results! Manufacture is low-precision work with modern high-tech machinery. A raw Corsair airframe cost about two hundred thousand dollars, not including plant cost, made this way. And –' here the Commodore spoke to Hicks, '– the plant cost Argentina nothing! This was the time of *la plata dulce*, as we call it; sweet, soft money from your banks, as much as we wanted, and no questions!'

'I did wonder!' Hicks replied. Piracy; larceny; now embezzlement! All on the grand scale, though – nothing mean! He looked around at the other Argentines, so urbane. They should have crossed bandoliers, sombreros and big grins, like the movies! Cheerful bandits! He liked them.

'And now there is a plant for the engines – also robotic, high-precision, so the new engines too are much better – like modern cars. When this is finished we can put the Corsair on the market – but not in South America! Eh! Not in South America!' He laughed. The bandits laughed with their leader. By 'this', presumably, he meant the Malvinas. Odd, thought Hicks, how Falklands doesn't sound right any more, already . . .

The small hours of Saturday, 10th April, saw the debut, in

Patagonia, of 'Eskimo Nell' and 'The Harlot of Jerusalem', courtesy of LeStrange and Finch respectively. Channing's 'Anthony Rowley' was well sung, but, too cerebral for the hour, failed to clear the language hurdle and was less heartily acclaimed. Hicks offered 'Old King Cole'. Tracey fell asleep.

Walking back alone, Hicks searched his memory for the damp, green smell of an English night. It wasn't there. Was it that long? The sky held a few stars, half a moon, and only the night wind, unboisterous. Was that the Southern Cross? Down there . . . above Tim's grave? Presently, unwilled, his steps veered off and took him down the hangar road; across the pan, dim Corsairs like sleeping beetles; out along the perimeter track, wide and empty, redolent of that night with Carla in the fog; the cliff track, rough and maritime-smelling; the neat, square, unfenced cemetery. He stayed until dawn.

When he got home, Carla was still elaborately unconscious in his bed. As with everything, she slept with great conviction and without reserve. He joined her.

Later, over a luxurious noon-time brunch in the *Rancho* – an excellent establishment run by and not for its staff, and much appreciated therefore by the British – Carla wanted to hear from him the Commodore's assessment of yesterday's raid: as Cormorán 11#3 she had watched *Hercules*'s twin-barrelled gun tracking her leader, then switch to #2, and presumably to her as she took final aim.

'The ECM was good,' he told her.

'How good?'

He gave her the details.

'Ten!' she laughed. 'The man is dreaming to think he can shoot down so many! – even without getting hit himself! And when he is hit, one, two bombs – peuff, he can shoot no more!' It seemed to Hicks a strange thing for such a small, high voice to be saying.

'I think you are right.'

'Anyway . . .' she made a face, 'I don't too much like this laydown. It is very accurate, I know, but for me the dive-bombing is more exciting!'

'Yes, dear,' Hicks caught himself saying, as he buttered a piece of toast. He smiled.

160

Chapter 17

Eagle reached the start position for Operation Barbary Coast late on Sunday, 18th April after a thundering seven-day ocean passage with *Cherryleaf* and the two frigates. They spent the night in Condition Two alert, refuelling. Then they circled, quiet on the empty ocean, crews dressed and briefed, aircraft armed and fuelled. Two thousand seven hundred miles north-east, fourteen Victor tankers of RAF Strategic Support Command, heavy with fuel, stood on the moonlit concrete acres of Ascension airfield. Armed guards kept watch.

The sun rose in London. Diplomats stirred. Another emergency debate was scheduled in the UN Security Council, at which Britain would again quote Resolution 501 and insist on the removal of Argentine troops from the Falkland Islands as a pre-condition for any negotiations. General Alexander Haig, mid-air en route to Buenos Aires on the latest leg of his diplomatic shuttle, passed Signor Perez de Cuellar, Argentina's UN Ambassador, flying north for the debate.

The British war cabinet met at nine o'clock. After a very full review by the Foreign Secretary of the current diplomatic situation, and some discussion, there was a long silence. The Prime Minister addressed the Secretary of State for Defence:

'And you say that with a fleet of World War Two aeroplanes at this base at Punta Deseada the Argentines are effectively depriving us of all our military options?'

'Yes, Prime Minister. That is unfortunately true – as long as the base and the aircraft are there. And there is another interesting point. They have not yet deployed any of these aircraft to the Falklands. This reinforces our interpretation of the project as an ambush. I strongly believe we are not supposed to know they are there. And the Foreign Secretary and I agree that, this being the case, and for two reasons, the Argentines are unlikely to make a public fuss if we destroy them: first, admitting their existence would expose their purpose and thus weaken Argentina's defence against charges of aggression; and secondly, if we do the job properly, the loss of face would be enormous.'

'Thank you. Well, gentlemen, it seems that having pre-empted us once with their invasion, they now want to do it again. My Latin is rusty, but do we think *caveat pre-emptor* would fit the case?'

Some winced. None dissented. The Prime Minister asked that the Chief of The Defence Staff should be sent in.

The Admiral reported *Eagle* on station and ready. HMS *Thunderer*, one of two hunter-killer SSN's diverted to the South Atlantic some time before, was off Punta Deseada reporting weather and standing by for SAR. Pressure in the area was fairly high and steady, and the submarine reported too that, for the second weekend in succession, there had been no observable air activity at the Corsair base.

'But,' he concluded, 'it is now of course too late to strike today.'

'Why?' asked the Prime Minister.

The Admiral, looking at his watch, said, 'Speaking in GMT, sunrise out there this morning is 1037. The lead time for the tankers is six hours from Ascension. Add another hour and a half for the Harriers to rendezvous, transit and attack. The tankers have to leave Ascension at about 0300, to strike at dawn.'

'Must it be dawn?'

'Yes, Prime Minister. We want these Corsairs on the ground.'

'We should decide now for tomorrow, then.' The room again filled with silence.

'The Rules of Engagement are quite clear?' the Prime Minister asked the Admiral.

'Absolutely. Visual attacks on aircraft, hangars and

162

support installations only. And we maintain a recall facility up to the moment of attack.'

'Very well, then. Make it so.'

The Harrier and Victor crews stood down, tried to rest through Monday. Barbary Coast would be their first operation without peacetime safety margins. Calculations of astronomical magnitude had been carried out to produce the group flight plan, whose aim was to get enough fuel overhead *Eagle* to top-up the Harriers after they had climbed to about 30,000 feet for the first part of their transit in, and again, after the attack, for their return to the ship. These two 'sharp-end' Victors would themselves then be unable to reach Ascension without refuelling from others that had already taken off once, given fuel to others, returned, landed, refuelled and taken off again to meet them. Fourteen Victor Tankers was the number demanded by the flight-planning computer for the task. There were no spares.

Without further word from London, the Victors started taking off at 0240 on Tuesday and proceeded silently southwest. One by one, leeched, they peeled off and returned, with nearly empty tanks, until after nearly six hours Esso Leader and his number two were alone, their inertial navigation showing some two hundred nautical miles to the rendezvous. Below, sixteen RAF Harrier Ground-attack pilots emerged cautiously from the island door onto *Eagle*'s dark flight-deck, an alien world to them, slippery with dew and reeking of salt and tractor fumes. They carefully checked their aircraft. When the flight-deck control light changed from red to amber they started their engines and signalled crews to remove their chain lashings. They could feel the trembling deck as the ship worked up speed and the heel as she swung into wind. She steadied. The light went steady green – the final executive signal for Operation Barbary Coast – and the Harriers taxied onto the dimly-lit centreline and launched up the ski-jump at 30-second intervals. Heavy with fuel and weapons, they laboured to height at full power, on course to the target, located the unlit tankers by TACAN beacon, refuelled and flew on in loose formation at high level, four hundred and fifty miles to go. Behind them, as the eastern sky paled, Esso One and Two took up a lazy, economical orbit at 33,000 feet.

Thunderer had detected a long-range ten-centimetre search radar at 'Newfield', but had reported that it was not switched on during the hours of darkness; it usually began radiating about 0730. Nevertheless, forty minutes after leaving the tankers, 220 miles to go, Pothecary began a slow descent and led the Harriers down to 500 feet, 300 knots. From sixty-five pounds a minute at 30,000 feet, fuel flow rose to eighty, and their speed over the ground was cut by a third. No word had been said since the pilots got in their planes on *Eagle*'s deck. All radar switches were off – not even standby. Their passive warning receivers had remained silent, indicating no radar emissions from any source in their area.

A hundred miles out, they passed close to the submerged *Thunderer* on her SAR station. Neither spoke. The Harriers navigated using their INAS/Inertial Navigation and could in theory bomb blind. 'Newfield's' details had been pinpointed within metres by satellite, the coordinates programmed into the Harriers' on-board computers, and their auto weapon-release facility should have been able to put the BL755's, at least, on to the target. The Rules of Engagement, however, prohibited this; and, anyway Pothecary was not convinced of the accuracy of *Eagle*'s INAS alignment, which depended upon the ship knowing exactly where it was.

Thirty miles, the Initial Point of the attack pattern. Pothecary's INAS display flashed the waypoint. He turned right six degrees, powered up to 480 knots, and let down to a hundred feet above the sea. Visibility was good under half-cover of strato-cumulus and the Patagonian coast changed quickly from a smudge to an outline. He was looking for a promontory, the one that enfolded the bay containing a small-craft jetty. The coast was familiar, from study of *Thunderer*'s facsimile photographs, and Pothecary soon picked out the bay, a little right of where it should have been – so, he'd have that drink off *Eagle*'s navigator! He relaxed, concentrating on the familiar routine of the attack pattern, 'Newfield's' tower plainly visible as a marker.

Pothecary plus seven carried BL755's to be laid down in an overlapping pattern of 70 by 200-metre ellipses across that half of the parking pan, nearest the hangars, where the Corsairs habitually parked. Five were armed with four pods each of mixed HE and incendiary-headed SNEB unguided rockets, for the hangars. One carried four 540lb HE bombs, for the 'fuel farm' which Bagshaw had pinpointed from satellite photographs by noting a focus of bowsers and their tyre-marks upon a point to the east of the pan. On the sixteenth Harrier, besides a photo-reconnaisance/PR pod, was a new weapon which the RAF's Tactical Weapons Unit was anxious to try out.

The PR aircraft was still twelve miles out over the sea when Pothecary crossed the grey cliffs on the attack heading of 244 degrees, down the axis of the parking pan. The tower very slightly left of the nose at two miles. The preferred attack heading for identifying and aiming, coming from inland, would have meant attacking into a low sun with salty windscreens – and would have given Roca more warning. As it was, from the cliffs to the eastern edge of the pan, 1,700 metres, took only six seconds. The BL755 dispenser unit parted from Pothecary's right wing, at about the moment he passed over Hicks' apartment, flew on descending shallowly until it was over the parking pan and then, with a loud crackle, flung out its load. One hundred and eighteen 3-kilogram bomblets fell like seeds upon the parked Corsairs nearest the tower.

Pothecary passed within feet of the control-tower belvedere, saw figures through the glass, banked hard left and pulled into a 5g level turn south across the runways and beyond, scalding the poor landscape with noise on his way to the sea. Then he was over the cliffs again, turning hard and descending. He snapped his wings level as his gyro compass hit the return heading, 068 degrees true, pulled the nose up and headed for the stratosphere.

After Pothecary, at about five-second intervals seven more BL755's rained 900-odd bomblets down on the out-parked Corsairs. Many were destroyed. None escaped damage.

Next the rocketeers, even lower, line-astern upon the bombers, along between the hangar fronts and the shambles on the pan, past the tower, out into the desert half a mile and then into a hard right turn, climbing to just below the cloudbase at 1,500 feet, heading back northeast. The airfield was now on their right, black smoke rolling away on the wind. Abreast the hangars, their leader, Flight Lieutenant Phillips, snapped right into a shallow dive and laid the bright diamond of his aiming-marker a shade right of No. 5 Hangar. As the west wind drifted him left with the smoke, the shining diamond moved towards the hangar. At 900 feet altitude the two coincided and he squeezed his trigger. Flames from the rocket-motors streamed from the four barrel-like pods under his wings and the rapidly diminishing distance between him and the green-drab hangar filled with a dense jostling pack of black arrows not unlike a medieval painting. But these arrows were supersonic and they were two-inch diameter steel tubes tipped with high-explosive or magnesium. They numbered 96 in all.

Phillips held his dive long enough to see them running true, then pulled hard up and left towards the sun and home. Behind him, jagged holes appeared in the roof and sides of Soto's hangar as rockets exploded on contact or passed through the flimsy metal to detonate inside against whatever solid object they first encountered in a maelstrom of fire and explosions.

No. 4 Hangar was next. It was easy work. These men were experts. And there had been, so far, no return fire. But the third rocketeer was unlucky. No. 3 Hangar was spared because, despite all the precautions, salt spray had penetrated the aircraft's electronics bay during *Eagle*'s passage south: engine heat had evaporated the water, leaving a tiny salt crystal holding open the relay connecting the firing circuits with the Harrier's AC bus-bar. Expletives being no substitute for explosives, Hangar No. 3 stood intact as the next two dissolved in flames.

'Red Leader, this is Blue Three . . . Total hangup! . . . Going round again!' The first words spoken on the radio that morning, a mix of disgust, anger and determination.

'Roger, Blue Three, One pass only. Advise clearing.' Pothecary, passing 20,000ft in the climb, replied.

'Wilco.' No more was said.

The rocketeers clear, except for Blue Three in his three-mile wide repeat pattern, three Harriers remained, Green section. Green Two put four 540lb GP bombs into the fuel farm, with limited success: two bowsers erupted into a satisfying conflagration among buildings and pipework, but the size

166

of the explosion suggested the underground tanks had escaped.

Simultaneously, Green Three with four pods of SNEB's located what Bagshaw had convinced the command might be an aircraft park or store, reasoning that if Corsairs were being manufactured in Argentina and shipped to 'Newfield' for assembly there would need to be a clearing-house or storage facility for the finished aircraft: these would almost certainly not be in the front-line hangars down on the 'waterfront'. He had found, in a computer-enhanced satellite photograph, a rectangle about the size of four hangars put together, on the northern outskirts of the field, and it was this that Flight-Lieutenant Apps now had in his sights.

With his rockets set to slow-ripple, Apps pressed his trigger at about 900 feet and held it, easing the nose of his Harrier up to hose the rockets along the low, flat-roofed building. Easy shooting. He couldn't miss. Ninety of his 96 rocket-projectiles struck home, most passing straight through the roof. Apps had to hold his aircraft in the dive longer than the other rocketeers, who had used fast-ripple, and as he bottomed out around 400 feet and began to pull up, a solid thump told him he had lost a gamble: a roof-girder, or some such solid object, had ricochetted a broken fragment of one of his rockets up into the underside of his aircraft with what effect he could not yet tell. He called, 'Green Three clear' and climbed out after the others.

Green Leader saw him go, too far away to notice the thin trail of fuel from his port wing, before turning in himself to run across the parking apron. He had already made one phot pass to the south, running his oblique camera over the target area; now he wanted verticals. And something else, too. Strike Command's Tactical Weapons Unit had offered a new weapon for Barbary Coast: a so-called Surface Denial Weapon. 'Just the job,' they had insisted, and eventually the weapon was included.

So with his weapon-selector set to a Dyno-tape 'SDW', Green Leader pressed his firing trigger as he passed abeam the control tower, and from a wing-pod a stream of glinting metal fell, not unlike snowflakes, upon the chaotic scene below. He saw movement on the ground, red vehicles, cars, then all was behind as he pulled up for home. He had seen enough.

'Red Leader this is Green Leader. *Barbarossa!* I say again *Barbarossa!* Acknowledge.'

The word was passed from Pothecary to Esso One, thence to *Eagle*, and within ten minutes the Cabinet Secretary excused himself to lay before the Prime Minister a note which read:

PM

From CDS

Operation Barbary Coast successfully accomplished at 1105GMT.

The Prime Minister's eyes closed, briefly. Then the interrupted discussions of the War Cabinet resumed – a little brisker and firmer, as it was later observed.

Eagle meanwhile was making thirty knots south-west towards the returning strike, flinging spray a hundred feet in the air and taking green water down the length of her flight deck. From the crowded bridge and its Flyco jetty down to the deep machinery spaces, tension gripped her company. At their action stations behind armoured doors and screwed-down hatches, depersonalised by their white anti-flash hoods and gloves, they felt in the ship's throbbing steel plates the new imperative that had displaced the niceties of peacetime naval life. The ship was being driven like a destroyer. Now and then, and unpredictably, her progress would be sharply disputed by an equal mass of water, an awkward swell intent on rolling east: a jarring shock of collision would travel through her and she would seem to stop: things fell and smashed, men staggered; then her 50,000 horsepower would reassert and she would corkscrew on her way. Five miles out on either bow, the frigates looked to be, for the most part, submerged in water and spray.

At the appropriate time, *Eagle* slowed and turned a little port into wind to launch four Sidewinder-armed Sea Harriers as Combat Air Patrol/CAP for the refuelling station, Point Bravo. They arrived – a welcome sight to the unarmed tanker crews, hoses already trailing – ten minutes before Pothecary plugged into Esso One. Refuelling was carried out in a wide continuous orbit to enable the tankers to maintain the position disciplined by ongoing distance-fuel analyses for themselves to Ascension and for the Harriers from-to Newfield and *Eagle*. There was much terse talk, now, on Strike Common, as *Eagle*'s Ops Officer, 'Delta Foxtrot', controlled the refuelling:

'Red Six. Ten miles.' . . . 'Red Six Delta Foxtrot, take Esso Two on north station and say your fuel.' . . . 'Red Six twelve hundred pounds remaining.' . . . 'Roger Red Six Bingo is two three zero zero pounds.' . . . 'Red Six twenty-three hundred' . . . 'Red Four pulling out' . . . 'Red Six clear in' . . . 'Red Six in. Fuel flowing' . . . Red Seven, ten miles' . . . 'Red Seven Delta Fox. Take Esso One on south station and say your fuel' . . . 'Red Seven has one thousand remaining' . . . 'Red Eight, ten miles' . . . 'Red Five is out, thank you. Do you take Access?' . . . 'Negative – South American Express only' . . . 'That will do nicely' . . . 'Red Seven is in. Fuel flowing' . . . 'Blue Leader, ten miles' . . . while 7,000 feet above, the four Sea Harriers racetracked, always two facing the threat, westward.

On another frequency, Strike Distress, a shorter exchange: 'Mayday, Mayday, Mayday . . . this is Green Three . . . I'm losing fuel . . . unable to make Point Bravo . . . intend ejecting in approximately ten minutes. Esso One acknowledge.' The Victor's navigator relayed Apps' call to *Eagle*, too far away to hear, as Apps, in a descending spiral, read out latitude and longitude from his INAS indicator. Below, Apps' voice loudspeakered through *Thunderer*'s control room. His figures were fed into her SINS equipment and within seconds the five-thousand ton submarine was in a steeply-banked accelerating turn under automatic con for rendezvous.

Apps' ejection and descent were uneventful. After a moment of panic in the water when a swath of parachute rigging lines enwrapped his leg and started pulling down, he methodically cut them away, inflated and boarded his dinghy, activated his UHF rescue beacon and set about making himself comfortable. This he had done when, sitting warm and dry in his immersion suit under the orange canopy but conscious of an edge of nausea and an excess of saliva, he became conscious too of an eerie low hum coming from the water. It grew louder until it emerged from the background of sea and wind noises and his bleeping beacon to assert a presence.

Apps, twisting to scan the hostile seascape, was quite astonished to find himself being regarded from about the length of a cricket pitch by an eye on a black pole. So disorientated was the flight lieutenant by his abrupt intimacy with things maritime, that it was some time before his brain could process what he was seeing. Then, noticing a UHF aerial on another pole a few yards away, he switched his PLB to 'Receive' and heard:

'Green Three, I presume?'

He pressed 'Transmit': 'Yes. I seem to have broken down.'

'Are you a member, sir?'

'No. But I'd like to join.'

'Stand by.'

The poles moved off a bit and then, with much less foaming and blowing than Apps would have imagined, *Thunderer* surfaced, shiny black and rolling in the swell. Figures emerged from her fin. Apps was grappled and unceremoniously boathooked up her slippery side and bundled below, where all was warmth, light and calm. Soon hot-showered and new-kitted, fortified with navy rum, he nevertheless shivered intermittently for two hours. The captain had explained that there was no question of a rendezvous with *Eagle* as all surface forces were withdrawing to Ascension: his stay on board would therefore be of indeterminate length. As he surveyed his bunk, which he was 'lucky not to have to share', about the size of a mortuary drawer and separated from the submarine's busy main-deck passage by a curtain, he thought back to his palatial 'hutch' in *Eagle* and said once more: 'Bloody hell!'

Chapter 18

Hicks' first waking thought was thunder. The second jet, 500 knots right overhead, was unmistakeable. His window looked east. He and Carla were there in time to see Red Three coming from their left, hot curling exhaust wrinkling the dawn sky. And two more behind. Above the brutal engine noise they heard the first explosions from the direction of the airfield.

Outside, still dressing, shoes undone, they ran with others towards the hangars. Smoke was already boiling up on the wind. The last bomber scoured overhead, roundels clearly visible. They watched its cluster-bomb separate and fly serenely on until, all in an instant at about a hundred feet, it assumed the personality of a detonating pepperpot and sneezed its bomblets out in all directions to fall beyond the hangar. They ran on, no thought of danger – the precision of the attack perhaps subconsciously reassuring.

A lull. Just the receding roar of the last bombers. Hicks caught Carla's arm and stopped, searching the sky all around, listening. Soon he saw what he was looking for, way out to the right, tiny yet and soundless, the rocketeers, pulling back in for their dive.

'Get back! *Get back!*' he yelled, pointing. 'Take cover!' Some around them stopped, most ran on. Hicks pulled Carla into the shelter of the nearest concrete building, still shouting, pointing at the first Harrier diving on the nearest hangar. Its pods flamed, and in milliseconds ninety-six projectiles were in flight, snaking, jostling down. The ear-splitting crackle of their sonic shock-waves drowned out the rising shriek of the

Harrier's engine. Hicks, still holding Carla, watched the rockets punch through the thin corrugated hangar, explode or ricochet as the Harrier pulled hard up and away. The concealed thud of a secondary explosion came from inside No. 5 and smoke was already feathering from its wounds as the next cascade of supersonic steel slammed into No. 4 with similar effect. The gut-twisting roar of jets and rockets and the savage accuracy of the attack exalted Hicks and he wanted to cheer. Oddly though, he felt glad one hangar had escaped destruction.

When they were sure it was over – Hicks recognised Green Three's two photographic passes though the silvery shower on the final run puzzled him – they went cautiously down between the flaming hulks of Nos. 4 and 5, already beginning to look like crashed and burning dirigibles, black-boned flaming hulks, to where they could see the pan. The belligerent echoes of Green Three's engine died away eastward, leaving the lesser roar of fires, sirens and high thin cries to fill the aural panorama. Cassián came around the corner behind them in his Mercedes, accelerating past them down the road. But before the car reached the pan it swerved violently and slewed to a stop. Cassián got out, looking at the ground, picked something up. Seeing Hicks and Carla running towards him he waved them to stop, pointing at the ground. Carla was the first to see a two-inch metal prong; Hicks picked it up. It was a four-pronged device of light metal, very strong, so made that it would always stand on three legs with the fourth vertical, deadly sharp. Hicks saw another. Then more. As they got towards the pan it became necessary to walk with care. Cassián's car had two flat tyres.

The half-dozen prongs Hicks collected fitted cleverly into each other, their bulk and weigh negligible, probably titanium. He could see that thousands could be packed and carried in a small dispenser. The weapon was new to him, but its efficacy soon became apparent as a fire-engine, driven with all the exuberance of the genre, swept out onto the pan from the access road at its north-east corner, flashing and wailing, heading for the nearest burning Corsair: in a racing turn, its two front tyres burst in quick succession and it lay over on its side and slid broadside with a loud bang into an intact Corsair.

It lay there, still flashing and mutedly wailing, as the bewildered crew climbed out. One jumped to the ground, screamed and fell, pointing around him at the dense scattering of prongs. The rest stayed on the useless fire engine, surrounded by an inferno. All the other vehicles attempting to approach the target area fared similarly. Roca's emergency services were crippled. Even walking, after the first rash of casualties, had to be slow and wary.

Cassián, unshaven and capless, surveyed the scene from where he stood with Hicks and Carla beside his useless car. Over a hundred of the Grupo's Corsairs were on the pan. Many were on fire, their merging palls of black smoke darkening the morning sky. Others showed torn metal, broken wings or tails, smashed undercarriages. A few seemed to have escaped but stood perilously close to burning, exploding neighbours or were threatened by spreading pools of blazing AvGas. The smoke passed low overhead to merge with that from the hangars and roll away upwards on the westerly wind. Around them, now, nobody moved.

Cassián got on his car radio. Fire services were to concentrate upon No. 3 hangar and 'the reserve'; sweeper-trucks were to clear the access to No. 3 before anything else approached. He ordered another car, to wait some distance back from the hangar area, for himself, and set off to meet it. Hicks and Carla went with him, eyes down, stepping round the vicious spikes.

'You know anything about this, Eeks?' the Commodore asked, as they walked.

'No.'

'No.' Eyes met briefly. They walked on. The prongs thinned out rapidly behind the hangars.

When they reached the car, all three got in. Hicks didn't know why: there had been no invitation. But it seemed unthinkable just to let the Commodore drive off alone.

Cassián turned to Hicks: 'How did they do it?'

'A carrier. It must be *Eagle. Invincible* and *Hermes* are supposed to be still at Ascension, according to the BBC.'

'Ah! ze *Eagle! Eagle* was not in our intelligence. She should be in the Mediterranean! And these were your Navy Harriers?'

'No, Royal Air Force. GR3's.'

'So. And their range?'

'With these weapons – maybe three hundred miles. Radius.' Hicks didn't feel obliged to mention, yet, that the Harriers had had their bolt-on refuelling probes fitted.

Cassián looked at his watch. They were driving north, out past the domestic site to a wired-off area where Hicks had never been. Smoke was rising here too, fire-engines already in place.

The Commodore changed radio channels and called Operations:

'Flag to Capitán Monegario.'

'Here, Contraalmirante.' After a short pause.

'I want a search and strike, maximum effort, as soon as possible. There is a carrier group at about three hundred miles. Get everybody on the base out to pick up these . . . *clavos*, these spikes! Everybody! I am at Reserve Storage.'

When the car stopped, Carla got out first, said urgently, 'I must go,' saluted the Commodore and ran off back towards the control tower leaving Hicks, hand involuntarily extended, looking after her. When she had gone ten paces she turned briefly, waved to him, ran on.

They were at the west end of the long, low building into which Green Three had poured his rockets. It was the size of four standard hangars end-to-end. Half way down it, a hundred and fity metres away, thick fountains of foam arched in among a mêlée of flame, smoke and flashing lights. Cassián led the way through a small door in the near end of the building.

Inside, in sterile, air-conditioned tranquillity, stood rows of Corsairs, so close there was no room to walk except in narrow passages like forest paths. About eighty, Hicks quickly guessed. Muted sounds of firefighting came from beyond the fire-curtain, but here all was order, fluorescent, smelling of paint, rubber, AvGas and virgin machinery. A senior technician saluted: 'Commodore! No problem here, so far! Sprinkler pressure is good if we need it.'

'Open the doors. Start getting them out!'

'But . . .'

'No buts. Get them *out*! I will send help. Jeff, on the radio.

174

Get Monegario. Tell him to send one or two hundred people here, quick, to push these planes.'

Hicks spoke to Operations from the car, then ran after the Commodore down towards the fire. The base engineer, Bolsano, was there, wet and dirty.

'. . . These are lost . . .' he was saying, indicating the blazing mid-section of the long hangar, '. . . sprinklers damaged . . . But if I keep the fire-curtains cool I hope to clear the other sections . . . I think I save most, now.' He flinched as the nearest burning Corsair exploded into a ball of dull red flame. 'But the most important now is the propellers – as you know, Commodore.'

'Yes. I have sent for help for you to push out. Now, Pedro, how long to get some of these ready to fly?'

'These planes are all reserve status, Commodore!' The engineer wiped a dollop of foam from his shirt-front.

'I know that.'

The engineer considered, ignoring another explosion. They all had to move hurriedly as a fire hose was dragged across the ground, foam flying everywhere. 'Two hours, Contraalmirante,' the engineer said at last. 'I give you ten aircraft in two hours – if they don't burn!'

'Do it, Pedro!' Cassián put a hand on the engineer's shoulder. 'We should make a return call on the British carrier before he is out of range, eh?'

The engineer looked at the blackened corpses of his brand-new charges. '*Si*. Contraalmirante!' he said with feeling.

Hicks went with Cassián to Operations. The Main Briefing Room was full already, the passage outside crowded with pilots. He couldn't see Carla.

In his office Monegario said: 'The No. 3 hangar is safe, Commodore. Twenty-eight Corsairs – twenty Bravos and eight Sierras, and the Skyhawks. The rest – very few left. See . . .' The operations block was alongside the tower, and from Monegario's window they looked north-east across the length of the parking pan. Hundreds of stooping figures moved slowly among the burning wreckage, picking up spikes. Hicks immediately thought it would have been better to organise them into lines and search methodically, was on the point of speaking – but then, this was the Argentine way!

'Twenty from No. 3, ten from reserve,' Cassián mused, surveying the ruins outside. He came to a decision, turned his back on the window and said to Monegario: 'Signal Defence Ministry. Private code for Admiral Anaya. Roca attacked 0730 local time by British Harrier GR3s. Considerable damage. Details will follow. Intend launch immediate armed search of NE sector to max range for British carrier group. Suggest similar from northern airfields cmm and specifically request Kondor assist location of target.'

When Mongario had gone out with the signal, Hicks felt impelled to say: 'Commodore, I think this will be a waste of time. The Harrier GR3 can flight-refuel, and I would expect the carrier to keep well out of range of your attack,' and did not fail to notice a new reticence in Cassián's answering glance.

'You are probably right, Eeks,' he said; 'but this . . .' he indicated the scene of devastation outside, 'calls for action. I cannot do nothing.'

'I understand.'

After a short silence, Cassián went on: 'Do not think, my friend, that I forget what you say at the beginning about defences at Roca. My opinion was, it is not necessary. I was wrong.' Monegario came back in.

'But you also were right,' said Hicks. He pointed outside. 'This is a compliment from the British government: you are their prime target!'

'But how did they know so much?' Monegario asked. 'Even the reserve!'

'Satellites! And you said yourself, there have been nuclear submarines in the area for a long time or you would have had *Las Malvinas* long ago!' Hicks paused and then added, for the unasked question still hung, 'Not from us. You know that! As for the Reserve – deductive intelligence: the operation predicates a reserve storage facility – and it *is* the biggest building at Roca.'

Cassián said to Monegario: 'I want a Combat Air Patrol, as many Sierras as you have, ten miles east, in case of re-attack. And as soon as the ground is clear of these spikes, *all* Corsairs to be dispersed around the field.' He looked at his watch.

'One hour since the strike. They will be on the ship soon. We can expect them again in two hours, if they come.'

The CAP of fifteen Sidewinder Sierras and the Skyhawks took off half an hour after the armed search departed, and remained on station all day, refuelling in relays. Air Force Mysteres and long-range Canberras fanned out over the ocean from Comodoro Rivadavia and other airfields around the naval base at Puerto Belgrano in Bahia Blanca. No trace of the British carrier until, late in the day, after the Corsair search had returned to Roca from their eight-hour patrols, the FAA's Boeing found the *Eagle* Task Group seven hundred miles from Roca and steaming away at high speed. The sudden appearance of two Sea Harriers, one close on each wingtip and hung with Sidewinders, startled the Boeing's crew who had not been told the reason for the hasty search. They were allowed to leave unmolested.

Hicks spent the whole day in the Operations Room, and was there at the end when a subdued meeting of Heads prepared a tally. At the start of the day, he learned, besides the 200 Corsairs on issue to the five 'waterfront' squadrons, there had been 337 completed airframes in store. Of this total, 174 had been destroyed, either incinerated in hangars or burned in the open. A further 65 were seriously damaged. There should thus have been nearly three hundred serviceable Corsairs still available to Cassián. But the situation was worse than these figures suggested. A high proportion of the Group's limited supply of propellers had been lost with the squadron aircraft, and of the reserve Corsairs, only eighty had propellers, The Group's total effective strength had thus been cut to about 130 Corsairs and four Skyhawks. One Corsair had failed to return from the search.

When arrangements had been outlined for re-equipping the squadrons from reserve, OC3, Burgos Alvarez, asked: 'Now there is no need for secrecy, Commodore, is it proposed we should move forward to the Malvinas and operate from there?'

'This sounds logical, but consider,' replied Cassián. 'The Grupo's strength is in numbers. Superior, even excessive numbers. Have you seen the Malvinas airfields? How can we provide, out there, for two hundred Corsairs? Fuel, engineering, weapons – even parking! No. We remain at Roca. Except maybe for patrol.'

After this, Cassián left them, to attend to the clamorous demands from Buenos Aires for information which he had been resisting all day. Hicks silently wished him well – his life's work and his career were in the balance – and set out to make his own way 'home'. He was hungry, and it was getting dark. He walked alone, with care, around the edge of the pan. The wind had lost its full strength, but was enough to swirl the stink of fire at him from all directions. Salvage teams worked on, arc-lit here and there. Corsairs were being towed by the tail to new dispersals around the field.

Carla was already home. She had flown the search. She was pale, her face long with exhaustion. She managed a smile. ''Allo, *querido mio*. Did you 'ave a good day at ze office?'

He took her in his arms and held her tight for a long time. She smelled of soap. Everything else stank of the smoke that had rolled over the domestic area all day. She clung to him, thin, immensely strong, but wonderfully feminine. He could feel her drawing strength from their embrace and, at long last, her mouth came up to his.

Later, she said: 'Eeks?'

'Yes?'

'What you do now?'

'I want some supper.' Staring at the ceiling.

'No! I mean what you do about zis war? You are on the wrong side!'

'*No es problema, querida!* There is no war!' It had just come to him in a flash. He sat up. *'No es guerra!'* He kissed her flat white belly, 'Come. Food,' he said, pulling her up.

'What you mean, *no es guerra*?' she protested.

'Later, I explain. Now, food.'

After supper in the Rancho, excited as a disturbed beehive, the *consejeros* met in Hicks' room. Carla was there.

'So where do we stand now?' Hicks addressed the question they had been carrying around all day. 'I'll tell you what I think. Two things have changed today. One, they know we're here – I mean, they know about Roca, and the Corsairs. Two, the numbers have changed, the equation is more balanced. We can forget about ambush, annihilation, massacre. Yes?'

All agreed.

'But now, there's something else,' he continued. This was his inspiration, and he'd had little time to think it through. 'The treason question. It's never been properly resolved – for me anyway. But after this morning, it suddenly came to me that this isn't war! Not formal War with a capital W. And if it's not War there's no treason, and with treason out of the way it becomes a business, open to anybody to make what they can out of it! Including us!'

The others looked baffled, as he expected. He went on: 'A war needs a cause. Just or unjust, real or imaginary. And in this case, the Falklands, there is no cause. There might have been, there would have been, if the invasion had been genuine, a prosecution of Argentina's claim which is from their point of view quite just. But the only purpose of this invasion was to rescue Galtieri's government. Pure and simple, first and last, a political exercise. So – no cause, no war!' His audience was beginning to fidget. Hicks held up his hand. 'Wait! Now consider this morning. And the Task Force. The UK government is going to enormous lengths to respond to Galtieri. The cost must be astronomical! But why? They've never before given the slightest indication they regarded the Falklands as important. Very much the opposite, in fact! And the islanders? Well the islands belong to the Falkland Islands Company, the FIC. The entire working population is employed by the FIC. They shop at the company store and drink at the company pub. British citizens, but what do they contribute except to the FIC shareholders? Shouldn't the FIC rescue them then! But no. An armada sails. Roca is taken out – a carrier task group and probably most of the Strategic Tanker Force. Magnificent! But again – why? Politics! I can think of no other reason for the UK to respond like this, no other possible justification – not even the so-called strategic Cape Horn route or the so-far mythical oil deposits – except that it will confer some political advantage upon the party in power. So again – no cause, no state necessity, no threat to national interests – no War! *No es guerra!* What do you say to

179

that? Personally I feel much better about the whole thing.' He did.

'That'll do me! I like it!' LeStrange said enthusiastically. 'But wasn't this morning absolutely *super*!'

'Miles?' Hicks needed to know what Channing thought.

'Well, treason is giving aid and comfort to the enemies of the Queen, and it would certainly be a long strength of the imagination to make the Argentines enemies of the Queen on the strength of the Falklands. I mean, a threat to the security of the realm? Is it? I don't think so. I think you're right, Jeff. And it's said that whatever you do against the state, if it's not treason, it's not morally wrong. I think we're just like Chaucer's old Knight who said, 'I will make war my work' – free to sell our skills. In fact if it weren't for people like us the politicians wouldn't be able to play these sort of games! No – I'm happier now, like you, especially now the pieces are on the board and the numbers down to something more manageable.'

'Me too,' said Tracey. 'That was as good as a cup final this morning!'

Carla, beside Hicks, had seemed asleep. Now she opened her eyes, frowned at Tracey, puzzled, made a little grimace of distaste, and relapsed.

'Doesn't matter a stuff to me,' Finch said in response to Hicks' enquiring glance. 'I was quite happy before. But this raid changes our position here. GEA was special. Now it's not. It'll be just part of the Argentine armed forces and our contract is with the Grupo, specifically. If they split up, and send a squadron here and a squadron there, and the Grupo ceases to exist, we're out of a job. My guess is they won't. The whole point of the Corsair thing is numbers, as Cassián said. He'll want to keep it going, and I hope he gets his way. He's our boss. I don't intend becoming just another Argentine joe working for somebody else.'

Later Hicks said to a sleepy Carla: 'Did you understand all that?'

'No. To me all is crazy. I fight for Argentina, my country! For you? You fight for what? For yourself I thought. But now, you say you fight for Cassián because he is your boss! You men I do not understand. When this is finish, I find ordinary man for 'osband, and 'ave some bebbies.' With which, Carla evanesced into unconsciousness leaving Hicks, in whose arms she lay, deeply and unaccountably lonely.

He hadn't convinced himself. After all the elation of the whirlwind day, that's what it came down to. How fiercely he envied Finch, for the certitude with which he lived his life! And how was it that this lovely woman in his arms had the knack of so painfully putting her finger on the sore patch on his soul?

Chapter 19

Eagle's photographic section rushed prints of Green Leader's film to the captain and the operations room. On deck, refuellers and armourers swarmed over the RAF Harriers. The ship held its breath while the captain with what experts he had pored over the still-damp photographs. They were nearly unanimous. He decided. Roca was neutralised and a re-strike was not necessary. The decision was broadcast to the ship's company. Tension eased, but *Eagle* kept on north-east at 28 knots.

Only Bagshaw seriously disagreed. 'Look,' he said, 'no question we've taken out a hundred on the pan, some in the hangars, and there's a good fire in the storage area – if that's what it is. But Barbary Coast was a response to several *hundred* Corsairs and if they've still got one or two hundred left, the threat remains! I think we should close and re-strike. Like they should have done at Pearl Harbour!'

'But where are they? We've wiped four of their hangars and hit the only other building big enough to hold the rest. Burning well – look!' The brilliant technical success of Barbary Coast was intoxicating; it was easy enough for *Eagle*'s officers to overvalue its results.

Within the hour, facsimile copies of the photographs were on the PI bench in Strike Command HQ. Here were experts aplenty. Using the latest analysis techniques, they confirmed *Eagle*'s interpretation: Newfield had been neutralised. They did add, however, that fax photographs were notoriously unclear.

Next day, when Captain Baldwin received a Staff signal conveying Bagshaw's doubts, he asked Strike to check. They did, and confirmed, pointing out that from the position and extent of the fire a few minutes after the attack, it was reasonable to extrapolate total destruction of the whole long building.

Baldwin paced, snarled and smoked half a packet of cigarettes as he considered this, and said at last: 'Well, my money's on Bagshaw!'

The RAF Harriers flew off *Eagle* five hundred miles out from Ascension. Ward and Bagshaw followed by Sea King from about three hundred miles, caught a returning VC10 and were in London before *Eagle* anchored in East Bay in the small hours of Friday, 23rd April.

'Don't sit down,' was Baldwin's greeting. 'Bring all your papers and come with me.' They left the seething MoD building and went by naval car to Northwood to see the Vice Chief of the Naval Staff, Baldwin's boss. In a far from quiet corner of the map room, while they waited their turn, they reviewed 'Newfield'; from Bagshaw's original, seminal paper, right up to the latest hour-old satellite photographs.

'Hello, Ozzy!' said the Vice Chief when they were admitted. 'Make it snappy, will you – the Boss is due in a few minutes. It's about Barbary Coast, yes?'

'Yes, sir,' Baldwin's mannerisms were forgotten. His thinning hair was rumpled and there was ash on his waistcoat. 'I'm not sure we've neutralised this Corsair threat.'

'Are we ever sure of anything?' The Admiral was sorting papers.

'Fair comment. But if the Task Force goes ahead on the assumption that Barbary Coast was an unqualified success, and it wasn't – then we lose. Of that much I can be sure.'

The Admiral stopped sorting his papers. 'Tell me,' he said. He looked fatigued, though less than the other three.

'All our evidence on Newfield indicates very large numbers of Corsairs. It's all here –' Baldwin tapped Bagshaw's brief case, '– but in summary, we estimated several hundred, you remember. Barbary Coast accounted for about a hundred positively destroyed, a further two hundred probables in the hangars. There could be one or two hundred left, maybe more.'

183

'But the strike leader signalled "Barbarossa". Mission accomplished.'

'And quite rightly, from his point of view, sir.' Baldwin felt for a cigarette, changed his mind. 'But I think, on reflection, the aim might have been unrealistic. And, we must note the Argentines have neither made any public comment on the raid, nor made any change in the disposition of the remaining Corsairs, like moving them forward to the Falklands.' He paused. 'And there's this –' Bagshaw handed over some large prints which Baldwin laid out before the Admiral; '– this is the Harrier's, just after the attack. This is the satellite shot, twenty-five minutes later – no change. But look at this, six hours later: the large hangar totally burnt out. And – you see this new bit here – previously empty ground covered with what my experts tell me is camouflage net. I think it very likely. It fits everything we know about Newfield. It's an ambush. We're expected to think we've neutralised him! He burnt the hangar as soon as he could get his aircraft out! Pound to a pinch of shit they're under the net!'

'Are they that clever?'

'This one is!'

That same afternoon, Ward and Bagshaw helicoptered back to Brize Norton. As the late dusk of the stratosphere closed about their Ascension-bound VC10, they both slept; content; mission accomplished. The Naval Staff had agreed Newfield was still a threat. *Eagle* had been placed under operational control of CinCFleet and assigned the task of dealing with it. She was to be available, as reserve, to the Task Force Commander. Tactics were to be decided locally. The special weapons and equipment ordered by NDA would be airlifted to Ascension next day. There would be no more help from the RAF, whose Harriers and tankers were now fully committed to Operation Corporate.

Lucky bastards, Baldwin muttered, watching his staff officers lifting off at Northwood. The first and probably the last war in his career. He went back to his Whitehall office.

*

184

'Revolutions two one zero. Steer one nine eight degrees.'

'Revolutions two one zero. Steer one nine eight degrees. Able Seaman Lewis on the wheel, sir.'

The Welsh helmsman's voice, relayed from far down in the ship, followed *Eagle*'s captain off the bridge as he made his way down to the ops room. Ascension Island was astern, the two frigates moving into station and their new oiler, *Oakleaf*, following at her best speed. Task Group 16 prepared for the discomfort of another fast passage south. The bridge emptied, leaving only the officer of the watch and the navigator and, out on the flying control wing, the usual 'goofers'. Two Sea Kings were still ashore, awaiting last-minute stores deliveries, mail, and Tuesday's papers. It was Wednesday, 28th April.

In the ops room now began the first of very many conferences, informal, irregular, and attended at one time or another by every weapons and tactics specialist in the ship.

The aim was simply put by Captain Carter. TG 16 was to eliminate the threat from 'Newfield'. And they had only the resources of the Group: six Sea Harriers, six Sea Kings, the two Type 22 frigates and their Wasp helicopters. SSN *Thunderer* was assigned to the Group for anti-submarine, ECM, anti-aircraft picket and SAR duties. Their orders, said the captain with a wry smile, make it clear that their role was to be, if necessary, sacrificial to the aim of all British naval forces in the South Atlantic – getting the Army and Marines ashore in the Falklands. Something about the way he said this made Bagshaw uneasy.

'I wonder if he's taking this seriously,' he said to Ward afterwards.

'Oh yes – up to a point,' replied Ward. 'But as a non-aviator he may not appreciate the threat as we do. Also, I suspect he's a bit miffed at being shunted into a siding. Missing the real action.'

'Do you think you should have a word with him?'

'Good God no!' Ward looked shocked. Then amused. It was just the sort of thing old Bagwash would say.

Not very long after this, in Moscow, at an inter-embassy cocktail party, an unusually slim Russian rear admiral hove purposefully alongside Capitán de Navio Hernando Frietes, the Argentine Naval Attaché.

'How would it suit you, my friend, to know of the departure of a British aircraft carrier group from the Ascension Islands. In the general direction of your country?' The Russian spoke casually. 'Today.'

A fast black car took Frietes though the deserted streets to the Embassy of the Argentine Republic in the Oktoberplatz. TG 16's position, course and speed were encyphered and radioed to Buenos Aires, together with details of the source of the information – Russia's Arktel Radar Ocean Reconnaissance Satellite – and a promise of more information to come.

The captains of two of the Armada's German-built diesel-electric submarines, I.14 and I.16, were called to the office of Contraalmirante Submarinos at Bahia Blanca and given new orders.

Cassián too was informed of *Eagle*'s movements. He had already deduced almost as much. He learned of the departure of the submarines. He hoped they did not succeed: he had come to regard the carrier as his private adversary. Anyway, he supposed a group of modern ships of the Royal Navy, world leaders in anti-submarine warfare, should have little difficulty in dealing with such primitive boats. His knowledge of *Thunderer*, too, was deductive. British SSN's had figured largely in the Junta's thinking on the Malvinas ever since 1976 and he was very much alive to the likelihood of Roca now being monitored from offshore. He proceeded accordingly.

Thus the two members of the SBS section, landed from *Thunderer* in the small hours of Sunday morning after the raid, spent three unrewarding days in an increasingly fetid hole in the ground beside the airfield without being able to see any more than the satellite. Without the benefit of high ground, they could not see the camouflaged aircraft park behind the burnt-out hangars, and counted only twenty-seven whole Corsairs parked about the field, well spread out. Frustrated in his nocturnal attempts to get to the main focus of interest, the storage area, their leader, following his orders, located Hicks.

Hicks was walking between the Rancho and his quarters on Wednesday evening around ten. Carla was with him. From a dark space between two buildings, as they passed, a low voice:

186

'Commander Hicks?'

Hicks felt Carla tense. He stopped.

'Sergeant Thomas. SBS.'

'What do you want?'

'Information.'

Hicks looked around. There was no one in sight.

'Well?'

'Come in here. Off the road.'

'No. What information?'

'Come off the street!'

'No. What do you want to know?'

There was exasperation in the pause.

'How many of these bleeding Corsairs have they got left? Just one figure.'

Carla had released his arm and was standing away, looking at his face.

'I don't know.'

'Roughly.'

Hicks had recovered from his surprise and was thinking now. I'm on the spot. I am a pivot. People will die. Who dies, how many, hangs on this moment. On me. This was the big leap. All the moral callisthenics of the last year, training for this. Watershed. Rubicon. He looked at Carla. Her face was blank.

He was conscious of having run on a black boulder of doubt. For the first time in weeks Pauline came into his thoughts, conjured by this English voice. And the voice with its undertone of trust and respect gave him another pang. Trying to think, and not to think, he felt himself being pulled across a line. It was unfair. A tug-of-war with the ground not level. He was giving, slipping. But this was a time for instinct, and when on a gust of wind he got a scent of the desert and remembered Tim, and Carla moved, still close enough for him to touch, Hicks dug in.

'Sergeant Thomas, believe me it's good to see you here! Wonderful! But I can't tell you anything. It wouldn't be right. Tell them that. They should understand. Now you'd better get away while you can. Quickly! Good luck!'

He said this to an imaginary blackfaced commando, beret, knife, sub-machine gun, in the black opening of the alley.

187

There was no reply. It needed a great effort of will to turn away from the menacing dark alleyway. Hicks took Carla's arm. She jerked it free, gave him a long look of puzzlement and anger, then turned and ran back towards the Rancho. Hicks looked after her for a few moments before his shoulders dropped and he turned and walked the other way.

Soon after, sirens sounded. Troops turned out. Nothing was found. Hicks described the encounter to Cassián whose eyebrows expressed recognition of the tacit declaration of fealty. The baffled Sergeant Thomas and his partner were picked up the next night by rubber boat. *Thunderer* embarked them safely before moving off to resume her patrol.

Hicks met LeStrange, who said to him, 'Well Jeff, I'm not sure I could have done it. Not when it comes to it, just like that.'

'I think you might have surprised yourself, Pierre. Like me.'

'Tell me something. Honest answer. Did it make any difference Carla being there?'

'Quote: no man does anything for one reason alone.'

LeStrange thought about that for a while, then said, 'Hmm. I believe you. And I'll tell you why. A year ago, six months ago, they could have pulled my fingernails out before I'd do what you just did. I mean it. And I'd have said anybody that did it should be shot. But do you know, from this distance, down here, that all seems a bit silly now. I mean,' his brow creased, 'are we men, or are we pawns?'

'Profound question, Pierre! I think it answers itself.'

'How's that?'

'Well, a pawn wouldn't ask, would it?' Hicks wasn't nearly as sanguine about his action as these glib answers suggested, but the benevolent pragratism that ruled his life admitted error and confusion and all the consequences. He couldn't expect to get it right every time. Fifty-one percent was his target. He weighed loss and pain against profit and happiness, aggregated them among all concerned and hoped to come out a nose ahead. Anything else was profit.

So he wasn't surprised when Carla moved out. In a period of tension, frustration and boredom at Roca, affecting every-one, Hicks felt something had to happen. An emotional

188

thunderstorm to clear the air. This was his. She had brought little with her, so her departure was quick and clean. And she gave no more an explanation of why she left than why she came, nor seemed to think one needed. He had thought himself prepared. She was nothing if not wayward. It was her charm. Yet Hicks, its willing victim, was devastated. Raw and callow in this, despite himself, he suffered twisting pangs of loss and took small comfort from the fact that Carla appeared to have no other attachment. Her breezy normality made it worse. He likened her to Masefield's stately Spanish galleon: the wind had changed, she had backed her yards and sailed off on another tack, unheeding of her wake.

He still saw a lot of her. She was a close friend of a girl who had, uniquely, engaged the affections of Tracey. Consuela Donován was another striking example of Argentina's racial blending: taller than ideal, with long oval face, strong nose, drooping eyes and dark hair from the depth of which, in certain lights, Celtic copper surfaced, she was a -S fighter section leader in 3 Squadron, and she was good. Drawn together in work, she deployed quite spontaneously around Tracey a mixture of respect and that innate erotic wisdom that Southern women have not lost, and he found this agreeable. They had lived together some weeks.

With so little to do – Cassián was permitting only a dozen or so flights per day – the *pulpería* became more than ever a social centre. Hicks could only avoid it at the cost of complete isolation, so he frequently came across Carla. She was friendly, and cheerful, but with never an echo of past intimacy. Hicks tried to match her uncanny insouciance, knowing he failed.

'Oh what can ail thee, knight-at-arms?' Miles Channing quoted quietly one day.

Hicks grinned ruefully. 'Is it that obvious?' When Channing didn't reply he added, 'Well I can tell you this – without her, no birds sing!'

189

Chapter 20

Apps was in the control room when the signal ordering *Thunderer* to leave her patrol area off Roca was handed to the Captain. 'Good-oh!' exclaimed the flight lieutenant. The submarine was assigned to TG 16 under *Eagle*'s tactical command, to rendezvous as soon as possible. Visions of fresh air, sky, space, expanded in Apps' head. *Thunderer*'s crew had been wonderfully hospitable, and it had been a very interesting experience, but twelve days as a sardine was enough. Now he would soon be out of the tin.

'You'll be lucky!' He gathered, when the laughter died down, that HM SSNs on patrol surface only for emergencies. Appendicitis, say.

He saw the problem fed into the Nav computer. The helm moved automatically, the deck tilted, and by the time the big submarine was settled on her new course the position and time of the rendezvous had been outprinted on the officer of the watch's table. Sunday, 2nd May. Three days to the next excitement. In the interest of his Service, Apps tried to keep a stiff upper lip, but it was hard. At the rendezvous he was allowed to look at *Eagle* through the periscope. He could see her deck park of Sea Harriers, a Sea King, rotors running, some people moving and close ahead the tanker, low in the water with her black hoses slung out. Apps remembered 'RAS' – replenishment at sea – from his own passage in *Eagle*. Passage to Purgatory. Perhaps he would write a book.

Thunderer went deep, made some bathytherm readings and then took station about three miles ahead of *Eagle* at a depth of ninety feet. The Group was making fourteen knots, base course 201 degrees. Roca was still over 2,000 miles ahead, but already *Eagle*'s Sea Kings and the frigates were deployed in an anti-submarine screen of which *Thunderer* became in effect the senior member. When the RAS was over, the group increased to eighteen knots, the two frigates eight miles abreast, *Thunderer* between them and a little ahead, and *Eagle* and *Oakleaf* in line astern well behind the submarine. Sea Kings hovered ahead with their transducers also at ninety feet, listening, lifting and moving forward every ten minutes or so to keep station on the group. The Argentine submarines' best submerged speed was only ten knots, so they could only threaten the Group from ahead. Two of them were known to be at sea, I-14 and I-16.

Squeezed into a corner of the tense control room, Apps witnessed the destruction of I-16. The regret in the captain's orders, 'Fire one! . . . Fire two!' The tension in the forty-second wait for the distant explosion. The hush that greeted it: *Thunderer*'s crew, like him, imagining the crashing inrush of water, quick horrible cold squeezing death. This was war. Paid fingers, like his, pressing buttons, articulating politics. Win some, lose some. Where for instance was the second Argentine sub? Out there? Somewhere in the water that was making his back cold . . .!

'Contact faded,' sonar reported. Fragments of I-16, torn apart by the wire-guided Tigerfish were drifting down towards the ocean bed.

'Resume station.' The regret was over. The submarine they had killed had been manoeuvring with unmistakably hostile intent. 'Now. Two questions:' the captain spoke to the generality; 'how did they know where we were? And where's the other bastard?'

The second question was soon answered. I-14 had used a cold layer to escape detection until very late. When she came to periscope depth for the attack, *Eagle*, having turned to evade I-16, was less than six miles away, bow on, at full speed. *Aurora*'s sonar acquired the submarine straight away. A flash warning apprised *Eagle*'s captain of the danger in his path. He ordered 'Steady as you go', and the 25,000-ton carrier charged on towards the submarine. Through his periscope, Capitán de Corbeta Buendías watched her coming as long as he dared before he crash-dived back into the shelter of the cold layer. *Eagle*'s propellers threshed overhead as he went down, then faded into silence. Silence. Motors stopped, hardly breathing, I-14 drifted down. They had heard I-16 go. There was no mistaking the single watery bang. A Tigerfish, an SSN, a hunter-killer. I-14's crew aged in the silence, two miles above the ocean floor.

But they were safe. 'Resume base course,' ordered *Eagle*'s captain. *Thunderer* was called off. The second submarine, now astern and deep, was no threat, could not possibly catch up. If it approached later, in the operating area, it would be dealt with.

'Make a signal.' The government was informed. No need to underline the implications of an intercept of a fast carrier group in mid-ocean by two slow submarines. TG 16 was being tailed. Satellite or nuke, Russian. Another card on the table. Argentina would be unwise to publish the loss.

'But they'll be more careful, in future,' said Captain Carter from his high swivel chair on the port side of *Eagle*'s bridge.

'Gutsy though – you have to admit, sir,' said Ward.

'There's a fine line between bravery and bravado. Difference is –' the captain sucked with noisy appreciation at a cup of tea, '– one is intelligent, the other isn't.'

'I think he's happier now,' said Ward to Bagshaw later. 'Congratulating himself, Task Group Commander, first blood.'

'Less disposed to caution, then, you think?'

'I would say so.'

'That's bad news,' predicted Bagshaw from his bunk.

The success of the strike depended upon good weather at Newfield, but the Task Group needed bad weather in the launch area. The Sea Harrier's unrefuelled range with a useful load was only about 250 miles, so for many hours either side of launch and recovery, *Eagle* would be well in range of attack by Corsairs, not to mention other Argentine air. To place the TG in this position in good weather for the best part of a whole day would be suicidal. The staff officers had joined *Eagle*'s Commander (Air) in advising caution.

But Captain Carter, very conscious of his unusual good

fortune in not having an admiral over him, and expanding into his new responsibility, took a wider view. The Invasion Force was on its way. *It* would have to come in range of Argentine air, eventually. The *Canberra*, thin-skinned and defenceless, thousands of soldiers. Supply ships, tankers, the whole armada. If the Corsair force was as powerful, and naval AA defences as weak, as was being suggested, then *their* mission surely would be suicidal – unless the Corsairs were destroyed. This was TG 16's task. And it was jeopardised by every hour of delay. As for waiting for the right weather, could anybody think of a part of the world with less met data than Southern Patagonia? He ordered preparations for an attack upon Newfield as soon as possible, leaving the details to the aviators.

'There is no point in our being here,' he told them, 'other than to strike. Hard. And first. Come what may.'

Ironically, Barbary Coast II was delayed by bad weather which set in from the south-west soon after the submarine encounter. Thick cloud hid the TG's movements but Carter had to reduce speed to avoid damage to deck-parked aircraft. In the afternoon of Thursday, 6th May he made a radical alteration to the east away from Roca, while *Thunderer* swept his wake. There was no shadowing Soviet. Confident that for so long as the cloud cover lasted his movements were secret, Carter refuelled all his ships and detached the oiler. The carrier and the two lean grey frigates dissolved into the dusk: unlit, blind and silent, making 30 knots direct for Roca, range 620 miles.

At 0830GMT, 0330 local time, *Eagle* slowed to launch two Sea Harriers into a southerly wind which though still strong had lost its anger. Before the second jet had vanished off the bow, starboard helm was on to bring the carrier back to base course, revolutions increasing. At 30 knots again, her over-hanging bow dealt roughly with the cross swell which retaliated by hurling what sounded like solid water up against the bridge windows. Far aft, six more jets, pre-armed and fuelled, stood chained down on the deserted flight deck, chocked and shrouded.

After half an hour or so, the carrier slowed again, turned

into wind while one of the Sea Harriers landed on. Impatience thick enough to cut filled the crowded silent bridge as engineers and armourers with shaded torches secured and refuelled it, dropped its buddy-pack refuelling pod and winched two 1000 lb bombs onto its outer wing stations. It didn't take long, but the BC II clock was set and running, seconds precious.

'Starboard twenty. Steer 248 degrees. Revolutions two three zero.' At last. Back on course, making thirty miles every hour, fifty knots of black wind and water over the deck, *Eagle* headed again for Newfield.

At 38,000 feet, first hints of dawn accentuated the loneliness of the tiny speck tipping a steel-grey contrail. Lieutenant Lee had never in his life felt so alone, so tenuous. The post-launch rendezvous and refuelling, zip-lipped, had left him sweating. Now in the velvet quiet of the stratosphere, he could hear his breath, the rhythmic gushes of oxygen, the little clicks of the valves in his mask. Familiar, comfortable. But not this isolation; this total silence; these vertiginous distances in an alien hemisphere. This compound of uncertainties.

Lieutenant Lee retreated from such thoughts, sought comfort in routine. Although there was little to do. The INS would take him to the target. If it didn't, his mission would abort: his two loads of SDW spikes would not be delivered; Newfield would not be disabled. Lee retreated too from that line of thought. The first faint indications from his Passive Warning Receiver, that he was entering the fringe of Newfield's search radar lobe, was comforting. Something human at last. He dropped below the lobe and went on.

Lieutenant Lee would have been, if possible, even less comfortable about his mission if he had known that at the moment he began his descent *Eagle* was in an emergency turn away from a submarine reported by the starboard screen frigate – a close-range surface sighting in poor light but emphatically a submarine, according to the look-out. Nearly forty minutes of confusion followed until, in improving light, the submarine became a school of whales. There was no way to make up the lost time, which translated into fifty miles extra flying for the

194

strike. Also, the wind was backing through south: *Eagle*'s flying course would take her away from the target, stretching the distance even further.

Carter considered delay, but it would be perilous for the ships. Four Sea Harriers launched on schedule at theoretical maximum range with two 1,000 lb air-burst fragmentation bombs each. The fifth jet – sixteen percent of *Eagle*'s striking power – hung askew in the starboard catwalk where the emergency turn, cross-swell, had thrown it, damaged beyond local repair. In silence the pilots climbed through the thick but lightening overcast, formed up on top and with INS computers locked to the Newfield co-ordinates, headed south-west.

But BCII was a total failure, and worse. The southern autumn threw a light south-westerly wind across a random eddy of the cold Falkland current. Blowing onshore at Roca, the wind carried thick sea-fog inland for miles.

'Red Leader this is Ploughman.' Lieutenant Lee. The first transmission of the day, on UHF Strike Common.

'Red Leader, go.' Dusty Miller, Sea-Jet squadron CO and strike leader.

'Ploughman is aborting. Target obscured. Fog. Tops about a thousand.'

'Roger Ploughman.' A pause. 'Any room underneath?'

'Negative. It's solid.'

And so it was. Miller checked. He had to. He let down off the coast and ran in on radar and radar altimeter. 100 feet, nothing. 50 feet and grey-white water flicking past below, the bottom of a goldfish-bowl of cotton wool. Miller pulled back up into the clear, made a quick circuit of the area, rocked his wings and climbed away northeast, followed by the others.

'Red Four. Leader has a bogey, seven o'clock, low.'

Miller banked left and looked down. He saw, just above the cloud-tops, a Corsair.

Chapter 21

Light sleepers at Roca had grown used to hearing the dawn-alert CAP warming engines. Four armed Corsair -S's out by the duty runway; start, run, shut-down; start, run, shut-down. From an hour before dawn, their engine temperatures were kept up, ready for instant scramble, pilots strapped in.

But on Friday, 7th May, even heavy sleepers were awake at dawn. There is menace in the howl of a Harrier's Pegasus, even muffled by thick fog. The noise was almost the first warning: the rolling roar of Lieutenant Lee's engine confirmed what Roca's radar operators could only suspect from the faint green flashes on their screen as he approached at twenty feet.

'Scramble!'

Four Pratt & Whitneys whined and coughed. Condensation, cold like rain, blew back off windscreens into pilots' faces. Sweet exhaust fumes mingled with sea-smelling mist. Gauges steadied. Gropingly, dangerously, four Corsairs followed the high-intensity lighting out onto the runway and took off in turn, blind. None of them could tell whether or not they stayed on the runway. It didn't matter.

The initial glamour of dawn-alert CAP had not lasted. After nearly four weeks, it was the pits, an asshole job. No. 2 of Mamba section that morning was Guardiamarina Margarita Madrigál, a plain serious girl of twenty-five with deep religious eyes, once a teacher and now an averagely competent -S pilot. She had no time to think during the scarey take-off. She retracted her gear as soon as she had a reading on her altimeter, put Armament Master ON, G.W. ARM, trimmed into the climb at 170 knots and flew the gauges.

It got rapidly lighter and then, abruptly, Guardiamarina Madrigál was in the clear on top, Mamba Leader half a mile ahead. She saw Miller's Harrier first, up ahead, and then the others, sharp silhouettes up against the alto-stratus. She jinked left, clawing towards her battle station half a mile abeam her leader. Looking back at the first Harrier, she saw two tiny black things fall away. Drop tanks. Or bombs. The jet banked left, holding its height a few thousand feet above, circling, looking down, curious. It was joined by another. The Corsairs, all four in the clear now, climbed on southeast, out over the hidden sea. 2,000 feet and now the two jets were behind. The others had vanished.

Mamba Leader turned ninety left, allowing the second pair of Corsairs to come abreast at two miles. Guardiamarina Madrigál slid under her leader onto his outside, eyes still on the two menacing jets. 3,000 feet. The Harriers were climbing with them, keeping their distance, slow and wary.

Then they swooped, one on each pair of Corsairs. Mamba Leader held his course, climbing straight northeast, drawing the cannon-armed Harriers into line astern. Calmly, Guard-iamarina Madrigál watched the sharp-nosed jet sliding down on her leader's tail. When it was at 500 metres, she called:

'Mamba – Break!'

Mamba Leader broke into a hard left turn, taking the Harrier with him. Guardiamarina Madrigál followed, but more leisurely to open the range. She had never flown a jet. They had been told about the Harrier and its vectored thrust. It didn't seem to like the instant 4½g of Mamba Leader's 150-knot Corsair. It rocked, probably on the stall buffet, and slid outside the Corsair's turn. She could see the jet's thick curling plume of exhaust smoke. Her Sidewinders acquired with a low growl that crescendoed as the Harrier's tail swung across her nose. There was no time to think. Guardiamarina Madrigál's well-drilled finger flipped up the safety cover and pulled the trigger. There was a flash, smoke, debris; a rearing, twisting fuselage; an ejection seat; and, as the dead Harrier tumbled into the cloud tops and disappeared, a parachute. All silent, and leaving Guardiamarina Madrigál open-mouthed with shock.

Lieutenant-Commander Miller too saw the explosion. Incredulity braked his reactions, and he nearly met the same fate. But he snap-rolled inverted, closed his throttle and pulled to the buffet two seconds before a pair of Sidewinders curved past just out of range. Miller dived for the fog bank and didn't emerge until he was ten miles out, homeward-bound, a little dazed and uncomfortably short of fuel.

The fog lasted until afternoon. The CAP remained overhead Roca for four hours before diverting to San Julian, down the coast, for fuel. They returned as soon as they could.

Guardiamarina Madrigál's first question was about the Harrier pilot. She was overjoyed to hear he had been rescued from the sea. He was in the base hospital with a broken arm and cuts. Diffidently, she went to see him.

Lieutenant Newson, a punchy young man though over-weight, was under sedation for shock. His arm had been set, his face stitched. A nurse told him: 'You have a visitor. The pilot who shoot you down. OK?'

Incomprehension. Who is this? This girl. The pilot rig, dirty face, ragged hair. He sniffed. She smelled of aeroplane. A shy smile twitched her sombre features. Concern was in her deep-set Catholic eyes.

'Allo,' she said.

'Hello.'

She tried again to smile, made a little gesture at his plastered arm.

'You OK?'

'Yeah. I'm fine.'

'I sorry.'

'What for?'

'I shoot you down.'

'You?' It was not said nicely.

'*Si*. Me.' The chin came up.

He looked at her, drowsily, for a long time. They were alone in the cool silence. The girl became conscious of herself, dishevelled, her sweat and aeroplane smell an intrusion in the sterile ward. She made an attempt to straighten her hair.

'What's your name?' he asked.

198

'I am Margarita Madrigál. I am guardiamarina in CANA.'

'Margarita Madrigál.' He said it slowly, making great stress on the final syllable. 'Margarita Madrigál.'

'Is it much pain?'

He smiled. Shook his head. 'No pain. No pain at all.' He reached, just a little, towards her with his undamaged hand.

She had no time to think. She took the hand in both of hers and squeezed it as she said, over and over: *Gracias a Dios! Gracias a Dios!* She kissed the hand. When she looked up, to ask him his name, Lieutenant Newson was asleep.

While Margarita Madrigál stood examining the bruised features of her victim, now in childlike repose, and still holding his hand, Hicks was beginning to observe, in Contraalmirante Cassián, signs of a behaviour pattern that surprised him.

Roca's response, long-planned, to *Eagle*'s approach, was an immediate maximum launch of Corsairs for an armed search. Sixty Bravos had taken off in fog, as they were readied, during the morning, and flown out on radial tracks, biased towards *Eagle*'s predicted position, to a range of 500 miles. They found nothing but a classic cyclonic wind pattern with precipitation and low cloud covering most of the search area. They would have had to be within half a mile, the returning pilots said, to pick up the carrier. They weren't that lucky.

Cassián knew about the depression. Long Range Maritime Patrol aircraft were available, C-130's, P2-V Neptunes and even the Navy's S2-F Trackers, all with radar that could have penetrated the cloud and rain and located the carrier with ease. The Commodore's staff urged him to use them.

'No,' he had said, 'this is GEA business. *I* will deal with this carrier!'

The *I* had been the first intimation, to Hicks, that Cassián was personalising. At the time it had seemed improbable, a slip. Now, with the bombers back – one crashed on take-off, another lost three hundred miles out with engine failure – it seemed more likely: the Commodore was unrepentant about not using LRMP, and ordered preparations for the search to be resumed at first light next day.

199

'But, Contraalmirante,' Monegario argued, 'that is twelve hours. The ships will be out of range!'

'Not so, my friend!' Greasy unshaven faces and crumpled clothes, signs of a day that had begun too early and too suddenly. 'Consider –' Cassián lit another cigar '– the captain of this carrier, this *Eagle*. He has come here for one reason. Only one. To kill the Corsair! You agree, Jeff?'

'Yes.' Kill Carla too, if he can.

'And so far, what has he done? Nothing! One Harrier is lost. He has how many more? Eight? Ten? It doesn't matter. He *must* try again! How can a commander come three thousand miles then turn around and go away after one attempt? Is this the Royal Navy? Jeff, I ask you this.'

'He will be concerned for the safety of his ship. He could be accused of bad judgement if he puts unprotected ships in range of land-based air.'

'Ah! Unprotected? But he has a squadron of the latest fighters, with the best weapons. He has also frigates with guided missiles. Unprotected?'

'You know, Commodore, he has no defence against the Corsair, in numbers.'

'*I* know that! *You* know that! But does *he*? Do *they* – those that send him?'

'I've said before: *they* must rate Roca and the Corsair very high!'

'Hm. Maybe. That does not mean they *really* know what I can do! I want to show them!' Cassián got up from the chair he had taken over in a corner of the Ops room, brushed the ash from his uniform as he looked around at the disordered desks and consoles, put on his cap. He pointed to the wall map, a large black area of which had just been cleaned of search tracks. 'Out there, tonight, he is planning, and wondering. Tomorrow –'

Without warning, several things happened at once. The building was rocked by a deafening explosion. Files, books, overfilled ashtrays, anything loose, rose into the air and scattered themselves on the floor. Hicks grabbed a table to steady himself, conscious through the ringing in his ears of the shriek of a Harrier passing overhead. Monegario sat down, involuntarily, in the chair he had just vacated. And Cassián staggered sideways into a radar console and gripped its rounded steel edge. That much Hicks saw before the lights went out.

Then from above the chilling sound of glass, and screams. Hicks made for the door in the dusty gloom. He could hear the incipient screech of the next jet. Frantic, he ran, thrusting unceremoniously down through the ant-like confusion of four flights of stairs until he was outside the main door. He *had* to see! Outside, he ran round the corner of the building until he could see to the east. He almost cheered the Harrier as it flashed overhead close enough for him to see its oily belly panels. He wanted to wave his arms and cheer. Fantastic!

Then another blast hit him like a fist and knocked him to the ground where he decided to stay; deaf, dizzy and dirty but choked with emotion. There would be another! Yes – there he is! Hammering in from the north-east; silent still – keeping up with his soundprint; 600 knots maybe; couple of hundred feet; two bombs; thousand-pounders; but parachutes! Retard bombs! Beautiful! Two tiny eggs, sown in the air a thousand yards from Hicks. As the Harrier went past, well out of danger, the bombs went off almost simultaneously. Hicks covered his ears.

He watched two more Harriers drop air-burst bombs off to his left in the direction of the storage area, then the fifth and last aircraft, slower than the others, showered the whole airfield with metal spikes from about two thousand feet. Then just the vanishing rumble of the last jet in the yellow evening sky. Hicks got up, brushed himself, looked around. He felt sheepish – not a familiar experience. Emotion was unprofessional, especially the gut-wrenching variety that had gripped him as the Harriers scalded Roca with their brutal sound and fury. He had wanted to dance and yell! But why? It was important to know. He decided it was plain relief: *Eagle* had been in grave danger, but with every bomb that burst above the airfield sending blast and shrapnel among the dispersed Corsairs that had so recently returned from hunting her, her prospects improved. Anyway, out of the emotion was born, willy-nilly, an idea.

Hicks composed himself and went to find the Commodore.

'Seventeen destroyed. Fifteen heavy damage. Some light damage.' Bolsano, the engineering boss, uniform streaked with oil, shrugged as he finished reading from a dirty piece of paper. They were in the ops room, tidied and swept in the two hours since the raid. 'It is very slow, because of these *clavos*, these spikes.'

'Propellers?' Monegario asked.

'We lose about twenty. I think. I will know better in daylight.'

After a pause, Monegario said: 'Contraalmirante, will you cancel the strike tomorrow morning? There will be few aircraft ready. And the spikes –'

'No!' Cassián had said little so far. 'It is no longer important, but the launch must go ahead, as many as possible.'

'No longer important, Contraalmirante?' Figari, OC One, asked.

'No. GEA has other interests now.' Hicks raised his eyebrows at Finch. Cassián went on: '*Eagle* will withdraw, after this. There will be no need to repeat, he will think, and it is dangerous to remain so close. So – we prepare now for the real battle. The British have big ships to carry their troops. You have heard. The liner *Canberra* has already left Ascension Island. Two thousand men. They hope to land on *Las Malvinas*, so they will have to come in range of the Corsairs of Roca, no?'

'*Si*, Contraalmirante!' The Argentines grinned.

'And then . . .' Cassián stood up, '. . . then, with even fifty Corsairs, forty, I make a carousel around this ship and – *wham!*' he punched his hand, 'Can you miss, a target so big? How will the British troops enjoy your bombs! Imagine the effect! Bomb after bomb down through the decks, in through the side of the ship. Exploding inside. Think of the luxury furniture, how well it will burn!'

Soto was still grinning, but Hicks caught flickers of doubt, even distaste, on the faces of one or two others. The room stank of dust and disturbance. The radar scopes were dead. From upstairs, again the sound of glass. Flying glass had caused horrific casualties up there. Everybody was dirty. Hicks was hungry and he wanted to get away from Cassián.

'This time,' the Commodore was saying, 'GEA will cooperate with other units to locate the target. Kondor Boeing will guide you, so Corsair effort will be all offensive, concentrated. Maximum numbers. The world will see your power! You have one week. Progress meetings daily. That is all.'

'Contraalmirante, in view of this new directive, will you reconsider tomorrow's strike? In my opinion, it can only jeopardize the main aim.'

'No!' said the usually mild Cassián, harshly. 'Maximum effort, armed search, at first light! Get these *clavos* . . .' he spat the word, 'off my airfield and fly! They will not expect it, and the forecast is good.'

'Very good, Contraalmirante,' Monegario replied politely, and they got up to go.

'The British will remain,' Cassián ordered.

'You will be glad to know,' he told them when the others had gone, 'that I have decided to terminate your contracts. From now.'

'Terminate? Or complete?' Finch asked, sharply.

'What is the difference?'

'The money.'

'You will be paid. You have done your work.' Cassián spoke, it seemed to Hicks, as if his mind were elsewhere. A cascade of glass came down the stairs outside the door as the clearing up went on. The lights flickered and dimmed, recovered. 'Training is complete. There is no need, now, for you to fly. You must of course to remain at Roca, until we finish this business.' Hicks heard the absence of interest in his voice.

Without comment they all went down to ground level and out the main door. Out on the darkened airfield, people moved in little pools of light, tending damaged planes. Mechanical sweepers, echelonned like minesweepers, were roaring up and down the parking apron. Other motor transport being paralysed, there was nothing for it but to walk carefully, with torches.

'Commodore,' said Hicks softly, 'if I were *Eagle*'s captain I would strike again tomorrow at dawn.' He said this almost against his will, but he was unable to suppress a picture of Carla, who was down to fly the next morning, sitting in a bombed-up Corsair out on the airfield when the Harriers arrived with their airburst frags.

203

Cassián walked on in silence. Hicks picked up a shining, evil-sharp prong from their path; he wished he could see the other's face.

'No,' came the reply at last. 'I don't think so.'

They parted. Hicks' idea had become an intention. But before anything, now, he wanted Carla. Hungry and dirty, he sought her, through the public rooms and finally, unmindful of curious stares in the corridors of the junior officers' block, he went to her room and knocked on the door.

Her hair was a mess and her thin legs inelegant. She had done a hurried job of covering her nakedness with a bathrobe. Her face was blank.

After a pause, he said, 'I can come in?'

A flicker. She held open the door.

'You are tired. You want some coffee?'

'Yes. Coffee would be good.' Hicks sat down on her warm bed. There wasn't much choice in the small room. Carla fiddled and produced the coffee.

'So.' She gave him the cup, sat down on a pile of clothes on a chair. They looked stonily at each other.

'You want to know why I come?' he asked.

'You want to sleep with me.'

Hicks thought about this for a moment. Then he began to laugh. As he hadn't laughed for a very long time. Carla looked severe. She took the mug which was in danger of spilling, put it on the desk. She stood up, still severe. But suddenly she caught the infectious emotion in Hicks's behaviour and her face split into a wide happy grin and she moved forward as she began to laugh and she took his head in her hands and she pressed his face into her belly to quiet him as his arms came around her.

After a long time, she stepped back and looked down at him.

'You do not have the *maldejada*?'

That set him off again, a mild hysteria of relief. When he could, he said: 'Will you come back?'

She made a moué, became serious, thought for a while.

'You want to know why I leave?'

'If you want to tell me.'

'Because I do not like a man to fight against his own country.'

204

'I understand that. *Comprendo muy bien*. But now, it is finished.' He explained.

'That is now. But you did what you did.'

'I did nothing – except help train the Grupo.'

'You refused information to the British soldier.'

'And I would again. I do not betray a trust.'

'Hm.' Carla shrugged her narrow shoulders.

A little later, in his rooms, Hicks said, 'I'm hungry!'

'Eeks, you're *always* hungry!' wailed Carla, as he dragged her out through the door, hoping the restaurant hadn't closed.

He didn't tell her why it was so important for him to eat just then.

Chapter 22

Carla was briefing next morning at 0400. Hicks got up too, saw her off, then after a hurried conference with Finch he made his way unobtrusively down to the dark offices, collected his flying kit and set out across the blacked-out airfield to the south side. When he remembered, he shuffled: to step on a prong now would be disastrous.

His plan was based upon his belief that *Eagle* would restrike this morning. The second strike yesterday, a brilliant stroke, had told him a lot about *Eagle*'s captain. Not a man to leave a job half done. One more raid would be risky, but not impossibly so, depending mainly upon the movement of the depression, and he would be surprised if such a daring commander failed to use his last chance. Surprised – and possibly dead, Hicks told himself melodramatically as he trudged across the dusty field.

But as he saw it, he too had just one window of opportunity, and he had decided to take it. He distrusted the decision: it owed more to impulse than to reason. Time would tell.

He found a lone Corsair. The ground crew hadn't arrived yet. He checked it out with his torch: full fuel, no bombs, but a splinter hole in the fuselage. Around the perimeter track to the next one. Full fuel, two bombs, no damage. Still dark, and some noise and movement here and there on the field. He BIT-tested the Corsair's IFF transponder, vital to his plan – such as it was! He would take off an hour before dawn.

He moved off into the darkness and sat down. The weather had improved. The damp sea-smell had gone and Roca smelled dry, continental, as Hicks remembered it from that

206

first day, but colder. It might be such a morning, when the sun came up. The first time he had seen her, and the image of her lean black-clad figure branded somewhere in him. A part of him ached, so he tried to move his mind onto the task ahead.

Presently, a truck came and dumped two engineers who pre-flighted the Corsair. When the time came, Hicks walked out of the darkness. *'Buenas días!'* He wore GEA flying kit and carried his 'bonedome'. One of them had a walkie-talkie. Hicks asked to borrow it, pretended to speak to the tower, fumbled and dropped the thing heavily, stamping on it in the dark for good measure before handing it back with apologies.

'It doesn't matter,' the man said good-humouredly.

'I'll use the aircraft radio.' Hicks' Spanish was imperfect – all verbs in the infinitive and no regard to gender, he had seen it once described.

He started up, aware of the curiosity – probably no higher than that – the premature noise would arouse. Infinitely slowly, since though the night had cracked into pre-dawn he could still barely see enough to avoid the other parked Corsairs, he taxied to the end of the nearest runway – Three Six, due north, and of course unlit. He took off, a long, long run across the invisible field with the south-west wind behind the heavy aircraft. Airborne at last, a little pool of light passed down his left side. Then just the empty Patagonian blackness, and a quivering array of green dials. He banked right towards the sea.

Out over the sea he dumped the bombs and set the Corsair up for fast cruise at 200 knots, 2,000 feet. This was a one-way ride and he wasn't interested in economy. He set the IFF transponder to Code 1234. If *Eagle* were out there, and if she was interrogating, 1234 would tell the operator the pilot was probably British, as it was a UK airspace code for non-controlled flights.

An hour passed, and it was light enough to see clouds ahead. When he could see the surface he noted the wind: northerly, moderate. The depression was to the east. The big P&W was running like a watch. The cloud was only broken cumulus, no high stuff except maybe way down to the south-east, to his right. He climbed above the cumulus layer, and then turned right. If *Eagle* were anywhere, she would be under what was left of the depression, not exposed out here in this brightening seascape.

An hour and a half. Stage II. Hicks switched IFF to Code 7700, international distress squawk. It would trigger an automatic alarm on any radar. If, etc etc etc . . . He changed frequency to 243.0 Mhz, international distress.

Two hours. Hicks flew on towards the cloudbank. He figured he could make land from 400 miles, if he found nothing. Dump the Corsair and hoof it. He was beginning to feel foolish. What would that have achieved, for God's sake? Except making life awkward for the other Brits.

Stage III. 'MAYDAY MAYDAY MAYDAY. This is Commander Hicks, Royal Navy, flying an Argentine Navy Corsair, I have vital information for the safety of the Falklands Task Force. Calling any British ship. I say again . . .'

Some twenty minutes later, Hicks was startled by a Sea Harrier, sharp-nosed, blue-grey and very close, sliding forward under his right wing. In his surprise and relief, he banked a little towards it, to get a better view. Instantly the jet seemed to stop in mid-air. It vanished astern. A voice, very loud, on the radio:

'Corsair 34. Keep straight and level!' Hicks flew very straight.

'Now rock your wings if you are reading me.' He did.

'I'm coming in below to check your wing-stations. Hold it steady.'

'Yankee Tango, Blue Leader. Single Corsair side number three four, clean. Heading one four five, speed two hundred.'

Another voice, almost as loud: 'Yankee Tango, roger. Corsair 34, this is Yankee Tango, what is your intention?'

Hicks turned down the volume. 'This is Commander Hicks, Jeff Hicks, last of 836 Squadron.'

'Go ahead.' Hostility and caution in the voice.

'I have information for you.'

A long pause, then: 'Who was your Senior Pilot in 836?'

'John Ward.' And the reply came back, with no hesitation:

'Turn right heading two six zero. Strangle parrot.' Hicks switched off the IFF as he turned, the Harrier still loose to starboard.

'Thirty-four what are your intentions?' Still in company with the Harrier after twenty minutes. Hicks sighted *Eagle* and the two frigates plunging towards him at high speed, under a shelf of cold front nimbo-stratus. The question came as they over-flew the carrier.

'Land on –or bale out,' he replied, eyes on the small wet pitching deck below him.

'What is your endurance?'

'Three hours.' At least.

'Stand by.' The Harrier landed on and Hicks was left circling alone.

'Thirty-four, what is your landing speed?'

'Ninety knots.'

'Roger. We can give you forty-five over the deck.'

Eagle was a standard CVS, much narrower and shorter than the CVAs of Hicks's day. She had no arrester wires. On the other hand, the CVS had the 'ski-jump' ramp for'd. If he touched down at 90 knots, his speed relative to the ship would be only 45. Landing well aft, he would have four hundred feet to stop, including the ski-jump. Feasible. Worth a try. Better than stepping out of a perfectly serviceable aircraft into thin air over deep water.

'Thirty-four, you clear the car park, I'll give it a go.' There were five Harriers and three Sea Kings on deck.

'Thirty-four, roger. Captain gives you ten minutes max.'

'Thirty-four, roger.' Then as an afterthought, 'Request captain's name?'

'Yankee Tango is Captain Carter.'

'*Cathy* Carter?' He couldn't resist it: Cathy short for catharsis short for shits; a midshipman tag. Flyco was silent. Hicks grinned.

The Sea Harriers and helicopters must have been on deck-alert. They were all airborne by the time Hicks made his first abortive approach. His first two attempts convinced him a normal deck-landing was impossible; as soon as he straightened up on finals the ship disappeared under the Corsair's nose. Sweating, he came round again. His time was up. He'd never done an old-style deck-landing, a continuous turn till you were over the deck, then cut and drop, but it was going to be that or nothing with this hose-nosed bastard of an aeroplane if he didn't want to get wet.

Low round the corner, tight, hanging on power and flaps a hundred feet above the waves he blinked sweat out of his eyes and swore. Tighten up, you fool! More bank, more power, 86 knots, bit slow, ease off, that's better, that's all I need is a salted-up bloody windscreen and the bloody sun dead ahead of course, now . . . now . . . ! ease off some more and *sidle* in, Jeff boy, sidle sidle 90 knots 90 knots 90 knots there's the wake nice and straight God bless that helmsman. Bloody hell, that *pitch*! Up she comes . . . up . . . wave-off? No? Thank you, Flyco. 88 knots *wow*! Some downdraught there – *power!* Not too much, got it, got it, here it comes we're over the deck 85 knots a beaut and level the wings and *cut*! Throttle shut, back on the stick and stall the bugger on, we're not going anywhere now but down and . . . and . . . *shit! Wham!* Jesus Christ! Hard back and full brake, no not too much, you'll lock the wheels, the deck's wet, better now, feel them pulling, pumping, pumping – what the hell, the nose is lifting, can't be, no, not at this speed, I don't believe it, I'm looking at the sky, is this it then . . . We've stopped! That's steel down there and check the other side bloody hell that was close that's water down there, but we've done it! We've done it! Sitting here like a praying mantis on the ski-slope. Oh you lovely Corsair, you lovely, lovely Corsair, I hope I didn't bend you!

'Well done, 34.' Very quietly, from Flyco.

Hicks unprised stiff fingers from around the throttle and stick, uncurled his toes and realised he was panting. By the time he had stopped the engine the Corsair was surrounded by flight deck personnel ready to secure it and the ship was turning hard starboard back towards the gloom and overcast from which it had emerged.

In the captain's small sea cabin off the bridge, calm and warm with the hum and tremble of distant machinery, Hicks' watery legs were very glad when he sat down. The coffee, the usual lousy NAAFI instant, was nectar.

'Pretty damn spectacular, Jeff!' said Carter, who had come down to the flight deck to meet him.

'Should have seen it from where I was sitting, quoth he!'

'And I like the Dan Dare outfit!' Hicks' black flying suit was a deal more dashing than NATO olive-drab. 'But aren't you a bit old for this sort of derring-do? And speaking of age,' said Carter with a big grin, 'if you mention that disgusting nickname again on my ship I'll have you keelhauled!'

Hicks held up a hand in surrender. 'Sorry, Phil. Slip of the tongue.' For a few moments the two old warriors studied one another.

'This must be pretty important,' said the Captain, businesslike.

'It is.' The muted thunder of a Harrier landing-on came through the curtained door. Hicks looked at the brass wall-clock. Nine-thirty. Six hours ago, he had had Carla tight in his arms.

There was so much to talk about they continued while Hicks used Carter's shower. How unreluctantly the suds, Carla and Roca, went down the drain on their way to the cold Atlantic. Yes, Carter had struck again that morning using Lepus rocket-flares to illuminate the field. Catch the bastards out. Nine thousand-pound frags, air-burst again, and the pilots reported about forty aircraft exposed. Hicks could see the photographs. Yes, Carter was expecting a search, but he'd been under good cloud cover for two days, moving fast all the time. And also he had included his last package of SDW in the morning's delivery. SDW? Those spikes. Slow the bastards down a bit, eh? 'But I'm 430 miles off the coast now. What's the range of these Corsairs. And what do they carry?'

Hicks got back into his clothes; remembering the last time he had put them on, Carla's paleness emphasizing the melancholy of the hour; trying not to dwell on the fragmentation bombs exploding a hundred feet above her armed Corsair.

The operations meeting lasted more than two hours, for most of which Hicks held the floor giving what was essentially a presentation on Roca and the Corsair. He caught himself enjoying his bizarre situation, three decks down in *Eagle*'s main briefing room, still in Argentine uniform. He had to explain the role of the British ashore. How much had changed in the last twenty-four hours! Not least, Cassián had signally failed to anticipate the consequences of terminating their contracts. Hadn't he?

The ship was at action stations and the meeting a fluid affair of comings and goings, telephones, buzzers and tannoy calls. Towards the end of the morning, as *Eagle* approached the limit of Corsair range, the captain reappeared, visibly more relaxed.

211

'From what you say, Jeff, if they've only got ten or twenty Corsairs left, with the tactics you describe, we could have a problem just defending ourselves, let alone the troop convoy!' Carter was brisk, matter-of-fact.

'Correct. Once they've located you and set up their attack, you won't stop them with the weapons you've got.'

'Well, location is inevitable, with the troopships. They can track them all the way down, with their LRMP Boeings. We think the Russians have put up a RORSAT too. So we're back where we started. The Corsairs have got to be destroyed on the ground. Do you think there's any chance they'll disperse, move them somewhere else?'

'Unlikely. They should have done it before, but the Commodore was obsessed with security. Now, thanks to you the outfit is in such bad shape my guess is nobody else would want anything to do with it. I think the Junta has always kept its distance, in case the thing flopped. There's also fuel – not many places in Patagonia selling 115-octane gasoline. No, he'll stick it out at Roca. He knows you can't hurt him much more than you already have.'

'Then I hope to prove him wrong,' Carter said. 'I want you and the staff here –' indicating Ward and Bagshaw '– and anybody else you need, to get together and work on the options. There isn't much time. Some sort of decision by this evening, but the sooner the better. And get rid of the Dan Dare suit, eh?'

'Aye-aye, sir,' replied Hicks, standing up as the Captain left the room.

About this time, an overworked Wren officer in Whitehall dropped the following signal into an overfull tray:

*

CONFIDENTAL
ROUTINE
071504z
Fm MOD (Navy)
TO EAGLE
=Commander JW HICKS Royal Navy is recalled to duty on the Active List with effect this date. Appointed EAGLE (additional). NoK informed.=

The tray was marked 'Non-Operational'. It's only personnel, she said.

*

Next day, in latitude 39.38S, longitude 42.30W, an RAF C130 dropped ten parachutes from two thousand feet in a line down *Eagle*'s port side, the Hercules already northbound for Ascension as six men and their equipment splashed down in the Atlantic.

Six ferret-eyed, hard young men, their leader a lieutenant of Marines, briefed, ate and slept before getting back into the same boats less than twenty-four hours later. The gleaming black fin of HMS *Thunderer* broke surface half a mile away as the boat-falls lowered them down the carrier's side. The men's speech seemed rationed: gritty expletives were necessary in the handling of their considerable baggage, apparently, but little else. Hicks, in the boat's sternsheets in his commando combat rig, felt excluded, as from a family. A very close family. The SBS unit knew each other so well that once they had an aim and a plan, all else was small-talk, thickly larded with the most shocking, high-octane profanity. It was apparent, and understandable, that he had been labelled 'not wanted on voyage'. Professional hooligans, the SBS, once embarked upon an operation, were a law unto themselves. 'Mayhem Inc' might have been their motto. They relied upon concealment and surprise. An unfit retired naval aviator was going to be an acute emcumbrance. A pain in the arse.

Hicks made a special effort to effect a sprightly transfer from the boat onto the submarine's hull and all but fell in the water. Saved by two life-jacketed sailors, he made his way below, squeezing past Flight Lieutenant Apps who, pale, bearded but ecstatic was going in the opposite direction as if towards the shining light of salvation itself.

Thunderer's CO made Hicks welcome and as comfortable as possible on the thirty-six hour high-speed submerged transit south-west. But it was not a comfortable voyage. Hicks was a naval officer, an aviator, not a commando. He did his best, as he and the SBS team talked over and over their plans for the demolition of Roca, to enter into the 'family' spirit –

213

knowing he could never succeed. They tried, too, but were so immured in their *cosa nostra* that they no longer had the knack of normal intercourse. He was their guide, a native to be spoken to slowly and distinctly in language other than their own hooligan patois. But he smiled to overhear, from behind a curtain, one of them say to another: 'Old fucker can't be total senile: you see that fucking plane he flew on board that fucking ship? Catch me doing that, mate! I reckon he's all fucking right!' 'Yeah?' replied the other as their voices faded down the pasage, 'well, you're the best fucker to look after 'im then!'

Their inflatables grounded, after a wild and very wet ride through heavy surf, on a steep shingle beach three miles south of Roca, a spot Hicks had chosen. He was very glad to get away from the black water, remembering the orcs he and Carla had seen there chasing seals, not so long ago. The boats hidden well above the high-water mark, the six commandos impossibly laden with their 'hooligan kit', Hicks led the way up the cliff ascent.

He had suggested, as a pied à terre, a shallow ravine on this, the south side of the field. 'No way!' the lieutenant had said 'Too obvious. First place they look. Also, what do you see from a ravine?' So he was to guide them to a spot half a mile south-west of the airfield perimeter where the ground rose a few feet. Here they would 'dig in' for the duration. They had about six hours of darkness left. Hicks could have told them the Patagonian desert was not meant to be walked in darkness. Lightly laden, carrying only his own gear, he just managed to keep his feet and maintain a compass course; but it was desperately tough going. Despite being soaked in sea water from the waist down he was soon sweating horribly and intensely annoyed at the way the SBS men, under their enormous loads, tripped along like cat-eyed ballet dancers in the dark. He suspected they were enjoying themselves. *He* it was, however, who had to navigate them to the low knoll they had chosen for their OP, and it was not proving easy. He very nearly fell into the ravine, a fifteen-foot drop. When they had traversed this the ground began to rise and the lights of Roca came in view, like a distant shore, enabling them to take compass bearings and thus, after what seemed to Hicks an endless ghastly battle against the

214

bloodymindedness of the Patagonian landscape, arrive at their destination. After a brief survey, and with characteristically little discussion, the SBS began to dig.

Filthy, damp and exhausted, Hicks watched animal-like, through a slit at ground level, the dawn of Tuesday, 11th May. He was looking north-east. In the foreground, a martian waste of pebbles and white sandy soil. Here and there a tussock of bunch-grass, or stunted cactus, and alarmingly close, the airfield. Even from this shallow elevation he could see it all: the nearside perimeter track a few hundred yards away, and over on the far side, the tower, No. 3 Hangar, the wreckage of the others, the tops of buildings behind. He hardly needed the binoculars to count aircraft. He got to seventy-five before he stopped, puzzled, and sat back. There must be over a hundred of them. But how . . . ?

'Er, excuse me, sir – you've just sat in me breakfast.'

Hicks apologised, but he had to remain sitting in whatever it was. There was nowhere to go. Thus his first lesson in the ergonomics of earth-living – no sudden moves. They were split four and three in two shallow trenches and there was, quite literally, no spare space in either. All but the smallest movement required advance notification and planning which the others did in coded grunts.

'I don't understand it,' Hicks said to the lieutenant. The other member of their threesome, upon whose breakfast he was sitting, was an earthy individual called Bodger. 'There shouldn't be anything like that many!'

'We don't have enough gear for a hundred, that's for sure,' replied the lieutenant, who was eating a marmalade pudding. 'But we're quite good at primitive vandalism, aren't we, Bodger?'

'Fucking right, sir!'

'For now, we can only watch, and rest. I suggest you get some sleep, sir.' Hicks picked up the edge of command in the young lieutenant's voice, and smiled to himself: this was commando business, and young lieutenant was in charge. *He* didn't sit in other people's breakfasts. Fair enough!

'All right. I'll take my turn though. A lot of those aircraft may be dummies – u/s. We need to know which.'

'Sure. I'll do the first watch. You two sleep.' After some squirming, and several minor avalanches of earth over both of them, Hicks and Bodger interlocked and fell asleep. Looks like an old badger, thought the lieutenant, looking down on Hicks' dusty bearded face. Game though, so far!

In excruciating discomfort and squalor, which the others seemed to notice not a whit, Hicks passed the day sleeping, keeping watch, squirming and scratching until, when it was dark enough, the lieutenant gave the signal and they emerged. Hicks felt relief beyond description, as one disinterred, resurrected, at being able to stand stiffly up, brush the earth off himself, and breath clean air. But cold, suddenly, in the Antarctic wind of early winter.

They pooled the results of the day's work with the others. Numbers agreed, and the positions of the hundred and five visible Corsairs were marked on the plan of Roca Hicks had made for them. Work had been carried out on these; these had been visited by fuel bowsers; these had run their engines – all ringed on the plan: twenty-two. Eighty-three had thus stood unattended all day. Forty at least of these had no propellers, and damage was apparent on about a dozen more.

The figures were close enough to Hicks's last estimate of the Grupo's effective strength – thirty to forty aircraft – to be encouraging. But there was a question mark, still. He buttoned his heavy parka and turned his back on the biting wind, looking out across the airfield at Roca's lights. On the left, behind the control tower, there was a glow of hidden, more powerful lights: the maintenance and storage area. If Cassián had more Corsairs up his crafty sleeve, that was where they were.

They ate, quickly and disgustingly. The lieutenant gave a few orders to the four occupants of the second trench and then he and Hicks, and Bodger, set off northwards around the airfield.

''Spect the fuckers can hear us coming already, in these fucking boots!' hissed Bodger. They were wearing thick, leather-soled boots, reputedly proof against SDW prongs, instead of the usual commando footwear. 'Shut up, Bodger, will you?' ordered the lieutenant, easily.

'Sir.'

216

Using a shallow fold in the ground, they crept towards the floodlit area until they were close enough to hear voices and the metallic sounds of tools, and pick out faces. Under a huge spread of camouflage netting dozens of men, heavily dressed against the cold, were working on forty Corsairs. Panels and cowlings lay around. The men swarmed with ant-like purpose, over, under and in the aircraft, all of which, to Hicks' eye, had the look of 'fliers'. Forty! He counted them again, studied the scene for a long time, then signalled the lieutenant to withdraw.

When they were safely back in the wilderness, Hicks said to the lieutenant, 'I think I ought to try to talk to the other Brits. They may know more, by now, of the Commodore's plans.' He had stopped walking as he spoke. The others halted in the dark.

After a long pause, the lieutenant said, 'I don't think that's a good idea, sir.' Hicks couldn't see his blackened face.

'Why not?'

'If you're caught, or seen, they'll know you're not alone. And we're here to destroy, not to spy. And if we do our job, that disposes of any plans the Commodore may have, surely?'

Hicks could not easily have explained why he had made such a foolish suggestion. It was improbable that the others were even at liberty, after his escape, or that they would have been told anything of importance. He stood looking through the dusty blackness at the distant lights. From somewhere came the notion that if he started walking towards them, he might not get far. Something in the lieutenant's voice?

He turned away. 'You're right, of course,' he said, and started walking into the wind.

For most of the night, huddled in a draughty gully, the lieutenant and his men planned the destruction of Cassián's remaining air power. The neology of hi-tech mayhem largely excluded Hicks, who was only consulted about such technicalities as lay outside the experience of the SBS: where were the Corsair's fuel tanks; and how best to cripple those aircraft they could not blow up, by cutting pipes and wiring looms, for instance. He could see that the task, considerably bigger than expected, was going to stretch their resources. He was asked

217

to draft a signal detailing what had been observed so far, and this was passed to *Thunderer*, together with the rendezvous time, on the unit's low-power radio. At last, towards dawn, they went to earth. The attack was planned for that evening.

Hicks, chilled to the bone and dog-tired, crept thankfully out of the rising wind, and the stink of earth and human dirt bothered him not at all as he and Bodger wriggled themselves together in their lair. The other trench was keeping watch until midday, so all three could sleep. But something had been bothering Hicks ever since their visit to the floodlit camouflage area, and now he said, as if to himself, 'Those forty Corsairs; why camouflage them by day, and then floodlight them at night? Especially as they've already been raided once in the dark!'

Bodger twitched. 'Well, they're only fucking wogs. What can y'expect!'

After a long pause, the lieutenant said, 'As you say, sir, they seem to have thrown away their black-out altogether. It only makes sense if they know there's no risk of them getting hit again – if they know the positions of our carriers.' The voice was disembodied in the blackness.

Hicks had already worked out that much. What bothered him was how much more did *they* know? He fell uneasily into sleep, Cassián's small round face and penetrating eyes taunting him in the dark.

'Stand absolutely still! Make no rapid movements! We are surrounded you!'

In the glare of sudden light from all around, Hicks and the SBS section became a frozen tableau. Only the wind moved.

They had emerged above ground soon after nightfall, spent an hour on last-minute adjustments to the 'kit', and were ready to move off when the lights and the metallic voice arrested them, the six heavily-laden, stocking-capped, black-faced SBS in a group, Hicks slightly apart.

'Is no good to resist. We are too many. Now, you will put down your weapons and equipment on the floor and put your hands up in the air!'

Swirling dust, silence, blinding light; Hicks squinted in the glare. The others, like him, were looking at the lieutenant. The lieutenant slowly swivelled his head around the perimeter of lights, so bright it was impossible to judge their distance or see anything beyond. He lowered his face for a moment, seemed to be considering, and then straightened up. 'Well,' he said conversationally, 'as my old mum always used to say, you can't fart in the face of thunder. Sorry, chaps.' He unslung his Uzi, dropped it, and began to wriggle out of his pack. As the others, with the utmost reluctance, followed suit, their anger and frustration vented in a volcanic display of *sotto voce* malediction: thus the Liverpudlian Bodger, throwing to the ground in disgust his carefully prepared pack of explosive, detonators and fuses – 'Well fuck my old boot!'

Chapter 23

'So now he knows what he could only guess before,' said Cassián. 'And after Captain Carter gets your message, he must have to come back. Like Henry V, he will say, "Once more!" I know him now.' The black eyes twinkled and the Contraalmirante took a sip of brandy.

'And you will have your battle,' Hicks said resignedly.

'At last!'

'And fill the sea up with our English dead?' Hicks's eyes were heavy with fatigue.

Cassián smiled. 'That is not the aim. You know that, my friend. The act and the consequences are different – we have talked on this before. We know our Aquinas and our Saint Augustine. Warlike action in a just war is moral. Only when the *intention* is to cause death, is it immoral. These men are paid soldiers.'

'And excessive force? That is immoral, for the same reason.'

'On this you win. There will be no excess. I have come to see, apart from moral questions, overkill would be bad for the Grupo. Our victory will be quick, clean, and clinical – I wish I could add painless. The rapier, not the bludgeon.'

'And we? What is to become of us?' Hicks was clean-smelling and wearing Argentine uniform.

'Why, nothing!' The little Commodore beamed. 'You have done valuable work, and you still have some little time with us.' He poured some more cognac. 'Look, I will explain. I have to admit the first Harrier attack was a shock. It was a brilliant operation! *Fantastico!* I cannot say how much I admire all those involved in it, from the planning to the flying.

I was completely surprised – and flattered, for, as you point out, it means your government puts a very high value upon my Grupo. But since then –' they were in the Commodore's quarters, where Hicks had been invited soon after his arrest and capture, and the steward was clearing away the remains of their meal; '– since then, although Captain Carter has kept us busy, I know, and he knows that I know, his limitations. He cannot come too close, nor stay too long, and he has few Harriers. He knows too it has never been possible to bomb an airfield out of commission. Captain Carter has an impossible task, but he has to try, as every hour the Task Force with its troop transports comes closer to my Corsairs.'

'Are you telling me you *planned* all this? My defection? The commando raid – ?' Hicks was desperately tired. The brandy fuddled his brain.

'Planned? No! Anticipated – yes!' Cassián's smugness took Hicks back to that night in Rotterdam, so long ago. 'When I said it was my intention to sink *Canberra*, I would be surprised if one of you did not try to take a warning. And disappointed. Allow me the wit to recognise the boundaries of artificial loyalty: I think you had adjusted to a gladiatorial combat against your own people, but *Canberra* would be different. You would say, "Now there is a new thing". Did it not seem strange, how easy it was to take a Corsair with no obstacle, no pursuit? Later,' he said, parenthetically, 'I want you to tell me all about your trip – it must have been very interesting.' He continued, 'So now, you are gone, and I expect you tell Captain Carter – by the way, I am very pleased to know the man's name – that without nuclear weapons the only way to neutralise the Corsair threat from Roca is a commando raid. So, we wait your return. *Eagle*'s position is discovered, too far for Harriers. We arrange our shop window for you. Our infra-red binoculars are very good! You stand out in the desert like the testicles of a dog, is that the expression? And when you have send your message on the radio, we say thank you, that is enough, you can come in now and have a hot bath and some food!'

'Dogs balls,' said Hicks bitterly, and looked in the other's face for evidence of patronising or gloating. He detected nothing but avid curiosity in the flashing black eyes. The excitement of the end-game! Just a few pieces left, each move crucial. He's played well though. He could so easily have suffered a failure of nerve. But his was the nerveless zeal of the messiah. Hicks had a new vision of Carter being played like a trout on a line, an unbreakable line of duty hundreds of miles long and even now being reeled relentlessly in. And where, in all these metaphors, was he himself? Pawn, or lure? Or were all of them just insects in Cassián's jamjar?

Warmed by the brandy, Hicks laughed out loud. 'Contraal-mirante, I take my hat off to you! And I can speak for Captain Carter. He would be proud to meet you. He would appreciate the joke!' Then, more soberly, 'And he would say, I think, that in this game that you and he must play, you have the better cards!'

'But of course! I deal!' The Commodore became serious. 'Now, you will want to meet your friends. And rest. They will tell you there have been changes here. The *ejercito* – the army command – have seen that GEA has not so many Corsairs now, and they have taken many of the young pilots to rein-force the Malvinas garrison.' Hicks heart sank. 'I have lost very many of the *tenientes* and *guardiamarinas*. This means more work for the rest, and . . .' The Commodore saw Hicks was not listening. He smiled. 'Is all right. It was mostly men they take, Eeks. Teniente Souza is still here.'

'Carla?'

'*Si*, as you say. Carla. And I think she has some news for you! But come now – go and see her yourself.' Cassián stood up.

At the door, as they shook hands, their eyes met, Hicks' red-rimmed with fatigue, the other's black, opaque and lively. Hicks could find nothing to say. But when he turned to go, he asked, 'And the *Canberra*?'

'That, my friend,' replied the Commodore, 'will not be my decision.'

A car took Hicks the short distance to his apartment block where, in a brief reunion meeting in 'Pete's Place' he told his story to the others. They in turn described to him the attack by *Eagle*'s Harriers shortly after he had taken off three days ago, and the sudden departure that morning of all but about fifty of the young Argentine pilots. Carla had not been taken away, as he probably knew? Yes. Something in the way they looked at him made Hicks uneasy, adding to his impatience. As soon as he could, he left and went to his own rooms.

Before his door, with its sign, 'Capitán de Fragata JW HICKS', he hesitated. He had seen no one during his brief escorted visit earlier in the evening to bathe and change. But by now, everybody on the base must know of his return, and the manner of it. He went in.

Carla was reading, under a soft light. Hidden speakers in dim corners of the room played quietly the Bach cantata he had once described as reminiscent of her particular beauty. 'Wachet Auf'. Deep and dark. Vibrant.

She looked up, smiling. Then she frowned. 'Eeks! You look terrible!' She stood up, and examined him severely for a few moments before holding out her arms. 'What you need?'

''Ug,' he said, and then they were holding each other, very tight.

Eventually, and unusually, Hicks was the first to move. Gently he detached Carla and held her out in front of him by her thin arms. She looked more beautiful than he ever remembered. But there was something else. A reserve. Bashfulness? Carla!

'You have something to tell me, Carla,' he said.

She didn't want to meet his eyes. He waited, knowing and yet not knowing what it was. He pulled her towards him again. She stiffened. He buried his face in her hair. He heard her say something.

'What? What did you say?' he asked softly in her ear.

She pushed away and stepped back, looked straight at him and said, 'I am 'aving bebbi.' Her eyes stayed on his face, a timorous defiance in her shoulders.

Although some instinct had already warned Hicks, he found himself at her words back for the second time in his life in that fan-vaulted world of wonder and stopped clocks; but this time, instead of confusion, it was a surging diapason of joy that took away his speech and reason.

A voice said, 'But when? When did you know?'

She said, 'The same day you went away.'

'But I thought . . . ?'

'So I think also.' Carla shrugged, with a little shrug. She stood quite still, a shy half-smile showing her small teeth, eyes searching his face.

'You know how I feel?' What a stupid question! He wanted to shout out, but he was paralysed by joy.

'No, you 'ave to tell me how you feel, Eeks.'

'I feel like I own the world. You have given me the world. I am the king. Oh, Carla, Carla, Carla – come.' He held out his arms.

'You don't . . . ?'

'Mind?' Did she think he would *mind*! 'Wonderful! Oh Carla, this is wonderful.'

Now she was smiling. Hicks thought her eyes were moist, but she hid her face in his shoulder as she began to talk. 'I did not mean to tell you, Eeks, but they come to take so many of us away, and me, they do not want because of the bebbi, so I stay here, and everybody know why, and now you are come back, and –'

'All right, all right. It's all right. Everything is all right now. Eeks is back.' He held her away from him again. 'And *I* have something to tell *you*.'

'What?' A frisson of apprehension.

'A very important message.'

'What!'

'I love you. *Te quiero.*' Nothing had ever been easier to say.

With a happy smile she said, 'I want you tell me all what 'appened. I was very surprise when you go, just like that – pouff! You didn't tell me! I ask Feench, he tell me why, and then I very 'appy.'

'Why? Why happy?'

'It is good thing to do, of course. Make me very proud – bebbi too!' She patted her stomach.

She had gone to the base doctor after landing from the last fruitless six-hour armed search on Friday, the morning of his departure, to have her suspicions confirmed. She was not officially grounded, but the army recruiters had not wanted her, so here she was! She told him of the Harriers in the dark, the sudden flares, the crashing bombs and flying splinters as she and the others were out on the airfield pre-flighting their aircraft. One had been killed and three others injured, but

224

eighteen Corsairs had still taken off on time with their bombs to search for *Eagle*.

'Yes, it was good,' she said proudly, 'to fly, after these bombings. But a pity not to find the ships. The sea is so *big*!'

'Well, no more flying now for you, my love!'

'Why no flying? It makes no difference. I still fly when I need, probably for the Malvinas war, and then I finish. It will be time to stop.'

'It is time to stop now!'

'No. There is no need. The doctor says.'

'*Al diablo con dottore!* To hell with the doctor! *Eso e ridicolo!*' Hicks stood up and walked about. 'You must not fly!'

'Eeks!' He stopped in front of her. She said, 'I understand your feeling. But this is my bebbi, it is inside of me. As you would say, it is my problem. In Argentina, until now, men always say do or not do, and the women have no decision. The body of a woman is for a man to make children, as he wants. But for me, I don't like this. I like to be *capitán* in my own sheep. So please, allow I make my decision, eh?' There was no compromise in the upturned face, so after a few moments he took it in both his hands and kissed her.

'*Si, capitán!*' he said gravely. Then, kissing her hands, 'And may I ask what rank I have in your sheep?'

'You are *primer oficial*, of course. But tonight, you sleep in the *capitán*'s cabin. Come, you are tired. And Eeks?'

'Yes?'

'I also love you.'

How true, that to know and to be told are different things, thought Hicks.

Chapter 24

Opinion among *Eagle*'s officers as to what the future held for TG 16 was divided more or less by age. To the young, the great majority, the Corsair was not to be taken seriously. Until is was pushed overboard, Hicks' machine had been an object of curiosity and derision, unsleek and ugly; most gauche, its huge propeller, connoting slowness and antiquity.

Young officers with hi-tech minds, conditioned to aircraft in penny numbers, understandably dismissed the Corsair as an apparition from the past, a comically aberrant product of 'dago mentality', and so were prevented from even trying to conceive a scenario in which it would not be dealt with by modern defences. Thus handicapped, they felt threatened, as *Eagle* and her consorts turned south-west again, more by Argentina's very considerable conventional air, and by her submarines, than by Corsairs.

But a few, while acknowledging the conventional air threat, and especially the dreaded Etendard-Exocet, against which *Eagle* was defenceless, could arithmeticize from Hicks' short signal and deduce that no matter how slowly they flew, fifty-plus aircraft carrying two 1,000 lb bombs each, and piloted with anything like average competence, coming upon TG 16 in the open sea, amounted to bloody defeat.

The carrier had no close-range weapons. She relied upon her escorts to deal with hostile aircraft that penetrated her AA screen of Harrier CAP and Sea Cat missiles. Sea Cat could only engage high-flying targets at 70–80 miles, and the Harrier's main air-to-air weapon, Sidewinder, was useless against the Corsair and its 30mm Aden cannon difficult to bring to bear. Anyway, the Harriers were for offence: they were all Carter had. And there were only five left.

As for the escorts, the Type 22 frigates had Sea-Wolf missiles, highly effective out to about three miles and certainly lethal to Corsairs. But each ship had only a single six-barrel launcher fore and aft, with a reload time of up to five minutes, and although it could be expected to take a toll of the first wave of bombers it was not good at dealing with multiple targets, and the 'reload window' would be more than enough to permit Cassián's Carousel to get in and strike: the Sea-Wolf's first salvo would probably be their last. Furthermore, Cassián's Sidearm anti-radar missiles could be fired from a safe distance to take out Sea-Wolf Type 909 fire-control radars before the bombers went in.

SECRET

IMMEDIATE

FROM: CINC FLEET,

TO: CTG16,

231425Z MAY

=In view your latest information from NEWFIELD cmm essential this facility is neutralised completely before 21 May.
2. TG 16 to proceed as required to accomplish this aim.
3. Timing and method of attack at your discretion, however intelligence suggests sooner the better.
4. ARTEMIS and ANTARES available as additional escort if required.
5. Good luck. =

Captain Carter re-read the signal. *Eagle* steamed south by west, her speed an economical eighteen knots. From his high chair, Carter scanned the sparkling scene beyond the bridge windows. Out on the wings, *Biter* and *Breakspear* lunged slimly through the long waves, and far out of sight ahead, Sea Kings hovered, listening in the water. *Thunderer* was in company, somewhere. A gin-clear day, just a fringe of cirrus and a faint darkening of the horizon ahead. Carter felt a little like a man hatless in a blazing desert – fatally exposed. Apart from Russian satellites, AAF Boeing 707s had been keeping the

South Atlantic under surveillance for the last month, despite being warned off by *Invincible*'s Sea Harriers on 20th April.

Carter flipped the signal back and handed the clip-board to his Executive Officer who shared it with Commander (Air) before passing it on to Ward and Bagshaw. The top signal on the board was MOD's latest update on the disposition of Argentine naval surface units.

'Well, Andrew,' said the captain to his XO, 'this is it. You can start straight away. I think we should aim for Zulu One by sunset.'

'Aye aye, sir.' Z1, the ship's highest state of readiness, crew at action stations, watertight doors and hatches shut, domestic compartments at and below the waterline evacuated, was also the highest state of discomfort for its crew. The XO left the bridge to begin his unpopular task.

'Now, John,' Carter turned to his Commander (Air), 'let's go over this again. You want two Harriers on CAP and three rippling with bombs. Convince me about the CAP. Are they going to make any difference, apart from confusing the missiles. We're talking about close-in, remember.'

'To be honest, sir, if there are forty or fifty Corsairs, and they shot down two or three each – and that's optimistic – the Sea-Jets are not going to save the day. But, I think their value is more than strictly numerical. They'll disrupt and distract. Without any air opposition, the Corsairs will have it just like a firing-range!'

'But from what Jeff Hicks tells us, if they have normal fighter escort, they're not going to have any difficulty in dealing with two Harriers anyway,' put in Commander Ward.

'While the bombers get on and do their thing,' added the captain.

'Two Harriers is forty percent of your offensive effort, sir,' Ops reminded.

'Thank you, Ops.' Carter rubbed his chin, musing with unseeing eyes on the blue-white ocean outside. A Sea-King, refuelled and re-crewed, lifted off with a muted clatter of blades, hovered a few seconds, hauled itself around to port and set out ahead of the ship. Then the bridge was quiet again.

'All right,' said the Captain, 'no CAP.'

There was a short silence as Carter and his officers absorbed the bizarre prospect that lay ahead of them in the next hours, one of Her Majesty's largest and most expensive war vessels confronting the technology of a bygone age. The captain's decision, inescapable in the context of their mission, underscored the paucity of their resources.

'What about *Artemis* and *Antares*, sir?' asked the operations officer.

'Would they make any difference?' Nobody answered. 'No, draft a signal.'

'Aye aye, sir.'

'And you want to ripple the bombers, John?'

'Yes, sir,' answered Commander (Air). 'Two, two and one will keep them busy. Less time to recuperate and regroup than five all at once.'

Thus it was decided. TG 16 would make a fast approach towards Punta Medanosa during the night, launch the first Harriers before daylight, the others at three-quarter hour intervals. The carrier would be close enough to the target for the jets to recycle back over Roca within two and a half hours, keeping Roca under continual bombardment. In this way, it was hoped to achieve a progressive reduction of the Corsair fleet and prevent it organising for a mass attack. But nobody on *Eagle*'s bridge had any illusions about the risks involved in coming so close to the Argentine coast.

*

'. . . *The Battle of Punta Medanosa*', the Official History of the Falklands War might begin, if the battle could have been acknowledged, '*took place over 14th and 15th May 1982. The prolonged nature of the engagement, occasioned by contrary weather, has tended to obscure the true significance of the Argentine victory.*

'. . . *The cirrus cloud seen by Captain Carter on the morning of the 13th was the advancing fringe of a deepening polar depression moving north into the area between Patagonia and the Falkland Islands. Pressure fell rapidly as the Task Group moved south, with wind steadily increasing to a north-westerly gale, cloud lowering and thickening from the south, and rain.*

In the early stages, weather favoured the Task Group, affording it good cover without either impeding its flying operations or seriously obscuring the target area, where the wind was offshore. In the warm sector of the depression, Captain Carter made the most of the excellent all-weather capabilities of his Harriers, but the passage of the cold front in the early hours of the 15th reversed the situation and the Argentine commander was quick to use the unanswerable argument of numbers. From this point, the outcome was inevitable.

'. . . Given good weather throughout, there seems no reason to doubt that the affair would have proceeded to the same conclusion, only more quickly. . . . First contact was made when three Sea Harriers from HMS 'Eagle', using Lepus flares for illumination, dropped fragmentation bombs on BAN Roca at 0413 local time on 14th May . . .

Two hours before this, using a facsimile relay via *Teatro de Operaciones del Atlantico Sur* of a Soviet RORSAT update, Cassián had launched four Corsair-S Sierras with orders to find the Task Group and lie in wait for returning Harriers. It was a long shot, and in the dark, but it suited Cassián's private purpose and besides, he could do nothing else offensive until daylight.

Roca at the time of launch had high overcast and strong winds, but the forecast for the target area was poor. Half an hour after take-off, lowering cloud forced the formation leader down to less than a thousand feet. Rain and turbulence in the narrowing gap between sea and cloud made formation flying, using only tiny blue formation-lights, increasingly difficult, so that one by one, exhausted by the strain and physical effort, the pilots lost contact with the lead aircraft, broke away and proceeded on their own, navigating by Kondor Tacan towards the Task Group's predicted position. Not surprisingly, the mission was a failure. Three of the Corsairs returned to Roca between 0700 and 0800. The No. 2 aircraft disappeared without trace.

Cobra 2 was Guardiamarina Margarita Madrigál. Breathing heavily and sweating and dangerously disorientated, she hauled her Corsair hard up and away when the lead aircraft lights, barely visible through the streaming perspex, vanished in a particularly violent pocket of turbulence. She righted herself on instruments, turned back onto course using her own Tacan, and gingerly descended until her radar altimeter showed 500 feet. She could see nothing – the cockpit canopy reflected only the ghostly green of her instruments – but she could hear the rain, the low roar of hard water on the windscreen. In these conditions she continued along the briefed bearing to the range which was supposed to correspond with the Task Group's position, and began a search. There were three other Corsairs doing the same thing, unlit in the rain, and perhaps Harriers.

Guardiamarina Madrigál flew a creeping line-ahead search until her eye was caught by the blinking of a signal lamp below her. She had found the Task Group. Narrowing her search, she located the blurred unlit outline of the carrier in the easing rain. She shadowed *Eagle* until, alerted by a sudden change of course, she saw dim lights on the deck and went into a steep bank to get a better look. But by this time, she had been flying for over three hours in appalling conditions and without knowing it she was near exhaustion. In the horizonless dark she overbanked and forgot her altimeter, two basic errors that a more experienced, or less tired, pilot might have avoided. The Corsair yawed horribly as the wingtip sliced into an unseen wave-top, the nose dug in and the aircraft slammed inverted into the sea. Guardiamarina Margarita Madrigál died instantly of a broken neck and sank with her aircraft to the bottom of the sea. Of all her friends, none mourned her loss longer or more deeply than Lieutenant Newson of the Royal Navy.

'. . . TG 16 kept the offensive throughout the 14th. At around 0830, Roca's search radar was destroyed by an anti-radar missile from a Harrier, possibly a prototype Hughes ALARM supplied by the US. This largely negated the threat to 'Eagle's' Harriers from the Sidewinder-armed Corsairs on Combat Air Patrol, since by approaching unseen from random directions at high speed they made it impossible for the Corsairs to achieve a missile firing solution in time. One Sea Harrier was shot down, however, and its pilot killed, when it unaccountably returned after its bombing run and engaged in single combat with a Corsair on CAP . . .'

Tracey's acolyte Guardiamarina Consuela Donován was an apt pupil, her flying an expression of an ancient warrior instinct that matched her hawkish features. He had taught her all he knew of how to fight an aeroplane. This day, she was flying CAP in the early afternoon, and Tracey, nothing better to do, was keeping an eye on her from a safe place on the ground. The usual CAP was at least two Corsairs, but the other had recently landed for some technical reason and not yet been replaced on patrol when a Sea Harrier, barely preceded by its thundering soundprint, streaked across the aircraft from the west and dropped its two bombs. It seemed to be alone. Consuela's Corsair was badly placed to respond, and although she saw it and turned hard towards, it was opening at ten miles a minute and would soon have been out of range if it had just kept going like all the rest. But this pilot, perhaps having seen only one Corsair, and having fuel to spare, pulled round hard right, decelerating.

Tracey got to his feet. The Harrier, hauling back towards the field, was still slowing, but the rolling roar of its engine was winding up. For a moment, Tracey was puzzled, but then, seeing it come well below normal flying speed with its exhaust plumes swinging down, he understood – the jet was coming to the hover! Barely a thousand feet above the centre of the airfield, with the smoke and dust of its bombs curling in its jetwash, the Sea Harrier sat poised uncannily on a pillar of raw sound, bellowing a challenge at Consuela's Corsair.

Guardiamarina Consuela Donován was perplexed. A head-on jet should be closing fast. Not like this! The situation was outside her experience. She was in to half a mile, 1,000 yards, before it clicked, and then only because she saw the vertical plumes of jet-gas. That gave her six seconds, roughly, before her own 300 knots brought her in range of the Harrier's cannon. Her Sidewinders were useless until she could get behind, but it could just pivot and follow whichever way she went! Up? Down? Left? Right? Instinctively she chose to dive, to give the Harrier pilot the most difficult aiming problem. At about 800 yards she pushed the Corsair's nose down as hard as she dared without ripping the wings off. As the Harrier's nose dipped to follow, she rolled hard left, paused, reversed right to pass under the jet and pulled the Corsair up

232

into a sixty degree climb, full power, heading for the base of the overcast at about 1,500 feet.

The next few seconds were the longest of her life. She couldn't see the Harrier; didn't know if it had been able to follow her manoeuvres. She was losing speed fast and the Harrier could accelerate like a rocket. She strained the throttle forward and steeled for the impact of cannon shells in her back. At last, with a tentative first wisp and then a firm grey clasp, the cloud enfolded her and she was safe, breathing hard, trembling with reaction. And furious.

All day these Harriers had been coming over with their bombs. Her friends had been killed and injured. Roca, once a busy, orderly and proud place, was a shambles. And now this one. Laughing at them, was he? *Gringo bravado* in his fancy jet! Consuela's Celtic eyes flashed fire. Recalling Tracey's advice she tried, with some success, to cool her panting fury – never get personal, keep it technical, he always said. Think . . . Harrier . . . jet . . . short of fuel . . . can't stay and wait . . . his base is east . . . so! Still in cloud, but with the careful abandon of high adrenalin, she rolled past the vertical, pulled around onto an easterly heading and put the Corsair into a shallow full-power dive. She re-checked her missile switches.

The cloud thinned, flicking glimpses of land below, the coast, then she was in the clear, 350 knots and looking . . . looking . . . looking . . . Aaah . . . how small it was, and how fast! Streaking out low across the sea, grey on grey. Tiny! A growl in her earphones, the Sidewinder acquisition tone. She squeezed the firing trigger hard. One missile, two, three – enough! She lifted her finger from the trigger. Orgasmic excitement gripped her. An ancient cry, half scream, half shout, came from the Celtic throat as the missiles sped away, her remaining Sidewinder growling, pleading for release, the grey jet all but vanished, on, on, then when all the missiles must have failed, a small flash, a short trail of twirling flame, and a splash, all silent.

Circling above, all she could see was a smear of oil-slicked water amid the breakers, and a few small bits of flotsam. The shape of the stain reminded her of a trodden insect, and Guardiamarina Consuela Donován felt sick.

*'. . . Contraalmirante Cassián, Commander of BAN Roca
and the Grupo Especiale d'Ataque, afterwards said he
regarded Task Group 16's mission as impossible. Given twice
the resources, Carter could not have inflicted sufficient damage
upon either the airfield or the widely-dispersed aircraft of the
Grupo, to stop it operating. The same truth was apparent to
Captain Carter and his officers by the afternoon of 14th May.
His orders, however, were clear, so he moved closer to Punta
Medanosa to reduce the range and step up the sortie rate of his
Harriers. By nightfall, TG 16 was only 150 miles from the
Argentine mainland. A cold front was expected to pass through
the area the next morning, bringing clear weather and exposing
the ships to air attack. Carter therefore kept up the bombing
throughout the hours of darkness. Roca's commander has
stated that this was of little more than nuisance value.'*

Guardiamarina Carmina Lopez had both legs amputed well
above the knees by a bomb splinter and nearly died from loss
of blood. She tried her best to die.

*'. . . Eagle lost a third Sea Harrier, badly damaged attempting
to land in heavy rain at about 0500 15th May. The pilot was
killed.'*

Lieutenant Taff Jones felt his guts tighten when, returning to
Eagle from his second bombing trip of the night, he ran into
rain and turbulence the like of which he had never met in
twelve years' flying. Rain like solid water and vicious,
frightening turbulence rocked his Harrier as he approached
the ship's position on his INS. Lightning flashed continually
around him in the thunderclouds and static crashed in his
earphones. With fifteen minutes fuel left, instrument lights
full up and visor down against a lightning strike, he slowed as
much as he dared and crept in the last mile towards the ship's
co-ordinates at 500 feet, radar on Search.

Half way round a slow orbit, he got the ship on radar, a mile
ahead. Overwhelmed with relief, Jones turned down the
panel lighting and raised his visor and with night-adapted
pupils wide open, was peering through the streaming windscreen when lightning struck. His eyes seemed to melt into

balls of seething fire. Totally blind, he flew by instinct and kept the Harrier crazily airborne until with a vestige of returning sight he relocated the carrier and came in to land, only to have the engine cut from fuel exhaustion in the final hover-descent to the deck. The Harrier dropped like a brick, smashed its undercarriage and slid into the port catwalk. Lieutenant Jones, dazed by the crash, saw the deck-edge coming and felt his Harrier began to tilt. Convinced he was going over the side, he ejected, the rocket seat taking him out to port of the ship in a shallow parabola at whose apogee it auto-separated and left him in his parachute a hundred feet above the water. Fit, he might have survived. Dazed and almost certainly broken-backed, Lieutenant Taff Jones had no strength left for the struggle with the freezing waves, the parachute shroud-lines, or even the toggle of his life-jacket. He drowned quickly and continued down in his parachute to the bottom of the sea.

'. . . *Contraalmirante Cassián and the other personnel of BAN Roca endured the intermittent bombing of the night 14/15th May comforted by the expectation of a cold front clearance soon after daybreak which would enable them to settle the score. Several were killed and many injured as maintenance crews worked through the night repairing bomb-damaged aircraft. No interdiction sorties were attempted against the carrier. Aircrew rested as they could until assembled for briefing at 0600.'*

Hicks lay awake most of the night. He thought from Carla's breathing she did too. Through long melancholy hours punctuated by the bombing of the airfield, he stared into the dark thinking of what the day would bring, his mind – or was it his soul? – turning on a spit between a fire of criticism and cooling alibi. Over and over again he had to justify himself to dancing devils the chief of whom were Weakness, Venality and Infidelity. And the greatest of these was Infidelity. But to whom or what this nagging unfaith? Hicks stockaded himself with all the old arguments and retreated to a pillar of principle that put him out of reach of his tormentors, the Hicks Declaration of Independence, namely this, that we hold it a self-evident truth that the most important thing a human has to do is to stand out and be different. And whom had he betrayed?

From his pillar Hicks surveyed with pity a generation of Englishmen whose only use for adrenalin was chasing profits. The whizz-kid generation! He thought of his younger son, lured to the city by the scent of money; lost among the new barbarians, pagans without temples. No, don't apologise for being a soldier, mercenary, call it what you like. And Pauline? She had no time for tame men!

At 0510 by his watch, while Lieutenant Taff Jones sank with infinite slowness, in his parachute, to join Guardia-marina Margarita Madrigál at the bottom of the sea, while Guardiamarina Carmina Lopez lay legless, trying to die, Hicks found Carla's hand beside him in the bed, and felt an answering press. He had been told, in as many words, and accepted, what Heloise told Abelard; that love, to be worthy of the name, must be disinterested.

*

'. . . At 0900 GMT, 15th May, Captain Carter, ComTaskGroup 16, made a lengthy signal to CINC FLEET containing a summary of his actions so far and his assessment of the results in terms of the aim he had been set, and the outlook. The Admiralty was left in no doubt that TG 16's task was far from complete, but that the ships, in attempting to continue operations so close to the Argentine coast during the coming day in improving weather, would be exposed to heavy air attack. The Naval Staff urged that the ships be withdrawn before daylight, but this was opposed, in the Defence Council, by the Army, who pointed out that the Invasion Force would be entering the reported radius of action of the Newfield-based Corsairs within two days, and that if TG 16 were unable to defend itself against Argentine air attack, there was little hope for the troop convoy. The War Cabinet, fearful of the political consequences of a loss of momentum, accepted the Army view. Despite a strong personal plea from the First Sea Lord, who made it clear that all three ships could well be lost, the Cabinet instructed that TG 16 continue to engage.'

Captain Carter peered around the darkened bridge. 'Pilot!' he called.

'Sir?' The navigating officer ducked through his black-out curtain.

'Set course for Punta Medanosa. Twenty-eight knots.'

'Aye-aye, sir.' The navigator disappeared again.

'Wings! Oh there you are!' Commander (Air) had been standing behind the captain's chair. 'No more launches. Get this next Sea-Jet aboard and secured, We're going in close and I want to hit them hard now. Two over two, in about two hours. Can do? They're going to have to work on deck as best they can – I'm not slowing down.'

Carter spoke to his ship's company in a tannoy broadcast that in places was hard to hear above the pounding of her engines and screws. He told them what to expect, and reminded them of Nelson's famous signal. Air mechanics and armourers fought in horizontal rain and spray to prepare the Harriers. Soon after they had finished, and with dramatic suddenness, the rain stopped the sky cleared, the wind backed off the bow and *Eagle* and the frigates were in a different world, cold and clear, pre-dawn.

'Fucking typical!' remarked the soaked, exhausted flight-deck crews.

A hearty breakfast was made for the 1445 men in the three surface ships, then the galley fires were damped. Radars, missiles and fire-control systems, damage control equipment, were tested and double-checked. Any weapon that could be used against aircraft was set up on deck or super-structure. Those on deck duties were cold, very cold, but counted themselves lucky – they could at least see what was coming.

'Bridge – Ops. Captain please,' on the talkback. 0743 local time.

'Captain. Go ahead.'

'Multiple aircraft contacts on 992, sir. Overhead Newfield.'

Carter was down in the Ops room in seconds. He peered long and intently at the big search radar scope, Commander (Air) beside him.

'Eighty-five miles! Well, Wings?'

'Forming up, sir. I make it thirty plus.'

'At least! We're too late!' Carter spoke rapidly. 'How long to get those bombs off and load Sidewinder?'

'Thirty minutes, sir, with luck.'

'Then do it. *Go!* And get the pilots in them – choppers too, I want everything off the deck. *Pilot!*' the last on talkback to the bridge.

'Pilot, sir!'

'Reverse course. Corpen one eight zero. Speed two eight!'

The ship heeled heavily to port. Feet clattered, tannoys, bullhorns and talkbacks blared and squawked as the Task Group changed its posture. 'What a fucking caper!' commented the weary armourers, wrestling again with their stock-in-trade just as they did at Agincourt. All eyes looked aft as the ships fled towards the rising sun.

'. . . *The best Argentine sources put the operational strength of GEA on the morning of 15th May at 64 aircraft: 52 Corsair-B bombers, 9 -S fighters, and 3 -E ECM variants. Losses had been heavy, and there is considerable evidence that Cassián had had great difficulty in maintaining the exclusivity of his duel with TG 16: Admiral Anaya, the Armada chief, and Brigadier Lami Dozo of the FAA, had been impressing upon the Junta with increasing urgency the folly of leaving the destruction of the Task Group to chance, as they saw it. They had little faith in the ability of GEA to do the job, and wanted to bring to bear their own modern weaponry. The Junta held to the view, however, that a decisive victory by the Corsair Grupo would bring not only kudos but considerable commercial gain from sales – one of the original aims of the project. This view prevailed in so far that the Grupo was given until noon on the 15th to accomplish its victory. Against this background Cassián, favoured by a period of excellent weather, finally launched his attack in the early forenoon. It will be recalled that the Grupo had made use of British advisers in its training. These were not used in the attack on the British ships, but in a gesture which has been described as characteristic of Cassián, he accompanied the attack as an airborne observer in a two-seat Corsair piloted by one of them, Commander JW Hicks RN.'*

238

From 17,000 feet, Roca's scars had faded, the field itself nearly lost in a vast perspective of desert and ocean. Hicks flew a wide left orbit outside loose sections of Corsairs spiralling slowly upwards. Turning through east, he winced as the low sun seared his eyes and splashed electric blue around the perspex. Cassián, enjoying himself immensely, said, 'Who was it said the sun shines always on the righteous?'

'I don't know,' Hicks replied. 'Presumably somebody who thought he had a monopoly of righteousness!'

'Like me?' Cassián laughed into his microphone.

'All aboard' at last, Monegario rolled out, heading into sun. Hicks took station above on the port side so that Cassián could see his whole armada down-sun. Hicks peered ahead. The Task Group's position had been updated just before take-off. There was no escape for them in this weather. He tried hard to feel neutral, telling himself over and over again there was nothing he could do to prevent what was going to happen. Nothing. And anything was better than sitting idle on the ground at Roca.

The bombers, thirteen four-ship divisions, fanned out behind Monegario in a three-mile arc, the Sierras in two lines across the rear, the three Echos in between. Hicks knew with great exactitude which among the apparently motionless mass of aircraft was Carla. The formation coasted out. The digital clock in Hicks' Corsair said 0801.

'. . . 'Eagle's' battle log commences with the reversal of course at 0749. Captain Carter's intention in turning away was to gain time. The easterly course also held out the possibility of reaching cover under the retreating cold front if the first massed air attack could be fought off. The first Sea Harrier was launched at 0803 with orders to engage and destroy the FAA Boeing 707 that Carter believed was shadowing his Group . . .'*

Lieutenant-Commander Nick Croft of 802 Squadron got the Boeing visual at twenty miles, a sun-silver speck in a cobalt sky, trailing heavily, going left-right. Croft eased left, climbing at Mach.85, and then swung right in a wide turn to roll in behind. Levelling at 38,000 feet, he held .85 and checked switches. The Boeing would be loitering, .72 maybe, plenty of overtake. It was huge in his Head-Up Display already and expanding, motionless, four engines pouring vapour. Acquisition tone. Don't think about it. Don't think. Just lift the trigger guard, like that, they won't know what hit them, and press, like that . . .

'. . . A Boeing 707 of Grupo 1 FAA based at BAM Commodoro Rivadavia was reported intercepted and destroyed by a Sea Harrier at 0816 while carrying out surveillance duties . . .'

Teniente de Aviación Carlos Gonzales, navigator of Kondor One Five, was bored. He yawned. How much longer? He pushed back the sleeve of his flight overall. But he never knew what time he died. Croft's AIM9-L chose the Boeing's No. 2 engine and buried its glass nose eagerly in the turbine disc. The explosion cracked the wing spar, which folded and then broke. One wing gone, the Boeing rolled, reluctant at such indignity, so by the time the first roll was complete it was nearly vertical and going sideways under the asymmetric thrust of its two left engines. It began to spin. One after the other, the two left engines tore away under centrifugal force before the wing snapped off at the root and tore the fuselage across like a corned beef can. But Teniente Gonzales and the other detritus that now surrounded him had several minutes of flight left to reach the surface of the sea. His relatives comforted themselves that he died instantly.

'. . . The first direct contact between TG 16 and GEA came at 0828 when a Sea Harrier, assumed to be the same one that had shot down the Boeing, intercepted the Corsair formation at high speed from the north . . .'

'Bogey! Bogey! Left ten o'clock high, closing!'
    Capitán de Corbeta Caballeros Figari, escort leader, jerked his head left, saw the Harrier, pressed his transmit button and said, 'Cobra Leader, contact, Maintain.' The Corsairs flew straight on. The Harrier arced out left, to come in behind. When it passed his wingtip Figari called, 'Cobra 4, Cobra 6, break port, go!' The two left-wing Sierras snapped

on ninety degrees of bank and pulled away towards the streaking Harrier. Figari hardly watched them go. 'Look for the others. Look for the other!' he called, admonishing, and suiting his actions to his words.

'. . . *'Eagle' launched her remaining Sea Harriers between 0815 and 0820 with orders to engage the incoming formation at maximum range. Carter then turned his Group right, onto south-east, in what he must have known was a futile attempt to evade detection. This was confirmed at 0828 when Lt-Commander Croft reported 'Fifty plus Corsairs, heading 090°, fifteen thousand feet' and read their position off his INS. Carter issued 'Air Raid Warning Red' to the Group, called the frigates into consort defence stations and ordered radars and fire-control systems activated. Meanwhile, Lt-Commander Croft had been shot down and killed attacking the approaching formation of Corsairs . . .'*

Cobras 4 and 6 turned so quickly they were beam-on to Croft almost before he realised it, coming in from his left, but loosely, as if to let him get ahead. He guessed they had Sidewinders, and this put him in a quandary: to continue on round behind for a cannon attack on the sprawling formation of bombers – or fight it out with these two? Duty, or inclination? He eased the turn, rolled out half a mile astern of the formation, throttled back, switched to 'Gun', placed his HUD aiming mark on the nearest Corsair and held it there, waiting for the range to come down to 400. It was only a question of time. A toss-up. His skin crawled; not fear, but a sensing of the total hostility of everything around him, and his own fragility. 500. Impatient, he was moving his throttle forward when Cobra 4's Sidewinder blew off his tail. The Harrier pitched up savagely to an instantaneous 12g, flicked and spun down towards the sea. Croft blacked out. Blind, helpless but dimly conscious, his last thought was merely 'What a bloody waste!'

'. . . *Three Sea Harriers intercepted GEA at 0830 and carried out a co-ordinated attack. They shot down two Corsairs – a bomber and one of the ECM aircraft. But in positioning for these attacks the Harriers were forced to expose themselves to the Sidewinder missiles of the nine fighter escorts lying astern of the main body. All but one of the Sea Harriers were destroyed in their first attacking pass . . .'*

It had been Blount's idea, the ring defence, Figari remembered, and like its creator it was sound but unexciting. The fighter boss scanned left and right, checking his squadron. The Harriers swooped in. A pair on each side? Discipline, Blount had said. None of your bloody gaucho heroics! Well, Figari was proud to watch his pilots holding the line. Four and Six were back in on the left. The Harriers too showed discipline, going for the main body, ignoring the outliers. Figari, not terribly well placed for a shot in his central sector, eased right a bit, against his rules, and was rewarded by an acquisition growl in his earphones as one of the Harriers slid into his twelve o'clock. He squeezed the trigger. Nothing happened. Again, harder. Nothing. *Madre de Dios!*

Lientenant-Commander Paul Reynolds, the Harrier squadron CO, had talked to Hicks, and he knew what the loose ring of Corsairs behind the main formation were. But this was no time for sport. There was only one job for him and his squadron, and that was to carve out as many of the bombers as possible before they got to the ships. Here I am, I can do no other. With a last glance over his left shoulder at the loitering fighters, he turned in, chose a Corsair, and lined up his gunsight, well aware that behind him sat eight or nine Corsairs with thirty-odd Sidewinders pointing at his tailpipe. He had the satisfaction of feeling his Aden cannon blast his chosen victim into a ball of fire before his own world detonated into a centrifuge of flame, ice-cold air, pain and darkness.

Like shooting fish in a barrel, thought the disgusted Figari, watching the striken Harrier twirling its streamer of fire down towards the ocean. What he really meant was, how unLatin. But this was the British way. He looked left. Another Corsair had been hit and was dropping out of the formation trailing smoke, and as he watched, the Harrier behind it torched like a firework, flew on, and then exploded into pieces as a second missile homed into the flames. This one's Number Two, seeing his leader's fate, zoomed hard up and away out of sight, and Figari was just in time to see, on his right, another Harrier disintegrating in a hail of missiles before it could fire a shot. He craned around, but couldn't see the other Harrier – the last one?

'Cobra 4, Cobra 6, drop back,' Figari instructed.

Lieutenant Bob White, shaken, loitered a few miles behind the Corsairs. From five thousand feet up. He had a plan view of Cobra 4 and 6 peeling off left, flying a tight orbit and rolling out in line abreast, two miles astern of the original rearguard, and he divined their intention: another line of defence, no doubt bristling with missiles. He discovered he was trembling, and cold. He was the last. There was a terrible implacability about the way this huge formation of strange aircraft flew on, carrying death and destruction towards the ship he had left only a few minutes ago. His home. And nothing he could do would stop it. To attack was suicide! If it were any use, he would gladly have hurled himself upon the formation and destroyed it – but one or two, what difference would that make? He spoke to *Eagle*:

'Kilo Victor, Red Three. Red Leader, Two and Four are splashed. I'm holding astern a formation of about sixty, repeat six zero, Corsairs, in gridref 045692, heading 090, speed one ninety, and standing by.'

'Kilo Victor, roger.' They could see well enough, *Eagle* on her 992R, the frigates, closed in to four cables on each beam, on their 967/968 surveillance radars. They had seen the ten-degree alteration Monegario made when his ECM pilots picked up the Task Groups change of course. Look-outs with binoculars strained aft, glasses shaking with the shuddering deckplates of the racing ships.

'. . . GEA pilots sighted TG 16 at 0844 at a range of about fifteen miles, and soon afterwards their leader, Capitán de Fregata Monegario, ordered the Grupo to assume 'Carousel' formation [see Diagram, Annex 9, the Official History might say]. Then, in what analysts regard as the masterstroke of the battle, Monegario sent his two remaining ECM Corsair-E's in from astern of the TG and ordered them to fire all eight Sidearms in salvo. Sidearm was basically Sidewinder AIM-9C

hardware fitted with a Motorola broadband RF homing head covering SAM acquisition and control frequencies. GEA had acquired a preproduction batch but had little or no data on their performance. The cluster of Mach-2 missiles was detected by the aft-facing Type 909 radars, and both frigates' GWS25 fire-control systems reacted by auto-launching Sea Wolf. Two explosions were seen some distance astern of the ships, but as Monegario had anticipated, several of the ARM's escaped destruction and continued to their targets. Both frigates' after 909 radars were demolished in this successful operational debut of the Motorola Sidearm (denigrated, up to this, by some, as the 'poor man's Shrike'). The TG was thus severely disabled before the battle proper had begun, its rear hemisphere defended only by manually-aimed, single-shot Sea Wolf, and it was from this direction that Monegario now began his attack.

The weather at 0900, from 'Eagle's' log, was: Wind, southerly force five; Cloud, nil; Visibility over 25km; Sea, moderate southerly; Swell, moderate westerly; Air temp, +3°C; Sea temp, +5°C . . .'

Chapter 25

Like a clockface six miles across, the Carousel held station on the speeding grey ships, Págalo dive-bombers at 15,000 feet, Cormor-ans down low on the water. Fifty-one bombers in all, mostly in pairs, all around the clock.

'Carousel, this is Aguila,' Monegario called 'Attack will commence!' And he read out twice the choreography of the attack. And their target: the westerly frigate first.

Págalo Ten Leader, Teniente Alberto Alvarez, rolled his wings level at 15,000 feet, smiled across and gave a thumbs-up sign to his wingman close aboard his starboard side, set his switches, put his prop up to 2,700 rpm and concentrated on assessing the relative wind and aiming problem. He was a serious 22-year-old, dark and religious but otherwise un-memorable, who had opted out of Cuyo University in Mendosa to join GEA, a refugee from cynicism. He crossed himself, rolled in, set his bombsight reflector over the tiny trio of ships, and lifted the trigger-guard.

Able Seaman Wayne Mitchell, *Breakspear*'s after Sea Wolf aimer, was a fair, gaunt nineteen-year-old from Swindon, clever in his way, but determined, after the rough and tumble of a single-parent upbringing and a lousy education, that whatever talents he might have were private property. 'Come on then, let's have you Dago bastards!' he yelled to the wind with the bravado of the street gang, settled himself back with joystick and trigger to track the first of the diving Corsairs.

Mitchell's Sea Wolf took Alvarez' Corsair on the wing-root, detonating itself, his fuel tanks and both his bombs in a gigantic plunging ball of fire. Págalo 10#2 was almost engulfed.

Thrown sideways by the blast he completed his dive but his bombs fell well astern of *Breakspear*.

'Missed, you bastard!' shouted Mitchell, shaking his fist at the Corsair's belly, pulling out overhead, but his grin of triumph froze when he looked astern again.

Coming straight up the wake, behind the wraiths of spray from the first bombs, were two more Corsairs in line astern, very low, and already close enough to hear their high metallic whine. Open-mouthed, Mitchell watched two bombs part company with the lead aircraft and descend towards him, black, round and not at all unfriendly-looking.

With no memories of war or experience of great violence, Mitchell's brain was not equipped to translate what he was seeing, and triggered no fear, only fascination. He was aware of the ship heeling hard, pushing him uncomfortably against the armrest of his steel seat, and of the deck trembling beneath his feet, but he could not take his eyes off the slanting bombs. They seemed to veer off right, flew past, went into the water fifty yards on the port beam and exploded. Cormorán 9#2 made a very late, rough correction when she saw *Breakspear*'s wake betraying a large rudder angle and her stern begin to swing, and her bombs near-missed the ship on the starboard side, springing several plates. Able Seaman Mitchell was icily drenched by falling spray. Enraged, spitting salt water and obscenities, he searched the sky astern for another target. Ignoring the call in his headphones to 'Engage high-level target Green 140!' (Págalo 8), Mitchell swung his mounting and attempted to bring the juddering sight to bear on Cormorán 10, now dead astern.

Págalo 8 Leader was Capitán de Corbeta Soler Martinez, OC 2 Squadron, GEA, a family-looking, short, bald man with a thin Latin moustache. His flat and unambitious personality had determined his naval career: at 45 his low rank was belied by his high standing as a naval aviator. He was a happy man. He loved his family, and his job, and he was very good in both. The TG's hard right turn added another variable to Martinez' aiming problem, but his logical mind worked calmly on the data and produced a prediction and an aiming-point. Martinez delayed release until the minimum safe height, pickled his bombs, and pulled out.

Able Seaman Mitchell squeezed his trigger with orgasmic fury and launched his second Sea Wolf horizontally at Cormorán 10, two miles astern, head-on. Grinding his teeth, he steered the missile marker on his TV tube towards the target in the centre. Steel-helmeted, white-cowled, he barely heard the short warning whistle of Martinez' bombs, One fell in the sea, close astern, the other on the frigate's quarterdeck, penetrating the deck-plates before exploding. The blast made a shambles of the upper, exposed part of Able Seaman Mitchell, opened *Breakspear*'s plates to the sea, distorted the port propeller-shaft A-bracket and started a fire. The loosened shaft, a hundred tons of whirling steel, flexed briefly and then broke, furthering the devastation of *Breakspear*'s after section. The frigate's steering failed and she swung out of the turn and slowed, settling by the stern.

Thrown upon its own resources by the demise of its master, Mitchell's Sea Wolf reverted to its onboard electronic wits for the final stages of its interception and was only able to achieve a near-miss. Its proximity fuse activated ten feet below the Corsair. Several of the short steel rods it ejected struck home, but Cormorán 10 came on. *Breakspear*, by now moving at only ten knots and almost broadside-on, took two more bombs low down on her port side. One failed to explode, but the other travelled through the ship and blew a large hole below the waterline on the starboard side, flooding the machinery spaces and stopping the ship.

'Check! Check! Check!' ordered Monegario, and the remainder of the twelve bombers he had allocated to *Breakspear* pulled off. Anticipating that Carter would continue to circle right, he now called in the bombers from one, two and three o'clock on the circle to take the other frigate in the rear as the ships turned through south. Hicks had placed himself just outside the Carousel to the east, nearest to Carla, although from 17,000 feet he had only caught a glimpse of her, Cormorán 3#2, circling with her Leader three miles below.

Biter's after Sea Wolf aimer was Leading Seaman John Dennis, a neat and conscientious 23-year-old whose dark, crinkly hair had earned him a lovely wife and two children in Rotherham. He had joined the Navy because he liked discipline and order, and enjoyed being trained. From where he

247

sat, concentrating hard upon his orders, he was unaware of *Breakspear*'s fate. He didn't fully understand how the GWS25 director behind him had come to be wrecked, but he was full of confidence in his own ability to aim the six missiles in his tubes, and there were plenty more below.

Págalo 1 Leader was his first target. Teniente Clarita Vargas had worked in a fashion store in Buenos Aires. She had a luscious, delicate beauty, rare among Latins, and her movements, which gave her the air of one walking in a minefield, excited protective instincts in men, whom she disliked. Although a football fanatic, she was highly intelligent, and she had joined GEA to confirm her view than she could do anything as well as a man. She died at 10,000 feet, in an instant of immense pain, when Dennis's first Sea Wolf exploded underneath her engine.

Dennis wasted no time watching or gloating, but set about zeroing his sight on Teniente Vargas' number two. Working calmly and without emotion, he tracked the diving Corsair, locked on, and fired. The missile erupted from its launcher and streaked away on its rocket plume. Dennis gathered the incandescent tailpipe into his sight and began steering it towards the target, still very calm – it was delicate work. *Whamm!* As if an angry giant had swung a preposterous hammer against the ship's side, *Biter* was slammed bodily sideways. Dennis found himself in the starboard scuppers, ears ringing, senses reeling, looking down at the blue water being sucked into *Biter*'s screws. He clutched fiercely at the guard-rail, hung for a moment, then remembered he had a job to do. It seemed perfectly natural that he couldn't walk, so he began to crawl, back towards his proper place as the after Sea Wolf aimer.

This time, Monegario had led with his low-level bombers. With *Biter*'s main armament dedicated to the high-level threat, Comorán 2 section encountered only light machine-gun fire on their approach up the frigate's wake and although she presented a narrow target, scored one hit and a near-miss with their four bombs. The one that struck the superstructure port side amidships caused only superficial damage and few casualties. It was not a vital part of the ship – but for one item: the blast distorted and partially closed the downtake to *Biter*'s port engine. The Olympus gas turbine, at full power, had a huge appetite for air that could no longer be supplied. It sucked fiercely, causing a partial vacuum that further collapsed the downtake duct, and its turbine temperature shot towards the red line. Before the machinery control room staff could react, the engine had auto-cut.

As the drag of her port screw made it impossible for *Biter* to match *Eagle*'s hard turn, and the distance between the two ships began to close, she was forced to reduce speed even further to avoid collision. Able Seaman Pascoe, a stolid Devonian whose grandfather had fought at Jutland and father at the Plate, was one of *Biter*'s after Sea Wolf loading numbers. He went to help Dennis. But the leading seaman couldn't move his legs. As Pascoe stood over him, irresolute, a pair of bombs whistled into the sea between *Biter* and *Eagle* and exploded with a hard, double boom.

Pascoe made up his mind. He'd failed the aimer's course, but always said he could do the job as well as most – except old Dennis who was shit-hot but now looked like a run-over dog. Ignoring the dangling headphones, Pascoe leaped into the vacant seat and scanned the sky for a target, fixing naturally upon another pair of Corsairs coming up the wake.

Cormorán 3 Leader was Teniente Miguel Castro, a 26-year-old from Buenos Aires with heavy, patrician good looks and sleepy eyes. Disgusted with his money-oriented life in the family firm, he had leapt at the chance of flying for GEA. Three miles to run, with two armed bombs and a British frigate in his sights, Castro was telling himself that no matter what happened in the rest of his life, this would be its crowning moment. His #2 was Teniente Carla Souza.

Able Seaman Pascoe indexed the third Sea Wolf and swung the mount to point astern. *Biter*'s asymmetric engines and large rudder angle shook her stern, making it impossible to focus the sight. Pascoe fought down a sense of panic – he knew how much now depended upon him. He fumbled and overcontrolled, finally managed to get a lock-on. He fired. Out low across the curving wake went the missile. But it was a very late shot. Pascoe had only two seconds in which to input steering commands before the proximity fuse exploded the Sea Wolf slightly above and ahead of Castro's Corsair.

249

Just one flailing steel rod struck Castro's left wingtip, displacing the aileron downwards and distorting the wingtip fairing so that the aileron was effectively jammed down. Castro's aircraft began to roll to the right. He tried to correct, but the stick wouldn't move to the left. Instinctively, he pulled up away from the water. The roll continued, and it was plain the Corsair was going to invert completely. Approaching *Biter*'s stern, he passed vertical bank, still rolling. Leaving the throttle at full power he pushed with both hands on the stick to get the Corsair's long nose up away from the water, but with a ton of bombs still on the wings he hadn't enough elevator power, and Castro knew he was going to die. Inexorably, the Corsair descended, still rolling. *Eagle* loomed ahead, very close. Castro had time to regret not having enough control to die in style, in a dive on the carrier. Then the water was coming up. But before the silver cord of his life was loosed, Miguel Castro had abundant time to call up a memory, a smoke-filled room of jangling telephones and VDU's, futures, indices, and exchange rates, the futilities of another life. He closed his eyes and whispered his last words: '*Gracias a Dios!*'

Able Seaman Pascoe tried to get the next plane in his sight, but it was no good. *Biter* had reversed her turn, and under emergency left rudder and full right engine was now swinging hard across *Eagle*'s stern. The bearing was changing too fast for Pascoe, Carla's Corsair now wide on the port quarter. She had seen the start of Castro's death-roll after the missile exploded, but now her whole concentration was on the spray-wreathed frigate ahead, turning hard left as if to escape, and although this made for a difficult slanting shot, it was steadily exposing more and more of its length. She jinked left, aimed at the empty ocean ahead of the ship, where she judged their paths would cross, levelled her wings and flew on. Three hundred, two hundred, the hull with its black number – F103 – began to pass under the Corsair's nose. Count . . . three . . . two . . . one . . . *Now!*' The Corsair lifted, a ton lighter, and Carla banked hard left away from the looming bulk of the carrier ahead and got down on the water with the sun behind her, heading for home.

It was only an old iron bomb, minus, by now, most of it factory green paint, but its performance was impeccable. Released from Carla's left wing it flew a mathematical descending curve, arming itself, and, as if it knew full well what it was about, found a spot on *Biter*'s port side aft between frames 134 and 135. Its hardened nose and blunt round shoulders peeled back the 13mm steel plate and thrust inside. Neatly parting various wiring looms and small pipes, it traversed a darkened store-room and went effortlessly through another thin bulkhead into the next compartment. Here, stimulated by its delay-fuse – a modern implant – the 35-year-old bomb, veteran of dumps, depots, and magazines in half a dozen diminishing countries, found fulfilment. Augmented by the twenty-eight missiles in *Biter*'s after Sea Wolf magazine, it blew her stern off.

Hicks had seen photographs and films like this. The flat-top carrier drawing a frantic circling wake; white bomb circles on the water; smoke plumes from crippled ships. But in those World War II shots, there had always been return fire, bursting AA shells and tracer. *Biter* lay dead in the water at the head of her twisting, evanescent wake, her stern gone, awash amidships. *Eagle* had come nearly full circle and was heading back towards *Breakspear*, also stopped and low by the stern, and burning. As Hicks watched, *Eagle* eased her turn and seemed to be making towards *Breakspear* – to protect, or for protection, from the frigate's for'd Sea Wolf battery? Carla had cleared. Hicks watched tensely to see her leave the scene of battle and climb out west. With her departure, the second phase of Monegario's attack plan was complete, and the remaining twelve sections of bombers circled on their Carousel stations, awaiting *Aguila*'s order of battle for the final assault on the carrier.

*

SECRET

FLASH.

151400Z.

FROM: CTG16.

TO: CINC FLEET.

=*Breakspear and Biter disabled by bombing. All Sea Harriers lost to enemy action. Eagle will continue to defend the flag. God save the Queen*=

'. . . The effect of this signal, placed before the Defence Council within ten minutes of transmission, was paralysing. Members have since testified that in the immediate discussion that followed, the word surrender 'hung in the air', but was never uttered. The scenario of the mortal battle in which TG 16 was at that moment engaged eight thousand miles away was clearly conveyed by the signal – the force of three ships and 1,500 men faced imminent and certain annihilation. But the option of ordering Carter to haul down his flag was 'never admittable' – and it cannot have escaped any member of the Council that with every minute of discussion, it became less relevant. It was as if, one member said, news of the peremptory defeat of a Task Group of modern warships by a Latin American force of vintage aircraft, and the fearful adumbrations this carried for the rest of the Falklands campaign, would be mitigated, when it was passed on to the Cabinet, and ultimately the public, by a heroic last stand. No return signal was sent to Admiral Carter . . .'

Sixteen thousand tons, £400 million, a thousand men, facing annihilation and nothing more than small-arms for defence. Hicks had warned him, but Carter still found the disablement of his frigates hard to take in. His attackers, he guessed, had so far used less than half of their resources. He looked down from his bridge upon the men ranged around *Eagle*'s catwalks, rifles and light machine-guns at the ready. They might as well be bows and arrows! What now? The classic choice for a commander *in extremis* was to fight or surrender. Fight? What with?

Surrender? A major war vessel of Her Britannic Majesty's Royal Navy strike her colours on the high seas? Unscathed and without firing a shot! When did that last happen? If the *Prince of Wales* and *Repulse* had surrendered – and their situation was as hopeless and politically inept as his – who would have understood? Who of those in England that were not here would condone such a disgrace? – the pride of the Royal Navy sailed into Buenos Aires by a prize crew of dagoes! That's what they would say. The name of Carter would stink down through the rest of naval history. Another name came to his mind – Whitelock, luckless commander of the expeditionary force sent to seize Buenos Aires for Britain just before independence in 1806. He was routed by the city's inhabitants and sent home in disgrace. Carter sympathized, now, with the plaintiveness of his report: '. . . every male inhabitant, whether free or slave, fought with a resolution and perseverance which could not have been expected even from the enthusiasm of religion and national prejudice, or the most inveterate and implacable hostility.' Then as now, there would be no understanding. But that's what senior officers were for, to stand in the hard places and take the rub. That much would be understood! The bridge clock stood at 1408GMT. Carter smiled wryly and thought, 'And those in England still at lunch, shall count themselves full glad they were not here!'

'Midships! Revolutions 180,' he ordered. 'Tell *Breakspear* I'm moving into her bow arc. And confirm she's still got power on those for'd missiles!'

An access of welling, helpless rage assailed Hicks at what was going to happen next. Rage at politicians, at the ductile doughfaced armed forces hierarchy, at the whole clawing scrum of self-seekers who had conspired to put two thousand of their countrymen in such a position. He considered interced-ing, with Cassián in the cockpit behind him, on behalf of the ships, but baulked at the impropriety of it – usurping Carter's privilege. He could only watch. *Eagle* was approaching *Breakspear* from astern, to pass her to starboard. Soon she would have some cover – if *Breakspear*'s missiles were still 'up'.

Breakspear was flooding, the thrashing port propeller-shaft had opened her up as far as the machinery spaces amidships, stopping all four gas turbines. Two emergency diesels further for'd were barely capable of supplying power to her opera-tional equipment, and all her pumps could not keep down rising water in several large midships compartments. While damage control parties fought below decks with timber shores and wedges, her company gathered on the upper decks where, in the unaccustomed silence and biting salt wind they tended the injured and burnt.

Not all were accounted for. Among the missing was 17-year-old Darren Gregory, a prissy young steward with the

253

looks of a divinity student, long chin and spectacles. He had joined the Navy subconsciously searching for the order so absent in his upbringing and education. His action station was in the after missile magazine, deep down in the frigate's stern, where, alone, he monitored a simple phase of the Sea Wolf auto-loading train. Since the first colossal bang, it had been very quiet – an unnatural stillness Gregory could feel even after he realised he was deaf. There had been a temporary power failure, then the stillness. He was getting cold. No air came through the trunking, and nothing had happened for a long time, but it was outside Gregory's nature to initiate use of his sound-powered phone, or to try to open the oval hatch above his head, the only way out.

The deck sloped. Gregory didn't know that his compartment was already deeply submerged; that he was the only living thing aft of *Breakspear*'s funnel.

'Págalo 5, Cormorán 6, Págalo 7, Cormorán 5, Págalo 6, Cormorán 7. Stand by!' Monegario read out the order twice. Hicks had been watching, when he could see it, the surviving Sea Harrier. Now, he thought, it must try, at least try. It was a few thousand feet above the Págalos, to the south, with all the Sierras down there too, holding it off. Hicks' aircraft was unarmed – not that he could have done anything. As he sat, warm, dry and safe in his cockpit, Hicks churned with rage, frustration, compassion and hate, and he vowed he would shout from the rooftops, when he got home, what he had seen. Dealers and manipulators and profiteers, all obsessed with their own foul bottom lines. Well here was the real Bottom Line – and the bankruptcy court for a sailor was the ocean bed two thousand fathoms down.

The southern bomber sections were still circling, waiting for the executive GO! from Monegario. He, evidently, was holding them back until he was sure of *Eagle*'s intention. He could take his time: there was no need to risk further Corsair losses. It seemed to Hicks that *Breakspear*'s stern was lower, without the bow coming up. She was settling – yes, an orange dot, and then another – liferafts, alongside. Oh God! And smoke, thin grey smoke, streaming out from *Biter*'s shattered stern. Hicks just wanted to close his eyes.

'Stop! Stop! Aguila, this is *El Comando* – Cease the attack! Acknowledge!' Cassián's voice, even muffled by an oxygen mask, was unmistakable.

Monegario did not reply immediately.

'Aguila, this is Contraalmirante Cassián. The attack is to be discontinued! Acknowledge!'

After a highly eloquent pause, Monegario came back, 'Aguila, Roger.' He paused again. 'Aguila, request further instructions?'

'Remaining bombers assemble in formation to the south. Fighters hold off the Harrier. If the Harrier attacks, I would prefer you evade, not shoot him down.' And to Hicks, 'We will join with the bombers, Eeks, please.'

Bewildered, Hicks did as he was bid. Beset by a new tangle of emotions, he didn't trust himself to speak to the man a few feet behind him. Was this reprieve? He dared not even give rein to hope, but what else?

Seeing the bombers withdrawing, the Harrier pilot made, at last and misguidedly, his attack upon Alvarez' fighters. He brought his speed down to match theirs, chose his target, and swooped in a fair imitation of his namesake. He used flap and vectored thrust and every trick in his young repertoire, but could not prevent Alvarez, who had had twenty years of practice, from sliding away from his aiming pipper just as he got in range. Emboldened by his continued survival – in contrast to the fate of his squadron-mates – he gave up chasing Alvarez and picked another target, hoping for something easier, and then another. He saw his cannon shells strike the fleeting tail of one aircraft, apparently without effect, but then a caution sounded off and his Master Warning System told him he was 'Low fuel' and he rolled inverted and accelerated away from the mêlée towards his ship. He was on *Eagle*'s deck in three minutes, baffled and puzzled at still being alive.

On instructions from Cassián, the phalanx of 26 Corsair bombers flew directly at the crippled Task Group from the south, at 3,000 feet. Monegario and Hicks, flying as a pair, were in the lead.

'How do you tell them to get ready to drop ze bombs?' Cassián asked Hicks when they still had five or six miles to run.

'You say "Make Switches".'

'Make Switches!' the Commodore transmitted. Then, two miles short of the carrier, 'Stand by to release bombs . . . stand by . . . *Now!*'

A rain of bombs from the close-packed Corsairs fell into the ocean well short of the ships with a rolling thunder of explosions that turned a square mile of sea into a carpet of geysering foam. The formation held its course, straight over the Task Group towards the north, into the frigates' bow arcs, and only then made a slow turn left for home. No words passed between Hicks and his passenger for the rest of the flight.

Eagle stopped. Her boats and Sea Kings picked up *Breakspear*'s crew. When rising water choked the frigate's diesel generators, Steward Gregory's light went out. Wide-eyed, blind now as well as deaf, he stood clutching the cold steel frame of his ammunition hoist looking at nothing through his useless glasses. The slope of the deck beneath his feet seemed to have increased, but it was very hard to be sure in the dark. Mercifully, he could not hear the bulkheads around him straining under the increasing pressure. When *Breakspear* finally quit the surface and began her last voyage to the bottom of the sea, stern-first, Gregory was sure his floor was tilting. But he couldn't hear the rising scream of tortured metal all around, and his end came with the merciful suddenness of a detonation, at about a hundred fathoms, just as he began to think of screaming.

*

SECRET

FLASH.

151416Z.

FROM: CTG16

TO: CINC FLEET.

=*Air attack terminated. Enemy withdrawn. Breakspear sunk. Biter heavily damaged and without power. Eagle undamaged and preparing tow*=

'. . . To this signal, CinC Fleet did reply, and quickly: 'If Biter unable move under own power within one hour she is to be abandoned and sunk. Eagle to proceed east at best speed. . .'

Eagle took off Biter's crew. Before they left, they opened her up to the sea, but she was slow to sink. Her crew, on Eagle's crowded flight deck pounding eastwards, were watching her slowly diminishing shape with fond pride, talking of the stubbornness of the old lady, when Thunderer's Tigerfish struck her amidships and tore her heart out. Within minutes she was gone.

Chapter 26

The Commodore, for the first time in Hicks' experience, was in the Rancho, standing on a low table with a large cigar, and around him the pilots of his Grupo. He held up his hand and there was quiet.

'Cormoráns, Págalos, Cobras – I contragulate you all!' Hicks was forced to smile at the Caesarian opening. He felt for Carla's hand beside him and squeezed it as Cassián went on: 'This was your day of fulfilment, and it was magnificent! For some, the ultimate – using the weapons you have practised with so long. For others, their weapons were not used, but their contribution was no less important. And for some, their fate was to die for their country: these will have a place on a very special roll of honour in the history of Argentina. For us, though, they were our friends, so let us pause a moment to remember them, and commit their souls to God.'

A very few times before in his life, Hicks had experienced the strange, tingling resonance that he felt about him in the long silence. The war thrill, gift of great commanders. Cassián, a great commander?

'*In nomine Patri, Fili, et Spiritu Sanctu.*' Cassián crossed himself. 'Yes, history indeed. All your names will be associated with this battle. You were there, at Punta Medanosa. And you must understand what happened. And what did not happen. People will ask – why did you not sink the British carrier when you had the chance, whose planes had attacked for days, whose bombs had killed and injured your comrades?' People had been asking nothing else since they got back! 'Well, we need to think: our business is war, but

258

what is the aim of war? Is it to kill people?' The commodore, eyebrows up, questioned the surrounding upturned faces. None replied. 'No. That is plainly absurd. The aim of war is peace. We fight to rectify a cause and to restore peace. Our cause here, which we hold just, is the Malvinas. And the British too feel they have just cause to commit their citizens to war for these islands, so we fight, each for his own aim. And this aim is the only justification of what we are paid to do; and it is only in pursuit of this one aim that it is moral to take life.

'Now consider. If you had sunk the *Eagle*, killing many defenceless men and leaving the rest in the sea with little hope of rescue, how would such an act of savagery have served our country? For that is how it would be seen! The British do not possess Sea Harriers to replace those they have lost. *Eagle* is no asset to them any more, in this war. She has become, as you last saw her, a liability.' The voice tailed off, and the crowded room was very quiet. Cassián contemplated the end of his cigar.

'Oh yes, it pays to think of history! Argentina aspires to the company of civilised nations. But even more than this, consider your own humanity. What is this thing that marks us out from monkeys? Reason, you will say, and reason – yes – but besides this an ability to challenge our instincts. When I looked down on that big ship, that big British warship that had been our adversary for so long and done us so much harm, my instinct was to kill – a very strong urge to kill. But then I thought, am I a monkey? Are we all performing chimpanzees that we must follow instinct? And I decided, for all of us, that we were not! I would like to think you will agree that your abstinence, your final elegant gesture of magnanimity, rather than diminishing your victory, underlined it, and will command far more respect than if you had merely smashed and killed like barbarians.'

One or two murmurs of assent could be heard in the ensuing pause. Cassián wound up his speech: 'So, for what you did, feel proud. For what you did not do, feel glad, feel magnanimous, feel civilised, feel human. I salute you all, *mis amigos!*' The little black eyes sparkled, and he stepped down.

'Are you leaving us then?' Hicks managed, not without difficulty, to talk privately with Cassián in the crush.

'I don't know, Eeks. It is too soon. But I expect to be removed, now.'

'Removed? But surely you should expect honour, now, and promotion!'

The Commodore smiled, indulgently. 'So speaks the gringo! Eeks, this is South America, and in South America success is as dangerous as failure! Ovid said it long ago: "What is highest is envy's mark: winds sweep the summit"! Many wanted me to fail anyway, and my supporters now will make GEA's success their own. For me, there is no future.'

Hicks looked hard for some sign of bitterness or rancour in Cassián's expression, but saw only the usual bantering serenity. 'Then why did you do it? All these years?'

'Very simple, my friend! A happy alignment of conviction and inclination. I have worked for Argentina, because I believe in her future. And for myself, to destroy the myth of modern arms. I have done it! I have proved my thesis. I have made many enemies, of course, but for me the satisfaction is complete. I will now enjoy to hear all the arguments about it!'

Carla insisted she was not tired, but she made only faint protest when Hicks took her early from the celebrations. A freezing south-easter cut through their clothes as they walked home.

'Oh, Eeks, it's cold!' Carla shuddered. Hicks took off his leather jacket and put it over her shoulders as they hurried on. Suddenly, she stopped, turned round into the wind and looked up at the stars. 'Eeks. All those men in the sheeps – you think they are all right?' He assured her they were, all heading east, safe now, onboard *Eagle*. But she still stood looking up at the cold sky, out over where they had fought the morning's battle. 'So cold! Just think, Eeks, if we 'ad sink the carrier, those men, they would be in the sea, in this cold! And only one man to stop us!' They walked quickly on with the wind. 'You know, Eeks, I 'ave, what you say, the willies, to think how close we are to barbarians when we fight a war! Even me, and my friends who I like. And you? Before, I think fighting is like a job – you have a war and somebody got to do it, yes like a job. But if Cassián did not stop us today we are all barbarians now, all ordinary good people. And me. I don't understand!'

260

Hicks ushered her into the warmth of his rooms. 'I don't understand either, Carla, except that war brings out the best and worst in people. It's big business, and people have a lot of power in war. Today, every GEA pilot felt the power of destruction that they had, and this is not good. Power corrupts. You should know!'

'And how should I know about this?' Carla was taking off her own pilot's jacket, and she held it a moment behind her in a way that tightened the front of her khaki shirt. Hicks matched, as best he could, the arch look on her face, and standing in front of her put his hands on her rib-cage and then, slowly, cupped her small breasts.

'"How should I know about this?"' he mimicked. 'You women. You have the real power. You should leave these other games to men. It's all we have!'

'Pah! Eeks, you speak *ridicolo*!' She smiled. But she covered his hands, and pressing them to her, kissed him lightly and said, 'I don't know what you mean!'

'The greatest power of all – to create. How is our child?' She was in his arms now, and he spoke into her hair with its redolence of aeroplane.

'He is very well, thank you. You see – he speak like Englishman already!'

'And Mama?' He cupped his hands behind her head, pushing up her hair. 'Mama is very beautiful. He is going to be a most fortunate child.' He brushed her cheeks, and then her lips, very lightly with his own. 'But Mama is also tired.' He examined her face seriously. 'Even more beautiful than before – but more tired too, than before. Carla, please, no more flying. You have done enough, after today!'

'But my darling – we 'ave decide! The doctor says no problem for a month. I must do my work for the Grupo, and then I finish.' A shadow crossed her face. 'You too will finish, Eeks. And then . . .' There had been no time to talk about this; little enough time for Hicks to think about it. But he knew without thinking, that his future, now, was here in Argentina, with Carla and the child. It was not a question to be decided: the alternative was unthinkable. Carla was looking back at him with that direct way she had, not asking nor pleading, just placing the question between them. Her arms

261

were by her sides, her neck still nestling in his hands. From this pose they had often started to make love, she standing passively to be undressed. And then . . . ?

'And then,' he said, 'before he is born, you will have time to teach me to speak Spanish properly.'

She didn't move, only her eyes on his face, probing. After a little while, she said, 'You stay in Argentina?'

'Yes.'

Quite still she stood, their eyes locked. Eventually: 'How long?'

'As long as you want me.'

Another long silence. Hicks began to wonder if she would ever react. And then he saw a glittering tear form in the corner of her eye. It ran its course down her cheek, and still she didn't move. Another one started. Hicks could bear it no longer, and he quietly folded her thin body to him and held her tight.

In a small gale of happiness, they discussed and planned, the way people do who don't really care what happens: everything is going to be all right, no matter what. And then they went at last to bed, where Hicks, doubly excited by Carla's happiness, the exquisite denial of her condition, and the events of the day, lay far from sleep. She too, for after a while she suddenly gripped his hand.

'Eeks!'

'*Sí, querida?*'

'I am thinking. About today. What happen if, say Cassián not there, and Monegario orders to attack the carrier, at the end, with all the bombers. What happen if somebody say no? They refuse, and give the same reasons as Cassián. This would not be good for them, I think!'

'No. Disobeying orders, in the field. Worst offence in military discipline. Very serious. Court martial. Why?'

'But this is horrible! Don't you see? We all agree Cassián was right, and we are glad, like he says, he stop us from being like *los bárbaros*. But if Cassián is not there, we must be *bárbaros* if this is the order! There is no choice! I did not understand this before. Is it right?'

'I'm afraid so. When you wear uniform, you don't make up your own mind how you will fight.'

'But this is the same as to say if you wear uniform you have no mind!'

He turned towards her in the bed and put his hand on her still-flat stomach. 'Carla, my love. That is one ugliness of war, but not the only one. This is why I say you two should not be in it any more. Our child should not start his life like that.'

She pressed his hand. 'But I must. To start a thing and then give up because you do not agree the rules, I don't like. I must finish my duty. Our son would want it, if he is a good Argentine. I know!'

'Or she?'

'She too. Like me!'

Carla, as always, had resolved her doubt, or cast if off. Soon the twitching of her hand told she was asleep.

'. . . *During the night* [the Official History might say], *taking advantage of a spell of calm, the re-invasion Task Force commander brought his ships together in latitude 53°S, a safe distance east of Punta Medanosa, in order to transfer men and supplies from the troopships and supply vessels into the ships to be used in the landing – a very considerable operation. The opportunity was taken to assemble subordinate commanders and brief them on the invasion plan which had, of necessity, been formulated on passage.*

'The convergence of ships was detected before dark by Soviet satellite and this information was passed, routinely, to Teatro de Operaciones del Atlantico Sur (TOAS) at Comodoro Rivadavia. After consultation with the Junta, TOAS decided at this point to deploy all available air resources in an attempt to forestall a landing. Instructions were issued immediately to all FAA and CANA bases to prepare for a co-ordinated search-and-destroy programme at first light. The Junta, as yet unaware of the true circumstances surrounding 'Eagle's escape, and pleased with the sinking of two frigates by what they regarded as a vestigial GEA, made known their wish that Cassián's Grupo was to be given a role in this operation. (It should be remembered that, up to this, the Grupo had been a well-kept secret; and there was considerable prejudice against it among the few orthodox senior

263

officers who knew of its existence). Accordingly, GEA was entrusted with the task for which the Corsairs were best suited, the initial armed search, while the shorter-endurance jets, AAF Daggers and Skyhawks, CANA Etendards, were to be kept on the ground until the Task Force had been fixed. LRMP Neptunes and Hercules were to be launched well before dawn . . .'

Hicks' phone rang early. Teniente de Souza to report for briefing in forty-five minutes. No, the *consejeros* were not required.

He met LeStrange and Finch in the Rancho for breakfast. The empty messrooms spoke of another major operation, but nobody yet knew what.

'Well, they won't get away with it again,' said Finch grimly. 'Now that Cassián's made his point, he's going to have to play to win!'

'Surely they'll stay out of range!' said LeStrange. 'After what you told them, Jeff!' From the BBC, they knew the Task Force was getting close.

'Well, they've got to come in some time. The islands are only 450 miles from here.' Hicks poured himself some tea. 'And when they do, and the Grupo find them, they're dead ducks! A massacre!'

'And those Type 22's are the best we have, AA-wise?' Finch asked.

'The latest and the best!'

'Jesus!' Finch's face was grim.

'What a way to run a railway!'

'Quite.'

The big room was quiet. Hicks had told them his feelings yesterday, watching the defenceless carrier awaiting slaughter. What he had not told them was that, ever since, he had felt himself started on a downward vista whose lower reaches went beyond his experience.

'I may be wrong, but isn't this just what we expected?' LeStrange put the question in his usual overdone way.

'Expecting and seeing are different things! You can't rationalise a thousand poor bloody sailors waiting to be blown out of the water, no matter who's to blame.' The irritable voice sounded to Hicks like somebody else's. Every word a click of the rachet. The others hadn't been there.

Tracey had joined them. 'Well, OK,' he said, breezily, 'it's tough on the navy – but at least it's their scene. It's the poor bloody pongoes I feel sorry for, when this lot catch them!'

'Is this it then? Is that what they're briefing for?' LeStrange asked.

'Well, the navy can't invade the bleeding islands, can they?' Tracey replied irritably. 'I think the Argeys are probably capable of working out that if they sink the troops, they win. And also that you lot are not discussing cricket scores – God's sake cheer up before we're all arrested for conspiracy!'

The few others eating breakfast were all non-combatants. Hicks smiled and raised a hand as the engineer of No. 3 Squadron got up and left, and then he heard his voice say casually, 'Now is the time for all good men to come to the aid of the party.'

Nobody replied for a while. Then Finch said, 'There's only the A4's.'

'And what are you going to do with four Skyhawks?' Le-Strange snorted.

'More than sitting on your fat ass here, stuffing buns!' retorted Tracey.

'I thought we were here for the money!' said Finch, with a rare crooked smile.

'Yeah, well . . .'

Seeing Carla walking up from the briefing, Hicks was struck how she stated her personality in the simplicity of her dress and bearing, and, as she got closer, how her small fine features had softened. So very beautiful! It was hard not to touch her as they walked. The weather in the target area was bad, she told him, and the Grupo was holding until LRMP could refine the Task Force's position. Carla had been assigned the lead of her section and she was very proud.

'But I 'ave a feeling, Eeks . . . not a good feeling. Yesterday, you were there with me, and everything is all right. But today, I go alone. A long way, alone without you . . .'

265

With Carla on readiness, they were confined to the vicinity of the operations room. Hicks took her for a coffee in the flight canteen.

'Everything will be all right,' he told her, managing unobviously to hold her hand as they sat together. 'You think of me, and I will think of you. That way, we will be together. But not too much! Best way to come back safe is to keep your mind on the job, and look behind you. Yes?'

'Yes.'

'Promise?'

'*Promiso.*' She smiled brightly, but her hand was cold and damp.

'*. . . On the morning of 17th May, a warm north-westerly airstream moving over the cold Falkland Current drew a veil of low cloud and drizzle over the Task Force marshalling area around 49°S 53°W. This further impeded the task of Argentine LRMP aircraft, already kept at arm's length by the menace of 'Hermes' and 'Invincible's' Sea Harriers, and denied TOAS the information needed to target attacks by conventional jet squadrons. Aware that reinvasion was imminent, and that to allow the Task Force to group and prepare unmolested would invite a dash under cover of darkness to a dawn landing, by 0900 TOAS decided they could delay no longer. Accordingly, GEA at Roca was instructed to launch its bombers on a search/ strike plan based upon a narrow fan of search tracks covering the area occupied by the Task Force. Their orders, to locate the troop transports and attack these first, carried an implication that TOAS, at least, regarded GEA as expendable.*'

'*Attencion! Attencion!* Pilots report to your squadrons! Pilots report to your squadrons. *Pronto!*'

Hicks had always detested tannoys. The metallic power-laden voice, instrusive as a knife, churned his stomach. Carla started, instinctively removing her hand as all about them pilots made noisily for the door. She stood up, irresolute. 'I 'ave to go . . . Eeks . . . goodbye . . . goodbye . . .'

As if sucked towards the door by the crowd, she started to draw away, Hicks watched, dazedly, until she was half way across the room, and then a flash of panic went through him.

He rushed to her, caught her. She resisted briefly, and then they were in each other's arms. She stiffened, and he let her go. The naked wistful longing in the deep brown eyes as she said, *'Adios*, Eeks. *Adios!'* nearly broke him. Then she was gone. She never heard his quiet *'Vaya con Dios, querida!'*

Oddly, no special orders had been issued regarding the custody of the Skyhawks which, since the bombing, had been casually dispersed about the base and largely neglected. It had been arranged that, after breakfast, Finch would ring No. 3 Squadron engineering office and ask for the four jets to be pre-flighted and signed up, and he told Hicks now, when they met by the control tower, that the request had caused no comment. In fact, on his way down, he had seen mechanics working on the one parked up the road behind the tower.

Hicks nodded, as if he understood without hearing, and the two men stood on the edge of the windswept airfield. But Hicks was in a world apart. He saw the scurrying trucks and jeeps distributing pilots, and the scattered Corsairs whirling their propellers into life one by one and start to move; he didn't know which one was Carla. He heard the rumble of engines and the howling of the *uligán* through the shattered glass of the belvedere above.

He could smell, would always smell, the blend of sweet burnt AvGas, concrete, desert and sea that was Roca. He could feel through him the throb of the first Corsairs labouring overhead, heavy with bombs and fuel. And he could taste Carla's last kiss, and it was this that had him, once again, trapped in a cathedral where the fluted columns and fan-vaulting and organ music were his own emotions and he desperately wanted to ask somebody – God should be here – was it his fault? Was he to be crucified now? And why? Had he sinned that much, who merely went through open doors where lights shone? He recognised his sin and named it Acquiescence. Was life then a trap, a price on every happiness, even unto this? The cathedral was huge, but its odorous coolness rang empty with his silent cries. He felt a touch on his arm.

'Jeff. You should stay here.' It was Finch. He was right, of course. Lay down the cross. Give it up. It was too much. 'We can't all go,' Finch was saying, 'and Miles is happy to make the foursome.'

Hicks heard his own voice, hollow, saying, 'No Mike. Miles is the best one to stay. He can tell the story.' Then by a huge effort of will he was outside his cathedral, watching the Grupo circling overhead, black swallows against the sullen cloud. He ought to know which one was Carla, but he didn't. Finch said, 'What's the plan?'

Hicks laughed shortly. 'Plan? You steal your aeroplane and head east. Suggested track is 100° magnetic. We go independently – unless we manage to join up. Keep low or they might send something out from San Julian or Rio Gallegos to pick us off. We have to hope if the Grupo find anything there'll be enough R/T for us to home onto the action with Green Silk. What you do then is up to you.'

'And afterwards? Splashdown and throw ourselves on the world-famous hospitality of the Royal Navy?'

'That's about it. No way you'll get back here in an A4.'

The Grupo was formed up now. Monegario rolled out of his left orbit and led the loose formation of Corsairs out over the coast. The wind swallowed the sound of their engines, and the aircraft diminished to specks and then disappeared. As the two men turned their backs on the deserted airfield, Hicks looked at his watch: 0928. He asked Finch, 'Why are you doing this, Mike?'

'I daren't stop to think,' was Finch's answer.

They had an hour, if they were to arrive in the target area at the same time as the Corsairs and not waste fuel loitering. Hicks went to his room to collect a few essentials and left quickly, shutting the door firmly behind him and not looking back. He went to his office to pick up his helmet and a life-jacket. He had the use of a jeep, and it was arranged that he, Finch and LeStrange should use this to get to the three Skyhawks parked out on the southern perimeter, while Tracey went on foot to the one behind the tower. The aim was a synchronised start-up, at 1025, and then every man for himself.

The base looked silent and deserted but Hicks knew how many windows would become eyes when the sound of jets was heard; lucky the tower was still boarded up. He wished he could board up his mind. Like a drowning man trying not to inhale the choking water, he struggled to eradicate Carla and the lost future. He found it calmed him to think of Pauline now, his other, older love. Her scaffolding would hold: there was a rock-steadiness about the world she inhabited that he found too difficult now to evoke, as if it were a galaxy away.

Expecting to be challenged any minute, they drove out around the perimeter track, eastwards so as not to pass the tower. Hicks slowed to drop off LeStrange and Finch at their aircraft, drew up behind his own, removed the chocks and covers and climbed into the high cockpit. Sitting on the hard dinghy-pack that formed the squab of the ejection seat, he pulled on his helmet and set the switches ready for start.

For a long fifty seconds Hicks watched the access roads on the far side of the airfield. Nothing moved. Just the sweep hand on his watch. When it touched twelve he put the fuel cock on and pressed the starter button. The three A-4s fired off with a prolonged roar. Three plumes of black smoke blew away on the wind and the low whine of jets spread across the field. Before their engines reached idling speed, four Skyhawks were moving. Hicks swung right towards the threshold of runway 30, closing his canopy. He could see Finch taxing towards him from the other side of the runway and also some movement near the control tower a mile away on his left. He took the sharp left turn onto the runway at a ridiculous speed and rammed the throttle fully forward, calling, 'Rolling, three zero, rolling, *go!*' while struggling to control an almost broadside skid. He managed to stay on the concrete, and then the turbine hit full RPM and the thrust came in with a big push in the back and he was accelerating down the runway and had time to look ahead.

Another Skyhawk was coming toward him, head-on. Tracey! And behind him a cloud of dust and a scurry of vehicles. Hicks ruddered left and swerved as far as he dared towards the edge of the runway. If Tracey did the same, there should be plenty of room for them to pass. So they had figured, anyway! Yes – he was moving over: no problem! On he came, on, on, and then he was past, very close and very audible; but what about *all those fucking vehicles!* A car and a

269

jeep, nearly abreast, and a long way behind, a lumbering fire-wagon, following Tracey down the runway! The fools! Well, he couldn't stop if he wanted to. Hicks swung the jet back onto the centreline and aimed directly at the advancing vehicles. The car and jeep, quite close, lost their nerve and slewed off left and right into the dirt, leaving the fire engine coming on alone. Bloody idiot! Hicks checked his speed: 105. 110. 115. Two hundred yards. 120. He kept the Skyhawk's nose down. One hundred yards. He could almost read the number-plate as he pulled back on the stick. The Skyhawk rotated eagerly and leapt into the air, clearing the fire engine by more than ten feet.

Hicks banked hard right, wheels coming up, and looked behind as he passed over the tower. Finch had followed him close behind and was just lifting off. He couldn't see Tracey. But the fire-wagon! The driver must have decided he'd had enough, because he was swinging left off 30 runway at the intersection and onto 24, LeStrange's runway. He saw the Skyhawk head-on at less than two hundred yards, and panicked. The heavy wagon, its front wheels on full lock, heeled over, lay on its side, and slid up the centre of the runway. LeStrange had no chance.

Hicks saw only the start of the fireball and then he had to look to his own affairs. Already nearing the coast and doing 340 knots, he throttled back and descended. Clearing the clifftops by less than twenty feet, he levelled just above the sea on course, 100° magnetic, and checked both compasses and his altimeters. A movement out to his left caught his eye: Finch, right down on the sea and looking very fast although he was holding station, at about a hundred yards. He rocked his wings in answer to Hicks.

It was good to have company. Hicks eased up a hundred feet and set about strapping himself in. He had put on a lot of warm clothing; he had a life-jacket, an ejection seat and a dinghy; but he had no illusions about surviving long in water at 3°C. When all the straps were done up, he withdrew the seat safety pins and put them tidily in the stowage. Finch had gone even higher. Good idea: salted-up windscreens wouldn't help. Hicks eased up to three hundred feet and settled down.

270

Chapter 27

And then, for a while, there was nothing to do but think.

In his left hand, the throttle lever, thrusting him away from the Argentine coast at five miles a minute; in his right hand, the stick – a tiny pressure would turn him back to safety. But throttle and controls held steady and the Skyhawk flew on eastwards. Why? What was it pushing him out into the deep South Atlantic with no hope of return? Resist? It would have been as easy to stop breathing. So what was it?

You put on a uniform, you don't choose how you fight, he had told Carla. Yes, you surrender your humanity to something that transcends and diminishes it. But maybe, too, enhances it? Why not? Anyway, several thousand pounds of engine thrust was driving him out like a vector over a hostile ocean, probably never to return, and it had become very important to give that vector a name. Patriotism? Not a fashionable word. Not an attractive idea. Old hat, like religion. What else? What else? There wasn't much time.

Look at all the others! Munro died sadly, Blount nobly by any standards, and now LeStrange was gone and the rest, bar one, committed to this hopeless joust, everything to lose and nothing to gain, on behalf of people, most of whom they wouldn't pass the time of day with but who happened to carry the same passport. There hadn't even been any discussion, for God's sake! The response had been instinctive, a moral knee-jerk, triggered by something that must have been there all along. But what? What? Something underrunning all their lives, an endemic of civilisation, that did this sort of thing to ordinary people?

Look at Finch, streaking parallel across the waves, steady on east! A patriot, Finch? The idea made Hicks smile. Some grey cloud whipped between them. Hicks peered through his windscreen, trying to gauge the weather. Low cloud already! – a poor outlook for the next four hundred miles! But, the worse the weather, the better for the Task Force. Finch came in to fifty yards.

Weaving and occasionally climbing or descending to avoid cottony puffs of low stratus, Hicks decided that there wasn't going to be time to solve the problem. He would go for patriotism. The silent obbligato of their lives! The mystery vector! The state confirms your existence with a passport, and for this you owe allegiance. So: patriotism, like it or not. Like country like mother's breast – hence the knee-jerk!

Nearly satisfied with this, Hicks re-checked his watch and fuel gauges and then led Finch down into a crevasse between two extending banks of cloud to check the base. A hundred and fifty feet. And just above the waves, he found, as expected, his altimeter needed adjusting up a couple of milli-bars. The wind had veered more to the north, still force five to six, and visibility below the stratus was good. Hicks took Finch back up to a thousand feet.

Some time later, they passed their point of no return. Hicks reckoned the Corsairs still seventy-five miles ahead. His UHF radio, tuned to the strike common frequency, remained silent. In the last hundred miles, another sign of rising pressure, the upper cloud had thinned away and disappeared, leaving the two Skyhawks between a brilliant blue sky and a limitless snow-white carpet of stratus. Out of the blue, Tracey appeared and slid silently alongside Hicks on the right with a grin and a thumbs-up.

The Plan? Hicks smiled wryly to himself. Their American-built A4's had no radar but were fitted with a UHF homing device codenamed, in British circles, Green Silk. A needle showed, very simply, whether a transmission was coming from left or right of the Skyhawk's nose. Given a long or frequent enough transmission, it was possible to get a precise bearing by pointing the aircraft until there was no deflection. The success of the Skyhawk 'mission' depended upon the assumption that when the Corsairs found a target there would be enough UHF chatter to allow them to home onto the scene of action. Then it would be jungle warfare in the low cloud.

Hicks flew on. Within an hour, he would be in the water, dead or alive. Strange then that the presence of two others in the same predicament should be so comforting! Belatedly, he selected guns, flipped up the safety and pressed the trigger briefly. Loudly, the cannons reassured him they were loaded. Now came another tincture of suspicion into Hicks' mind – hadn't it all been too easy? Four Skyhawks fuelled, armed and pre-flighted without question; and only a few individuals, it seemed, had made any attempt to stop them taking off. A face drifted into his mind's-eye, small, dark, round. And there never was a time, he realised now, with something of a shock, that there had not been humour in the glittering eyes and the disorderly lips. Cassián!

With new-mint clarity Hicks saw Cassián's secret. He was God! Well, that was a bit over the top. Junior partner, local agent. Rival? That was how he saw himself, anyway. He had been playing God with Hicks's life ever since – even before! – they first met. He'd brought him into a new world, appointed him a role, laid down the rules and, most god-like, left him choice and free-will and then stood back! And he had been playing God for years with his Corsairs – a plague on wayward nations! Good God! Hicks laughed aloud, until a thought choked him. Carla!

Was Carla planned? She was up ahead somewhere, not far now. Not up here in the sunshine, but probable down in that murky sandwich of air between sea and cloud, looking with her almond brown eyes for British ships. Hicks sensed an implacable convergence taking place. He squirmed against it, physically, resenting the tiny cockpit and confining straps, resenting too the little commodore-god's half-smile as he watched his players work through their parts: he'd known that the very qualities he had selected them for in the first place would impel his British *consejeros* to revert to type when the chips were down for the last hand: far better than they, he understood patriotism! But Carla?

Was Carla, too, a contrivance of the Commodore? A shift in the centre of a man's inner universe like that! Could that be a manipulation? Unbelievable! And yet – the convergence

273

was real: their two lives apexing out here, geometrically, inexorably. Theorem: given an Argentine Navy A-4 Skyhawk, prove that when two converging lives intersect, neither is broken. Or both! The Commodore's eyes twinkling with anticipation. He would soon know!

'Damn you! Damn you, Cassián!' Hicks shouted into the pristine emptiness of the South Atlantic. The cry travelled no further than the perspex bubble in which he sat.

He checked watch and fuel gauges. They had come four hundred miles. They had the world to themselves, a dome of blue on a carpet of brilliant white, the sun hot on his left cheek. He trimmed back to 220 knots, loiter speed, and flew on east. They must be getting close, and the lower speed would save fuel for when it was needed. Hicks noticed that the other two, like him, were looking around a lot. He signalled them to move out to a thousand yards.

Ten minutes or so later, as he was wondering why Carla had become so unreal and he himself so calm – as if the chief part of him had detached and gone on ahead into oblivion – Hicks' eye was caught by a flash out to his right. Finch's aircraft, still on course, was torching a massive trail of flame out of a small cloud of smoke and debris. The rocket trail was still visible, coming up from ahead out of the stratus. Finch started to go down. Hicks watched, fascinated, his skin crawled with anticipation of the next missile, which he could do nothing to avoid if it were coming his way. Finch ejected. The canopy first, then man and seat together, small drogue chute then the long, streaming main parachute, nearly horizontal, snapping suddenly into a mushroom, the seat falling away and Finch suspended in the morning air above the cloudplain, all in silent slow-motion.

A Sea Wolf! A British ship down there, under the sea-fog, firing on radar. Hicks' IFF transponder was on Code 4321 – obviously this had not reassured them. He didn't blame them, only wondered why he himself was still alive – Sea Wolves came in sixes. Tracey was still all right, though he had broken hard away to port, away from the hidden ship. Feeling it was only a token, Hicks did the same. Rolling left and down, he didn't see the missile that passed under his belly just outside fusing distance and he followed Tracey in a wide arc to the

274

north around the ship. Almost certainly an AA picket, and they had flown right over it – a fair sign they were on track for the main body of the Task Force, maybe fifty miles to go. They steadied up and flew on east. Finch would be in the water now. They might pick him up.

'Aguila, Aguila, this is Cormorán Three Leader. Cormorán Three Leader.'

The Spanish voice was loud and clear. Hicks swung left ten degrees and got a bearing as it continued: 'I have two ships, two frigates, on course zero nine zero, speed two five. Request instructions.' A lanky youth, spotty, British-looking, but called Mendoza. Hicks knew him well.

'Cormorán Three Leader, this is Aguila. Roger.' Monegario. 'What is the weather?'

'We have low cloud, sometimes on the surface in fog; and drizzle. Visibility three kilometres to nothing. The wind is north, six. Over.'

'Roger, Cormorán Three Leader. Stay in contact. Do not attack. Do not attack. Report any change of course. Acknowledge!' C3L acknowledged, and silence again filled the empty scene ahead. Hicks held his height, and the new heading, about twenty degrees to the left of their original course. Monegario would be weighing the implications of two frigates heading east at high speed: with the Corsairs nearing the limit of their range, he would soon have to decide his tactics.

'Search Combine, this is Aguila . . .' and in a long series of directives Monegario altered all the Corsairs' search tracks, moving the axis of the search northwards. Listening, and incidentally checking the bearing of Monegario's aircraft, Hicks saw that he had decided to convert the fan-shaped search pattern into a criss-cross grid covering a box to the east of the speeding frigates – and that in doing so he was breaking his own rules on fuel reserves.

'Cormorán Five Leader, Roger.' Carla! The high voice acknowledging her new track was too short for a bearing, but she was somewhere out to the right, down in this appalling weather with their fetal child. But why did he feel so numb about everything? Was there some sort of emotional narcosis, like shock, that suppressed the pain beyond a certain threshold? He would never know. He had thirty-five minutes' fuel.

Using the broad spread of Corsair transmissions, Hicks had established his own position relative to the search plan. Another ten degrees left, he judged would take them directly to the centre of the Monegario's new box. He eased up close to Tracey, pointed deliberately at himself, then down, then ahead. Tracey nodded, signalled that he would follow, and gave a final thumbs-up in encouragement before dropping back out of sight.

Hicks let down cautiously into the mattress of stratus, not knowing how thick it was now. At a hundred feet a minute descent, he should see the water before he hit it, even in fog. Without the sun, it was instantly cold, though not enough to cause the shiver that he felt. Down, down, slowly down. The radar altimeter, when it began reading at four hundred feet, was seventy feet higher than the barometric – as it ought to be if the pressure had gone on rising. God, this was thick! Really thick, wet clammy mist. Little rivulets of it ran back along the canopy, and he couldn't even see the nose of the Skyhawk beyond the windscreen. He reduced his rate of descent even further: stupid to come all this way to fly into the side of a wave.

The mist parted, hesitantly, a net curtain whipped back a few times and then pulled firmly shut again. Enough though for Hicks to catch a glimpse of the sea, very close, confirming his radar altimeter reading of just under a hundred feet. Carefully, he levelled off and flew on. What the hell was anybody going to be able to do in this, all their attention taken up just avoiding flying into the sea!

With fifteen minutes fuel left and his radio still silent, Hicks was beginning to succumb to a penetrating melancholy. The little cockpit seemed saturated with it and he no longer cared to resist its creeping progress nor argue with the suffocating sense of futility that bred it. Moribund himself, he was emotionally deceased already, and worst of all, he realised it and knew that for the rest of his life – thank God it would not be long – he would be a sub-human primitive. Collapse of emotional infrastructure! What's the clinical term for that, he was wondering with a rueful half-smile as his watch told him the Corsairs had been airborne three hours and must now turn for home. Monegario had already used their emergency fuel reserves and the whole Grupo could be jeopardised by a change of wind. Minutes passed. It seemed unfair to Carla, and the child. The thought lit a fuse of anger inside Hicks and he wanted to yell, but Monegario, the man he knew well and liked, had dissolved and his atoms swirled in the generality of the history of Hicks and there was nothing to yell at.

The weather had improved, a little, with a more definite cloud base at about two hundred feet and below this only scattered blocks of mist, like icebergs. It wasn't surprising they hadn't found anything, though, because a grey drizzle held visibility down to less than two miles.

At last: 'Roca Combine this is Aguila. Return to base. I say again, return to base. Acknowledge.' Hicks listened eagerly as, one by one, from out of the greyness, the section leaders replied. 'Cormorán Five Leader, Return to Base, out.' Carla! The Green Silk needled swung right and Hicks had turned instinctively about thirty degrees, towards her, before she released her transmit button.

And then he saw *Canberra*.

Chapter 28

The liner's graceful stern was sliding into a fogbank a mile away, huge, incongruously white. Hicks, in his surprise, had missed Monegario's reply to Carla's sighting report, but Carla was saying, 'Roger. Cormorán Five section is attacking!'

She must be within a mile of him! Frantically he searched all around, fuming at the salty drizzle that blurred his windscreen. The escalator must be near the bottom. Next stop hell. Thinking he saw a Corsair, Hicks banked savagely right, a clumsy manoeuvre that took him down within a few feet of the tumbling seas and gave him a start of fright that set his heart hammering. He recovered to a safe height. If there had been a Corsair, it had vanished, as had the ship, and Hicks, disorientated by the hard turn, no longer knew which way to look. He decided to turn back left to his original course, and almost immediately saw a Corsair off to his right, coming towards.

Canberra had been steering roughly south. Carla must have seen the liner from the other side then, and flown around the patch of mist across her bows intending to attack from this, the westerly side. Hicks throttled back and pointlessly checked his fuel: with the needles this low he couldn't trust them, but any time in the next ten minutes the engine would stop. He was turning right to put himself between Carla and the ship, and incidentally to get behind her, when he saw another Corsair a hundred yards astern – Carla's number two. Done bloody well to hang on in this weather, Hicks couldn't help thinking as he eased his turn to get behind him, when a pinpoint of light appeared in the gloom beyond. Almost stationary at first, it accelerated too fast for the eye to see and passed between Hicks and the second Corsair leaving a pencil-line of grey smoke in the air. A second missile also missed, but as all three aircraft dived towards the surface a third Sea Wolf from the invisible ship slammed into Carla's number two. Hicks felt the concussion and jinked hard to avoid the debris. He levelled off at absolute minimum height and then went down another ten feet until the seas flicked underneath close enough to touch.

Ahead, the cranked wings of Carla's Corsair were so close to the waves that Hicks could see no gap. A flicker of inattention at this height would put either of them into the water. But there were no more missiles. Carla banked gently right, raising her fuselage just enough to keep her wingtip out of the water. Hicks followed, three men: pilot robotic; patriot reluctant; lover already dead; but an *alter ego*, survivor of the seismic rupture of his personality, thought on. Carla was circling the fog-patch into which *Canberra* had disappeared: she knew it was limited in extent, having just flown around it, and she was going to ambush the liner when it emerged again to the south.

They were flying away from the missile-firing ship, too. Hicks closed up to fifty yards on the outside of the turn, nearly line-astern. Carla eased up a little more and increased her bank, and when they had turned through something more than half a circle Hicks saw Canberra again a mile out to their right. She was nearly stern-on, turning hard right at full speed in a welter of spray, her superstructure hidden in mist. A quick glance at his compass told Hicks the liner, with two thousand troops, was making a dash for the protection of the AA frigate. Carla straightened up and began opening on Canberra's beam for her attack.

Canberra too steadied up. Steering roughly north-west, and still at full speed, she had come out of the mist and was visible in her surreal white entirety for the first time. A part of Hicks knew, then, why he was here.

Carla had increased to her attack speed, 240 knots. She flew on until she was just ahead of the beam of the plunging liner, climbed to a hundred feet and turned in. *Canberra*'s bows went into a patch of sea-fog and for a few seconds Hicks thought she was safe, but it was only a small gobbet that wreathed itself back around the ship, mingling with the flying spray, and she steamed on plainly visible.

This was the bottom line. The pilot of the A-4 lined up the gunsight. The patriot thumbed back the safety-catch. The third man braced himself for the immolating hammer of the cannon.

A spark of light caught Hicks' eye, out to the left, and almost before he could blink, a missile streaked across in front of him. In front of Carla too; her propeller was whirling through the rocket-trail when the next missile exploded below her and the Corsair started pouring black smoke and dark red flame. It flew on. *Canberra* was less than half a mile ahead. Time slowed to the consistency of thick molasses. Hicks' whole life had been lived for this moment, to prevent those two bombs on Carla's wings punching in through *Canberra*'s thin plates and setting off a holocaust. He dropped down, clear of her trailing smoke, eased the Skyhawk's nose up until his gunsight aiming mark was on the Corsair's under-belly. To make doubly sure of a clean kill with his two cannon, he opened the throttle to bring the range down even further, finger tense on the trigger.

His engine cut and died. The Skyhawk pitched nose-down, pulling the gunsight down off aim. Momentarily uncom-prehending, Hicks shoved the useless throttle fully forward and hauled the nose back up to point at the receding shape of Carla's smoking Corsair. He had taken a half-pressure on the trigger when his eye detected a movement to his left. In infinitely slow, freeze-frame sequences, he saw clearly the white, finned missile homing on the Corsair at 1,400 mph with silent, deadly purpose. His mind made it poise, and when the Sea Wolf hurled itself with the speed of a bullet into the side of the Corsair Hicks was already inside his cathedral and making its compline calm ring with his screams. God! . . . God! . . . *God!*

Confused, concussed and speechless with cold after ten minutes in the water, Hicks could only rage inwardly as he was grappled roughly into the grey seaboat. To the crew of the boat, he looked like a man who had no further use for life.

'. . . *The Corsair search failed. The Task Force Commander made good use of Mufax data and kept his ships where the weather was thickest while the massive transhipment operation went ahead. The conditions, low cloud, visibility nil to poor, drizzle and fog, were described as 'impossible' for offensive air operations, and the TF was, according to intelligence, outside Corsair range. Nevertheless, Corsairs were tracked on TF radars combing the whole area, and some interruptions to the transhipment programme resulted. One Corsair was brought down well to the west by a radar picket. Two shadowed an anti-submarine frigate for an hour before being shaken off. And two more, chancing upon 'Canberra' after turning back from extreme range, were destroyed by an escorting AA frigate (HMS 'Buckler'). (In this action, an Argentine A-4 Skyhawk was also brought down. Its British pilot was rescued but refused to disclose his role in the operation or why he had been flying so far beyond the Skyhawk's normal operating radius). Argentine sources throw no light on this, but suggest that about a quarter of the Corsairs, too, failed to return as a direct result of exceeding their prudent limit of endurance in their attempts to find the British fleet. The Argentines made no further use of Corsairs in the conflict . . .'*

*

'I'm not surprised,' said Captain Pollard. Burberry occupied an old Parker Knoll in the corner, his summer seat. His master's voice was familiar, as were all the others, except one.

'Cassián seems to have been playing his own game all along!' Pollard continued.

'According to this –' Captain Laski waved a paper, 'that's their way of doing things!' The document was an eighty-page report on the Argentine Corsair project from its inception, beginning with a resumé of Cassián's philosophy of numbers and concluding with an evaluation of the Corsair in the contemporary battle scene. It was addressed to the Director of Naval Intelligence and signed M. Channing.

'If,' said the voice Burberry had not heard before, 'we had taken the trouble to find out more about "their way of doing things", it seems to me the whole affair could probably have been avoided.' This was Rear Admiral Carter, late of HMS *Eagle*. 'But that is by the by.' He helped himself from a decanter of Quinta do Noval. Summer rain ran down the mullioned windows. 'I'm waiting to hear how you all seem to know so much about it.'

After a pause, Captain Sargent spoke. 'George was approached by Cassián, back in '79, for pilots. He told us no more than that he was attempting something radical, a departure, away from the hyper-expensives, back to basics, with the emphasis on numbers. The idea appealed, so we gave him names.'

'Jeff Hicks?' Carter interrupted.

'Yes. And Channing, and several others. It was up to them, but if they chose to go, we figured, we stood to gain by their experience. We wanted intelligence. To them it was just a job. Nobody expected an invasion, much less Operation Corporate!'

'We?' Carter looked enquiringly at Pollard their host.

'We three. A caucus, Philip. A cabal if you like. We think ship design has gone fundamentally wrong. We're not alone, of course. The arguments have been public for years but nobody, anywhere, seems able to resist the follow-on imperative – every new gadget needs another new gadget to either outperform or neutralise it, and each one costs more than the last so you get fewer of them. The RAF predict that by 2020 it will take their entire annual budget to buy one fighter, for God's sake! And yet it goes on! We were interested in Cassián's idea. We even thought it worth contriving a small action to bring people up short and make them look at alternatives, but that plan was overtaken by events. Classic case of getting more than we bargained for! So, we got our intelligence.' Pollard indicated the Channing report lying among the coffee cups. 'What we want from you, Philip, to flesh it out, is – how it looked from the receiving end.' Sargent put the question very quietly.

Carter thought for a long time, examining his glass this way and that as if the answer might be found in its wine-dark contents. Then he looked up, out through the leaded-light window, into some dimension far beyond the damp evening outside; and in the corner of the silent room Burberry lifted his head too, as though to listen.

At length, unhurriedly, Carter began to speak.

'I'll tell you how it looked. I saw two frigates, with the best AA weapons in the fleet, put down. Put down. Very economical, no fuss, just a surgical operation. There was some blood; I saw three Corsairs shot down – but there were dozens more. I saw my Harriers annihilated, effortlessly. I saw dagoes, as we are wont to call them, fighting with the precision of a ballet chorus, with the courage of samurai, with skill, cunning, intelligence and daring. And finally, I saw, in these same dagoes, a humanity that we might look in vain to find among ourselves. That's how it looked.' Carter paused and looked into the faces of the other men.

'As to how it felt – put yourself in my place! Pinnacle of your career, sea-going command of a capital ship, and all that goes with it. You've been stripped of your fighters and your escorts and your capital ship is not provided with any weapons and you've blown up your life-jacket and you're standing there with your ship's company watching forty-odd World War Two planes coming at you with bombs, and then –' Carter put out both hands as if in supplication, '– and then –' there was a difficulty in his throat with the words. '– they drop their fucking bombs in the sea! They do that, then they fly sedately overhead, as if it was a fucking parade, and disappear. Leaving me to pick up survivors and run! I'll tell you how I felt! I felt ashamed!' Burberry jumped, as Carter's fist crashed on the table. 'I never felt such shame. Nobody should. That, between us, is why I resigned. I was ashamed!' With the air of a man who had more to say, Carter drained his glass and poured some more.

'World War Two aeroplanes for God's sake! What a joke, eh? Well I'll tell you what I think about that! I think the real hero of the war was Sam Baldwin.' Carter was speaking more quickly now. 'If this is true –' he put a finger on Channing's report, 'and they started with four or five hundred of these things, then without Barbary Coast we would have been wiped out. There were fifty-five of them at Medanosa. We shot down four or five, and they took out *Breakspear* and *Biter* with less than a dozen. Imagine a hundred of them, or two hundred, at San Carlos! If Sam hadn't had the guts to take this to the top, they'd still have the Falklands and we would

283

now be looking very foolish. Of that I am sure. But that's not the end of it, is it.'

'No it's not, Philip.' Laski spoke. 'At least that is our aim. This has opened up the can of worms. All the latest technology rubbished by Red Indians! Question is, now the can is open, is anybody prepared to look into it? The Cassián Thesis!'

Another long silence ensued. The only movement in the room was Burberry licking a hind paw.

'Where's Jeff Hicks now?' asked Carter of the generality. Nobody knew.

*

On the strength of his British passport, he spent some time in the Falklands. He resisted, politely and firmly and finally angrily, all efforts to repatriate him. He made himself useful in the aftermath of the war and earned enough to live simply. He seldom spoke, and if anybody had cared to follow him when he disappeared for long periods they would have seen him sitting, heedless of wind or rain, on top of the low cliffs of Cape Victoria, staring fixedly north-east across the sea.

In September, as southern winter eased into spring, he disappeared altogether. And so did a Phantom F-4M from RAF Stanley. In the dark, he took the engine blanks, covers and chocks from the unguarded aircraft and got in. From his time on the Navy F-4K, he knew how to start its Speys on its own batteries. As soon as there was light enough to see he made a full afterburner take-off and vanished north, low and supersonic. The dumbfounded alert crews were minutes behind, too far.

He flew a number of dog-legs at an economical 400 knots, then circled for some time over an empty patch of ocean before turning west. After nearly six hundred miles flying he approached the Argentine coast at zero feet, zoom-climbed over the Patagonian cliffs to get his bearings. There was no sign of life at Roca. No windsock. He landed on Runway 30, pulling the tail-chute handle just before he reached the fire-black stain near the intersection, stopped without difficulty in the strong wind, taxied to the pan and shut down.

284

Roca was deserted. In front of him, flanked by the blackened dirigible wreckage of the other hangars, Number 3 stood empty, open to the rattling wind. A piece of hoarding on the control tower flapped irritably. The oily concrete under his feet had a thin film of grey sand, moving with the wind, spreading fingers of the desert. He could smell only dryness.

With the hasteless air of a man who is retired, he went about the place. Not much, apart from engineering equipment, had been removed when the Grupo left. He found no doors locked, many banging emptily day and night. He visited rooms, staying longer in some than others. When the helicopter came with a crew to remove the Phantom, he was at the cliff-top cemetery and concealed himself until they had gone.

The length of his stay at Roca was non-dimensional. One day he left. With a few essentials, he started walking north. On that day the Patagonian wind, the *uligán*, blew unusually from the north and had a vicious quality that stung his face with flying grit and seemed to press him back. Occasionally, the sheer ferocity of it made him stagger, but always, with the air of a man who has an appointment, he forced on up the narrow road. He never once looked back.

At Roca, on a bed, in a room whose door carries the label 'Capitán de Fregata J. Hicks', there lies, probably to this day, a sea-stained British passport.

Did you find what I sang erewhile so hard to follow?
. . . go lull yourself with what you can understand, and with piano-tunes,
For I lull nobody, and you will never understand me.

Walt Whitman, 'To a Certain Civilian'

285